Bestselling author Tess Gerritsen is also a doctor, and she brings to her novels her first-hand knowledge of emergency and autopsy rooms.

But her interests span far wider than medical topics. As an anthropology undergraduate at Stanford University, she catalogued centuries-old human remains, and she continues to travel the world, driven by her fascination with ancient cultures and bizarre natural phenomena.

Now a full-time novelist, she lives with her husband in Maine.

For more information about Tess Gerritsen and her novels, visit her website at www.tessgerritsen.co.uk

HAVE YOU READ THEM ALL?

The thrillers featuring
Jane Rizzoli and Maura Isles are:

THE SURGEON

Introducing Detective Jane Rizzoli of the Boston Homicide Unit

In Boston, there's a killer on the loose. A killer who targets
lone women and performs ritualistic acts of torture
before finishing them off...

'A read-in-one-go novel if ever there was one'
Independent on Sunday

THE APPRENTICE

The surgeon has been locked up for a year, but his
chilling legacy still haunts the city, and especially Boston
homicide detective Jane Rizzoli...

'Gerritsen has enough in her locker to seriously worry
Michael Connelly, Harlan Coben and even the great
Dennis Lehane. Brilliant'
Crime Time

THE SINNER

Long-buried secrets are revealed as Dr Maura Isles and
detective Jane Rizzoli find themselves part of an investigation
that leads to the awful truth.

'Gutsy, energetic and shocking'
Manchester Evening News

BODY DOUBLE

Dr Maura Isles has seen more than her share of corpses.
But never has the body on the autopsy table been her own...

'It's scary just how good Tess Gerritsen is. This is crime
writing at its unputdownable, nerve-tingling best'
Harlan Coben

VANISH

When medical examiner Maura Isles looks down at the body
of a beautiful woman she gets the fright of her life.
The corpse opens its eyes...

'A horrifying tangle of rape, murder and blackmail'
Guardian

THE MEPHISTO CLUB

Can you really see evil when you look into someone's eyes?
Dr Maura Isles and detective Jane Rizzoli encounter
evil in its purest form.

'Gruesome, seductive and creepily credible'
The Times

KEEPING THE DEAD

She's Pilgrim Hospital's most unusual patient – a mummy
thought to have been dead for centuries. But when Dr Maura
Isles attends the CT scan, it reveals the image
of a very modern bullet...

'A seamless blend of good writing and pulse-racing tension'
Independent

THE SURGEON

Tess Gerritsen

BANTAM BOOKS

LONDON • TORONTO • SYDNEY • AUCKLAND • JOHANNESBURG

TRANSWORLD PUBLISHERS
61–63 Uxbridge Road, London W5 5SA
A Random House Group Company
www.rbooks.co.uk

THE SURGEON
A BANTAM BOOK: 9780553824551

First published in Great Britain
in 2001 by Bantam Press
an imprint of Transworld Publishers
Bantam edition published 2002
Bantam edition reissued 2010

Addresses for Random House Group Ltd companies outside the UK
can be found at: www.randomhouse.co.uk
The Random House Group Ltd Reg. No. 954009

Penguin Random House is committed to a sustainable future for
our business, our readers and our planet. This book is made from
Forest Stewardship Council® certified paper.

MIX
Paper from
responsible sources
FSC® C018179

Printed and bound in Great Britain by Clays Ltd, Elcograf S.p.A.

Typeset in Sabon by Falcon Oast Graphic Art Ltd.

14

Acknowledgements

I owe a very special thanks to:

Bruce Blake and Detective Wayne R. Rock of the Boston Police Department, and to Chris Michalakes, M.D., for their technical assistance.

Jane Berkey, Don Cleary, and Andrea Cirillo for their helpful comments on the first draft.

My editor, Linda Marrow, for gently pointing the way.

My guardian angel, Meg Ruley. (Every writer needs a Meg Ruley!)

And to my husband, Jacob. Always, to Jacob.

Prologue

Today they will find her body.

I know how it will happen. I can picture, quite vividly, the sequence of events that will lead to the discovery. By nine o'clock, those snooty ladies at the Kendall and Lord Travel Agency will be sitting at their desks, their elegantly manicured fingers tapping at computer keyboards, booking a Mediterranean cruise for Mrs Smith, a ski vacation at Klosters for Mr Jones. And for Mr and Mrs Brown, something different this year, something exotic, perhaps Chiang Mai or Madagascar, but nothing too rugged; oh no, adventure must, above all, be comfortable. That is the motto at Kendall and Lord: 'Comfortable adventures.' It is a busy agency, and the phone rings often.

It will not take long for the ladies to notice that Diana is not at her desk.

One of them will call Diana's Back Bay residence, but the phone will ring, unanswered. Maybe Diana is in the shower and can't hear it. Or she has already left for work but is running late. A dozen perfectly benign possibilities will run through the caller's mind. But as the day wears on, and repeated calls go unanswered, other, more disturbing possibilities, will come to mind.

9

I expect it's the building superintendent who will let Diana's coworker into the apartment. I see him nervously rattling his keys as he says, 'You're her friend, right? You sure she won't mind? 'Cause I'm gonna have to tell her I let you in.'

They walk into the apartment, and the coworker calls out: 'Diana? Are you home?' They start up the hall, past the elegantly framed travel posters, the superintendent right behind her, watching that she doesn't steal anything.

Then he looks through the doorway, into the bedroom. He sees Diana Sterling, and he is no longer worried about something as inconsequential as theft. He wants only to get out of that apartment before he throws up.

I would like to be there when the police arrive, but I am not stupid. I know they will study every car that creeps by, every face that stares from the gathering of spectators on the street. They know my urge to return is strong. Even now, as I sit in Starbucks, watching the day brighten outside the window, I feel that room calling me back. But I am like Ulysses, safely lashed to my ship's mast, yearning for the sirens' song. I will not dash myself against the rocks. I will not make that mistake.

Instead I sit and drink my coffee while, outside, the city of Boston comes awake. I stir three teaspoons of sugar into my cup; I like my coffee sweet. I like everything to be just so. To be perfect.

A siren screams in the distance, calling to me. I feel like Ulysses straining against the ropes, but they hold fast.

Today they will find her body. Today they will know we are back.

One

One year later

Detective Thomas Moore disliked the smell of latex, and as he snapped on the gloves, releasing a puff of talcum, he felt the usual twinge of anticipatory nausea. The odor was linked to the most unpleasant aspects of his job, and like one of Pavlov's dogs, trained to salivate on cue, he'd come to associate that rubbery scent with the inevitable accompaniment of blood and body fluids. An olfactory warning to brace himself.

And so he did, as he stood outside the autopsy room. He had walked in straight from the heat, and already sweat was chilling on his skin. It was July 12, a humid and hazy Friday afternoon. Across the city of Boston, air conditioners rattled and dripped, and tempers were flaring. On the Tobin Bridge, cars would already be backed up, fleeing north to the cool forests of Maine. But Moore would not be among them. He had been called back from his vacation, to view a horror he had no wish to confront.

He was already garbed in a surgical gown,

11

which he'd pulled from the morgue linen cart. Now he put on a paper cap to catch stray hairs and pulled paper booties over his shoes, because he had seen what sometimes spilled from the table onto the floor. The blood, the clumps of tissue. He was by no means a tidy man, but he had no wish to bring any trace of the autopsy room home on his shoes. He paused for a few seconds outside the door and took a deep breath. Then, resigning himself to the ordeal, he pushed into the room.

The draped corpse lay on the table – a woman, by the shape of it. Moore avoided looking too long at the victim and focused instead on the living people in the room. Dr Ashford Tierney, the Medical Examiner, and a morgue attendant were assembling instruments on a tray. Across the table from Moore stood Jane Rizzoli, also from the Boston Homicide Unit. Thirty-three years old, Rizzoli was a small and square-jawed woman. Her untamable curls were hidden beneath the paper O.R. cap, and without her black hair to soften her features, her face seemed to be all hard angles, her dark eyes probing and intense. She had transferred to Homicide from Vice and Narcotics six months ago. She was the only woman in the homicide unit, and already there had been problems between her and another detective, charges of sexual harassment, countercharges of unrelenting bitchiness. Moore was not sure he liked Rizzoli, or she him. So far they had kept their interactions strictly business, and he thought she preferred it that way.

Standing beside Rizzoli was her partner, Barry Frost, a relentlessly cheerful cop whose bland and beardless face made him seem much younger than his thirty years. Frost had worked with Rizzoli for two months now without complaint, the only man in the unit placid enough to endure her foul moods.

As Moore approached the table, Rizzoli said, 'We wondered when you'd show up.'

'I was on the Maine Turnpike when you beeped me.'

'We've been waiting here since five.'

'And I'm just starting the internal exam,' Dr Tierney said. 'So I'd say Detective Moore got here right on time.' One man coming to the defense of another. He slammed the cabinet door shut, setting off a reverberating clang. It was one of the rare occasions he allowed his irritation to show. Dr Tierney was a native Georgian, a courtly gentleman who believed ladies should behave like ladies. He did not enjoy working with the prickly Jane Rizzoli.

The morgue attendant wheeled a tray of instruments to the table, and his gaze briefly met Moore's with a look of, *Can you believe this bitch?*

'Sorry about your fishing trip,' Tierney said to Moore. 'It looks like your vacation's canceled.'

'You're sure it's our boy again?'

In answer, Tierney reached for the drape and pulled it back, revealing the corpse. 'Her name is Elena Ortiz.'

Though Moore had been braced for this sight, his first glimpse of the victim had the impact of a physical blow. The woman's black hair, matted stiff with blood, stuck out like porcupine quills

13

from a face the color of blue-veined marble. Her lips were parted, as though frozen in mid-utterance. The blood had already been washed off the body, and her wounds gaped in purplish rents on the gray canvas of skin. There were two visible wounds. One was a deep slash across the throat, extending from beneath the left ear, transecting the left carotid artery, and laying open the laryngeal cartilage. The coup de grace. The second slash was low on the abdomen. This wound had not been meant to kill; it had served an entirely different purpose.

Moore swallowed hard. 'I see why you called me back from vacation.'

'I'm the lead on this one,' said Rizzoli.

He heard the note of warning in her statement; she was protecting her turf. He understood where it came from, how the constant taunts and skepticism that women cops faced could make them quick to take offense. In truth he had no wish to challenge her. They would have to work together on this, and it was too early in the game to be battling for dominance.

He was careful to maintain a respectful tone. 'Could you fill me in on the circumstances?'

Rizzoli gave a curt nod. 'The victim was found at nine this morning, in her apartment on Worcester Street, in the South End. She usually gets to work around six a.m. at Celebration Florists, a few blocks from her residence. It's a family business, owned by her parents. When she didn't show up, they got worried. Her brother went to check on her. He found her in the bed-room. Dr Tierney estimates the time of death was somewhere between midnight and four this morning. According to the family, she had no current boyfriend, and no one in her apartment building recalls seeing any male visitors. She's just a hardworking Catholic girl.'

Moore looked at the victim's wrists. 'She was immobilized.'

'Yes. Duct tape on the wrists and ankles. She was found nude. Wearing only a few items of jewelry.'

'What jewelry?'

'A necklace. A ring. Ear studs. The jewelry box in the bedroom was untouched. Robbery was not the motive.'

Moore looked at the horizontal band of bruising across the victim's hips. 'The torso was immobilized as well.'

'Duct tape across the waist and the upper thighs. And across her mouth.'

Moore released a deep breath. 'Jesus.' Staring at Elena Ortiz, Moore had a disorienting flash of another young woman. Another corpse – a blonde, with meat-red slashes across her throat and abdomen.

'Diana Sterling,' he murmured.

'I've already pulled Sterling's autopsy report,' said Tierney. 'In case you need to review it.'

But Moore did not; the Sterling case, on which he had been lead detective, had never strayed far from his mind.

A year ago, thirty-year-old Diana Sterling, an employee at the Kendall and Lord Travel Agency, had been discovered nude and strapped to her bed with duct tape. Her throat and lower abdomen

15

were slashed. The murder remained unsolved.

Dr Tierney directed the exam light onto Elena Ortiz's abdomen. The blood had been rinsed off earlier, and the edges of the incision were a pale pink.

'Trace evidence?' asked Moore.

'We picked off a few fibers before we washed her off. And there was a strand of hair, adhering to the wound margin.'

Moore looked up with sudden interest. 'The victim's?'

'Much shorter. A light brown.'

Elena Ortiz's hair was black.

Rizzoli said, 'We've already requested hair samples from everyone who came into contact with the body.'

Tierney directed their attention to the wound. 'What we have here is a transverse cut. Surgeons call this a *Maylard* incision. The abdominal wall was incised layer by layer. First the skin, then the superficial fascia, then the muscle, and finally the pelvic peritoneum.'

'Like Sterling,' said Moore.

'Yes. Like Sterling. But there are differences.'

'What differences?'

'On Diana Sterling, there were a few jags in the incision, indicating hesitation, or uncertainty. You don't see that here. Notice how cleanly this skin has been incised? There are no jags at all. He did this with absolute confidence.' Tierney's gaze met Moore's. 'Our unsub is learning. He's improved his technique.'

'If it's the same unknown subject,' Rizzoli said.

'There are other similarities. See the squared-off

16

margin at this end of the wound? It indicates the track moves from right to left. Like Sterling. The blade used in this wound is single-edged, non-serrated. Like the blade used on Sterling.'

'A scalpel?'

'It's consistent with a scalpel. The clean incision tells me there was no twisting of the blade. The victim was either unconscious, or so tightly restrained she couldn't move, couldn't struggle. She couldn't cause the blade to divert from its linear path.'

Barry Frost looked like he wanted to throw up. 'Aw, jeez. Please tell me she was already dead when he did this.'

'I'm afraid this is not a postmortem wound.' Only Tierney's green eyes showed above the surgical mask, and they were angry.

'There was antemortem bleeding?' asked Moore.

'Pooling in the pelvic cavity. Which means her heart was still pumping. She was still alive when this . . . procedure was done.'

Moore looked at the wrists, encircled by bruises. There were similar bruises around both ankles, and a band of petechiae – pinpoint skin hemorrhages – stretched across her hips. Elena Ortiz had struggled against her bonds.

'There's other evidence she was alive during the cutting,' said Tierney. 'Put your hand inside the wound, Thomas. I think you know what you're going to find.'

Reluctantly Moore inserted his gloved hand into the wound. The flesh was cool, chilled from several hours of refrigeration. It reminded him of

17

how it felt to thrust his hand into a turkey carcass and root around for the package of giblets. He reached in up to his wrist, his fingers exploring the margins of the wound. It was an intimate violation, this burrowing into the most private part of a woman's anatomy. He avoided looking at Elena Ortiz's face. It was the only way he could regard her mortal remains with detachment, the only way he could focus on the cold mechanics of what had been done to her body.

'The uterus is missing.' Moore looked at Tierney.

The M.E. nodded. 'It's been removed.'

Moore withdrew his hand from the body and stared down at the wound, gaping like an open mouth. Now Rizzoli thrust her gloved hand in, her short fingers straining to explore the cavity.

'Nothing else was removed?' she asked.

'Just the uterus,' said Tierney. 'He left the bladder and bowel intact.'

'What's this thing I'm feeling here? This hard little knot, on the left side,' she said.

'It's suture. He used it to tie off blood vessels.'

Rizzoli looked up, startled. 'This is a *surgical* knot?'

'Two-oh plain catgut,' ventured Moore, looking at Tierney for confirmation.

Tierney nodded. 'The same suture we found in Diana Sterling.'

'Two-oh catgut?' asked Frost in a weak voice. He had retreated from the table and now stood in a corner of the room, ready to bolt for the sink. 'Is that like a – a brand name or something?'

'Not a brand name,' said Tierney. 'Catgut is a

18

type of surgical thread made from the intestines of cows or sheep.'

'So why do they call it catgut?' asked Rizzoli.

'It goes back to the Middle Ages, when gut strings were used on musical instruments. The musicians referred to their instruments as their *kit*, and the strings were called *kitgut*. The word eventually became *catgut*. In surgery, this sort of suture is used to sew together deep layers of connective tissue. The body eventually breaks down the suture material and absorbs it.'

'And where would he get this catgut suture?' Rizzoli looked at Moore. 'Did you trace a source for it on Sterling?'

'It's almost impossible to identify a specific source,' said Moore. 'Catgut suture's manufactured by a dozen different companies, most of them in Asia. It's still used in a number of foreign hospitals.'

'Only foreign hospitals?'

Tierney said, 'There are now better alternatives. Catgut doesn't have the strength or durability of synthetic sutures. I doubt many surgeons in the U.S. are currently using it.'

'Why would our unsub use it at all?'

'To maintain his visual field. To control the bleeding long enough so he can see what he's doing. Our unsub is a very neat man.'

Rizzoli pulled her hand from the wound. In her gloved palm was cupped a tiny clot of blood, like a bright red bead. 'How skillful is he? Are we dealing with a doctor? Or a butcher?'

'Clearly he has anatomical knowledge,' said Tierney. 'I have no doubt he's done this before.'

Moore took a step backward from the table, recoiling from the thought of what Elena Ortiz must have suffered, yet unable to keep the images at bay. The aftermath lay right in front of him, staring with open eyes.

He turned, startled, as instruments clattered on the metal tray. The morgue attendant had pushed the tray next to Dr Tierney, in preparation for the Y-incision. Now the attendant leaned forward and stared into the abdominal wound.

'So what happens to it?' he asked. 'Once he whacks out the uterus, what does he do with it?'

'We don't know,' said Tierney. 'The organs have never been found.'

Two

Moore stood on the sidewalk in the South End neighborhood where Elena Ortiz had died. Once this had been a street of tired rooming houses, a shabby backwater neighborhood separated by railroad tracks from the more desirable northern half of Boston. But a growing city is a ravening creature, always in search of new land, and railroad tracks are no barrier to the hungry gaze of developers. A new generation of Bostonians had discovered the South End, and the old rooming houses were gradually being converted to apartment buildings.

Elena Ortiz lived in just such a building. Though the views from her second-story apartment were uninspiring – her windows faced a Laundromat across the street – the building did offer a treasured amenity rarely found in the city of Boston: tenant parking, crammed into the adjacent alley.

Moore walked down that alley now, scanning the windows in the apartments above, wondering who at that moment was looking down at him. Nothing moved behind the windows' glassy eyes.

The tenants facing this alley had already been interviewed; none had offered any useful information.

He stopped beneath Elena Ortiz's bathroom window and stared up at the fire escape leading to it. The ladder was pulled up and latched in the retracted position. On the night Elena Ortiz died, a tenant's car had been parked just beneath the fire escape. Size 8½ shoe prints were later found on the car's roof. The unsub had used it as a stepping-stone to reach the fire escape.

He saw that the bathroom window was shut. It had not been shut the night she met her killer.

He left the alley, circled back to the front entrance, and let himself into the building.

Police tape hung in limp streamers across Elena Ortiz's apartment door. He unlocked the door and fingerprint powder rubbed off like soot on his hand. The loose tape slithered across his shoulders as he stepped into the apartment.

The living room was as he remembered it from his walk-through the day before, with Rizzoli. It had been an unpleasant visit, simmering with undercurrents of rivalry. The Ortiz case had started off with Rizzoli as lead, and she was insecure enough to feel threatened by anyone challenging her authority, especially an older male cop. Though they were now on the same team, a team that had since expanded to five detectives, Moore felt like a trespasser on her turf, and he'd been careful to couch his suggestions in the most diplomatic terms. He had no wish to engage in a battle of egos, yet a battle was what it had become. Yesterday he'd tried to focus on this crime scene, but her resentment kept pricking his bubble of concentration.

Only now, alone, could he completely focus his attention on the apartment where Elena Ortiz had died. In the living room he saw mismatched furniture arranged around a wicker coffee table. A desktop computer in the corner. A beige rug patterned with leafy vines and pink flowers. Since the murder, nothing had been moved, nothing altered, according to Rizzoli. The last light of day was fading in the window, but he did not turn on the lights. He stood for a long time, not even moving his head, waiting for complete stillness to fall across the room. This was the first chance he'd had to visit the scene alone, the first time he'd stood in this room undistracted by the voices, the faces, of the living. He imagined the molecules of air, briefly stirred by his entry, now slowing, drifting. He wanted the room to speak to him.

He felt nothing. No sense of evil, no lingering tremors of terror.

The unsub had not come in through the door. Nor had he gone wandering through his newly claimed kingdom of death. He had focused all his time, all his attention, on the bedroom.

Moore walked slowly past the tiny kitchen and started up the hallway. He felt the hairs on the back of his neck begin to bristle. At the first doorway he paused and stared into the bathroom. He turned on the light.

Thursday is a warm night. It is so warm that all across the city, windows are left open to catch every stray breeze, every cool breath of air. You crouch on the fire escape, sweating in your dark clothes, staring into this bathroom. There is no sound; the woman is asleep in the bedroom. She has to be up early for her job at the florist's, and at this hour her sleep cycle is passing into its deepest, most unarousable phase.

She doesn't hear the scratch of your putty knife as you pry open the screen.

Moore looked at the wallpaper, adorned with tiny red rose-buds. A woman's pattern, nothing a man would choose. In every way this was a woman's bathroom, from the strawberry-scented shampoo, to the box of Tampax under the sink, to the medicine cabinet crammed with cosmetics. An aqua-eye-shadow kind of gal.

You climb in the window, and fibers of your navy-blue shirt catch on the frame. Polyester. Your sneakers, size 8½, leave prints coming in on the white linoleum floor. There are traces of sand, mixed with crystals of gypsum. A typical mix picked up from walking the city of Boston.

Maybe you pause, listening in the darkness. Inhaling the sweet foreignness of a woman's space. Or maybe you waste no time but proceed straight to your goal.

The bedroom.

The air seemed fouler, thicker, as he followed in the intruder's footsteps. It was more than just an imagined sense of evil; it was the smell.

He came to the bedroom door. By now the hairs on the back of his neck were standing straight out. He already knew what he would see inside the room; he thought he was prepared for it. Yet when he turned on the lights, the horror assailed him once again, as it had the first time he'd seen this room.

24

The blood was now over two days old. The cleaning service had not yet come in. But even with their detergents and steam cleaners and cans of white paint, they could never fully erase what had happened here, because the air itself was permanently imprinted with terror.

You step through the doorway, into this room. The curtains are thin, only an unlined cotton print, and light from the street lamps shines through the fabric, onto the bed. Onto the sleeping woman. Surely you must linger a moment, studying her. Considering with pleasure the task that lies ahead. Because it is pleasurable for you, isn't it? You are growing more and more excited. The thrill moves through your bloodstream like a drug, awakening every nerve, until even your fingertips are pulsing with anticipation.

Elena Ortiz did not have time to scream. Or, if she did, no one heard her. Not the family in the unit next door, nor the couple below.

The intruder brought his tools with him. Duct tape. A rag soaked in chloroform. A collection of surgical instruments. He had come fully prepared.

The ordeal would have lasted well over an hour. Elena Ortiz was conscious for at least part of that time. The skin on her wrists and ankles was chafed, indicating she had struggled. In her panic, her agony, she had emptied her bladder, and urine had soaked into the mattress, mingling with her blood. The operation was a delicate one, and he took the time to do it right, to take only what he wanted, nothing more.

He did not rape her; perhaps he was incapable of doing so.

25

When he'd finished his terrible excision, she was still alive. The pelvic wound continued to bleed, the heart to pump. How long? Dr Tierney had guessed at least half an hour. Thirty minutes, which must have seemed an eternity to Elena Ortiz.

What were you doing during that time? Putting your tools away? Packing your prize in a jar? Or did you merely stand here, enjoying the view?

The final act was swift and businesslike. Elena Ortiz's tormentor had taken what he wanted, and now it was time to finish things. He'd moved to the head of the bed. With his left hand he'd grasped a handful of her hair, yanking backward so hard he tore out more than two dozen strands. These were found later, scattered on the pillow and floor. The bloodstains shrieked out the final events. With her head immobilized and the neck fully exposed, he'd made a single deep slash starting at the left jaw and moving rightward, across the throat. He had severed the left carotid artery and the trachea. Blood spurted. On the wall to the left of the bed were dense clusters of small circular drops flowing downward, characteristic of arterial spray as well as exhalation of blood from the trachea. The pillow and sheets were saturated from downward dripping. Several cast-off droplets, thrown off as the intruder swung away the blade, had spattered the windowsill.

Elena Ortiz had lived long enough to see her own blood spurt from her neck and hit the wall in a machine-gun spray of red. She had lived long enough to aspirate blood into her severed trachea, to hear it gurgle in her lungs, to cough it out in explosive bursts of crimson phlegm.

She had lived long enough to know she was dying.

And when it was done, when her agonal struggles had ceased, you left us a calling card. You neatly folded the victim's nightshirt, and you left it on the dresser. Why? Is it some twisted sign of respect for the woman you've just slaughtered? Or is it your way of mocking us? Your way of telling us that you are in control?

Moore returned to the living room and sank into an arm-chair. It was hot and airless in the apartment, but he was shivering. He didn't know if the chill was physical or emotional. His thighs and shoulders ached, so maybe it was just a virus coming on. A summer flu, the worst kind. He thought of all the places he'd rather be at that moment. Adrift on a Maine lake, his fishing line whicking through the air. Or standing at the seashore, watching the fog roll in. Anywhere but this place of death.

The chirp of his beeper startled him. He shut it off and realized his heart was pounding. He made himself calm down first before he took out the cell phone and punched in the number.

'Rizzoli,' she answered on the first ring, her greeting as direct as a bullet.

'You paged me.'

'You never told me you got a hit on VICAP,' she said.

'What hit?'

'On Diana Sterling. I'm looking at her murder book now.'

VICAP, the Violent Criminals Apprehension

Program, was a national database of homicide and assault information gathered from cases across the country. Killers often repeated the same patterns, and with this data investigators could link crimes committed by the same perpetrator. As a matter of routine, Moore and his partner at the time, Rusty Stivack, had initiated a search on VICAP.

'We turned up no matches in New England,' said Moore. 'We ran down every homicide involving mutilation, night entry, and duct tape bindings. Nothing fits Sterling's profile.'

'What about the series in Georgia? Three years ago, four victims. One in Atlanta, three in Savannah. All were in the VICAP database.'

'I reviewed those cases. That perp is not our unsub.'

'Listen to this, Moore. Dora Ciccone, age twenty-two, graduate student at Emory. Victim first subdued with Rohypnol, then restrained to the bed with nylon cord—'

'Our boy here uses chloroform and duct tape.'

'He sliced open her abdomen. Cut out her uterus. Performed a coup de grace – a single slash across the neck. And finally – get this – he folded her nightclothes and left them on a chair by the bed. I'm telling you, it's too goddamn close.'

'The Georgia cases are closed,' said Moore. 'They've been closed for two years. That perp is dead.'

'What if Savannah PD blew it? What if he *wasn't* their killer?'

'They had DNA to back it up. Fibers, hairs. Plus there was a witness. A victim who survived.'

'Oh yeah. The survivor. Victim number five.'

Rizzoli's voice held a strangely taunting note.

'She confirmed the perp's identity,' said Moore.

'She also conveniently shot him to death.'

'So what, you want to arrest his ghost?'

'Did you ever talk to that surviving victim?' Rizzoli asked.

'No.'

'Why not?'

'What would be the point?'

'The point is that you might've learned something interesting. Like the fact she left Savannah soon after that attack. And guess where she's living now?'

Through the hiss of the cell phone, he could hear the whoosh of his own pulse. 'Boston?' he asked softly.

'And you're not gonna believe what she does for a living.'

Three

Dr Catherine Cordell sprinted down the hospital corridor, the soles of her running shoes squeaking on the linoleum, and pushed through the double doors into the emergency room.

A nurse called out: 'They're in Trauma Two, Dr Cordell!'

'I'm there,' said Catherine, moving like a guided missile straight for Trauma Two.

Half a dozen faces flashed her looks of relief as she stepped into the room. In one glance she took stock of the situation, saw jumbled instruments glittering on a tray, the IV poles with bags of Ringer's lactate hanging like heavy fruit on steel-rod trees, blood-streaked gauze and torn packaging scattered across the floor. A rapid sinus rhythm twitched across the cardiac monitor – the electrical pattern of a heart racing to stay ahead of Death.

'What've we got?' she asked as personnel moved aside to let her pass.

Ron Littman, the senior surgical resident, gave her a rapid-fire report. 'John Doe Pedestrian, hit-and-run. Rolled into the E.R. unconscious. Pupils are equal and reactive, lungs are clear, but the abdomen's distended. No bowel sounds. BP's down to sixty over zip. I did a paracentesis. He's got blood in his belly. We've got a central line in, Ringer's lactate wide open, but we can't keep his pressure up.'

'O neg and fresh frozen on the way?'

'Should be here any minute.'

The man on the table was stripped naked, every intimate detail mercilessly exposed to her gaze. He appeared to be in his sixties, already intubated and on a ventilator. Toneless muscles sagged in folds on gaunt limbs, and his ribs stood out like arching blades. A preexisting chronic illness, she thought; cancer would be her first guess. The right arm and hip were abraded and bloody from scraping across pavement. On his right lower chest a bruise formed a purple continent on the white parchment of skin. There were no penetrating wounds.

She slipped on her stethoscope to verify what the resident had just told her. She heard no sounds in the belly. Not a growl, not a tinkle. The silence of traumatized bowel. Moving the stethoscope diaphragm to the chest, she listened for breath sounds, confirming that the endotracheal tube was properly placed and that both lungs were being ventilated. The heart battered like a fist against the chest wall. Her exam took only a matter of seconds, yet she felt as though she were moving in slow motion, that around her the room full of personnel stood frozen in time, awaiting her next action.

A nurse called out: 'I'm barely getting the systolic at fifty!'

31

Time sprang ahead at a frightening pace.

'Get me a gown and gloves,' said Catherine. 'Open the laparotomy tray.'

'What about taking him to the O.R.?' said Littman.

'All rooms are in use. We can't wait.' Someone tossed her a paper cap. Swiftly she tucked in her shoulder-length red hair and tied on a mask. A scrub nurse was already holding out a sterile surgical gown. Catherine slipped her arms into the sleeves and thrust her hands into gloves. She had no time to scrub, no time to hesitate. She was in charge, and John Doe was crashing on her.

Sterile drapes were whisked onto the patient's chest and pelvis. She grabbed hemostats from the tray and swiftly clamped the drapes in place, squeezing the steel teeth with a satisfying *snap, snap*.

'Where's that blood?' she called out.

'I'm checking with the lab now,' said a nurse.

'Ron, you're first assist,' Catherine said to Littman. She glanced around the room and focused on a pasty-faced young man standing by the door. His nametag read: *Jeremy Barrows, Medical Student*. 'You,' she said. 'You're second assist!'

Panic flashed in the young man's eyes. 'But – I'm only in my second year. I'm just here to—'

'Can we get another surgical resident in here?'

Littman shook his head. 'Everyone's spread thin. They've got a head injury in Trauma One and a code down the hall.'

'Okay.' She looked back at the student.

'Barrows, you're it. Nurse, get him a gown and gloves.'

'What do I have to do? Because I don't really know—'

'Look, you want to be a doctor? Then *glove up*!'

He flushed bright red and turned to don a gown. The boy was scared, but in many ways Catherine preferred an anxious student like Barrows to an arrogant one. She'd seen too many patients killed by a doctor's overconfidence.

A voice crackled on the intercom: 'Hello, Trauma Two? This is the lab. I have a hematocrit on John Doe. It's fifteen.'

He's bleeding out, thought Catherine. 'We need that O neg now!'

'It's on its way.'

Catherine reached for a scalpel. The weight of the handle, the contour of steel, felt comfortable in her grasp. It was an extension of her own hand, her own flesh. She took a quick breath, inhaling the scent of alcohol and glove talc. Then she pressed the blade to the skin and made her incision, straight down the center of the abdomen.

The scalpel sketched a bright bloody line on the canvas of white skin.

'Get the suction and laparotomy pads ready,' she said. 'We've got a belly full of blood.'

'BP's barely palpable at fifty.'

'O neg and fresh frozen plasma's here! I'm hanging it now.'

'Someone keep an eye on the rhythm. Let me know what it's doing,' said Catherine.

'Sinus tach. Rate's up to one-fifty.'

She sliced through the skin and subcutaneous

fat, ignoring the bleeding from the abdominal wall. She wasted no time with minor bleeders; the most serious hemorrhage was inside the abdomen, and it had to be stopped. A ruptured spleen or liver was the most likely source.

The peritoneal membrane bulged out, tight with blood.

'It's about to get messy,' she warned, her blade poised to penetrate. Though she was braced for the gush, that first piercing of the membrane released such an explosive spout she felt a flash of panic. Blood spilled onto the drapes and streamed to the floor. It splattered her gown, its warmth like that of a copper-scented bath soaking through her sleeves. And still it continued to flow out in a satiny river.

She thrust in retractors, widening the wound's gap and exposing the field. Littman inserted the suction catheter. Blood gurgled into the tubing. A stream of bright red splashed into the glass reservoir.

'More laparotomy pads!' Catherine yelled over the scream of suction. She had stuffed half a dozen of the absorptive pads into the wound and watched as they magically turned red. Within seconds they were saturated. She pulled them out and inserted fresh ones, packing them into all four quadrants.

A nurse said, 'I'm seeing PVCs on the monitor!'

'Shit, I've already sucked two liters into the reservoir,' said Littman.

Catherine glanced up and saw that bags of O neg blood and fresh frozen plasma were rapidly dripping into the IVs. It was like pouring blood into a sieve. In through the veins, out through the wound. They could not keep up. She could not clamp vessels that were submerged in a lake of blood; she could not operate blind.

She pulled out the lap pads, heavy and dripping, and stuffed in more. For a few precious seconds she made out the land-marks. The blood was oozing from the liver, but there was no obvious point of injury. It seemed to be leaking from the entire surface of the organ.

'I'm losing his pressure!' a nurse called out.

'Clamp!' said Catherine, and the instrument was instantly slapped in her hand. 'I'm going to try a Pringle maneuver. Barrows, pack in more pads!'

Startled into action, the medical student reached toward the tray and knocked over the stack of laparotomy pads. He watched in horror as they tumbled off.

A nurse ripped open a fresh packet. 'They go in the patient, not on the floor,' she snapped. And her gaze met Catherine's, the same thought mirrored in both women's eyes.

That one's going to be a doctor?

'Where do I put them?' Barrows asked.

'Just clear the field. I can't see with all the blood!'

She gave him a few seconds to sponge the wound; then she reached in and tore apart the lesser omentum. Guiding the clamp from the left side, she identified the hepatic pedicle, through which the liver's artery and portal vein coursed. It was only a temporary solution, but if she could cut off the blood flow at that point, she might control the hemorrhage. It would buy them precious time to stabilize the pressure, to pump more blood and plasma into his circulation.

She squeezed the clamp shut, closing off the vessels in the pedicle.

To her dismay, the blood continued to ooze out, unabated.

'Are you sure you got the pedicle?' said Littman.

'I *know* I got it. And I know it's not coming from the retroperitoneum.'

'Maybe the hepatic vein?'

She grabbed two lap pads from the tray. This next maneuver was a last resort. Placing the lap pads on the liver's surface, she squeezed the organ between her gloved hands.

'What's she doing?' asked Barrows.

'Hepatic compression,' said Littman. Sometimes it can close off the edges of hidden lacerations. Hold off exsanguination.'

Every muscle in her shoulders and arms went taut as she strained to maintain the pressure, to squeeze back the flood.

'It's still pooling,' said Littman. 'This isn't working.'

She stared into the wound and saw the steady reaccumulation of blood. Where the hell is he bleeding from? she thought. And suddenly noticed there was blood oozing steadily from other sites as well. Not just the liver, but also the abdominal wall, the mesentery. The incised edges of skin.

She glanced at the patient's left arm, which poked out from beneath the sterile drapes. The gauze dressing over the IV site was soaked with blood.

'I want six units of platelets and fresh frozen

plasma STAT,' she ordered. 'And start a heparin infusion. Ten thousand units IV bolus, then a thousand units an hour.'

'Heparin?' said Barrows in bewilderment. 'But he's bleeding out—'

'This is DIC,' said Catherine. 'He needs anti-coagulation.'

Littman was staring at her. 'We don't have the labs yet. How do you know it's DIC?'

'By the time we get the coag studies, it'll be too late. We've got to move *now*.' She nodded to the nurse. 'Give it.'

The nurse plunged the needle into the IV's injection port. Heparin was a desperate toss of the dice. If Catherine's diagnosis was correct, if the patient was suffering from DIC – disseminated intravascular coagulation – then throughout his bloodstream, massive numbers of thrombi were forming like a microscopic hailstorm, consuming all his precious coagulation factors and platelets. Severe trauma, or an underlying cancer or infection, could set off an uncontrolled cascade of thrombus formation. Because DIC used up coagulation factors and platelets, both necessary for blood to clot, the patient would begin to hemorrhage. To halt the DIC, they had to administer heparin, an anti-coagulant. It was a strangely paradoxical treatment. It was also a gamble. If Catherine's diagnosis was wrong, the heparin would make the bleeding worse.

As if things could get any worse. Her back ached and her arms were trembling from the effort to maintain pressure on the liver. A drop of sweat slid down her cheek and soaked into her mask.

Lab was back on the intercom. 'Trauma Two, I've got STAT results on John Doe.'

'Go ahead,' the nurse said.

'The platelet count's down to a thousand. Prothrombin time's way up at thirty, and he's got fibrin degradation products. Looks like your patient's got a roaring case of DIC.'

Catherine caught Barrows's glance of amazement. *Medical students are so easy to impress.*

'V tach! He's in V tach!'

Catherine's gaze shot to the monitor. A whip-sawing line traced jagged teeth across the screen. 'Any pressure?'

'No. I've lost it.'

'Start CPR. Littman, you're in charge of the code.'

The chaos built like a storm, swirling around her with ever more violence. A courier whooshed in with fresh frozen plasma and platelets. Catherine heard Littman call out orders for cardiac drugs, saw a nurse place her hands on the sternum and begin pumping on the chest, head nodding up and down like a mechanical sipping bird. With every cardiac compression, they were perfusing the brain, keeping it alive. They were also feeding the hemorrhage.

Catherine stared down into the patient's abdominal cavity. She was still compressing the liver, still holding back the tidal wave of blood. Was she imagining it, or did the blood, which had trickled like glossy ribbons through her fingers, seem to be slowing?

'Let's shock him,' said Littman. 'One hundred joules—'

'No, wait. His rhythm's back!'

Catherine glanced at the monitor. Sinus tachycardia! The heart was pumping again, but it was also forcing blood into the arteries.

'Are we perfusing?' she called out. 'What's the BP?'

'BP is . . . ninety over forty. *Yes!*'

'Rhythm's stable. Maintaining sinus tach.'

Catherine looked into the open abdomen. The bleeding had slowed to a barely perceptible ooze. She stood cradling the liver in her grasp and listened to the steady beep of the monitor. Music to her ears.

'Folks,' she said. 'I think we have a save.'

Catherine stripped off her bloody gown and gloves and followed the gurney bearing John Doe out of Trauma Two. The muscles in her shoulders quivered with fatigue, but it was a good fatigue. The exhaustion of victory. The nurses wheeled the gurney into the elevator, to bring their patient to the Surgical Intensive Care Unit. Catherine was about to step onto the elevator as well when she heard someone call out her name.

She turned and saw a man and a woman approaching her. The woman was short and fierce-looking, a coal-eyed brunette with a gaze direct as lasers. She was dressed in a severe blue suit that made her look almost military. She seemed dwarfed by her much taller companion. The man was in his mid-forties, and threads of silver streaked his dark hair. Maturity had carved deeply sober lines into what was still a strikingly handsome face. It was his eyes that Catherine focused on. They were a soft gray, unreadable.

'Dr Cordell?' he asked.

'Yes.'

'I'm Detective Thomas Moore. This is Detective Rizzoli. We're from the homicide unit.' He held up his badge, but it might as well have been dime-store plastic. She scarcely looked at it; her focus was entirely on Moore.

'May we talk to you in private?' he asked.

She glanced at the nurses waiting with John Doe in the elevator. 'Go ahead,' she called to them. 'Dr Littman will write the orders.'

Only after the elevator door had closed did she address Detective Moore. 'Is this about the hit-and-run that just came in? Because it looks like he's going to survive.'

'We're not here about a patient.'

'You did say you're from Homicide?'

'Yes.' It was the quiet tone of his voice that alarmed her. A gentle warning to prepare herself for bad news.

'Is this – oh god, I hope this isn't about someone I know.'

'It's about Andrew Capra. And what happened to you in Savannah.'

For a moment she could not speak. Her legs suddenly felt numb and she reached back toward the wall, as though to catch herself from falling.

'Dr Cordell?' he said with sudden concern. 'Are you all right?'

'I think . . . I think we should talk in my office,' she whispered. Abruptly she turned and walked out of the E.R. She did not look back to see if the detectives were following her; she just kept walking, fleeing toward the safety of her office, in the adjoining clinic building. She heard their footsteps right behind her as she navigated through the sprawling complex that was Pilgrim Medical Center.

What happened to you in Savannah?

She did not want to talk about it. She had hoped never to talk about Savannah to anyone, ever again. But these were police officers, and their questions could not be avoided.

At last they reached a suite with the plaque:

Peter Falco, M.D.
Catherine Cordell, M.D.
General and Vascular Surgery.

She stepped into the front office, and the receptionist looked up with an automatic smile of greeting. It froze half-formed on her lips when she saw Catherine's ashen face and noticed the two strangers who had followed her in.

'Dr Cordell? Is something wrong?'

'We'll be in my office, Helen. Please hold my calls.'

'Your first patient's coming in at ten. Mr Tsang, follow-up splenectomy—'

'Cancel it.'

'But he's driving all the way from Newbury. He's probably on his way.'

'All right, then have him wait. But please, don't put any calls through.'

Ignoring Helen's bewildered look, Catherine headed straight to her office, Moore and Rizzoli following right behind her. Immediately she

41

reached for her white lab coat. It was not hanging on the door hook, where she always kept it. It was only a minor frustration, but added to the turmoil she was already feeling, it was almost more than she could handle. She glanced around the room, searching for the lab coat as though her life depended on it. She spotted it draped over the filing cabinet and felt an irrational sense of relief as she snatched it up and retreated behind her desk. She felt safer there, barricaded behind the gleaming rosewood surface. Safer and in control.

The room was a carefully ordered place, the way everything in her life was carefully ordered. She had little tolerance for sloppiness, and her files were organized in two neat stacks on the desk. Her books were lined up alphabetically by author on the shelves. Her computer hummed softly, the screen saver building geometric patterns on the monitor. She slipped on the lab coat to cover her bloodstained scrub top. The additional layer of uniform felt like another shield of protection, another barrier against the messy and dangerous vagaries of life.

Sitting behind her desk, she watched Moore and Rizzoli glance around the room, no doubt taking the measure of its occupant. Was that automatic for police officers, that quick visual survey, the appraisal of the subject's personality? It made Catherine feel exposed and vulnerable.

'I realize this is a painful subject for you to revisit,' said Moore as he sat down.

'You have no idea how painful. It's been two years. Why has this come up now?'

'In relation to two unsolved homicides, here in Boston.'

Catherine frowned. 'But I was attacked in Savannah.'

'Yes, we know. There's a national crime database called VICAP. When we did a search of VICAP, looking for crimes similar to our homicides here, Andrew Capra's name came up.'

Catherine was silent for a moment, absorbing this information. Building the courage to pose the next logical question. She managed to ask it calmly. 'What similarities are we talking about?'

'The manner in which the women were immobilized and controlled. The type of cutting instrument used. The . . .' Moore paused, struggling to phrase his words with the most delicacy possible. 'The choice of mutilation,' he finished quietly.

Catherine gripped the desk with both hands, fighting to contain a sudden surge of nausea. Her gaze dropped to the files stacked so neatly in front of her. She spotted a streak of blue ink staining the sleeve of her lab coat. *No matter how much you try to maintain order in your life, no matter how careful you are to guard against mistakes, against imperfections, there is always some smudge, some flaw, lurking out of sight. Waiting to surprise you.*

'Tell me about them,' she said. 'The two women.'

'We're not at liberty to reveal very much.'

'What can you tell me?'

'No more than what was reported in Sunday's *Globe*.'

It took a few seconds for her to process what he

had just said. She stiffened in disbelief. 'These Boston murders – they're *recent*?'

'The last one was early Friday.'

'So this has nothing to do with Andrew Capra! Nothing to do with me.'

'There are striking similarities.'

'Then they're purely coincidental. They have to be. I thought you were talking about old crimes. Something Capra did years ago. Not last week.' Abruptly she shoved back her chair. 'I don't see how I can help you.'

'Dr Cordell, this killer knows details that were never released to the public. He has information about Capra's attacks that no one outside the Savannah investigation knows.'

'Then maybe you should look at those people. The ones who do know.'

'You're one of them, Dr Cordell.'

'In case you've forgotten, I was a *victim*.'

'Have you spoken in detail about your case to anyone?'

'Just the Savannah police.'

'You haven't discussed it at length with your friends?'

'No.'

'Family?'

'No.'

'There must be someone you've confided in.'

'I don't talk about it. I never talk about it.'

He fixed her with a disbelieving gaze. 'Never?'

She looked away. 'Never,' she whispered.

There was a long silence. Then Moore asked, gently, 'Have you ever heard of the name Elena Ortiz?'

'No.'

'Diana Sterling?'

'No. Are they the women . . .'

'Yes. They're the victims.'

She swallowed hard. 'I don't know their names.'

'You didn't know about these murders?'

'I make it a point to avoid reading about anything tragic. It's just something I can't deal with.' She released a weary sigh. 'You have to understand, I see so many terrible things in the emergency room. When I get home, at the end of the day, I want peace. I want to feel safe. What happens in the world – all the violence – I don't need to read about it.'

Moore reached into his jacket and produced two photographs, which he slid across the desk to her. 'Do you recognize either of these women?'

Catherine stared at the faces. The one on the left had dark eyes and a laugh on her lips, the wind in her hair. The other was an ethereal blonde, her gaze dreamy and distant.

'The dark-haired one is Elena Ortiz,' said Moore. 'The other is Diana Sterling. Diana was murdered a year ago. Do these faces look at all familiar?'

She shook her head.

'Diana Sterling lived in the Back Bay, only half a mile from your residence. Elena Ortiz's apartment is just two blocks south of this hospital. You may very well have seen them. Are you absolutely sure you don't recognize either woman?'

'I've never seen them before.' She held out the photos to Moore and suddenly saw that her hand was trembling. Surely he noticed it as he took back

45

the photos, as his fingers brushed hers. She thought he must notice a great deal; a policeman would. She'd been so focused on her own turmoil that she had scarcely registered much about this man. He'd been quiet and gentle, and she had not felt in any way threatened. Only now did she realize he'd been studying her closely, waiting for a glimpse of the inner Catherine Cordell. Not the accomplished trauma surgeon, not the cool and elegant redhead, but the woman beneath the surface.

Detective Rizzoli spoke now, and, unlike Moore, she made no effort to soften her questions. She simply wanted answers, and she didn't waste any time going after them. 'When did you move here, Dr Cordell?'

'I left Savannah a month after I was attacked,' said Catherine, matching Rizzoli's businesslike tone.

'Why did you choose Boston?'

'Why not?'

'It's a long way from the South.'

'My mother grew up in Massachusetts. She brought us to New England every summer. It felt like . . . I was coming home.'

'So you've been here over two years.'

'Yes.'

'Doing what?'

Catherine frowned, perplexed by the question. 'Working here at Pilgrim, with Dr Falco. On Trauma Service.'

'I guess the *Globe* got it wrong, then.'

'Excuse me?'

'I read the article about you a few weeks ago.

The one on women surgeons. Great photo of you, by the way. It said you've been working here at Pilgrim for only a year.'

Catherine paused, then said, calmly, 'The article was correct. After Savannah, I took some time to . . .' She cleared her throat. 'I didn't join Dr Falco's practice until last July.'

'And what about your first year in Boston?'

'I didn't work.'

'What did you do?'

'Nothing.' That answer, so flat and final, was all she'd damn well say. She was not going to reveal the humiliating truth of what that first year had been like. The days, stretching into weeks, when she was afraid to emerge from her apartment. The nights when the faintest sound could leave her shaking in panic. The slow and painful journey back into the world, when just riding an elevator, or walking at night to her car, was an act of sheer courage. She'd been ashamed of her vulnerability; she was still ashamed, and her pride would never allow her to reveal it.

She looked at her watch. 'I have patients coming in. I really have nothing more to add.'

'Let me re-check my facts here.' Rizzoli opened a small spiral-bound notebook. 'A little over two years ago, on the night of June fifteenth, you were attacked in your home by Dr Andrew Capra. A man you knew. An intern you worked with in the hospital.' She looked up at Catherine.

'You already know the answers.'

'He drugged you, stripped you. Tied you to your bed. Terrorized you.'

'I don't see the point of—'

47

'Raped you.' The words, though spoken quietly, had an impact as brutal as a slap.

Catherine said nothing.

'And that's not all he planned to do,' continued Rizzoli.

Dear god, make her stop.

'He was going to mutilate you in the worst possible way. As he mutilated four other women in Georgia. He cut them open. Destroyed precisely what made them women.'

'That's enough,' said Moore.

But Rizzoli was relentless. 'It could have happened to you, Dr Cordell.'

Catherine shook her head. 'Why are you doing this?'

'Dr Cordell, there is nothing I want more than to catch this man, and I would think you'd want to help us. You'd want to stop it from happening to other women.'

'This has nothing to do with me! Andrew Capra is dead. He's been dead for two years.'

'Yes, I've read his autopsy report.'

'Well, I can guarantee he's dead,' Catherine shot back. 'Because I'm the one who blew that son of a bitch away.'

Four

Moore and Rizzoli sat sweating in the car, warm air roaring from the AC vent. They'd been stuck in traffic for ten minutes, and the car was getting no cooler.

'Taxpayers get what they pay for,' said Rizzoli. 'And this car's a piece of junk.'

Moore shut off the AC and rolled down his window. The odor of hot pavement and auto exhaust blew into the car. Already he was bathed in perspiration. He didn't know how Rizzoli could stand keeping her blazer on; he had shed his jacket the minute they'd stepped out of Pilgrim Medical Center and were enveloped in a heavy blanket of humidity. He knew she must be feeling the heat, because he saw sweat glistening on her upper lip, a lip that had probably never made the acquaintance of lipstick. Rizzoli was not bad-looking, but while other women might smooth on makeup or clip on earrings, Rizzoli seemed determined to downplay her own attractiveness. She wore grim dark suits that did not flatter her petite frame, and her hair was a careless mop of black curls. She was who she was, and either you

accepted it or you could just go to hell. He understood why she'd adopted that up-yours attitude;
she probably needed it to survive as a female cop.
Rizzoli was, above all, a survivor.

Just as Catherine Cordell was a survivor. But Dr
Cordell had evolved a different strategy:
Withdrawal. Distance. During the interview, he'd
felt as though he were looking at her through
frosted glass, so detached had she seemed.

It was that detachment that irked Rizzoli.
'There's something wrong with her,' she said.
'Something's missing in the emotions department.'

'She's a trauma surgeon. She's trained to keep
her cool.'

'There's cool, and then there's ice. Two years
ago she was tied down, raped, and almost gutted.
And she's so friggin' calm about it now. It makes
me wonder.'

Moore braked for a red light and sat staring
at the grid-locked intersection. Sweat trickled
down the small of his back. He did not function
well in the heat; it made him feel sluggish and
stupid. It made him long for summer's end, for the
purity of winter's first snowfall . . .

'Hey,' said Rizzoli. 'Are you listening?'

'She is tightly controlled,' he conceded. But not
ice, he thought, remembering how Catherine
Cordell's hand had trembled as she gave him
back the photos of the two women.

Back at his desk, he sipped lukewarm Coke and
re-read the article printed a few weeks before in
the *Boston Globe*: 'Women Holding the Knife.' It
featured three female surgeons in Boston – their
triumphs and difficulties, the special problems

50

they faced in their specialty. Of the three photos, Cordell's was the most arresting. It was more than the fact she was attractive; it was her gaze, so proud and direct that it seemed to challenge the camera. The photo, like the article, reinforced the impression that this woman was in control of her life.

He set aside the article and sat thinking of how wrong first impressions can be. How easily pain can be masked by a smile, an upward tilting chin.

Now he opened a different file. Took a deep breath and re-read the Savannah police report on Dr Andrew Capra.

Capra made his first known kill while he was a senior medical student at Emory University in Atlanta. The victim was Dora Ciccone, a twenty-two-year-old Emory graduate student, whose body was found tied to the bed in her off-campus apartment. Traces of the date-rape drug Rohypnol were found in her system on autopsy. Her apartment showed no signs of forced entry.

The victim had invited the killer into her home.

Once drugged, Dora Ciccone was tied to her bed with nylon cord, and her screams were muffled with duct tape. First the killer raped her. Then he proceeded to cut.

She was alive during the operation.

When he had completed the excision, and had taken his souvenir, he administered the coup de grace: a single deep slash across the neck, from left to right. Though the police had DNA from the killer's semen, they had no leads. The investigation was complicated by the fact Dora was known as a party girl who liked to cruise the local bars and often brought home men she'd only just met.

On the night she died, the man she brought home was a medical student named Andrew Capra. But Capra's name did not come to the attention of the police until three women had been slaughtered in the city of Savannah, two hundred miles away.

Finally, on a muggy night in June, the killings ended.

Thirty-one-year-old Catherine Cordell, the chief surgical resident in Savannah's Riverland Hospital, was startled by someone knocking at her door. When she opened it, she found Andrew Capra, one of her surgery interns, standing on her porch. Earlier that day, in the hospital, she had reprimanded him about a mistake he'd made, and now he was desperate to find out how he could redeem himself. Could he please come in to talk about it?

Over a few beers, they'd reviewed Capra's performance as an intern. All the errors he'd made, the patients he might have harmed because of his carelessness. She did not sugarcoat the truth: that Capra was failing and would not be allowed to finish the surgery program. At some point in the evening, Catherine left the room to use the toilet, then returned to resume the conversation and finish her beer.

When she regained consciousness, she found herself stripped naked and tied to the bed with nylon cord.

The police report described, in horrifying detail, the nightmare that followed.

Photographs taken of her in the hospital

revealed a woman with haunted eyes, a bruised and horribly swollen cheek. What he saw, in these photos, was summed up in the generic word: *victim.*

It was not a word that applied to the eerily composed woman he had met today.

Now, re-reading Cordell's statement, he could hear her voice in his head. The words no longer belonged to an anonymous victim, but to a woman whose face he knew.

I don't know how I got my hand free. My wrist is all scraped now, so I must have pulled it through the cord. I'm sorry, but things aren't clear in my mind. All I remember is reaching for the scalpel. Knowing that I had to get the scalpel off the tray. That I had to cut the cords, before Andrew came back . . .

I remember rolling toward the side of the bed. Falling half onto the floor and hitting my head. Then I was trying to find the gun. It's my father's gun. After the third woman was killed in Savannah, he insisted I keep it.

I remember reaching under my bed. Grabbing the gun. I remember footsteps, coming into the room. Then – I'm not sure. That must be when I shot him. Yes, that's what I think happened. They told me I shot him twice. I guess it must be true.

Moore paused, mulling over the statement. Ballistics had confirmed that both bullets were fired from the weapon, registered to Catherine's father, that was found lying beside the bed. Blood tests in the hospital confirmed the presence of

Rohypnol, an amnesiac drug, in her bloodstream, so she might very well have blank spots in her memory. When Cordell was brought to the E.R., the doctors described her as confused, either from the drug or from a possible concussion. Only a heavy blow to the head could have left such a bruised and swollen face. She did not recall how or when she received that blow.

Moore turned to the crime scene photos. On the bedroom floor, Andrew Capra lay dead, flat on his back. He had been shot twice, once in the abdomen, once in the eye, both times at close range.

For a long time he studied the photos, noting the position of Capra's body, the pattern of the bloodstains.

He turned to the autopsy report. Read it through twice.

Looked once again at the crime scene photo.

Something is wrong here, he thought. Cordell's statement does not make sense.

A report suddenly landed on his desk. He glanced up, startled, to see Rizzoli.

'Did you get a load of this?' she asked.

'What is it?'

'The report on that strand of hair found in Elena Ortiz's wound margin.'

Moore scanned down to the final sentence. And he said: 'I have no idea what this means.'

In 1997, the various branches of the Boston Police Department were moved under one roof, located inside the brand-new complex at One Schroeder Plaza in Boston's rough-and-tumble Roxbury neighborhood. The cops referred to their new digs as 'the marble palace' because of the extensive use of polished granite in the lobby. 'Give us a few years to trash the place, and it'll feel like home' was the joke. Schroeder Plaza bore little resemblance to the shabby police stations seen on TV cop shows. It was a sleek and modern building, brightened by large windows and skylights. The homicide unit, with its carpeted floors and computer workstations, could have passed for a corporate office. What the cops liked best about Schroeder Plaza was the integration of the various BPD branches.

For homicide detectives, a visit to the crime lab was only a walk down the hallway, to the south wing of the building.

In Hair and Fiber, Moore and Rizzoli watched as Erin Volchko, a forensic scientist, sifted through her collection of evidence envelopes. 'All I had to work with was that single hair,' said Erin. 'But it's amazing what one hair can tell you. Okay, here it is.' She'd located the envelope with Elena Ortiz's case number, and now she removed a microscope slide. 'I'll just show you what it looks like under the lens. The numerical scores are in the report.'

'These numbers?' said Rizzoli, looking down at the long series of scoring codes on the page.

'Correct. Each code describes a different characteristic of hair, from color and curl to microscopic features. This particular strand is an A01 – a dark blond. Its curl is B01. Curved, with a curl diameter of less than eighty. Almost, but not quite, straight. The shaft length is four centimeters. Unfortunately, this strand is in its telogen phase, so there's no epithelial tissue adhering to it.'

'Meaning there's no DNA.'

'Right. Telogen is the terminal stage of root growth. This strand fell out naturally, as part of the shedding process. In other words, it was not yanked out. If there were epithelial cells on the root, we could use their nuclei for DNA analysis. But this strand doesn't have any such cells.'

Rizzoli and Moore exchanged looks of disappointment.

'But,' added Erin, 'we do have something here that's pretty damn good. Not as good as DNA, but it might hold up in court once you nail a suspect. It's too bad we don't have any hairs from the Sterling case to compare.' She focused the microscope lens, then scooted aside. 'Take a look.'

The scope had a teaching eyepiece, so both Rizzoli and Moore could examine the slide simultaneously. What Moore saw, peering through the lens, was a single strand beaded with tiny nodules.

'What are the little bumps?' said Rizzoli. 'That's not normal.'

'Not only is it abnormal, it's rare,' said Erin. 'It's a condition called *Trichorrhexis invaginata*, otherwise known as 'bamboo hair.' You can see how it gets its nickname. Those little nodules make it look like a stalk of bamboo, don't they?'

'What are the nodules?' asked Moore.

'They're focal defects in the hair fiber. Weak spots which allow the hair shaft to fold back on itself, forming a sort of ball and socket. Those little bumps are the weak spots, where the shaft has telescoped on itself, making a bulge.'

'How do you get this condition?'

'Occasionally it can develop from too much hair processing. Dyes, permanents, that sort of thing. But since we're most likely dealing with a male unsub, and since I see no evidence of artificial bleaching, I'm inclined to say this is not due to processing, but to some sort of genetic abnormality.'

'Like what?'

'Netherton's Syndrome, for instance. That's an autosomal recessive condition that affects keratin development. Keratin is a tough, fibrous protein found in hair and nails. It's also the outer layer of our skin.'

'If there's a genetic defect, and the keratin doesn't develop normally, then the hair is weakened?'

Erin nodded. 'And it's not just the hair that can be affected. People with Netherton's Syndrome may have skin disorders as well. Rashes and flaking.'

'We're looking for a perp with a bad case of dandruff?' said Rizzoli.

'It may be even more obvious than that. Some of these patients have a severe form known as *icthyosis*. Their skin can be so dry it looks like the hide of an alligator.'

Rizzoli laughed. 'So we're looking for *reptile man*! That should narrow down the search.'

'Not necessarily. It's summertime.'

'What does that have to do with it?'

'This heat and humidity improves skin dryness. He may look entirely normal this time of year.'

Rizzoli and Moore glanced at each other, simultaneously struck by the same thought.

57

Both victims were slaughtered during the summertime.

'As long as this heat holds up,' said Erin, 'he probably blends right in with everyone else.'

'It's only July,' said Rizzoli.

Moore nodded. 'His hunting season's just begun.'

John Doe now had a name. The E.R. nurses had found an ID tag attached to his key ring. He was Herman Gwadowski, and he was sixty-nine years old.

Catherine stood in her patient's SICU cubicle, methodically surveying the monitors and equipment arrayed around his bed. A normal EKG rhythm blipped across the oscilloscope. The arterial waves spiked at 110/70, and the readings from his central venous pressure line rose and fell like swells on a windblown sea. Judging by the numbers, Mr Gwadowski's operation was a success.

But he's not waking up, thought Catherine as she flashed her penlight into the left pupil, then the right. Nearly eight hours after surgery, he remained in a deep coma.

She straightened and watched his chest rise and fall with the cycling of the ventilator. She had stopped him from bleeding to death. But what had she really saved? A body with a beating heart and no functioning brain.

She heard tapping on the glass. Through the cubicle window she saw her surgical partner, Dr Peter Falco, waving to her, a concerned expression on his usually cheerful face.

Some surgeons are known to throw temper tantrums in the O.R. Some sweep arrogantly into the operating suite and don their surgical gowns the way one dons royal robes. Some are coldly efficient technicians for whom patients are merely a bundle of mechanical parts in need of repair.

And then there was Peter. Funny, exuberant Peter, who sang earsplittingly off-key Elvis songs in the O.R., who organized paper airplane contests in the office and happily got down on his hands and knees to play Lego with his pediatric patients. She was accustomed to seeing a smile on Peter's face. When she saw him frowning at her through the window, she immediately stepped out of her patient's cubicle.

'Everything all right?' he asked.

'Just finishing rounds.'

Peter eyed the tubes and machinery bristling around Mr Gwadowski's bed. 'I heard you made a great save. A twelve-unit bleeder.'

'I don't know if you'd call it a save.' Her gaze returned to her patient. 'Everything works but the gray matter.'

They said nothing for a moment, both of them watching Mr Gwadowski's chest rise and fall.

'Helen told me two policemen came by to see you today,' said Peter. 'What's going on?'

'It wasn't important.'

'Forgot to pay those parking tickets?'

She forced a laugh. 'Right, and I'm counting on you to bail me out.'

They left the SICU and walked into the hallway, lanky Peter striding beside her in that easy lope of his. As they rode the elevator, he asked:

'You okay, Catherine?'

'Why? Don't I look okay?'

'Honestly?' He studied her face, his blue eyes so direct she felt invaded. 'You look like you need a glass of wine and a nice dinner out. How about joining me?'

'A tempting invitation.'

'But?'

'But I think I'll stay in for the night.'

Peter clutched his chest, as though mortally wounded. 'Shot down again! Tell me, is there any line that works on you?'

She smiled. 'That's for you to find out.'

'How about this one? A little bird told me it's your birthday on Saturday. Let me take you up in my plane.'

'Can't. I'm on call that day.'

'You can switch with Ames. I'll talk to him.'

'Oh, Peter. You know I don't like to fly.'

'Don't tell me you have phobias about flying?'

'I'm just not good at relinquishing control.'

He nodded gravely. 'Classic surgical personality.'

'That's a nice way of saying I'm uptight.'

'So it's a no-go on the flying date? I can't change your mind?'

'I don't think so.'

He sighed. 'Well, that's it for my lines. I've gone through my entire repertoire.'

'I know. You're starting to recycle them.'

'That's what Helen says, too.'

She shot him a look of surprise. 'Helen's giving you tips on how to ask me out?'

'She said she couldn't stand the pathetic

spectacle of a man banging his head against an impregnable wall.'

They both laughed as they stepped off the elevator and walked to their suite. It was the comfortable laugh of two colleagues who knew this game was all tongue-in-cheek. Keeping it on that level meant no feelings were hurt, no emotions were at stake. A safe little flirtation that kept them both insulated from real entanglements. Playfully he'd ask her out; just as playfully she'd turn him down, and the whole office was in on the joke.

It was already five-thirty, and their staff was gone for the day. Peter retreated to his office and she went into hers to hang up her lab coat and get her purse. As she put the coat on the door hook, a thought suddenly occurred to her.

She crossed the hallway and stuck her head in Peter's office. He was reviewing charts, his reading glasses perched on his nose. Unlike her own neat office, Peter's looked like chaos central. Paper airplanes filled the trash can. Books and surgery journals were piled on chairs. One wall was nearly smothered by an out-of-control philodendron. Buried in that jungle of leaves were Peter's diplomas: an undergraduate degree in aeronautical engineering from MIT, an M.D. from Harvard Medical School.

'Peter? This is a stupid question . . .'

He glanced up over his glasses. 'Then you've come to the right man.'

'Have you been in my office?'

'Should I call my lawyer before I answer that?'

'Come on. I'm serious.'

He straightened, and his gaze sharpened on hers. 'No, I haven't. Why?'

'Never mind. It's not a big deal.' She turned to leave and heard the creak of his chair as he stood up. He followed her into her office.

'What's not a big deal?' he asked.

'I'm being obsessive-compulsive, that's all. I get irritated when things aren't where they should be.'

'Like what?'

'My lab coat. I always hang it on the door, and somehow it ends up on the filing cabinet, or over a chair. I know it's not Helen or the other secretaries. I asked them.'

'The cleaning lady probably moved it.'

'And then it drives me crazy that I can't find my stethoscope.'

'It's still missing?'

'I had to borrow the nursing supervisor's.'

Frowning, he glanced around the room. 'Well, there it is. On the bookshelf.' He crossed to the shelf, where her stethoscope lay coiled beside a bookend.

Silently she took it from him, staring at it as though it were something alien. A black serpent, draped over her hand.

'Hey, what's the matter?'

She took a deep breath. 'I think I'm just tired.' She put the stethoscope in the left pocket of her lab coat – the same place she always left it.

'Are you sure that's all? Is there something else going on?'

'I need to get home.' She walked out of her office, and he followed her into the hall.

'Is it something to do with those police officers?

Look, if you're in some kind of trouble – if I can help out—'

'I don't *need* any help, thank you.' Her answer came out cooler than she'd intended, and she was instantly sorry for it. Peter didn't deserve that.

'You know, I wouldn't mind if you did ask me for favors every so often,' he said quietly. 'It's part of working together. Being partners. Don't you think?'

She didn't answer.

He turned back to his office. 'I'll see you in the morning.'

'Peter?'

'Yes?'

'About those two police officers. And the reason they came to see me—'

'You don't have to tell me.'

'No, I should. You'll just wonder about it if I don't. They came to ask me about a homicide case. A woman was murdered Thursday night. They thought I might have known her.'

'Did you?'

'No. It was a mistake, that's all.' She sighed. 'Just a mistake.'

Catherine turned the dead bolt, felt it drive home with a satisfying thud, and then slid the chain in place. One more line of defense against the unnamed horrors that lurked beyond her walls. Safely barricaded in her apartment, she removed her shoes, set her purse and car keys down on the cherrywood butler's table, and walked in stockinged feet across the thick white carpet of her living room. The flat was pleasantly cool, thanks to the miracle of central air-conditioning. Outside it was eighty-six degrees, but in here the temperature never wavered above seventy-two in the summer or below sixty-eight in the winter. There was so little in one's life that could be pre-set, predetermined, and she strove to maintain what order she could manage within the circumscribed boundaries of her life. She had chosen this twelve-unit condominium building on Commonwealth Avenue because it was brand-new, with a secure parking garage. Though not as picturesque as the historic redbrick residences in the Back Bay, neither was it plagued by the plumbing or electrical uncertainties that come with older buildings. Uncertainty was something Catherine did not tolerate well. Her flat was kept spotless, and except for a few startling splashes of color, she'd chosen to furnish it mostly in white. White couch, white carpets, white tile. The color of purity. Untouched, virginal.

In her bedroom she undressed, hung up her skirt, set aside the blouse to be dropped off at the dry cleaner's. She changed into loose slacks and a sleeveless silk blouse. By the time she walked barefoot into the kitchen, she was feeling calm, and in control.

She had not felt that way earlier today. The visit by the two detectives had left her shaken, and all afternoon she had caught herself making careless mistakes. Reaching for the wrong lab slip, writing the incorrect date on a medical chart. Only minor errors, but they were like faint ripples that mar the surface of waters that are deeply disturbed. For the last two years she had managed to suppress all

64

thoughts of what had happened to her in Savannah. Every so often, without warning, a remembered image might return, as sharp as a knife's slash, but she would dance away from it, deftly turning her mind to other thoughts. Today, she could not avoid the memories. Today, she could not pretend that Savannah had never happened.

The kitchen tiles were cool under her bare feet. She fixed herself a screwdriver, light on the vodka, and sipped it as she grated Parmesan cheese and chopped tomatoes and onions and herbs. She had not eaten since breakfast, and the alcohol sluiced straight into her bloodstream. The vodka buzz was pleasant and anesthetizing. She took comfort in the steady rap of her knife against the cutting board, the fragrance of fresh basil and garlic. Cooking as therapy.

Outside her kitchen window, the city of Boston was an overheated cauldron of gridlocked cars and flaring tempers, but in here, sealed behind glass, she calmly sautéed the tomatoes in olive oil, poured a glass of Chianti, and heated a pot of water for fresh angel-hair pasta. Cool air hissed from the air-conditioning vent.

She sat down with her pasta and salad and wine and ate to the background strains of Debussy on the CD player. Despite her hunger and the careful attention to the preparation of her meal, everything seemed tasteless. She forced herself to eat, but her throat felt full, as though she had swallowed something thick and glutinous. Even drinking a second glass of wine could not dislodge the lump in her throat. She put down her fork and stared at her half-eaten dinner. The music swelled and swept over her in breaking waves.

She dropped her face in her hands. At first no sound came out. It was as if her grief had been bottled up so long, the seal had permanently frozen shut. Then a high keening escaped her throat, the thinnest thread of sound. She gasped in a breath, and a cry burst forth as two years' worth of pain came pouring out all at once. The violence of her emotions scared her, because she could not hold them back, could not fathom how deep her pain went or if there would ever be an end to it. She cried until her throat was raw, until her lungs were stuttering with spasms, the sound of her sobbing trapped in that hermetically sealed apartment.

At last, drained of all tears, she lay down on the couch and fell at once into a deep and exhausted sleep.

She came sharply awake to find herself in darkness. Her heart was pounding, her blouse soaked in sweat. Had there been a noise? The crack of glass, the tread of a footstep? Was that what had startled her from such a deep sleep? She dared not move a muscle, for fear she would miss the telltale sound of an intruder.

Moving lights shone through the window, the headlights of a passing car. Her living room briefly brightened, then slid back into darkness. She listened to the hiss of cool air from the vent, the growl of the refrigerator in the kitchen. Nothing alien. Nothing that should inspire this crushing sense of dread.

She sat up and summoned the courage to turn

on the lamp. Imagined horrors instantly vanished in the warm glow of light. She rose from the couch, moving deliberately from room to room, turning on lights, looking into closets. On a rational level, she knew that there was no intruder, that her home, with its sophisticated alarm system and its dead bolts and its tightly latched windows, was as protected as any home could be. But she did not rest until this ritual had been completed and every dark nook had been searched. Only when she was satisfied that her security had not been breached did she allow herself to breathe easily again.

It was ten-thirty. A Wednesday. *I need to talk to someone. Tonight I cannot deal with this alone.*

She sat down at her desk, booted up her computer, and watched as the screen flickered on. It was her lifeline, her therapist, this bundle of electronics and wires and plastic, the only safe place into which she could pour her pain.

She typed in her screen name, CCORD, signed onto the Internet, and with a few clicks of the mouse, a few words typed on the keyboard, she navigated her way into the private chat room called, simply: *womanhelp*.

Half a dozen familiar screen names were already there. Faceless, nameless women, all of them drawn to this safe and anonymous haven in cyberspace. She sat for a few moments, watching the messages scroll down the computer screen. Hearing, in her mind, the wounded voices of women she had never met, except in this virtual room.

LAURIE45: So what did you do then?

VOTIVE: I told him I wasn't ready. I was still having flash-backs. I told him if he cared about me, he'd wait.

HBREAKER: Good for you.

WINKY98: Don't let him rush you.

LAURIE45: How did he react?

VOTIVE: He said I should just GET OVER IT. Like I'm a wimp or something.

WINKY98: Men should get raped!!!!

HBREAKER: It took me two years before I was ready.

LAURIE45: Over a year for me.

WINKY98: All these guys think about are their dicks. It's all about them. They just want their THING satisfied.

LAURIE45: Ouch. You're pissed off tonight, Wink.

WINKY98: Maybe I am. Sometimes I think Lorena Bobbitt had the right idea.

HBREAKER: Wink's getting out her cleaver!

VOTIVE: I don't think he's willing to wait. I think he's given up on me.

WINKY98: You're worth waiting for. You're WORTH IT!

A few seconds passed, with the message box blank. Then,

LAURIE45: Hello, CCord. It's good to see you back.

Catherine typed.

CCORD: I see we're talking about men again.
LAURIE45: Yeah. How come we can't ever get off this tired subject?
VOTIVE: Because they're the ones who hurt us.

There was another long pause. Catherine took a deep breath and typed.

CCORD: I had a bad day.
LAURIE45: Tell us, CC. What happened?

Catherine could almost hear the coo of female voices, gentle, soothing murmurs through the ether.

CCORD: I had a panic attack tonight. I'm here, locked in my house, where no one can touch me and it still happens.
WINKY98: Don't let him win. Don't let him make you a prisoner.
CCORD: It's too late. I am a prisoner. Because I realized something terrible tonight.
WINKY98: What's that?
CCORD: Evil doesn't die. It never dies. It just takes on a new face, a new name. Just because we've been touched by it once, it doesn't mean we're immune to ever being hurt again. Lightning can strike twice.

No one typed anything. No one responded.
No matter how careful we are, evil knows where we live, she thought. It knows how to find us.
A drop of sweat slid down her back.

And I feel it now. Closing in.

Nina Peyton goes nowhere, sees no one. She has not been to her job in weeks. Today I called her office in Brookline, where she works as a sales representative, and her colleague told me he doesn't know when she will return to them. She is like a wounded beast, holed up in her cave, terrified of taking even one step out into the night. She knows what the night holds for her, because she has been touched by its evil, and even now she feels it seeping like vapor through the walls of her home. The curtains are closed tight, but the fabric is thin, and I see her moving about inside. Her silhouette is balled up, arms squeezed to her chest, as though her body has folded into itself. Her movements are jerky and mechanical as she paces back and forth.

She is checking the locks on the doors, the latches on the windows. Trying to shut out the darkness.

It must be stifling inside that little house. The night is like steam, and there are no air conditioners in any of her windows. All evening she has stayed inside, the windows closed despite the heat. I picture her gleaming with sweat, suffering through the long hot day and into the night, desperate to let in fresh air, but afraid of what else she might let in.

She walks past the window again. Stops. Lingers there, framed by the rectangle of light. Suddenly the curtains flick apart, and she reaches through to unlock the latch. She slides up the window. Stands before it, taking in hungry gulps of fresh air. She has finally surrendered to the heat.

There is nothing so exciting to a hunter as the scent of wounded prey. I can almost smell it wafting out, the scent of a bloodied beast, of defiled flesh. Just as she breathes in the night air, so, too, am I breathing in her scent. Her fear.

My heart beats faster. I reach into my bag, to caress the instruments. Even the steel is warm to my touch.

She closes the window with a bang. A few deep gulps of fresh air was all she dared allow herself, and now she retreats to the misery of her stuffy little house.

After a while, I accept disappointment and I walk away, leaving her to sweat through the night in that oven of a bedroom.

Tomorrow, they say, it will be even hotter.

Five

'This unsub is a classic picquerist,' said Dr Lawrence Zucker. 'Someone who uses a knife to achieve secondary or indirect sexual release. Picquerism is the act of stabbing or cutting, any repeated penetration of the skin with a sharp object. The knife is a phallic symbol – a substitution for the male sexual organ. Instead of performing normal sexual intercourse, our unsub achieves his release by subjecting his victim to pain and terror. It's the power that thrills him. Ultimate power, over life and death.'

Detective Jane Rizzoli was not easily spooked, but Dr Zucker gave her the creeps. He looked like a pale and hulking John Malkovich, and his voice was whispery, almost feminine. As he spoke, his fingers moved with serpentine elegance. He was not a cop but a criminal psychologist from Northeastern University, a consultant for the Boston Police Department. Rizzoli had worked with him once before on a homicide case, and he'd given her the creeps then, too. It was not just his appearance but the way he so thoroughly insinuated himself into the perp's mind and the obvious pleasure he derived from wandering in that satanic dimension. He *enjoyed* the journey. She could hear that almost subliminal hum of excitement in his voice.

She glanced around the conference room at the other four detectives and wondered if anyone else was spooked by this weirdo, but all she saw was tired expressions and varying shades of five o'clock shadows.

They were all tired. She herself had slept scarcely four hours last night. This morning she'd awakened in the dark pre-dawn, her mind zooming straight into fourth gear as it processed a kaleidoscope of images and voices. She had absorbed the Elena Ortiz case so deeply into her subconscious that in her dreams she and the victim had engaged in a conversation, albeit a non-sensical one. There had been no supernatural revelations, no clues from beyond the grave, merely images generated by the twitches of brain cells. Still, Rizzoli considered the dream significant. It told her just how much this case meant to her. Being lead detective on a high-profile investigation was like walking the high wire without a net. Nail the perp, and everyone applauded. Screw up, and the whole world watched you splat.

This was now a high-profile case. Two days ago, the headline hit the front page of the local tabloid: 'The Surgeon Cuts Again.' Thanks to the *Boston Herald*, their unsub had his own moniker, and even the cops were using it. *The Surgeon.*

God, she'd been ready to take on a high-wire act, ready for the chance to either soar or crash on her own merits. A week ago, when she'd walked into Elena Ortiz's apartment as lead detective, she had known, in an instant, that this was the case that would make her career, and she was anxious to prove herself.

How quickly things changed.

Within a day, her case had ballooned into a much wider investigation, led by the unit's Lieutenant Marquette. The Elena Ortiz case had been folded into the Diana Sterling case, and the team had grown to five detectives, in addition to Marquette: Rizzoli and her partner, Barry Frost; Moore and his heavyset partner, Jerry Sleeper; plus a fifth detective, Darren Crowe. Rizzoli was the only woman on the team; indeed, she was the only woman in the entire homicide unit, and some men never let her forget it. Oh, she got along fine with Barry Frost, despite his irritatingly sunny disposition. Jerry Sleeper was too phlegmatic to get anybody pissed off at him or to be pissed off at anyone else. And as for Moore – well, despite her initial reservations, she was actually beginning to like him and truly respect him for his quietly methodical work. Most important, he seemed to respect *her*. Whenever she spoke, she knew that Moore listened.

No, it was the fifth cop on the team, Darren Crowe, she had issues with. Major issues. He sat across the table from her now, his tanned face wearing its usual smirk. She'd grown up with boys like him. Boys with lots of muscle, lots of girl-friends. Lots of ego.

She and Crowe despised each other.

A stack of papers came around the table. Rizzoli took a copy and saw it was a criminal profile that Dr Zucker had just completed.

'I know some of you think my work is hocus-pocus,' said Zucker. 'So let me explain my reasoning. We know the following things about our unknown subject. He enters the victim's residence through an open window. He does this in the early morning hours, sometime between midnight and two a.m. He surprises the victim in her bed. Immediately incapacitates her with chloroform. He removes her clothes. He restrains her by binding her to the bed using duct tape around her wrists and ankles. He reinforces that with strips across her upper thighs and mid-torso. Finally, he tapes her mouth shut. Utter control is what he achieves. When the victim awakens shortly thereafter, she cannot move, cannot scream. It's as though she's paralyzed, yet she's awake and aware of everything that happens next.

'And what happens next is surely anyone's worst nightmare.' Zucker's voice had faded to a monotone. The more grotesque the details, the softer he spoke, and they were all leaning forward, hanging on his words.

'The unsub begins to cut,' said Zucker. 'According to the autopsy report, he takes his time. He is meticulous. He slices through the lower abdomen, layer by layer. First the skin, then the subcutaneous layer, the fascia, the muscle. He uses suture to control the bleeding. He identifies and removes only the organ he wants. Nothing more. And what he wants is the womb.'

Zucker looked around the table, taking note of their reactions. His gaze fell on Rizzoli, the only cop in the room who possessed the organ of which they spoke. She stared back, resentful that her gender had caused him to focus on her.

'What does that tell us about him, Detective Rizzoli?' he asked.

'He hates women,' she said. 'He cuts out the one thing that makes them women.'

Zucker nodded, and his smile made her shudder. 'It's what Jack the Ripper did to Annie Chapman. By taking the womb, he defeminizes his victim. He steals her power. He ignores their jewelry, their money. He wants just one thing, and once he's harvested his souvenir, he can proceed to the finale. But first, there is a pause before the ultimate thrill. The autopsy on both victims indicates that he stops at this point. Perhaps an hour passes, as the victims continue to bleed slowly. A pool of blood collects in their wound. What is he doing during that time?'

'Enjoying himself,' said Moore softly.

'You mean, like jerking off?' said Darren Crowe, posing the question with his usual crudeness.

'There was no ejaculate left at either crime scene,' pointed out Rizzoli.

Crowe tossed her an *aren't you smart* look. 'The absence of *e-jac-u-late*', he said, sarcastically emphasizing every syllable, 'doesn't rule out jerking off.'

'I don't believe he *was* masturbating,' said Zucker. 'This particular unsub would not relinquish that much control in an unfamiliar environment. I think he waits until he's in a safe place to achieve sexual release. Everything about the crime scene screams *control*. When he proceeds to the final act, he does it with confidence and authority. He cuts the victim's throat with a single deep slash. And then he performs one last ritual.'

Zucker reached into his briefcase and took out two crime scene photos, which he laid on the table. One was of Diana Sterling's bedroom, the other of Elena Ortiz's.

'He meticulously folds their nightclothes and places them near the body. We know the folding was done after the slaughter, because blood splatters were found on the inside folds.'

'Why does he do that?' asked Frost. 'What's the symbolism there?'

'Control again,' said Rizzoli.

Zucker nodded. 'That's certainly part of it. By this ritual, he demonstrates he's in control of the scene. But at the same time, the ritual controls *him*. It's an impulse he may not be able to resist.'

'What if he's prevented from doing it?' asked Frost. 'Say he's interrupted and can't complete it?'

'It will leave him frustrated and angry. He may feel compelled to immediately start hunting for the next victim. But so far, he's always managed to complete the ritual. And each killing has been satisfying enough to tide him over for long periods of time.' Zucker looked around the room. 'This is the worst kind of unsub we can face. He went a whole year between attacks – that's extremely rare. It means he can go months between hunts. We could run ourselves ragged looking for him, while he sits patiently waiting for the next kill. He is careful. He is organized. He will leave few, if any, clues behind.' He glanced at Moore, seeking confirmation.

'We have no fingerprints, no DNA, at either crime scene,' Moore said. 'All we have is a single strand of hair, collected from Ortiz's wound. And a few dark polyester fibers from the window frame.'

'I take it you've found no witnesses, either.'

'We had thirteen hundred interviews on the Sterling case. One hundred eighty interviews so far on the Ortiz case. No one saw the intruder. No one was aware of any stalker.'

'But we have had three confessions,' said Crowe. 'They all walked in off the street. We took their statements and sent them on their way.' He laughed. 'Wackos.'

'This unsub is not insane,' said Zucker. 'I would guess he appears perfectly normal. I believe he's a white male in his late twenties or early thirties. Neatly groomed, of above-average intelligence. He is almost certainly a high school graduate, perhaps with a college education or even more. The two crime scenes are over a mile apart, and the murders were committed at a time of day when there was little public transportation running. So he drives a car. It will be neat and well maintained. He probably has no history of mental health problems, but he may have a juvenile record of burglary or voyeurism. If he's employed, it will be a job that requires both intelligence and meticulousness. We know he is a planner, as demonstrated by the fact he carries his murder kit with him – scalpel, suture, duct tape, chloroform. Plus a container of some kind in which to bring his souvenir home. It could be as simple as a Ziploc bag. He works in a field that requires attention to

78

detail. Since he obviously has anatomical knowledge, and surgical skills, we could be dealing with a medical professional.'

Rizzoli met Moore's gaze, both struck by the same thought: There were probably more doctors per capita in the city of Boston than anywhere else in the world.

'Because he is intelligent,' said Zucker, 'he knows we're staking out the crime scenes. And he will resist the temptation to return. But the temptation is there, so it's worth continuing the stakeout of Ortiz's residence, at least for the near future.

'He is also intelligent enough to avoid choosing a victim in his immediate neighborhood. He's what we call a "commuter", rather than a "marauder". He goes outside his neighborhood to hunt. Until we have more data points to work with, I can't really do a geographical profile. I can't pinpoint which areas of the city you should focus on.'

'How many data points do you need?' asked Rizzoli.

'A minimum of five.'

'Meaning, we need five murders?'

'The criminal geographic targeting program I use requires five to have any validity. I've run the CGT program with as few as four data points, and sometimes you can get an offender residence prediction with that, but it's not accurate. We need to know more about his movements. What his activity space is, where his anchor points are. Every killer works inside a certain comfort zone. They're like carnivores hunting. They have their territory, their fishing holes, where they find their prey.' Zucker looked around the table at the detectives' unimpressed faces. 'We don't know enough about this unsub yet to make any predictions. So we need to focus on the victims. Who they were, and why he chose them.'

Zucker reached into his briefcase and took out two folders, one labeled *Sterling*, the other *Ortiz*. He produced a dozen photographs, which he spread out on the table. Images of the two women when they were alive, some dating all the way back to childhood.

'You haven't seen some of these photos. I asked their families to provide them, just to give us a sense of the history of these women. Look at their faces. Study who they were as people. Why did the unsub choose *them*? Where did he see them? What was it about them that caught his eye? A laugh? A smile? The way they walked down a city street?'

He began to read from a typewritten sheet.

'Diana Sterling, thirty years old. Blond hair, blue eyes. Five foot seven, one hundred twenty-five pounds. Occupation: travel agent. Workplace: Newbury Street. Residence: Marlborough Street in the Back Bay. A graduate of Smith College. Her parents are both attorneys, who live in a two-million-dollar home in Connecticut. Boyfriends: none at the time of her death.'

He put that sheet of paper down, picked up another.

'Elena Ortiz, twenty-two years old. Hispanic. Black hair, brown eyes. Five foot two, one hundred four pounds. Occupation: retail clerk in her family's floral business in the South End. Residence: an apartment in the South End.

Education: high school graduate. Has lived all her life in Boston. Boyfriends: none at the time of her death.'

He looked up. 'Two women who lived in the same city but moved in different universes. They shopped at different stores, ate at different restaurants, and had no friends in common. How does our unsub find them? *Where* does he find them? Not only are they different from each other; they're different from the usual sex crime victim. Most perps attack the vulnerable members of society. Prostitutes or hitchhikers. Like any hunting carnivore, they stalk the animal who's at the edge of the herd. So why choose these two?' Zucker shook his head. 'I don't know.'

Rizzoli looked at the photos on the table, and an image of Diana Sterling caught her eye. It showed a beaming young woman, the brand-new Smith College grad in her cap and gown. The golden girl. What would it be like to be a golden girl? Rizzoli wondered. She had no idea. She'd grown up the scorned sister of two strappingly handsome brothers, the desperate little tomboy who only wanted to be one of the gang. Surely Diana Sterling, with her aristocratic cheekbones and her swan neck, had never known what it was like to be shut out, excluded. She'd never known what it was like to be ignored.

Rizzoli's gaze paused on the gold pendant dangling around Diana's throat. She picked up the photo and took a closer look. Pulse accelerating, she glanced around the room to see if any of the other cops had registered what she had just noticed, but no one was looking at her or the photos; they were focused on Dr Zucker.

He had unfurled a map of Boston. Overlaid on the grid of city streets were two shaded areas, one encompassing the Back Bay, the other limited to the South End.

'These are the known activity spaces for our two victims. The neighborhoods they lived in and worked in. All of us tend to conduct our day-to-day lives in familiar areas. There's a saying among geographic profilers: *Where we go depends upon what we know, and what we know depends on where we go.* This is true for both victims and perps. You can see, from this map, the separate worlds in which these two women lived. There's no overlap. No common anchor point or node in which their lives intersected. This is what puzzles me most. It's key to the investigation. What is the link between Sterling and Ortiz?'

Rizzoli's gaze dropped back to the photo. To the gold pendant dangling at Diana's throat. *I could be wrong. I can't say anything, not until I'm certain, or it'll be one more thing Darren Crowe will use to ridicule me.*

'You're aware there's another twist to this case?' said Moore. 'Dr Catherine Cordell.'

Zucker nodded. 'The surviving victim from Savannah.'

'Certain details about Andrew Capra's killing spree were never released to the public. The use of catgut suture. The folding of the victims' nightclothes. Yet our unsub here is reenacting those very details.'

'Killers do communicate with each other. It's a twisted brotherhood, of sorts.'

'Capra's been dead two years. He can't communicate with anyone.'

'But while he was alive, he may have shared all the gruesome details with our unsub. That's the explanation I'm hoping for. Because the alternative is far more disturbing.'

'That our unsub had access to the Savannah police reports,' said Moore.

Zucker nodded. 'Which would mean he's someone in law enforcement.'

The room fell silent. Rizzoli couldn't help looking around at her colleagues – all of them men. She thought about the kind of man who is drawn to police work. The kind of man who loves the power and authority, the gun and the badge. The chance to control others. *Precisely what our unsub craves.*

When the meeting broke up, Rizzoli waited for the other detectives to leave the conference room before she approached Zucker.

'Can I hold on to this photo?' she asked.

'May I ask why?'

'A hunch.'

Zucker gave her one of his creepy John Malkovich smiles. 'Share it with me?'

'I don't share my hunches.'

'It's bad luck?'

'Protecting my turf.'

'This is a team investigation.'

'Funny thing about teamwork. Whenever I share my hunches, someone else always gets the credit.' With photo in hand, she walked out of the room and immediately regretted making that last comment. But all day she had been irritated by her male colleagues, by their little remarks and snubs that together added up to a pattern of disdain. The last straw was the interview that she and Darren Crowe had conducted of Elena Ortiz's next-door neighbor. Crowe had repeatedly interrupted Rizzoli's questions to ask his own. When she'd yanked him out of the room and called him on his behavior, he'd shot back the classic male insult:

'I guess it's that time of month.'

No, she was going to keep her hunches to herself. If they didn't pan out, then no one could ridicule her. And if they bore fruit, she would rightfully claim credit.

She returned to her workstation and sat down to take a closer look at Diana Sterling's graduation photo. Reaching for her magnifying glass, she suddenly focused on the bottle of mineral water she always kept on her desk, and her temper boiled up when she saw what had been shoved inside.

Don't react, she thought. Don't let 'em see they've gotten to you.

Ignoring the water bottle and the disgusting object it contained, she aimed the magnifying glass on Diana Sterling's throat. The room seemed unusually hushed. She could almost feel Darren Crowe's gaze as he waited for her to explode.

It ain't gonna happen, asshole. This time I'm gonna keep my cool.

She focused on Diana's necklace. She had almost missed this detail, because the face was what had initially drawn her attention, those gorgeous cheekbones, the delicate arch of the

84

eyebrows. Now she studied the two pendants dangling from the delicate chain. One pendant was in the shape of a lock; the other was a tiny key. The key to my heart, thought Rizzoli.

She rifled through the files on her desk and found the photos from the Elena Ortiz crime scene. With the magnifying glass, she studied a close-up shot of the victim's torso. Through the layer of dried blood caked on the neck, she could just make out the fine line of the gold chain; the two pendants were obscured.

She reached for the phone and dialed the M.E.'s office.

'Dr Tierney is out for the afternoon,' said his secretary. 'Can I help you?'

'It's about an autopsy he did last Friday. Elena Ortiz.'

'Yes?'

'The victim was wearing an item of jewelry when she was brought into the morgue. Do you still have it?'

'Let me check.'

Rizzoli waited, tapping her pencil on the desk. The water bottle was right there in front of her, but she steadfastly ignored it. Her anger had given way to excitement. To the exhilaration of the hunt.

'Detective Rizzoli?'

'Still here.'

'The personal effects were claimed by the family. A pair of gold stud earrings, a necklace, and a ring.'

'Who signed for them?'

'Anna Garcia, the victim's sister.'

'Thank you.' Rizzoli hung up and glanced at her watch. Anna Garcia lived all the way out in Danvers. It meant a drive through rush hour traffic . . .

'Do you know where Frost is?' asked Moore.

Rizzoli glanced up, startled, to see him standing beside her desk. 'No, I don't.'

'He hasn't been around?'

'I don't keep the boy on a leash.'

There was a pause. Then he asked, 'What's this?'

'Ortiz crime scene photos.'

'No. The thing in the bottle.'

She looked up again and saw a frown on his face. 'What does it look like? It's a fucking tampon. *Someone* around here has a real sophisticated sense of humor.' She glanced pointedly at Darren Crowe, who suppressed a snicker and turned away.

'I'll take care of this,' Moore said and picked up the bottle.

'Hey. *Hey!*' she snapped. 'Goddamnit, Moore. Forget it!'

He walked into Lieutenant Marquette's office. Through the glass partition she saw Moore set the bottle with the tampon on Marquette's desk. Marquette turned and stared in Rizzoli's direction.

Here we go again. Now they'll be saying the bitch can't take a practical joke.

She grabbed her purse, gathered up the photos, and walked out of the unit.

She was already at the elevators when Moore called out: 'Rizzoli?'

'Don't fight my fucking battles for me, okay?' she snapped.

'You weren't fighting. You were just sitting there with that . . . thing on your desk.'

'Tampon. Can you say the word nice and loud?'

'Why are you angry with me? I'm trying to stick up for you.'

'Look, *Saint* Thomas, this is how it works in the real world for women. I file a complaint, I'm the one who gets the shaft. A note goes in my personnel record. *Does not play well with boys.* If I complain again, my reputation's sealed. Rizzoli the whiner. Rizzoli the wuss.'

'You're letting them win if you *don't* complain.'

'I tried it your way. It doesn't work. So don't do me any favors, okay?' She slung her purse over her shoulder and stepped onto the elevator.

The instant the door closed between them, she wanted to take back those words. Moore didn't deserve such a rebuke. He had always been polite, always the gentleman, and in her anger she had flung the unit's nickname for him in his face. *Saint Thomas.* The cop who never stepped over the line, never swore, never lost his cool.

And then there were the sad circumstances of his personal life. Two years ago, his wife, Mary, had collapsed from a cerebral hemorrhage. For six months she'd hung on in the twilight zone of a coma, but until the day she actually died Moore had refused to give up hope that she'd recover. Even now, a year and a half after Mary's death, he did not seem to accept it. He still wore his wedding ring, still kept her photo on his desk. Rizzoli had watched the marriages of too many other cops disintegrate, had watched the changing gallery of women's photos on her colleagues' desks. On Moore's desk, the image of Mary remained, her smiling face a permanent fixture.

Saint Thomas? Rizzoli gave a cynical shake of the head. If there were any real saints in the world, they sure as hell wouldn't be cops.

One wanted him to live, the other wanted him to die, and both claimed to love him more. The son and daughter of Herman Gwadowski faced each other across their father's bed, and neither was willing to give in.

'You weren't the one who had to take care of Dad,' Marilyn said. 'I cooked his meals. I cleaned his house. I took him to the doctor every month. When did you even *visit* him? You always had better things to do.'

'I live in L.A., for god's sake,' snapped Ivan. 'I have a business.'

'You could have flown out once a year. How hard was that?'

'Well, I'm here now.'

'Oh, right. Mr Big Shot swoops in to save the day. You couldn't be bothered to visit before. But now you want *everything* done.'

'I can't believe you'd just let him go.'

'I don't want him to suffer anymore.'

'Or maybe you just want him to stop draining his bank account.'

Every muscle in Marilyn's face snapped taut. 'You bastard.'

Catherine could listen no more, and she cut in: 'This isn't the place to be discussing it. Please, can you both step out of the room?'

For a moment, brother and sister eyed each

other in hostile silence, as though just the act of being the first to leave was a surrender. Then Ivan stalked out, an intimidating figure in a tailored suit. His sister, Marilyn, looking every bit the tired suburban housewife she was, gave her father's hand a squeeze and followed her brother.

In the hallway, Catherine laid out the grim facts.

'Your father has been in a coma since the accident. His kidneys are now failing. Because of his long-term diabetes, they were already impaired, and the trauma made things worse.'

'How much was due to surgery?' asked Ivan. 'The anesthetic you gave him?'

Catherine suppressed her rising temper and said, evenly: 'He was unconscious when he came in. Anesthesia was not a factor. But tissue damage puts a strain on kidneys, and his are shutting down. Plus, he has a diagnosis of prostate cancer that's already spread to his bones. Even if he does wake up, those problems remain.'

'You want us to give up, don't you?' said Ivan.

'I simply want you to re-think his code status. If his heart should stop, we don't have to resuscitate him. We can let him go peacefully.'

'You mean, just let him die.'

'Yes.'

Ivan gave a snort. 'Let me tell you something about my dad. He's not a quitter. And neither am I.'

'For god's sake, Ivan, this isn't about winning or losing!' said Marilyn. 'It's about when to let go.'

'And you're so quick to do that, aren't you?' he said, turning to face her. 'The first sign of difficulty, little Marilyn always gives up and lets

Daddy bail her out. Well, he never bailed me out.'

Tears glistened in Marilyn's eyes. 'It's not about Dad, is it? It's about you having to win.'

'No, it's about giving him a fighting chance.' Ivan looked at Catherine. 'I want everything done for my father. I hope that's absolutely clear.'

Marilyn wiped tears from her face as she watched her brother walk away. 'How can he say he loves him, when he never came to see him?' She looked at Catherine. 'I don't want my dad resuscitated. Can you put that in the chart?'

This was the sort of ethical dilemma every doctor dreaded. Although Catherine sided with Marilyn, the brother's last words had carried a definite threat.

She said, 'I can't change the order until you and your brother agree on this.'

'He'll never agree. You heard him.'

'Then you'll have to talk to him some more. Convince him.'

'You're afraid he'll sue, aren't you? That's why you won't change the order.'

'I know he's angry.'

Sadly Marilyn nodded. 'That's how he wins. It's how he always wins.'

I can stitch a body back together again, thought Catherine. But I cannot mend this broken family.

The pain and hostility of that meeting still clung to her when she walked out of the hospital a half hour later. It was Friday afternoon and a free weekend stretched ahead, yet as she drove out of the medical center parking garage she felt no sense of liberation. It was even hotter today than yesterday, in the nineties, and she looked forward to the coolness of her apartment, to sitting down with an iced tea and the TV tuned to The Discovery Channel.

She was waiting at the first intersection for the light to turn green when her gaze drifted to the name of the cross street. Worcester.

It was the street where Elena Ortiz had lived. The victim's address had been mentioned in the *Boston Globe* article, which Catherine had finally felt compelled to read.

The light changed. On impulse, she turned onto Worcester Street. She'd never had reason to drive this way before, but something drew her onward. The morbid need to see where the killer had struck and to see the building where her own personal nightmare had come to life for another woman. Her hands were damp, and she could feel her pulse quickening as she watched the numbers on the buildings climb.

At Elena Ortiz's address, she pulled over to the curb.

There was nothing distinctive about this edifice, nothing that shouted to her of terror and death. She saw just another three-story brick building.

She stepped out of her car and stared at the windows of the upper floors. Which apartment had been Elena's? The one with the striped curtains? Or the one with the jungle of hanging plants? She approached the front entrance and looked at the tenant names. There were six apartments; Apartment 2A's tenant name was blank. Already Elena had been erased, the victim purged from the ranks of the living. No one wanted to be reminded of death.

According to the *Globe*, the killer had gained access by way of a fire escape. Backing up onto the sidewalk, Catherine spotted the steel lattice snaking up the alley side of the building. She took a few steps into the gloom of the alley, then abruptly halted. The back of her neck was prickling. She turned to look at the street and saw a truck rattle by, a woman jogging. A couple getting into their car. Nothing that should make her feel threatened, yet she could not ignore the silent shouts of panic.

She returned to her car, locked the doors, and sat clutching the steering wheel, repeating to herself: 'Nothing is wrong. Nothing is wrong.' As cold air blasted from the car vent, she felt her pulse gradually slow. At last, with a sigh, she leaned back.

Her gaze turned, once again, to Elena Ortiz's apartment building.

Only then did she focus on the car, parked in the alley. On the license plate mounted on its rear bumper.

POSEY5.

In an instant she was fumbling through her purse for the detective's business card. With shaking hands she dialed his number on her car phone.

He answered with a businesslike, 'Detective Moore.'

'This is Catherine Cordell,' she said. 'You came to see me a few days ago.'

'Yes, Dr Cordell?'

'Did Elena Ortiz drive a green Honda?'

'Excuse me?'

'I need to know her license number.'

'I'm afraid I don't understand—'

'Just *tell me*!' Her sharp command startled him. There was a long silence on the line.

'Let me check,' he said. In the background she heard men talking, phones ringing. He came back on the line.

'It's a vanity plate,' he said. 'I believe it refers to the family's flower business.'

'POSEY FIVE,' she whispered.

A pause. 'Yes,' he said, his voice strangely quiet. Alert.

'When you spoke to me, the other day, you asked if I knew Elena Ortiz.'

'And you said you didn't.'

Catherine released a shuddering breath. 'I was wrong.'

Six

She was pacing inside the E.R., her face pale and tense, her coppery hair a tangled mane about her shoulders. She looked at Moore as he stepped into the waiting area.

'Was I right?' she said.

He nodded. 'Posey Five was her Internet screen name. We checked her computer. Now tell me how you knew this.'

She glanced around the bustling E.R. and said: 'Let's go into one of the call rooms.'

The room she took him to was a dark little cave, windowless, furnished with only a bed, a chair, and a desk. For an exhausted doctor whose single goal is sleep, the room would be perfectly sufficient. But as the door swung shut, Moore was acutely aware of how small the space was, and he wondered if the forced intimacy made her as uncomfortable as it did him. They both glanced around for places to sit. At last she settled on the bed, and he took the chair.

'I never actually *met* Elena,' said Catherine. 'I didn't even know that was her name. We belonged to the same Internet chat room.

You know what a chat room is?'

'It's a way to have a live conversation on the computer.'

'Yes. A group of people who are online at the same time can meet over the Internet. This is a private room, only for women. You have to know all the right keywords to get into it. And all you see on the computer are screen names. No real names or faces, so we can all stay anonymous. It lets us feel safe enough to share our secrets.' She paused. 'You've never used one?'

'Talking to faceless strangers doesn't much appeal to me, I'm afraid.'

'Sometimes,' she said softly, 'a faceless stranger is the only person you *can* talk to.'

He heard the depth of pain in that statement and could think of nothing to say.

After a moment, she took a deep breath and focused not on him but on her hands, folded in her lap. 'We meet once a week, on Wednesday nights at nine o'clock. I enter by going on-line, clicking the chat-room icon, and typing in first *PTSD*, and then: *womanhelp*. And I'm in. I communicate with other women by typing messages and sending them through the Internet. Our words appear onscreen, where we can all see them.'

'PTSD? I take it that stands for—'

'Post-traumatic stress disorder. A nice clinical term for what the women in that room are suffering.'

'What trauma are we talking about?'

She raised her head and looked straight at him. 'Rape.'

The word seemed to hang between them for a

moment, the very sound of it charging the air. One brutal syllable with the impact of a physical blow.

'And you go there because of Andrew Capra,' he said gently. 'What he did to you.'

Her gaze faltered, dropped away. 'Yes,' she whispered. Once again she was looking at her hands. Moore watched her, his anger building over what had happened to Catherine. What Capra had ripped from her soul. He wondered what she was like before the attack. Warmer, friendlier? Or had she always been so insulated from human contact, like a bloom encased in frost?

She drew herself straighter and forged ahead. 'So that's where I met Elena Ortiz. I didn't know her real name, of course. I saw only her screen name, Posey Five.'

'How many women are in this chat room?'

'It varies from week to week. Some of them drop out. A few new names appear. On any night, there can be anywhere from three to a dozen of us.'

'How did you learn about it?'

'From a brochure for rape victims. It's given out at women's clinics and hospitals around the city.'

'So these women in the chat room, they're all from the Boston area?'

'Yes.'

'And Posey Five, was she a regular visitor?'

'She was there, off and on, over the last two months. She didn't say much, but I'd see her name on the screen and I knew she was there.'

'Did she talk about her rape?'

'No. She just listened. We'd type hellos to her.

96

And she'd acknowledge the greetings. But she wouldn't talk about herself. It's as if she was afraid to. Or just too ashamed to say anything.'

'So you don't know that she *was* raped.'

'I know she was.'

'How?'

'Because Elena Ortiz was treated in this emergency room.'

He stared at her. 'You found her record?'

She nodded. 'It occurred to me that she might have needed medical treatment after the attack. This is the closest hospital to her address. I checked our hospital computer. It has the name of every patient seen in this E.R. Her name was there.' She stood up. 'I'll show you her record.'

He followed her out of the call room and back into the E.R. It was a Friday evening, and the casualties were rolling in the door. The TGIF-er, clumsy with booze, clutching an ice bag to his battered face. The impatient teenager who'd lost his race with a yellow light. The Friday night army of the bruised and bloodied, stumbling in from the night. Pilgrim Medical Center was one of the busiest E.R.'s in Boston, and Moore felt as though he was walking through the heart of chaos as he dodged nurses and gurneys and stepped over a fresh splash of blood.

Catherine led him into the E.R. records room, a closet-sized space with wall-to-wall shelves containing three-ring binders.

'This is where they temporarily store the encounter forms,' said Catherine. She pulled down the binder labeled: *May 7–May 14*. 'Every time a patient is seen in the E.R., a form is generated. It's usually only a page long, and it contains the doctor's note, and the treatment instructions.'

'There's no chart made up for each patient?'

'If it's just a single E.R. visit, then no hospital chart is ever put together. The only record is the encounter form. These eventually get moved to the hospital's medical records room, where they're scanned and stored on disk.' She opened the May 7–May 14 binder. 'Here it is.'

He stood behind her, looking over her shoulder. The scent of her hair momentarily distracted him, and he had to force himself to focus on the page. The visit was dated May 9, 1:00 a.m. The patient's name, address, and billing information were typed at the top; the rest of the form was handwritten in ink. Medical shorthand, he thought, as he struggled to decipher the words and could make out only the first paragraph, which had been written by the nurse:

22-year-old Hispanic female, sexually assaulted two hours ago. No allergies, no meds. BP 105/70, P 100, T 99.

The rest of the page was indecipherable.

'You'll have to translate for me,' he said.

She glanced over her shoulder at him, and their faces were suddenly so close he felt his breath catch.

'You can't read it?' she asked.

'I can read tire tracks and blood splatters. This I can't read.'

'It's Ken Kimball's handwriting. I recognize his signature.'

98

'I don't even recognize it as English.'

'To another doctor, it's perfectly legible. You just have to know the code.'

'They teach you that in medical school?'

'Along with the secret handshake and the decoder ring instructions.'

It felt strange to be trading quips over such grim business, even stranger to hear humor come from Dr Cordell's lips. It was his first glimpse of the woman beneath the shell. The woman she'd been before Andrew Capra had inflicted his damage.

'The first paragraph is the physical exam,' she explained. 'He uses medical shorthand. *HEENT* means head, ears, eyes, nose, and throat. She had a bruise on her left cheek. The lungs were clear, the heart without murmurs or gallops.'

'Meaning?'

'Normal.'

'A doctor can't just write: 'The heart is normal'?'

'Why do cops say "vehicle" instead of just plain 'car'?'

He nodded. 'Point taken.'

'The abdomen was flat, soft, and without organomegaly. In other words—'

'Normal.'

'You're catching on. Next he describes the . . . pelvic exam. Where things are not normal.' She paused. When she spoke again, her voice was softer, drained of all humor. She took a breath, as though to draw in the courage to continue. 'There was blood in the introitus. Scratches and bruising on both thighs. A vaginal tear at the four o'clock position, indicating this was not a consensual act.

At that point Dr Kimball says he stopped the exam.'

Moore focused on the final paragraph. This he could read. This contained no medical shorthand.

Patient became agitated. Refused collection of rape kit. Refused to cooperate with any further intervention. After baseline HIV screen and VDRL drawn, she dressed and left before authorities could be called.

'So the rape was never reported,' he said. 'There was no vaginal swab. No DNA collected.'

Catherine was silent. She stood with head bowed, her hands clutching the binder.

'Dr Cordell?' he said, and touched her shoulder. She gave a start, as though he had burned her, and he quickly took his hand away. She looked up, and he saw rage in her eyes. There was a fierceness radiating from her that made her, at that moment, every bit his equal.

'Raped in May, butchered in July,' she said. 'It's a fine world for women, isn't it?'

'We've spoken to every member of her family. No one said anything about a rape.'

'Then she didn't tell them.'

How many women keep their silence? he wondered. How many have secrets so painful they cannot share them with the people they love? Looking at Catherine, he thought about the fact that she, too, had sought comfort in the company of strangers.

She took the encounter out of the binder for him to photocopy. As he took it, his gaze fell on the

100

doctor's name, and another thought occurred to him.

'What can you tell me about Dr Kimball?' he said. 'The one who examined Elena Ortiz?'

'He's an excellent physician.'

'He usually works the night shift?'

'Yes.'

'Do you know if he was on duty last Thursday night?'

It took her a moment to register the significance of that question. When she did, he saw she was shaken by the implications. 'You don't really think—'

'It's a routine question. We look at all the victim's prior contacts.'

But the question was not routine, and she knew it.

'Andrew Capra was a doctor,' she said softly. 'You don't think another doctor—'

'The possibility has occurred to us.'

She turned away. Took an unsteady breath. 'In Savannah, when those other women were murdered, I just assumed I didn't know the killer. I assumed that if I ever did meet him, I'd know it. I'd feel it. Andrew Capra taught me how wrong I was.'

'The banality of evil.'

'That's exactly what I learned. That evil can be so ordinary. That a man I'd see every day, say hello to every day, could smile right back at me.' She added, softly: 'And be thinking of all the different ways he'd like to kill me.'

It was dusk when Moore walked back to his car,

but the heat of day still radiated from the black-top. It would be another uncomfortable night. Across the city, women would sleep with windows left open to the night's fickle breezes. The night's evils.

He stopped and turned toward the hospital. He could see the bright red 'ER' light, glowing like a beacon. A symbol of hope and healing.

Is that your hunting ground? The very place where women go to be healed?

An ambulance glided in from the night, lights flashing. He thought of all the people who might pass through an E.R. in the course of a day. EMTs, doctors, orderlies, janitors.

And cops. It was a possibility he never wanted to consider, yet it was one he could never dismiss. The profession of law enforcement holds a strange allure for those who hunt other human beings. The gun, the badge, are heady symbols of domination. And what greater control could one exercise than the power to torment, to kill? For such a hunter, the world is a vast plain teeming with prey.

All one has to do is choose.

There were babies everywhere. Rizzoli stood in a kitchen that smelled like sour milk and talcum powder as she waited for Anna Garcia to finish wiping apple juice from the floor. One toddler was clinging to Anna's leg; a second was pulling pot lids out of a kitchen cabinet and clanging them together like cymbals. An infant was in a high chair, smiling through a mask of creamed spinach. And on the floor, a baby with a bad case of cradle

102

cap was crawling around on a treasure hunt for anything dangerous to put in his greedy little mouth. Rizzoli did not care for babies, and it made her nervous to be surrounded by them. She felt like Indiana Jones in the snake pit.

'They're not all mine,' Anna was quick to explain as she limped over to the sink, the toddler hanging on like a ball and chain. She wrung out the dirty sponge and rinsed her hands. 'Only this one's mine.' She pointed to the baby on her leg. 'That one with the pots, and the one in the high chair, they belong to my sister Lupe. And the one crawling around, I baby-sit him for my cousin. As long as I'm home with mine, I thought I might as well watch a few more.'

Yeah, what's another smack on the head? thought Rizzoli. But the funny thing was, Anna did not look unhappy. In fact, she scarcely seemed to notice the human ball and chain or the clang-clang of the pots slamming against the floor. In a situation that would give Rizzoli a nervous break-down, Anna had the serene look of a woman who is exactly where she wants to be. Rizzoli wondered if this was what Elena Ortiz would have been like one day, had she lived. A mama in her kitchen, happily wiping up juice and drool. Anna looked very much like the photos of her younger sister, just a little plumper. And when she turned toward Rizzoli, the kitchen light shining directly on her forehead, Rizzoli had the chilling sensation that she was staring at the same face that had looked up at her from the autopsy table.

'With these little guys around, it takes me for-ever to do the smallest thing,' said Anna. She picked up the toddler hanging on her leg and propped him expertly on one hip. 'Now, let me see. You came for the necklace. Let me get the jewelry box.' She walked out of the kitchen, and Rizzoli felt a moment of panic, left alone with three babies. A sticky hand landed on her ankle and she looked down to see the crawler chewing on her pant cuff. She shook him off and quickly put a safe distance between her and that gummy mouth.

'Here it is,' said Anna, returning with the box, which she set on the kitchen table. 'We didn't want to leave it in her apartment, not with all those strangers going in and out cleaning the place. So my brothers thought I should keep the box until the family decides what to do with the jewelry.' She lifted the lid, and a melody began to tinkle. 'Somewhere My Love.' Anna seemed momentarily stunned by the music. She sat very still, her eyes filling with tears.

'Mrs Garcia?'

Anna swallowed. 'I'm sorry. My husband must have wound it up. I wasn't expecting to hear . . .'

The melody slowed to a few last sweet notes and stopped. In silence Anna gazed down at the jewelry, her head bent in mourning. With sad reluctance she opened one of the velvet-lined compartments and withdrew the necklace.

Rizzoli could feel her heartbeat quickening as she took the necklace from Anna. It was as she'd remembered it when she'd seen it around Elena's neck in the morgue, a tiny lock and key dangling from a fine gold chain. She turned over the lock and saw the eighteen-karat stamp on the back.

'Where did your sister get this necklace?'

'I don't know.'

'Do you know how long she's owned it?'

'It must be something new. I never saw it before the day . . .'

'What day?'

Anna swallowed. And said softly: 'The day I picked it up at the morgue. With her other jewelry.'

'She was also wearing earrings and a ring. Those you've seen before?'

'Yes. She's had those a long time.'

'But not the necklace.'

'Why do you keep asking about it? What does it have to do with . . .' Anna paused, horror dawning in her eyes. 'Oh god. You think *he* put it on her?'

The baby in the high chair, sensing something was wrong, let out a wail. Anna set her own son down on the floor and scurried over to pick up the crying infant. Hugging him close, she turned away from the necklace as though to protect him from the sight of that evil talisman. 'Please take it,' she whispered. 'I don't want it in my house.'

Rizzoli slipped the necklace into a Ziploc bag. 'I'll write you a receipt.'

'No, just take it away! I don't care if you keep it.'

Rizzoli wrote the receipt anyway and placed it on the kitchen table next to the baby's dish of creamed spinach. 'I need to ask one more question,' she said gently.

Anna kept pacing the kitchen, jiggling the baby in agitation.

'Please go through your sister's jewelry box,' said Rizzoli. 'Tell me if there's anything missing.'

'You asked me that last week. There isn't.'

'It's not easy to spot the *absence* of something. Instead, we tend to focus on what doesn't belong. I need you to go through this box again. Please.'

Anna swallowed hard. Reluctantly she sat down with the baby in her lap and stared into the jewelry box. She took out the items one by one and laid them on the table. It was a sad little assortment of department store trinkets. Rhinestones and crystal beads and faux pearls. Elena's taste had run toward the bright and gaudy.

Anna laid the last item, a turquoise friendship ring, on the table. Then she sat for a moment, a frown slowly forming on her face.

'The bracelet,' she said.

'What bracelet?'

'There should be a bracelet, with little charms on it. Horses. She used to wear it every day in high school. Elena was crazy about horses . . .' Anna looked up with a stunned expression. 'It wasn't worth anything! It was just made of tin. Why would he take it?'

Rizzoli looked at the Ziploc bag containing the necklace – a necklace she was now certain had once belonged to Diana Sterling. And she thought, *I know exactly where we'll find Elena's bracelet: around the wrist of the next victim.*

Rizzoli stood on Moore's front porch, triumphantly waving the Ziploc bag containing the necklace.

'It belonged to Diana Sterling. I just spoke to

her parents. They didn't realize it was missing until I called them.'

He took the bag but didn't open it. Just held it, staring at the gold chain coiled inside the plastic.

'It's the physical link between both cases,' she said. 'He takes a souvenir from one victim. Leaves it with the next.'

'I can't believe we missed this detail.'

'Hey, we *didn't* miss it.'

'You mean *you* didn't miss it.' He gave her a look that made her feel ten feet taller. Moore wasn't a guy who'd slap your back or shout your praises. In fact, she could not remember ever hearing him raise his voice, either in anger or in excitement. But when he gave her *that look*, the eyebrow raised in approval, the mouth tilted in a half smile, it was all the praise she'd ever need.

Flushing with pleasure, she reached down for the bag of take-out food she'd brought. 'You want dinner? I stopped in at that Chinese restaurant down the street.'

'You didn't have to do that.'

'Yeah, I did. I figure I owe you an apology.'

'For what?'

'For this afternoon. That stupid deal with the tampon. You were just standing up for me, trying to be the good guy. I took it the wrong way.'

An awkward silence passed. They stood there, not sure of what to say, two people who don't know each other well and are trying to get past the rocky start of their relationship.

Then he smiled, and it transformed his usually sober face into that of a much younger man. 'I'm starved,' he said. 'Bring that food in here.'

With a laugh, she stepped into his house. It was her first time here, and she paused to glance around, taking in all the womanly touches. The chintz curtains, the floral watercolors on the wall. It was not what she expected. Hell, it was more feminine than her own apartment.

'Let's go into the kitchen,' he said. 'My papers are in there.'

He led her through the living room, and she saw the spinet piano.

'Wow. You play?' she asked.

'No, it's Mary's. I've got a tin ear.'

It's Mary's. Present tense. It struck her then that the reason this house seemed so feminine was that it was still present-tense-Mary, a house waiting, unaltered, for its mistress to come home. A photo of Moore's wife was displayed on the piano, a sunburned woman with laughing eyes and hair in windblown disarray. Mary, whose chintz curtains still hung in the house she would never return to.

In the kitchen, Rizzoli set the bag of food on the table, next to a stack of files. Moore shuffled through the folders and found the one he was searching for.

'Elena Ortiz's E.R. report,' he said, handing it to her.

'Cordell dug this up?'

He gave an ironic smile. 'I seem to be surrounded by women more competent than I am.'

She opened the folder and saw a photocopy of a doctor's chicken-scratch handwriting. 'You got the translation on this mess?'

'It's pretty much what I told you over the phone.

Unreported rape. No kit collected, no DNA. Even Elena's family didn't know about it.'

She closed the folder and set it down on his other papers. 'Jeez, Moore. This mess looks like my dining table. No place left to eat.'

'It's taken over your life, too, has it?' he said, clearing away the files to make space for their dinner.

'What life? This case is all there is to mine. Sleep. Eat. Work. And if I'm lucky, an hour at bedtime with my old pal Dave Letterman.'

'No boyfriends?'

'Boyfriends?' She snorted as she took out the food cartons and laid napkins and chopsticks on the table. 'Oh yeah. Like I gotta beat 'em all off.' Only after she said it did she realize how self-pitying that sounded – not at all the way she meant it. She was quick to add: 'I'm not complaining. If I need to spend the weekend working, I can do it without some guy whining about it. I don't do well with whiners.'

'Hardly surprising, since you're the opposite of a whiner. As you made painfully clear to me today.'

'Yeah, yeah. I thought I apologized for that.'

He got two beers from the refrigerator, then sat down across from her. She'd never seen him like this, with his shirtsleeves rolled up and looking so relaxed. She liked him this way. Not the forbidding Saint Thomas but a guy she could shoot the breeze with, a guy who'd laugh with her. A guy who, if he just bothered to turn on the charm, could knock a girl's socks off.

'You know, you don't always have to be tougher than everyone else,' he said.

'Yes, I do.'

'Why?'

'Because *they* don't think I am.'

'Who doesn't?'

'Guys like Crowe. Lieutenant Marquette.'

He shrugged. 'There'll always be a few like that.'

'How come I always end up working with them?' She popped open her beer and took a swig. 'That's why you're the first one I told about the necklace. You won't hog the credit.'

'It's a sad day when it gets down to who claims credit for this or that.'

She picked up her chopsticks and dug into the carton of kung pao chicken. It was burn-your-mouth spicy, just the way she liked it. Rizzoli was no wimp when it came to hot peppers, either.

She said, 'The first really big case I worked on in Vice and Narcotics, I was the only woman on a team with five men. When we cracked it, there was this press conference. TV cameras, the whole nine yards. And you know what? They mentioned every name on that team but mine. Every other goddamn name.' She took another swallow of beer. 'I make sure that doesn't happen anymore. You guys, you can focus all your attention on the case and the evidence. But I waste a lot of energy just trying to make myself heard.'

'I hear you fine, Rizzoli.'

'It's a nice change.'

'What about Frost? You have problems with him?'

'Frost is cool.' She winced at the unintended quip. 'His wife's got him well trained.'

They both laughed at that. Anyone who overheard Barry Frost's meek *yes dear, no dear* phone conversations with his wife had no doubt who was boss in the Frost household.

'That's why he's not gonna move up very far,' she said. 'No fire in the belly. Family man.'

'There's nothing wrong with being a family man. I wish I'd been a better one.'

She glanced up from the carton of Mongolian beef and saw that he wasn't looking at her but was staring at the necklace. There'd been a note of pain in his voice, and she didn't know what to say in response. Figured that it was best not to say anything.

She was relieved when he turned the subject back to the investigation. In their world, murder was always a safe topic.

'There's something wrong here,' he said. 'This jewelry thing doesn't make sense to me.'

'He's taking souvenirs. Common enough.'

'But what's the point of taking a souvenir if you're going to give it away?'

'Some perps take the vic's jewelry and give it to their own wives or girlfriends. They get a secret thrill from seeing it around their girlfriend's neck, and being the only one who knows where it really comes from.'

'But our boy's doing something different. He leaves the souvenir at the *next* crime scene. He doesn't get to keep seeing it. Doesn't get the recurrent thrill of being reminded of his kill. There's no emotional gain that I can see.'

'A symbol of ownership? Like a dog, marking his territory. Only he uses a piece of jewelry to mark his next victim.'

111

'No. That's not it.' Moore picked up the Ziploc bag and weighed it in his palm, as though divining its purpose.

'The main thing is, we're onto the pattern,' she said. 'We'll know exactly what to expect at the next crime scene.'

He looked up at her. 'You just answered the question.'

'What?'

'He's not marking the victim. He's marking the crime scene.'

Rizzoli paused. All at once, she understood the distinction. 'Jesus. By marking the scene . . .'

'This isn't a souvenir. And it's not a mark of ownership.' He set down the necklace, a tangled filigree of gold that had skimmed the flesh of two dead women.

A shudder went through Rizzoli. 'It's a calling card,' she said softly.

Moore nodded. 'The Surgeon is talking to us.'

A place of strong winds and dangerous tides.

This is how Edith Hamilton, in her book Mythology, describes the Greek port of Aulis. Here lie the ruins of the ancient temple of Artemis, the goddess of the hunt. It was at Aulis where the thousand Greek black ships gathered to launch their attack on Troy. But the north wind blew, and the ships could not sail. Day after day, the wind was relentless and the Greek army, under the command of King Agamemnon, grew angry and restless. A soothsayer revealed the reason for the ill winds: the goddess Artemis was angry, because Agamemnon had slain one of her beloved creatures, a wild hare. She would not allow the Greeks to depart unless Agamemnon offered up a terrible sacrifice: his daughter, Iphigenia.

And so he sent for Iphigenia, claiming that he had arranged for her a great marriage to Achilles. She did not know she was coming instead to her death.

Those fierce north winds were not blowing on the day you and I walked the beach near Aulis. It was calm, the water was green glass, and the sand was as hot as white ash beneath our feet. Oh, how we envied the Greek boys who ran barefoot on the sun-baked shore! Though the sand scorched our pale tourist skin, we reveled in the discomfort, because we wanted to be like those boys, our soles like toughened leather. Only through pain and hard wear do calluses form.

In the evening, when the day had cooled, we went to the Temple of Artemis.

We walked among the lengthening shadows, and came to the altar where Iphigenia was sacrificed. Despite her prayers, her cries of 'Father, spare me!,' the warriors carried the girl to the altar. She was stretched over the stone, her white neck bared to the blade. The ancient playwright Euripides writes that the soldiers of Atreus, and all the army, stared at the ground, unwilling to watch the spilling of her virgin blood. Unwilling to witness the horror.

Ah, but I would have watched! And so, too, would you have. And eagerly, too.

I pictured the silent troops assembled in the gloom. I imagined the beating of drums, not the lively throb of a wedding celebration, but a

113

somber march toward death. I saw the procession, winding its way into the grove. The girl, white as a swan, flanked by soldiers and priests. The drumming stops.

They carry her, shrieking, to the altar.

In my vision, it is Agamemnon himself who holds the knife blade, for why call it sacrifice if you are not the one who draws the blood? I see him approach the altar, where his daughter lies, her tender flesh exposed to all eyes. She pleads for her life, to no avail.

The priest grasps her hair and pulls it back, baring her throat. Beneath the white skin the artery pulses, marking the place for the blade. Agamemnon stands beside his daughter, looking down at the face he loves. In her veins runs his blood. In her eyes he sees his own. By cutting her throat, he cuts his own flesh.

He raises the knife. The soldiers stand silent, statues among the sacred grove of trees. The pulse in the girl's neck is fluttering.

Artemis demands sacrifice, and this Agamemnon must do.

He presses the blade to the girl's neck, and slices deep.

A fountain of red spurts, splashing his face with hot rain.

Iphigenia is still alive, her eyes rolled back in horror as the blood pumps from her neck. The human body contains five liters of blood, and it takes time for such a volume to be discharged from a single severed artery. As long as the heart continues to beat, the blood pumps out. For at least a few seconds, perhaps even a minute *or more, the brain functions. The limbs thrash.*

As her heart beats its last, Iphigenia watches the sky darken, and feels the heat of her own blood spout on her face.

The ancients say that almost immediately the north wind ceased to blow. Artemis was satisfied. At last the Greek ships sailed, and armies fought, and Troy fell. In the context of that greater bloodshed, the slaughter of one young virgin means nothing.

But when I think of the Trojan War, what comes to my mind is not the wooden horse or the clang of swords or the thousand black ships with sails unfurled. No, it is the image of a girl's body, drained white, and the father standing beside her, clutching the bloody knife.

Noble Agamemnon, with tears in his eyes.

Seven

'It's pulsating,' said the nurse.

Catherine stared, dry-mouthed with horror, at the man lying on the trauma table. A foot-long iron rod protruded straight up from his chest. One medical student had already fainted at the sight, and the three nurses stood with mouths agape. The rod was embedded deep in the man's chest, and it was pulsing up and down in rhythm with his heartbeat.

'What's our BP?' Catherine said.

Her voice seemed to snap everyone into action mode. The blood pressure cuff whiffed up, sighed down again.

'Seventy over forty. Pulse is up to one-fifty!'

'Turning both IVs wide open!'

'Breaking open the thoracotomy tray—'

'Somebody get Dr Falco down here STAT. I'm going to need help.' Catherine slipped into a sterile gown and pulled on gloves. Her palms were already slippery with sweat. The fact the rod was pulsing told her the tip had penetrated close to the heart – or, even worse, was actually embedded in it. The worst thing she could do was pull it out. It might open a hole through which he could exsanguinate in minutes.

The EMTs at the scene had made the right decision: they had started an IV, intubated the victim, and brought him to the E.R. with the rod still in place. The rest was up to her.

She was just reaching for the scalpel when the door swung open. She looked up and gave a sigh of relief as Peter Falco walked in. He halted, his gaze taking in the patient's chest, with the rod protruding like a stake through a vampire's heart.

'Now that's something you don't see every day,' he said.

'BP's bottoming out!' a nurse called.

'There's no time for bypass. I'm going in,' said Catherine.

'I'll be right with you.' Peter turned and said, in an almost casual tone, 'Can I have a gown, please?'

Catherine swiftly opened an anterolateral incision, which would allow the best exposure to the vital organs of the thoracic cavity. She was feeling calmer, now that Peter had arrived. It was more than just having the extra pair of skilled hands; it was Peter himself. The way he could walk into a room and size up the situation with just a glance. The fact he never raised his voice in the O.R., never showed a hint of panic. He had five years' more experience than she did on the front lines of trauma surgery, and it was with horrifying cases like this one where his experience showed.

He took his place across the table from Catherine, his blue eyes zeroing in on the incision. 'Okeydoke. We having fun yet?'

'Barrel of laughs.'

He got right down to business, his hands working in concert with hers as they tore into the chest with almost brutal force. He and Catherine had operated as a team so many times before, each automatically knew what the other one needed and could anticipate moves ahead of time.

'Story on this?' asked Peter. Blood spurted, and he calmly snapped a hemostat over the bleeder.

'Construction worker. Tripped and fell on the site and got himself skewered.'

'That'll ruin your day. Burford retractor, please.'

'Burford.'

'How we doing on blood?'

'Waiting on the O neg,' a nurse answered.

'Is Dr Murata in-house?'

'His bypass team's on its way in.'

'So we just need to buy a little time here. What's our rhythm?'

'Sinus tach, one-fifty. A few PVCs—'

'Systolic's down to fifty!'

Catherine shot a glance at Peter. 'We're not going to make it to bypass,' she said.

'Then let's just see what we can do here.'

There was sudden silence as he stared into the incision.

'Oh god,' said Catherine. 'It's in the atrium.'

The tip of the rod had pierced the wall of the heart, and with every beat fresh blood squirted out around the edge of the puncture site. A deep pool of it had already collected in the thoracic cavity.

'We pull it out, we're going to have a real gusher,' said Peter.

'He's already bleeding out around it.'

The nurse said, 'Systolic's barely palpable!'

'Ho-kay,' said Peter. No panic in his voice. No sign of any fear whatsoever. He said to one of the nurses, 'Can you hunt me down a sixteen French Foley catheter with a thirty cc balloon?'

'Uh, Dr Falco? Did you say a *Foley*?'

'Yep. A urinary catheter.'

'And we'll need a syringe with ten cc's of saline,' said Catherine. 'Stand by to push it.' She and Peter didn't have to explain a thing to each other; they both understood what the plan was.

The Foley catheter, a tube designed for insertion into a bladder to drain urine, was handed to Peter. They were about to put it to a use for which it was never intended.

He looked at Catherine. 'You ready?'

'Let's do it.'

Her pulse was throbbing as she watched Peter grasp the iron rod. Saw him gently pull it out of the heart wall. As it emerged, blood exploded from the puncture site. Instantly Catherine thrust the tip of the urinary catheter into the hole.

'Inflate the balloon!' said Peter.

The nurse pressed down the syringe, injecting ten cc's of saline into the balloon at the tip of the Foley.

Peter pulled back on the catheter, jamming the balloon against the inside of the atrium wall. The gush of blood cut off. Barely a trickle oozed out.

'Vitals?' called out Catherine.

'Systolic's still at fifty. The O neg's here. We're hanging it now.'

Heart still pounding, Catherine looked at Peter

and saw him wink at her through his protective goggles.

'Wasn't that fun?' he said. He reached for the clamp with the cardiac needle. 'You want to do the honors?'

'You bet.'

He handed her the needle holder. She would sew together the edges of the puncture, then pull out the Foley before she closed off the hole entirely. With every deep stitch she took, she felt Peter's approving gaze. Felt her face flush with the glow of success. Already she felt it in her bones: This patient would live.

'Great way to start the day, isn't it?' he said. 'Ripping open chests.'

'This is one birthday I'll never forget.'

'My offer's still on for tonight. How about it?'

'I'm on call.'

'I'll get Ames to cover for you. C'mon. Dinner and dancing.'

'I thought the offer was for a ride in your plane.'

'Whatever you want. Hell, let's do peanut butter sandwiches. I'll bring the Skippy.'

'Ha! I always knew you were a big spender.'

'Catherine, I'm serious.'

Hearing the change in his voice, she looked up and met his steady gaze. Suddenly she noticed that the room had hushed and that everyone else was listening, waiting to find out if the unattainable Dr Cordell would finally succumb to Dr Falco's charms.

She took another stitch as she thought about how much she liked Peter as a colleague, how much she respected him and he respected her. She didn't want that to change. She didn't want to endanger that precious relationship with an ill-fated step toward intimacy.

But oh, how she missed the days when she could enjoy a night out! When an evening was something to look forward to, not dread.

The room was still silent. Waiting.

At last she looked up at him. 'Pick me up at eight.'

Catherine poured a glass of Merlot and stood by the window, sipping wine as she gazed out at the night. She could hear laughter and could see people strolling below on Commonwealth Avenue. Fashionable Newbury Street was only one block away, and on a Friday night in summer this Back Bay neighborhood was a magnet for tourists. Catherine had chosen to live in the Back Bay for just that reason; she took comfort in knowing that other people were around, even if they were strangers. The sound of music and laughter meant she was not alone, not isolated.

Yet here she was, behind her sealed window, drinking her solitary glass of wine, trying to convince herself that she was ready to join that world out there.

A world Andrew Capra stole from me.

She pressed her hand to the window, fingers arched against the glass, as though to shatter her way out of this sterile prison.

Recklessly she drained her wine and set the glass down on the windowsill. I will not stay a victim, she thought. I won't let him win.

She went into her bedroom and surveyed the

clothes in her closet. She pulled a green silk dress from her closet and zipped herself into it. How long had it been since she'd worn this dress? She couldn't remember.

From the other room came a cheery: 'You've got mail!' announcement over her computer. She ignored the message and went into the bathroom to put on makeup. War paint, she thought as she brushed on mascara, dabbed on lipstick. A mask of courage, to help her face the world. With every stroke of the makeup brush, she was painting on confidence. In the mirror she saw a woman she scarcely recognized. A woman she had not seen in two years.

'Welcome back,' she murmured, and smiled.

She turned off the bathroom light and walked out to the living room, her feet reacquainting themselves with the torment of high heels. Peter was late; it was already eight-fifteen. She remembered the 'You've got mail' announcement she'd heard from the bedroom and went to her computer to click on the mailbox icon.

There was one message from a sender named SavvyDoc, with the subject heading: 'Lab Report.' She opened the e-mail.

Dr Cordell,
   Attached are pathology photos which will interest you.

It was unsigned.

She moved the arrow to the 'download file' icon, then hesitated, her finger poised on the mouse. She did not recognize the sender,

SavvyDoc, and normally she would not download a file from a stranger. But this message was clearly related to her work, and it had addressed her by name.

She clicked 'download.'

A color photograph materialized on the screen.

With a gasp, she jerked from her seat as though scalded, and the chair toppled to the floor. She stumbled backward, hand clasped over her mouth.

Then she ran for the phone.

Thomas Moore stood in her doorway, his gaze tight on her face. 'Is the photo still on the screen?'

'I haven't touched it.'

She stepped aside and he walked in, all business, always the policeman. He focused at once on the man who was standing beside the computer.

'This is Dr Peter Falco,' said Catherine. 'My partner in the practice.'

'Dr Falco,' said Moore, as the two men shook hands.

'Catherine and I were planning to go out for dinner tonight,' said Peter. 'I was held up at the hospital. Got here just before you did, and . . .' He paused and looked at Catherine. 'I take it dinner's off?'

She answered with a sickly nod.

Moore sat down at the computer. The screen saver had activated and bright tropical fish swam across the monitor. He nudged the mouse.

The downloaded photograph appeared.

At once Catherine turned away and went to the window, where she stood hugging herself, trying

123

to block out the image she'd just seen on the monitor. She could hear Moore tapping on the keyboard behind her. Heard him make a phone call and say, 'I've just forwarded the file. Got it?' The darkness below her window had fallen strangely silent. Is it already so late? she wondered. Looking down at the deserted street, she could scarcely believe that only an hour ago she'd been ready to step out into that night and rejoin the world.

Now she wanted only to bolt the doors and hide.

Peter said, 'Who the hell would send you something like this? It's sick.'

'I'd rather not talk about it,' she said.

'Have you gotten stuff like this before?'

'No.'

'Then why are the police involved?'

'Please *stop*, Peter. I don't want to discuss it!'

A pause. 'You mean you don't want to discuss it with me.'

'Not now. Not tonight.'

'But you will talk about it with the police?'

'Dr Falco,' said Moore, 'it really would be better if you left now.'

'Catherine? What do you want?'

She heard the hurt in his voice, but she did not turn to look at him. 'I'd like you to go. Please.'

He didn't answer. Only when the door closed did she know Peter had left.

A long silence passed.

'You haven't told him about Savannah?' asked Moore.

'No. I could never bring myself to tell him.'

124

Rape is a subject too intimate, too shameful, to talk about. Even with someone who cares about you.

She asked: 'Who is the woman in the picture?'

'I was hoping you could tell me.'

She shook her head. 'I don't know who sent it, either.'

The chair creaked as he stood up. She felt his hand on her shoulder, his warmth penetrating the green silk. She had not changed clothes and was still dressed up, glossied up for the evening. The whole idea of stepping out on the town now struck her as pitiful. What had she been thinking? That she could go back to being like everyone else? That she could be whole again?

'Catherine,' he said. 'You need to talk to me about this photo.'

His fingers tightened on her shoulder, and she was suddenly aware that he'd called her by her first name. He was standing close enough for her to feel his breath warm her hair, yet she did not feel threatened. Any other man's touch would have seemed like an invasion, but Moore's was genuinely comforting.

She nodded. 'I'll try.'

He pulled up another chair and they both sat down in front of the computer. She forced herself to focus on the photograph.

The woman had curly hair, splayed out like corkscrews on the pillow. Her lips were sealed beneath a silvery strip of duct tape, but her eyes were open and aware, the retinas reflecting blood-red in the camera's flash. The photograph showed her from the waist up. She was bound to the bed, and she was nude.

'Do you recognize her?' he asked.

'No.'

'Is there anything about this photo that strikes you as familiar? The room, the furniture?'

'No. But . . .'

'What?'

'He did it to me, too,' she whispered. 'Andrew Capra took photos of me. Tied to my bed . . .' She swallowed, humiliation washing over her, as though it were her own body so intimately exposed to Moore's gaze. She found herself crossing her arms over her chest, to shield her breasts from further violation.

'This file was transmitted at seven fifty-five p.m. And the sender's name, SavvyDoc – do you recognize it?'

'No.' She focused again on the woman, who stared back with bright red pupils. 'She's awake. She knows what he's about to do. He waits for that. He *wants* you to be awake, to feel the pain. You have to be awake, or he won't enjoy it . . .' Although she was talking about Andrew Capra, she had somehow slipped into the present tense, as though Capra were still alive.

'How would he know your e-mail address?'

'I don't even know who *he* is.'

'He sent this to *you*, Catherine. He knows what happened to you in Savannah. Is there anyone you can think of who might do this?'

Only one, she thought. But he's dead. Andrew Capra is dead.

Moore's cell phone rang. She almost jumped out of her chair. 'Jesus,' she said, her heart pounding, and sank back again.

126

He flipped open the phone. 'Yes, I'm with her now . . .' He listened for a moment and suddenly looked at Catherine. The way he was staring alarmed her.

'What is it?' asked Catherine.

'It's Detective Rizzoli. She says she traced the source of the e-mail.'

'Who sent it?'

'You did.'

He might as well have slapped her in the face. She could only shake her head, too shocked to respond.

'The name "SavvyDoc" was created this evening, using *your* America Online account,' he said.

'But I keep two separate accounts. One is for my personal use—'

'And the other?'

'For my office staff, to use during . . .' She paused. 'The office. He used the computer in my *office*.'

Moore lifted the cell phone to his ear. 'You got that, Rizzoli?' A pause, then: 'We'll meet you there.'

Detective Rizzoli was waiting for them right outside Catherine's medical suite. A small group had already gathered in the hallway – a building security guard, two police officers, and several men in plainclothes. Detectives, Catherine assumed.

'We've searched the office,' said Rizzoli. 'He's long gone.'

'Then he was definitely here?' said Moore.

'Both computers are turned on. The name

SavvyDoc is still on the America Online sign-on screen.'

'How did he gain entry?'

'The door doesn't appear to be forced. There's a housekeeping service under contract to clean these offices, so there are a number of passkeys floating around. Plus there are the employees who work in this suite.'

'We have a billing clerk, a receptionist, and two clinic assistants,' said Catherine.

'And there's you and Dr Falco.'

'Yes.'

'Well, that makes six more keys that could've been lost or borrowed,' was Rizzoli's brusque reaction. Catherine did not care for this woman, and she wondered if the feeling was mutual.

Rizzoli gestured toward the suite. 'Okay, let's take you through the rooms, Dr Cordell, and see if anything's missing. Just don't touch anything, okay? Not the door, not the computers. We'll be dusting them for prints.'

Catherine looked at Moore, who placed a reassuring arm around her shoulder. They stepped into her suite.

She spared only a brief glance around the patient waiting room, then went into the receptionist's area, where the office staff worked. The billing computer was on. The A drive was empty; the intruder had not left any floppy disks behind.

With a pen, Moore tapped the computer mouse to inactivate the screen saver, and the AOL sign-on window appeared. 'SavvyDoc' was still in the 'selected name' box.

'Does anything in this room look different to you?' asked Rizzoli.

Catherine shook her head.

'Okay. Let's go in your office.'

Her heart was pounding faster as she walked up the hallway, past the two exam rooms. She stepped into her office. Instantly her gaze shot to the ceiling. With a gasp, she jerked backward, almost colliding with Moore. He caught her in his arms and held her steady.

'That's where we found it,' said Rizzoli, pointing to the stethoscope dangling from the overhead light. 'Just hanging there. I take it that's not where you left it.'

Catherine shook her head. She said, her voice muted by shock: 'He's been in here before.'

Rizzoli's gaze sharpened on hers. 'When?'

'The last few days. I've been finding things missing. Or moved around.'

'What things?'

'The stethoscope. My lab coat.'

'Look around the room,' said Moore, gently coaxing her forward. 'Has anything else changed?'

She scanned the bookshelves, the desk, the filing cabinet. This was her private space, and she'd organized every inch of it. She knew where things should be and where they should not be.

'The computer's on,' she said. 'I always turn it off when I leave for the day.'

Rizzoli tapped on the mouse, and the AOL screen appeared, with Catherine's screen name, 'CCord,' in the sign-on box.

'This is how he got your e-mail address,' said

Rizzoli. 'All he had to do was turn on your computer.'

She stared at the keyboard. *You typed on these keys. You sat in my chair.*

Moore's voice gave her a start.

'Is anything missing?' he asked. 'It's likely to be something small, something very personal.'

'How do you know that?'

'It's his pattern.'

So it had happened to the other women, she thought. The other victims.

'It might be something you'd wear,' said Moore. 'Something you alone would use. A piece of jewelry. A comb, a key chain.'

'Oh god.' Immediately she reached down to yank open the top desk drawer.

'Hey!' said Rizzoli. 'I said not to touch anything.'

But Catherine was already thrusting her hand into the drawer, frantically searching among the pens and pencils. 'It's not here.'

'What isn't?'

'I keep a spare key ring in my desk.'

'Which keys are on it?'

'An extra key to my car. To my hospital locker . . .' She paused, and her throat was suddenly dry. 'If he's been in my locker during the day, then he's had access to my purse.' She looked up at Moore. 'To my house keys.'

The techs were already dusting for prints when Moore returned to the medical suite.

'Tucked her in bed, did you?' said Rizzoli.

'She's going to sleep in the E.R. call room. I

130

don't want her going home until it's secure.'

'You gonna personally change all her locks?'

He frowned, reading her expression. Not liking what he saw there. 'You have a problem?'

'She's a nice-looking woman.'

I know where this is headed, he thought, and gave a tired sigh.

'A little damaged. A little vulnerable,' said Rizzoli. 'Jeez, it makes a guy want to rush right in and protect her.'

'Isn't that our job?'

'Is that all it is, a job?'

'I'm not going to talk about this,' he said, and walked out of the suite.

Rizzoli followed him into the hallway like a bulldog snapping at his heels. 'She's at the center of this case, Moore. We don't know if she's being straight with us. Please don't tell me you're getting involved with her.'

'I'm not involved.'

'I'm not blind.'

'What do you see, exactly?'

'I see the way you look at her. I see the way she looks at you. I see a cop who's losing his objectivity.' She paused. 'A cop who's going to get hurt.'

Had she raised her voice, had she said it with hostility, he might have responded in kind. But she had said those last words quietly, and he could not muster the necessary outrage to fight back.

'I wouldn't say this to just anyone,' said Rizzoli. 'But I think you're one of the good guys. If you were Crowe, or some other asshole, I'd say sure, go get your heart reamed out, I don't give a shit. But I don't want to see it happen to you.'

They regarded each other for a moment. And Moore felt a twinge of shame that he could not look past Rizzoli's plainness. No matter how much he admired her quick mind, her unceasing drive to succeed, he would always focus on her utterly average face and her shapeless pantsuits. In some ways he was no better than Darren Crowe, no better than the jerks who stuffed tampons in her water bottle. He did not deserve her admiration.

They heard the sound of a throat being cleared and turned to see the crime scene tech standing in the doorway.

'No prints,' he said. 'I dusted both computers. The keyboards, the mice, the disk drives. They've all been wiped clean.'

Rizzoli's cell phone rang. As she flipped it open, she muttered: 'What did we expect? We're not dealing with a moron.'

'What about the doors?' asked Moore.

'There's a few partials,' said the tech. 'But with all the traffic that probably comes in and out of here – patients, staff – we're not going to be able to ID anything.'

'Hey, Moore,' said Rizzoli, and she clapped her cell phone shut. 'Let's go.'

'Where?'

'Headquarters. Brody says he's gonna show us the miracle of pixels.'

'I put the image file on the Photoshop program,' said Sean Brody. 'The file takes up three megabytes, which means it's got lots of detail. No fuzzy pics for this perp. He sent a quality image, right down to the victim's eyelashes.'

Brody was the BPD's techno-wiz, a pasty-faced youngster of twenty-three who now slouched in front of the computer screen, his hand practically grafted to the mouse. Moore, Rizzoli, Frost, and Crowe stood behind him, all gazing over his shoulder at the monitor. Brody had an irritating laugh, like a jackal's, and he gave little chortles of delight as he manipulated the image on the screen.

'This is the full-frame photo,' said Brody. 'Vic tied to the bed. Awake, eyes open, bad case of red eye from the flash. Looks like duct tape on her mouth. Now see, down here in the left-hand corner of the pic, there's the edge of the night-stand. You can see an alarm clock sitting on top of two books. Zoom in, and see the time?'

'Two twenty,' said Rizzoli.

'Right. Now the question is, a.m. or p.m.? Let's go up to the top of the photo, where you see a corner of the window. The curtain's closed, but you can just make out this little chink here, where the edges of the fabric don't quite meet. There's no sunlight coming through. If the time on that clock is correct, this photo was taken at two-twenty a.m.'

'Yeah, but which day?' said Rizzoli. 'This could have been last night or last year. Hell, we don't even know if the Surgeon's the guy who snapped this pic.'

Brody tossed her an annoyed glance. 'I'm not done yet.'

'Okay, what else?'

'Let's just slide lower down the image. Check out the woman's right wrist. It's got duct tape

133

obscuring it. But see that dark little blotch there? What do you suppose that is?' He pointed and clicked, and the detail got larger.

'Still doesn't look like anything,' said Crowe.

'Okay, we'll zoom in again.' He clicked once more. The dark lump took on a recognizable shape.

'Jesus,' said Rizzoli. 'It looks like a tiny horse. That's Elena Ortiz's charm bracelet!'

Brody glanced back at her with a grin. 'Am I good or what?'

'It's him,' said Rizzoli. 'It's the Surgeon.'

Moore said, 'Go back to the nightstand.'

Brody clicked back to the full frame and moved the arrow to the lower left corner. 'What do you want to look at?'

'We've got the clock telling us it's two-twenty. And then there's those two books under the clock. Look at their spines. See how that top book jacket reflects light?'

'Yeah.'

'That has a clear plastic cover protecting it.'

'Okay . . .' said Brody, clearly not understanding where this was headed.

'Zoom in on the top spine,' said Moore. 'See if we can read that book title.'

Brody pointed and clicked.

'Looks like two words,' said Rizzoli. 'I see the word *the*.'

Brody clicked again, zooming in closer.

'The second word begins with an S,' said Moore. 'And look at this.' He tapped on the screen. 'See this little white square here, at the base of the spine?'

'I know what you're getting at!' Rizzoli said, her voice suddenly excited. 'The title. Come on; we need the goddamn title!'

Brody pointed and clicked one last time.

Moore stared at the screen, at the second word on the book's spine. Abruptly he turned and reached for the telephone.

'What am I missing?' asked Crowe.

'The title of the book is *The Sparrow*,' said Moore, punching in 'O.' 'And that little square on the spine – I'm betting that's a call number.'

'It's a library book,' said Rizzoli.

A voice came on the line. 'Operator.'

'This is Detective Thomas Moore, Boston PD. I need an emergency contact number for the Boston Public Library.'

'Jesuits in space,' said Frost, sitting in the back-seat. 'That's what the book's about.'

They were speeding down Centre Street, Moore at the wheel, emergency lights flashing. Two cruisers were leading the way.

'My wife belongs to this reading group, see,' said Frost. 'I remember her talking about *The Sparrow*.'

'So it's science fiction?' asked Rizzoli.

'Naw, it's more like deep religious stuff. What's the nature of God? That kind of thing.'

'Then I don't need to read it,' said Rizzoli. 'I know all the answers. I'm Catholic.'

Moore glanced at the cross street and said, 'We're close.'

The address they sought was in Jamaica Plain, a west Boston neighborhood tucked between

Franklin Park and the bordering town of Brookline. The woman's name was Nina Peyton. A week ago, she had borrowed a copy of *The Sparrow* from the library's Jamaica Plain branch. Of all the patrons in the greater Boston area who had checked out copies of the book, Nina Peyton was the only one who, at 2:00 a.m., was not answering her telephone.

'This is it,' said Moore, as the cruiser just ahead of them turned right onto Eliot Street. He followed suit and, a block later, pulled up behind it.

The cruiser's dome light shot surreal flashes of blue into the night as Moore, Rizzoli, and Frost stepped through the front gate and approached the house. Inside, one faint light glowed.

Moore shot a look at Frost, who nodded and circled toward the rear of the building.

Rizzoli knocked on the front door and called out: 'Police!'

They waited a few seconds.

Again Rizzoli knocked, harder. 'Ms. Peyton, this is the police! Open the door!'

There was a three-beat pause. Suddenly Frost's voice crackled over their com units: 'There's a screen prised off the back window!'

Moore and Rizzoli exchanged glances, and without a word the decision was made.

With the butt of his flashlight, Moore smashed the glass panel next to the front door, reached inside, and slid open the bolt.

Rizzoli was first into the house, moving in a semicrouch, her weapon sweeping an arc. Moore was right behind her, adrenaline pulsing as he registered a quick succession of images. Wood floor. An open closet. Kitchen straight ahead, living room to the right. A single lamp glowing on an end table.

'The bedroom,' said Rizzoli.

'Go.'

They started up the hallway, Rizzoli taking the lead, her head swiveling left and right as they passed a bathroom, a spare bedroom, both empty. The door at the end of the hall was slightly ajar; they could not see past it, into the dark bedroom beyond.

Hands slick on his weapon, heart thudding, Moore edged toward the door. Gave it a nudge with his foot.

The smell of blood, hot and foul, washed over him. He found the light switch and flicked it on. Even before the image hit his retinas, he knew what he would see. Yet he was not fully prepared for the horror.

The woman's abdomen had been flayed open. Loops of small bowel spilled out of the incision and hung like grotesque streamers over the side of the bed. Blood dribbled from the open neck wound and collected in a spreading pool on the floor.

It took Moore an eternity to process what he was seeing. Only then, as he fully registered the details, did he understand their significance. The blood, still fresh, still dripping. The absence of arterial spray on the wall. The ever-widening pool of dark, almost black blood.

At once he crossed to the body, his shoes tracking straight through the blood.

'Hey!' yelled Rizzoli. 'You're contaminating the scene!'

He pressed his fingers to the intact side of the victim's neck.

The corpse opened her eyes.

Dear god. She's still alive.

Eight

Catherine jerked rigid in bed, heart slamming in her chest, every nerve electric with fear. She stared at the darkness, struggling to quell her panic.

Someone was pounding on the door of the call room. 'Dr Cordell?' Catherine recognized the voice of one of the E.R. nurses. 'Dr Cordell!'

'Yes?' said Catherine.

'We have a trauma case coming in! Massive blood loss, abdominal and neck wounds. I know Dr Ames is covering for trauma tonight, but he's delayed. Dr Kimball could use your help!'

'Tell him I'll be there.' Catherine turned on the lamp and stared at the clock. It was 2:45 a.m. She'd slept only three hours. The green silk dress was still draped over the chair. It looked like something foreign, from another woman's life, not her own.

The scrub suit she'd worn to bed was damp with sweat, but she had no time to change. She gathered her tangled hair in a ponytail and went to the sink to splash cold water on her face. The woman staring back at her from the mirror was a shell-shocked stranger. *Focus. It's time to let go of the fear. Time to go to work.* She slipped her bare feet into the running shoes she'd retrieved from her hospital locker and, with a deep breath, stepped out of the call room.

'ETA two minutes!' called the E.R. clerk. 'Ambulance says pressure's down to seventy systolic!'

'Dr Cordell, they're setting up in Trauma One.'

'Who've we got on the team?'

'Dr Kimball and two interns. Thank god you're already in-house. Dr Ames's car conked out and he can't get in . . .'

Catherine pushed into Trauma One. In a glance she saw the team had prepared for the worst. Three poles were hung with Ringer's lacate; IV tubes were coiled and ready for connection. A courier was standing by to run blood tubes to the lab. The two interns stood on either side of the table, clutching IV catheters, and Ken Kimball, the E.R. doc on duty, had already broken the tape sealing the laparotomy tray.

Catherine pulled on a surgical cap, then thrust her arms into the sleeves of a sterile gown. A nurse tied the gown in back and held open the first glove. With every piece of the uniform came another layer of authority and she was feeling stronger, more in control. In this room, she was the savior, not the victim.

'What's the story on the patient?' she asked Kimball.

'Assault. Trauma to the neck and abdomen.'

'Gunshot?'

'No. Stab wounds.'

Catherine paused in the act of snapping on the

140

second glove. A knot had suddenly formed in her stomach. *Neck and abdomen. Stab wounds.*

'Ambulance is pulling in!' a nurse yelled through the doorway.

'Blood and guts time,' said Kimball, and he stepped out to meet the patient.

Catherine, already in sterile garb, stayed right where she was. The room had suddenly gone silent. Neither the two interns flanking the table nor the scrub nurse, poised to hand Catherine surgical instruments, said a word. They were focused on what was happening beyond the door.

They heard Kimball yell: 'Go, go, *go!*'

The door flew open, and the gurney wheeled in. Catherine caught a glimpse of blood-soaked sheets, of a woman's matted brown hair and a face obscured by the tape holding an ET tube in place.

With a *one-two-three!* they slid the patient onto the table.

Kimball pulled off the sheet, baring the victim's torso.

In the chaos of that room, no one heard Catherine's sharp intake of breath. No one noticed her take a stumbling step backward. She stared at the victim's neck, where the pressure dressing was saturated a deep red. She looked at the abdomen, where another hastily applied dressing was already peeling free, spilling trickles of blood down the naked flank. Even as everyone else sprang into action, connecting IVs and cardiac leads, squeezing air into the victim's lungs, Catherine stood immobilized by horror.

Kimball peeled off the abdominal dressing.

Loops of small bowel spilled out and plopped onto the table.

'Systolic's barely palpable at sixty! She's in sinus tach—'

'I can't get this IV in! Her vein's collapsed!'

'Go for a subclavian!'

'Can you toss me another catheter?'

'Shit, this whole field's contaminated . . .'

'Dr Cordell? Dr Cordell?'

Still in a daze, Catherine turned to the nurse who'd just spoken and saw the woman frowning at her over the surgical mask.

'Do you want lap pads?'

Catherine swallowed. Took a deep breath. 'Yes. Lap pads. And suction . . .' She re-focused on the patient. A young woman. She had a disorienting flashback to another E.R., to the night in Savannah when she herself had been the woman lying on the table.

I won't let you die. I won't let him claim you.

She grabbed a handful of sponges and a hemostat from the instrument tray. She was fully focused now, the professional back in control. All the years of surgical training automatically kicked into gear. She turned her attention first to the neck wound and peeled off the pressure dressing. Dark blood dribbled out and splattered the floor.

'The carotid!' said one of the interns.

Catherine slapped a sponge against the wound and took a deep breath. 'No. No, if it was the carotid she'd already be dead.' She looked at the scrub nurse. 'Scalpel.'

The instrument was slapped in her hand. She paused, steadying herself for the delicate task, and placed the tip of the scalpel on the neck. Maintaining pressure on the wound, Catherine swiftly slit through the skin and dissected upward toward the jaw, exposing the jugular vein. 'He didn't cut deep enough to reach the carotid,' she said. 'But he did get the jugular. And this end's retracted up into the soft tissue.' She tossed down the scalpel and grabbed the thumb forceps. 'Intern? I need you to sponge. *Gently!*'

'You going to re-anastomose?'

'No, we're just going to tie it off. She'll develop collateral drainage. I need to expose enough vein to get suture around it. Vascular clamp.'

Instantly the instrument was in her hand.

Catherine positioned the clamp and snapped it over the exposed vessel. Then she released a sigh and glanced at Kimball. 'This bleeder's down. I'll tie it off later.'

She turned her attention to the abdomen. By now Kimball and the other intern had cleared the field using suction and lap pads, and the wound was fully exposed. Gently Catherine nudged aside loops of bowel and stared into the open incision. What she saw made her sick with rage.

She met Kimball's stunned gaze across the table.

'Who would do this?' he said softly. 'Who the hell are we dealing with?'

'A monster,' she said.

'The vic's still in surgery. She's still alive.' Rizzoli snapped her cell phone shut and looked at Moore and Dr Zucker. 'We now have a witness. Our unsub's getting careless.'

'Not careless,' said Moore. 'Rushed. He didn't

143

have time to finish the job.' Moore stood by the bedroom door, studying the blood on the floor. It was still fresh, still glistening. *It's had no time to dry. The Surgeon was just here.*

'The photo was e-mailed to Cordell at seven fifty-five P.M.,' said Rizzoli. 'The clock in the photo said two-twenty.' She pointed to the clock on the nightstand. 'That's set at the correct time. Which means he must have taken the photo *last* night. He kept that victim alive, in this house, for over twenty-four hours.'

Prolonging the pleasure.

'He's getting cocky,' said Dr Zucker, and there was an unsettling note of admiration in his voice. An acknowledgment that here was a worthy opponent. 'Not only does he keep the victim alive for a whole day; he actually *leaves* her here, for a time, to send that e-mail. Our boy is playing mind games with us.'

'Or with Catherine Cordell,' said Moore.

The victim's purse was lying on top of the dresser. With gloved hands, Moore went through the contents. 'Wallet with thirty-four dollars. Two credit cards. Triple A card. Employee ID badge for Lawrence Scientific Supplies, Sales Department. Driver's license, Nina Peyton, twenty-nine years old, five foot four, a hundred thirty pounds.' He flipped over the license. 'Organ donor.'

'I think she just donated,' said Rizzoli.

He unzipped a side pocket. 'There's a datebook.'

Rizzoli turned to look at him with interest. 'Yes?'

He opened the book to the current month. It

was blank. He flipped backward until he found an entry, written nearly eight weeks before: *Rent due*. He flipped further back and saw more entries: *Sid's B-day. Dry cleaning. Concert 8:00. Staff meeting.* All the mundane little details that make up a life. Why had the entries suddenly stopped eight weeks ago? He thought of the woman who had written these words, printing neatly in blue ink. A woman who had probably looked ahead to the blank page for December and pictured Christmas and snow with every reason to believe she would be alive to see it.

He closed the book and was so overwhelmed by sadness that for a moment he could not speak.

'There's nothing at all left behind in the sheets,' said Frost, crouched by the bed. 'No loose surgical threads, no instruments, nothing.'

'For a guy who was supposedly in a hurry to leave,' said Rizzoli, 'he did a good job of cleaning up after himself. And look. He had time to fold the nightclothes.' She pointed to a cotton nightgown, which lay neatly folded on a chair. 'This doesn't go along with his being in a rush.'

'But he left his victim alive,' said Moore. 'The worst possible mistake.'

'It doesn't make sense, Moore. He folds the nightgown, picks up after himself. And then he's so careless as to leave behind a witness? He's too smart to make this mistake.'

'Even the smartest ones screw up,' said Zucker. 'Ted Bundy got careless at the end.'

Moore looked at Frost. 'You're the one who called the victim?'

'Yeah. When we were running down that list of

145

phone numbers the library gave us. I called this residence around two, two-fifteen. I got the answering machine. I didn't leave any message.'

Moore glanced around the room but saw no answering machine. He walked out to the living room and spotted the phone on the end table. It had a caller ID box, and the memory button was smeared with blood.

He used the tip of a pencil to press the button, and the phone number of the last caller was displayed on the digital readout.

Boston PD 2:14 A.M.

'Is that what spooked him?' asked Zucker, who'd followed him into the living room.

'He was right here when Frost called. There's blood on the caller ID button.'

'So the phone rang. And our unsub wasn't finished. He hadn't achieved satisfaction. But a phone call in the middle of the night must have rattled him. He came out here, into the living room, and saw the number on the caller ID box. Saw it was the police, trying to reach the victim.' Zucker paused. 'What would *you* do?'

'I'd clear out of here.'

Zucker nodded, and a smile twitched at his lips.

This is all a game to you, thought Moore. He went to the window and looked out at the street, which was now a bright kaleidoscope of flashing blue lights. Half a dozen cruisers were parked in front of the house. The press was out there, too; he could see the local TV vans setting up their satellite feeds.

'He didn't get to enjoy it,' Zucker said.

'He completed the excision.'

'No, that's just the souvenir. A little reminder of his visit. He wasn't here just to collect a body part. He came for the ultimate thrill: to feel a woman's life drain away. But this time he didn't achieve it. He was interrupted, distracted by fear that the police were coming. He didn't stay long enough to watch his victim die.' Zucker paused. 'The next one's going to come very soon. Our unsub is frustrated, and the tension is getting unbearable for him. Which means he's already on the hunt for a new victim.'

'Or he's already chosen her,' said Moore. And thought: Catherine Cordell.

The first streaks of dawn were lightening the sky. Moore had not slept in nearly twenty-four hours, had been going full throttle for most of the night, fueled only by coffee. Yet as he looked up at the brightening sky, what he felt was not exhaustion but renewed agitation. There was some connection between Catherine and the Surgeon that he did not understand. Some invisible thread that bound her to that monster.

'Moore.'

He turned to see Rizzoli and instantly picked up on the excitement in her eyes.

'Sex Crimes just called,' she said. 'Our victim is a very unlucky lady.'

'What do you mean?'

'Two months ago, Nina Peyton was sexually assaulted.'

The news stunned Moore. He thought of the blank pages in the victim's datebook. Eight weeks ago, the entries had stopped. That was when Nina Peyton's life had screeched to a halt.

'There's a report on file?' said Zucker.

'Not just a report,' said Rizzoli. 'A rape kit was collected.'

'*Two* rape victims?' said Zucker. 'Could it be this easy?'

'You think their rapist comes back to kill them?'

'It's got to be more than random chance. Ten percent of serial rapists later communicate with their victims. It's the perp's way of prolonging the torment. The obsession.'

'Rape as foreplay to murder.' Rizzoli gave a disgusted snort. 'Nice.'

A new thought suddenly occurred to Moore. 'You said a rape kit was collected. So there was a vaginal swab?'

'Yep. DNA's pending.'

'Who collected that swab? Did she go to the emergency room?' He was almost certain that she'd say: *Pilgrim Hospital*.

But Rizzoli shook her head. 'Not the E.R. She went to Forest Hills Women's Clinic. It's right down the road.'

On a wall in the clinic waiting room, a full-color poster of the female genital tract was displayed beneath the words: *Woman. Amazing Beauty.* Though Moore agreed that a woman's body was a miraculous creation, he felt like a dirty voyeur, staring at that explicit diagram. He noticed that several women in the waiting room were eyeing him the way gazelles regard a predator in their midst. That he was accompanied by Rizzoli did not seem to alter the fact he was the alien male.

He was relieved when the receptionist finally said, 'She'll see you now, Detectives. It's the last room on the right.'

Rizzoli led the way down the hall, past posters with *The 10 signs your partner is abusive* and *How do you know if it's rape?* With every step he felt as if another stain of male guilt had attached itself to him, like dirt soiling his clothes. Rizzoli felt none of this; she was the one on familiar ground. The territory of women. She knocked on the door that said: 'Sarah Daly, Nurse Practitioner.'

'Come in.'

The woman who stood up to greet them was young and hip-looking. Under her white coat she wore blue jeans and a black tee shirt, and her boyish haircut emphasized dark gamine eyes and elegant cheekbones. But what Moore could not stop focusing on was the small gold hoop in her left nostril. For much of the interview, he felt as if he were talking to that hoop.

'I reviewed her medical chart after you called,' said Sarah. 'I know a police report *was* filed.'

'We've read it,' said Rizzoli.

'And your reason for coming here?'

'Nina Peyton was attacked last night, in her home. She's now in critical condition.'

The woman's first reaction was shock. And then, fast on its heels, rage. Moore saw it in the way her chin jutted up and her eyes glittered. 'Was it *him*?'

'Him?'

'The man who raped her?'

'It's a possibility we're considering,' said Rizzoli. 'Unfortunately, the victim is comatose and can't talk to us.'

'Don't call her the *victim*. She does have a name.'

Rizzoli's chin jutted up as well, and Moore knew she was pissed off. It was not a good way to start an interview.

He said, 'Ms. Daly, this was an incredibly brutal crime, and we need—'

'Nothing is incredible,' retorted Sarah. 'Not when we're talking about what men do to women.' She picked up a folder from her desk and held it out to him. 'Her medical record. The morning after she was raped, she came to this clinic. I was the one who saw her that day.'

'Were you also the one who examined her?'

'I did everything. The interview, the pelvic exam. I took the vaginal swabs and confirmed there was sperm under the microscope. I combed the pubic hair, collected nail clippings for the rape kit. Gave her the morning-after pill.'

'She didn't go to the E.R. for any other tests?'

'A rape victim who walks in our door gets everything taken care of in this building, by one person. The last thing she needs is a parade of changing faces. So I draw the blood and send it out to the lab. I make the necessary calls to the police. If that's what the victim wants.'

Moore opened the folder and saw the patient information sheet. Nina Peyton's date of birth, address, phone number, and employer were listed. He flipped to the next page and saw it was filled with small, tight handwriting. The date of the first entry was May 17.

Chief Complaint: Sexual assault
History of Present Illness: 29-year-old white female, believes she was sexually assaulted. Last night while having drinks at the Gramercy Pub, she felt dizzy and remembers walking to the bathroom. She has no memory of any events that followed . . .

'She woke up at home, in her own bed,' said Sarah. 'She didn't remember how she got home. Didn't remember getting undressed. She certainly didn't remember tearing her own blouse. But there she was, stripped of her clothes. Her thighs were caked with what she thought was semen. One eye was swollen, and she had bruises on both wrists. She figured out pretty quick what had happened. And she had the same reaction other rape victims have. She thought: 'It's my fault. I shouldn't have been so careless.' But that's how it is with women.' She looked directly at Moore. 'We blame ourselves for everything, even when it's the man who does the fucking.'

In the face of such anger, there was nothing he could say. He looked down at the chart and read the physical exam.

Patient is a disheveled, withdrawn female who speaks in a monotone. She is unaccompanied, and has walked to the clinic from her home . . .

'She kept talking about her car keys,' said

151

Sarah. 'She was battered, one eye was swollen shut, and all she could focus on was the fact she'd lost her car keys and she needed to find them or she couldn't drive to work. It took me a while to get her to break out of that repeating loop and talk to me. This is a woman who'd never had anything really bad happen to her. She was educated, independent. A sales rep for Lawrence Scientific Supplies. She deals with people every day. And here she was, practically paralyzed. Obsessed with finding her stupid car keys. Finally we opened her purse and searched through all the pockets, and the keys were there. Only after we found them could she focus on me, and tell me what happened.'

'And what did she say?'

'She went into the Gramercy Pub around nine o'clock to meet a girlfriend. The friend never showed, so Nina hung around for a while. Had a martini, talked to a few guys. Look, I've been there, and every night it's a busy place. A woman would feel safe.' She added, on a bitter note: 'As if there *is* any safe place.'

'Did she remember the man who took her home?' asked Rizzoli. 'That's what we really need to know.'

Sarah looked at her. 'It's all about the criminal, isn't it? That's all those two cops from Sex Crimes wanted to hear about. The perp gets the attention.'

Moore could feel the room heating up with Rizzoli's temper. He said, quickly: 'The detectives said she was unable to provide a description.'

'I was in the room when they interviewed her.

She asked me to stay, so I heard the whole story twice. They kept after her about what he looked like, and she just couldn't tell them. She honestly could not remember anything about him.'

Moore turned to the next page in the chart. 'You saw her a second time, in July. Only a week ago.'

'She came back for a follow-up blood test. It takes six weeks after exposure for an HIV test to become positive. That's the ultimate atrocity. First to be raped, and then to find out your attacker has given you a fatal disease. It's six weeks of agony for these women, waiting to find out if they'll get AIDS. Wondering if the enemy is inside you, multiplying in your blood. When they come for their follow-up test, I have to give them a pep talk. And swear that I'll call them the instant I get the results back.'

'You don't analyze the tests here?'

'No. It all gets sent out to Interpath Labs.'

Moore turned to the last page of the chart and saw the sheet of results. *HIV screen: Negative. VDRL (syphilis): Negative.* The page was tissue-thin, a sheet from a printed carbon form. The most important news of our lives, he thought, so often arrives on such flimsy paper. Telegrams. Exam scores. Blood tests.

He closed the chart and laid it on the desk. 'When you saw Nina the second time, the day she came in for the follow-up blood test, how did she strike you?'

'Are you asking me if she was still traumatized?'

'I have no doubt she was.'

His quiet answer seemed to puncture Sarah's

153

swelling bubble of rage. She sat back, as though, without anger, she had lost some vital fuel. For a moment she considered his question. 'When I saw Nina the second time, she was like one of the walking dead.'

'How so?'

'She sat in that chair where Detective Rizzoli is now, and I felt as if I could almost see straight through her. As if she was transparent. She hadn't been to work since the rape. I think it was hard for her to face people, especially men. She was paralyzed by all these strange phobias. Afraid to drink tap water, or anything that hadn't been sealed. It had to be in an unopened bottle or can, something that couldn't be poisoned or drugged. She was afraid that men could look at her and see she'd been violated. She was convinced her rapist had left sperm on her bedsheets and clothes, and she was spending hours every day washing things over and over. Whoever Nina Peyton used to be, that woman was dead. What I saw in her place was a ghost.' Sarah's voice had trailed off, and she sat very still, staring toward Rizzoli, seeing another woman in that chair. A succession of women, different faces, different ghosts, a parade of the damaged.

'Did she say anything about being stalked? About the attacker reappearing in her life?'

'A rapist never disappears from your life. For as long as you live, you're always his property.' Sarah paused. And added, bitterly: 'Maybe he just came to claim what was his.'

Nine

It was not virgins the Vikings sacrificed, but harlots.

In the year of our lord 922, the Arab diplomat ibn Fadlan witnessed just such a sacrifice among the people he called the Rus. He described them as tall and blond, men of perfect physique who traveled from Sweden, down the Russian rivers, to the southern markets of Kazaria and the Caliphate, where they traded amber and furs for the silk and silver of Byzantium. It was on that trade route, in a place called Bulgar, at the bend of the Volga, that a dead Viking man of great importance was prepared for his final journey to Valhalla.

Ibn Fadlan witnessed the funeral.

The dead man's boat was hauled ashore and placed on posts of birch wood. A pavilion was built on the deck, and in this pavilion was a couch covered in Greek brocade. The corpse, which had been buried ten days, was then disinterred.

To ibn Fadlan's surprise, the blackened flesh did not smell.

The newly dug-up corpse was then adorned in

fine clothes: trousers and stockings, boots and a tunic, and a caftan of brocade with gold buttons. They placed him on the mattress inside the pavilion, and propped him up with cushions in a sitting position. Around him they placed bread and meat and onions, intoxicating drink, and sweet-smelling plants. They slew a dog and two horses, a rooster and a hen, and all these, too, they placed inside the pavilion, to serve his needs in Valhalla.

Last, they brought a slave girl.

For the ten days that the dead man had lain buried in the ground, the girl had been given over to whoredom. Dazed with drink, she was brought from tent to tent to service every man in the encampment. She lay with legs spread beneath a succession of sweating, grunting men, her well-used body a communal vessel into which the seed of all the tribesmen was spilled. In this way was she defiled, her flesh corrupted, her body made ready for sacrifice.

On the tenth day, she was brought to the ship, accompanied by an old woman whom they called the Angel of Death. The girl removed her bracelets and finger rings. She drank deeply to intoxicate herself. Then she was brought into the pavilion, where the dead man sat.

There, upon the brocade-draped mattress, she was defiled yet again. Six times, by six men, her body passed among them like shared meat. And when it was done, when the men were sated, the girl was stretched out at the side of her dead master. Two men held her feet, two men held her hands, and the Angel of Death looped a cord

156

around the girl's neck. While the men pulled the cord taut, the Angel raised her broad-bladed dagger and plunged it into the girl's chest.

Again and again the blade came down, spilling blood the way a grunting man spills seed, the dagger reenacting the ravishment that came before, sharp metal piercing soft flesh.

A brutal rutting that delivered, with its final thrust, the rapture of death.

'She required massive transfusions of blood and fresh frozen plasma,' said Catherine. 'Her pressure's stabilized, but she's still unconscious and on a ventilator. You'll just have to be patient, Detective. And hope she wakes up.'

Catherine and Detective Darren Crowe stood outside Nina Peyton's SICU cubicle and watched three lines trace across the cardiac monitor. Crowe had been waiting by the O.R. door when the patient was wheeled out, had stuck right beside her in the Recovery Room and later during the transfer to SICU. His role was more than merely protective; he was eager to take the patient's statement, and for the last few hours he had made a nuisance of himself, demanding frequent progress reports and hovering outside the cubicle.

Now, once again, he repeated the question he'd been asking all morning: 'Is she going to live?'

'All I can tell you is that her vital signs are stable.'

'When can I talk to her?'

Catherine gave a tired sigh. 'You don't seem to understand how critical she was. She lost more than a third of her blood volume before she even

157

got here. Her brain may have been deprived of crucial circulation. When and if she *does* regain consciousness, there's a chance she won't remember anything.'

Crowe looked through the glass partition. 'Then she's useless to us.'

Catherine stared at him with mounting dislike. Not once had he expressed concern for Nina Peyton, except as a witness, as someone he could use. Not once, all morning, had he referred to her by name. He'd called her *the victim* or *the witness*. What he saw, looking into the cubicle, wasn't a woman at all but simply a means to an end.

'When will she be moved from ICU?' he asked.

'It's too early to ask that question.'

'Could she be transferred to a private room? If we keep the door closed, limit the personnel, then no one has to know she can't talk.'

Catherine knew exactly where this was going. 'I won't have my patient used as bait. She needs to stay here for round-the-clock observation. You see those lines on the monitor? That's the EKG, the central venous pressure, and the arterial pressure. I need to stay on top of every change in her status. This unit is the only place to do it.'

'How many women could we save if we stop him now? Have you thought about that? Of all people, Dr Cordell, you know what these women have gone through.'

She went rigid with anger. He had struck a blow at her most vulnerable spot. What Andrew Capra had done to her was so personal, so intimate, that she could not speak of the loss, even with her own father. Detective Crowe had ripped open that wound.

'She may be the only way to catch him,' said Crowe.

'This is the best you can come up with? Use a comatose woman as bait? Endanger other patients in this hospital by inviting a killer to show up here?'

'What makes you think he isn't already here?' Crowe said, and he walked away.

Already here. Catherine could not help but glance around the unit. She saw nurses bustling between patients. A group of resident surgeons gathered near the bank of monitors. A phlebotomist carrying her tray of blood tubes and syringes. How many people walked in and out of this hospital every day? How many of them did she truly know as people? No one. That much Andrew Capra had taught her: that she could never really know what lurked in a person's heart.

The ward clerk said, 'Dr Cordell, telephone call.'

Catherine crossed to the nurses' station and picked up the phone.

It was Moore. 'I hear you pulled her through.'

'Yes, she's still alive,' Catherine answered bluntly. 'And no, she's not talking yet.'

A pause. 'I take it this is a bad time to call.'

She sank into a chair. 'I'm sorry. I just spoke to Detective Crowe, and I am not in a good mood.'

'He seems to have that effect on women.'

They both laughed, tired laughs that melted any hostility between them.

'How are you holding up, Catherine?'

'We had some hairy moments, but I think I've got her stablilized.'

'No, I mean *you*. Are you okay?'

It was more than just a polite inquiry; she heard real concern in his voice, and she did not know what to say. She knew only that it felt good to be cared about. That his words had brought a flush to her cheeks.

'You won't go home, right?' he said. 'Until your locks are changed.'

'It makes me so angry. He's taken away the one place I felt safe.'

'We'll make it safe again. I'll see about getting a locksmith over there.'

'On a Saturday? You're a miracle worker.'

'No. I just have a great Rolodex.'

She leaned back, the tension easing from her shoulders. All around her, the SICU hummed with activity, yet her attention was focused completely on the man whose voice now soothed her, reassured her.

'And how are you?' she asked.

'I'm afraid my day's just beginning.' A pause as he turned to answer someone's question, something about which evidence to bag. Other voices were talking in the background. She imagined him in Nina Peyton's bedroom, the evidence of horror all around him. Yet his voice was quiet and unruffled.

'You'll call me the instant she wakes up?' said Moore.

'Detective Crowe's hanging around here like a vulture. I'm sure he'll know it before I do.'

'Do you think she *will* wake up?'

160

'Honest answer?' said Catherine. 'I don't know. I keep saying that to Detective Crowe, and he doesn't accept it, either.'

'Dr Cordell?' It was Nina Peyton's nurse, calling from the cubicle. The tone of her voice instantly alarmed Catherine.

'What is it?'

'You've got to come look at this.'

'Is something wrong?' Moore said over the phone.

'Hang on. Let me check.' She set down the receiver and went into the cubicle.

'I was cleaning her off with a washcloth,' the nurse said. 'They brought her down from the O.R. with blood still caked all over her. When I turned her on her side, I saw it. It's behind her left thigh.'

'Show me.'

The nurse grasped the patient's shoulder and hip and rolled her onto her side. 'There,' she said softly.

Fear skewered Catherine to the spot. She stared at the cheery message that had been written in black felt-tip ink on Nina Peyton's skin.

HAPPY BIRTHDAY. DO YOU LIKE MY GIFT?

Moore found her in the hospital cafeteria. She was seated at a corner table, her back to the wall, assuming the position of one who knows she is threatened and wants to see any attack coming. She was still wearing surgeon's scrubs, and her hair was tied back in a ponytail, exposing her strikingly angular features, the unadorned face, the glittering eyes. She had to be nearly as exhausted as he was, but fear had heightened her alertness, and she was like a feral cat, watching his every move as he approached the table. A half-empty cup of coffee sat in front of her. How many refills had she had? he wondered, and saw that she trembled as she reached for the cup. Not the steady hand of a surgeon, but the hand of a frightened woman.

He sat down across from her. 'There'll be a patrol car parked outside your building all night. Did you get your new keys?'

She nodded. 'The locksmith dropped them off. He told me he put in the Rolls-Royce of dead bolts.'

'You'll be fine, Catherine.'

She looked down at her coffee. 'That message was meant for me.'

'We don't know that.'

'It was my birthday yesterday. He knew. And he knew I was scheduled to be on call.'

'If he's the one who wrote it.'

'Don't bullshit me. You *know* it was him.'

After a pause, Moore nodded.

They sat without speaking for a moment. It was already late afernoon, and most of the tables were empty. Behind the counter, cafeteria workers cleared away the serving pans, and steam rose in wispy columns. A lone cashier cracked open a fresh package of coins, and they clattered into the register drawer.

'What about my office?' she said.

'He left no fingerprints.'

'So you have nothing on him.'

162

'We have nothing,' he admitted.

'He moves in and out of my life like air. No one sees him. No one knows what he looks like. I could put bars on all my windows, and I'll still be afraid to fall asleep.'

'You don't have to go home. I'll bring you to a hotel.'

'It doesn't matter where I hide. He'll know where I am. For some reason, he's chosen me. He's told me I'm next.'

'I don't think so. It would be an incredibly stupid move on his part, warning his next victim. The Surgeon is not stupid.'

'Why did he contact me? Why write me notes on . . .' She swallowed.

'It could be a challenge to *us*. A way of taunting the police.'

'Then the bastard should have written to *you*!' Her voice rang out so loudly that a nurse pouring a cup of coffee turned and stared at her.

Flushing, Catherine rose to her feet. She'd embarrassed herself by that outburst, and she was silent as they walked out of the hospital. He wanted to take her hand, but he thought she would only pull away, interpreting it as a condescending gesture. Above all, he did not want her to think him condescending. More than any woman he'd ever met, she commanded his respect.

Sitting in his car, she said quietly: 'I lost it in there. I'm sorry.'

'Under the circumstances, anyone would have.'

'Not you.'

His smile was ironic. 'I, of course, never lose my cool.'

163

'Yes, I've noticed.'

And what did that mean? he wondered as they drove to the Back Bay. That she thought him immune to the storms that roil a normal human heart? Since when had clear-eyed logic meant the absence of emotions? He knew his colleagues in the homicide unit referred to him as Saint Thomas the Serene. The man you turned to when situations became explosive and a calm voice was needed. They did not know the other Thomas Moore, the man who stood before his wife's closet at night, inhaling the fading scent of her clothes. They saw only the mask he allowed them to see.

She said, with a note of resentment, 'It's easy for you to be calm about this. You're not the one he's fixated on.'

'Let's try to look at this rationally—'

'Look at my own death? Of *course* I can be rational.'

'The Surgeon has established a pattern he's comfortable with. He attacks at night, not during the day. At heart he's a coward, unable to confront a woman on equal terms. He wants his prey vulnerable. In bed and asleep. Unable to fight back.'

'So I should never fall asleep? That's an easy solution.'

'What I'm saying is, he'll avoid attacking anyone during daylight hours, when a victim is able to defend herself. It's after dark when everything changes.'

He pulled up in front of her address. While the building lacked the charm of the older brick residences on Commonwealth Avenue, it had the advantage of a gated and well-lit underground garage. Access to the front entrance required both a key as well as the correct security code, which Catherine punched into the keypad.

They entered a lobby, decorated with mirrors and polished marble floors. Elegant, yet sterile. Cold. An unnervingly silent elevator whisked them to the second floor.

At her apartment door, she hesitated, the new key in hand.

'I can go in and take a look first, if that would make you feel better,' he said.

She seemed to take his suggestion as a personal affront. In answer, she thrust the key in the lock, opened the door, and walked in. It was as if she had to prove to herself that the Surgeon had not won. That she was still in control of her life.

'Why don't we go through all the rooms, one by one,' he said. 'Just to make sure nothing has been disturbed.'

She nodded.

Together they walked through the living room, the kitchen. And last, the bedroom. She knew the Surgeon had taken souvenirs from other women, and she meticulously went through her jewelry box, her dresser drawers, searching for any sign of a trespasser's hand. Moore stood in the doorway watching her sort through blouses and sweaters and lingerie. And suddenly he was hit with an unsettling memory of another woman's clothes, not nearly as elegant, folded in a suitcase. He remembered a gray sweater, a faded pink blouse. A cotton nightgown with blue cornflowers. Nothing brand-new, nothing expensive. Why had he never bought Mary anything extravagant?

What did he think they were saving for? Not what the money had eventually gone to. Doctors and nursing home bills and physical therapists.

He turned from the bedroom doorway and walked out to the living room, where he sat down on the couch. The late afternoon sun streamed through the window and its brightness stung his eyes. He rubbed them and dropped his head in his hands, afflicted by guilt that he had not thought of Mary all day. For that he felt ashamed. He felt even more ashamed when he raised his head to look at Catherine and all thoughts of Mary instantly vanished. He thought: This is the most beautiful woman I've ever known.

The most courageous woman I've ever known.

'There's nothing missing,' she said. 'Not as far as I can tell.'

'Are you sure you want to stay here? I'd be happy to bring you to a hotel.'

She crossed to the window and stared out, her profile lit by the golden light of sunset. 'I've spent the last two years being afraid. Locking out the world with dead bolts. Always looking behind doors and searching closets. I've had enough of it.' She looked at him. 'I want my life back. This time I won't let him win.'

This time, she had said, as though this was a battle in a much longer war. As though the Surgeon and Andrew Capra had blended into a single entity, one she had briefly subdued two years ago but had not truly defeated. Capra. The Surgeon. Two heads of the same monster.

'You said there'd be a patrol car outside tonight,' she said.

166

'There will be.'

'You guarantee it?'

'Absolutely.'

She took a deep breath, and the smile she gave him was an act of sheer courage. 'Then I have nothing to worry about, do I?' she said.

It was guilt that made him drive toward Newton that evening instead of going straight home. He had been shaken by his reaction to Cordell and troubled by how thoroughly she now monopolized his thoughts. In the year and a half since Mary's death, he had lived a monk's existence, feeling no interest whatsoever in women, all passions dampened by grief. He did not know how to deal with this fresh spark of desire. He only knew that, given the situation, it was inappropriate. And that it was a sign of disloyalty to the woman he had loved.

So he drove to Newton to make things right. To assuage his conscience.

He was holding a bouquet of daisies as he stepped into the front yard and latched the iron gate behind him. It's like carrying coals to Newcastle, he thought, looking around at the garden, now falling into the shadows of evening. Every time he visited, there seemed to be more flowers crammed into this small space. Morning glory vines and rose canes had been trained up the side of the house, so that the garden seemed to be expanding skyward as well. He felt almost embarrassed by his meager offering of daisies. But daisies were what Mary had loved best, and it was almost a habit for him now, to choose them at the

167

flower stand. She'd loved their cheery simplicity, the fringes of white around lemony suns. She'd loved their scent – not sweet and cloying like other flowers, but pungent. Assertive. She'd loved the way they sprang up wild in vacant lots and road-sides, reminders that true beauty is spontaneous and irrepressible.

Like Mary herself.

He rang the bell. A moment later the door swung open, and the face that smiled at him was so much like Mary's, he felt a familiar twinge of pain. Rose Connelly had her daughter's blue eyes and round cheeks, and although her hair was almost entirely gray and age had etched its mark on her face, the similarities left no doubt that she was Mary's mother.

'It's so good to see you, Thomas,' she said. 'You haven't been by lately.'

'I'm sorry about that, Rose. It's hard to find time lately. I hardly know which day it is.'

'I've been following the case on the TV. What a terrible business you're in.'

He stepped into the house and handed her the daisies. 'Not that you need any more flowers,' he said wryly.

'One can never have too many flowers. And you know how much I love daisies. Would you like some iced tea?'

'I'd love some, thank you.'

They sat in the living room, sipping their tea. It tasted sweet and sunny, the way they drank it in South Carolina where Rose was born. Not at all like the somber New England brew that Moore had grown up drinking. The room was sweet as well, hopelessly old-fashioned by Boston standards. Too much chintz, too many knick-knacks. But oh, how it reminded him of Mary! She was everywhere. Photos of her hung on the walls. Her swimming trophies were displayed on the bookshelves. Her childhood piano stood in the living room. The ghost of that child was still here, in this house where she had been raised. And Rose was here, the keeper of the flame, who looked so much like her daughter that Moore sometimes thought he saw Mary herself gazing from Rose's blue eyes.

'You look tired,' she said.

'Do I?'

'You never went on vacation, did you?'

'They called me back. I was already in the car, heading up the Maine Turnpike. Had my fishing poles packed. Bought a new tacklebox.' He sighed. 'I miss the lake. It's the one thing I look forward to all year.'

It was the one thing Mary had always looked forward to as well. He glanced at the swimming trophies on the bookshelf. Mary had been a sturdy little mermaid who would happily have lived her life in the water had she been born with gills. He remembered how cleanly and powerfully she had once stroked across the lake. Remembered how those same arms had wasted away to twigs in the nursing home.

'After the case is solved,' said Rose, 'you could still go to the lake.'

'I don't know that it will be solved.'

'That doesn't sound like you at all. So discouraged.'

'This is a different sort of crime, Rose. Committed by someone I can't begin to understand.'

'You always manage to.'

'Always?' He shook his head and smiled. 'You give me too much credit.'

'It's what Mary used to say. She liked to brag about you, you know. *He always gets his man.*'

But at what cost? he wondered, his smile fading. He remembered all the nights away at crime scenes, the missed dinners, the weekends when his mind was occupied only by thoughts of work. And there had been Mary, patiently waiting for his attention. *If I had just one day to relive, I would spend every minute of it with you. Holding you in bed. Whispering secrets beneath warm sheets.*

But God grants no such second chances.

'She was so proud of you,' Rose said.

'I was proud of her.'

'You had twenty good years together. That's more than most people can say.'

'I'm greedy, Rose. I wanted more.'

'And you're angry you didn't get it.'

'Yes, I suppose I am. I'm angry that she had to be the one with the aneurysm. That she was the one they couldn't save. And I'm angry that—' He stopped. Released a deep breath. 'I'm sorry. It's just hard. Everything is so hard these days.'

'For both of us,' she said softly.

They gazed at each other in silence. Yes, of course it would be even harder for widowed Rose, who had lost her only child. He wondered whether she would forgive him if he ever remarried. Or would she consider it a betrayal? The

170

consignment of her daughter's memory to an even deeper grave?

Suddenly he found he could not hold her gaze, and he glanced away with a twinge of guilt. The same guilt he'd felt earlier that afternoon when he'd looked at Catherine Cordell and felt the unmistakable stirring of desire.

He set down his empty glass and rose to his feet. 'I should be going.'

'So it's back to work already?'

'It doesn't stop until we catch him.'

She saw him to the door and stood there as he walked through the tiny garden to the front gate. He turned and said, 'Lock your doors, Rose.'

'Oh, you always say that.'

'I always mean it, too.' He gave a wave and walked away, thinking: *Tonight more than ever.*

Where we go depends on what we know, and what we know depends on where we go.

The rhyme kept repeating in Jane Rizzoli's head like an irritating childhood ditty as she stared at the Boston map tacked on a large corkboard on her apartment wall. She had hung the map the day after Elena Ortiz's body was discovered. As the investigation wore on, she had stuck more and more colored pins on the map. There were three different colors representing three different women. White for Elena Ortiz. Blue for Diana Sterling. Green for Nina Peyton. Each marked a known location within the woman's sphere of activity. Her residence, her place of employment. The homes of close friends or relatives. Which medical facility she visited. In short, the habitat of the prey. Somewhere in the course of her day-to-day activities, each woman's world had intersected with the Surgeon's.

Where we go depends on what we know, and what we know depends on where we go.

And where did the Surgeon go? she wondered. What made up *his* world?

She sat eating her cold supper of a tuna sandwich and potato chips washed down with beer, studying the map as she chewed. She had hung the map on the wall next to her dining table, and every morning when she drank her coffee, every evening when she had dinner – provided she got home for dinner – she would find her gaze inexorably drawn to those colored pins. While other women might hang pictures of flowers or pretty landscapes or movie posters, here she was, staring at a death map, tracing the movements of the deceased.

This is what her life had come to: eat, sleep, and work. She'd been living in this apartment for three years now, but there were few decorations on the walls. No plants (who had time to water 'em?), no stupid knickknacks, not even any curtains. Only venetian blinds on the windows. Like her life, her home was streamlined for work. She loved, and lived for, her job. Had known she'd wanted to be a cop since she was twelve years old, when a woman detective visited her school on Career Day. First the class had heard from a nurse and a lawyer, then a baker and an engineer. The students' fidgeting got louder. Rubber bands shot between rows and a spitball sailed across the room. Then the woman cop stood up, weapon holstered at her waist, and the class suddenly hushed.

Rizzoli never forgot that. She never forgot how even the boys gazed in awe at a *woman*.

Now she was that woman cop, and while she could command the awe of twelve-year-old boys, the respect of adult men often eluded her.

Be the best was her strategy. Outwork them, outshine them. So here she was, working even as she ate her dinner. Homicide and tuna fish sandwiches. She took a long pull of beer, then leaned back, staring at the map. There was something creepy about seeing the human geography of the dead. Where they'd lived their lives, the places that were important to them. At yesterday's meeting, the criminal psychologist Dr Zucker had tossed out a number of profiling terms. Anchor points. Activity nodes. Target backcloths. Well, she didn't need Zucker's fancy words or a computer program to tell her what she was looking at and how to interpret it. Gazing at the map, what she imagined was a savanna teeming with prey. The color pins defined the personal universes of three unlucky gazelles. Diana Sterling's was centered in the north, in the Back Bay and Beacon Hill. Elena Ortiz's was in the South End. Nina Peyton's was to the southwest, in the suburb of Jamaica Plain. Three discrete habitats, with no overlap.

And where is your habitat?

She tried to see the city through his eyes. Saw canyons of skyscrapers. Green parks like swaths of pastureland. Paths along which herds of dumb prey moved, unaware that a hunter was watching them. A predatory traveler who killed across both distance and time.

173

The phone rang and she gave a start, tipping the beer bottle on its side. Shit. She grabbed a roll of paper towels and dabbed up the spill as she answered the phone.

'Rizzoli.'

'Hello, Janie?'

'Oh. Hey, Ma.'

'You never called me back.'

'Huh?'

'I called you a few days ago. You said you'd call back and you didn't.'

'It slipped my mind. I'm up to my eyeballs in work.'

'Frankie's coming home next week. Isn't that great?'

'Yeah.' Rizzoli sighed. 'That's great.'

'You see your brother once a year. Couldn't you sound a little more excited?'

'Ma, I'm tired. This Surgeon case is going round-the-clock.'

'Have the police caught him?'

'I *am* the police.'

'You know what I mean.'

Yeah, she knew. Her mother probably pictured little Janie answering the phones and bringing coffee to those all-important *male* detectives.

'You're coming for dinner, right?' said her mother, sliding right out of the topic of Jane's work. 'Next Friday.'

'I'm not sure. It depends on how the case goes.'

'Oh, you can be here for your own brother.'

'If things heat up, I may have to do it another day.'

'We can't do it another day. Mike's already agreed to drive down Friday.'

Well of course. Let's cater to brother Michael.
'Janie?'
'Yeah, Ma. Friday.'

She hung up, her stomach churning with unspent anger, a feeling that was all too familiar. God, how had she survived her childhood?

She picked up her beer and swallowed the few drops that hadn't spilled. Looked up at the map again. At that moment, catching the Surgeon had never been more important to her. All the years of being the ignored sister, the trivial girl, made her focus her rage on *him*.

Who are you? Where are you?

She went very still for a moment, staring. Thinking. Then she picked up the package of pins and chose a new color. Red. She stabbed one red pin on Commonwealth Avenue, another in the location of Pilgrim Hospital, in the South End.

The red marked Catherine Cordell's habitat. It intersected both Diana Sterling's and Elena Ortiz's. Cordell was the common factor. She moved through the worlds of both victims.

And the life of the third victim, Nina Peyton, now rests in her hands.

Ten

Even on a Monday afternoon, the Gramercy Pub was a happening place. It was 7:00 P.M., and the corporate singles were out on the town and ready to play. This was their playpen.

Rizzoli sat at a table near the entrance and felt puffs of hot city air blow into the room every time the door swung open to admit yet another GQ clone, another office Barbie swaying in three-inch heels. Rizzoli, wearing her usual boxy pantsuit and sensible flats, felt like the high school chaperone. She saw two women walk in, sleek as cats, trailing mingled scents of perfume. Rizzoli never wore perfume. She owned one tube of lipstick, which was stored somewhere in the back of her bathroom cabinet, along with the dried-up mascara wand and the bottle of Dewy Satin foundation. She'd purchased the makeup five years ago at a department store cosmetics counter, thinking that perhaps, with the right tools of illusion, even she could look like cover girl Elizabeth Hurley. The salesgirl had creamed and powdered, stroked and sketched, and when it was over had triumphantly handed Rizzoli a mirror and asked, smiling, 'What do you think of your new look?'

What Rizzoli thought, staring at her own image, was that she hated Elizabeth Hurley for giving women false hope. The brutal truth was, there are some women who will never be beautiful, and Rizzoli was one of them.

So she sat unnoticed and sipped her ginger ale as she watched the pub gradually fill with people. It was a noisy crowd, with much chatter and clinking of ice cubes, the laughter a little too loud, a little too forced.

She rose and worked her way toward the bar. There she flashed her badge at the bartender and said, 'I have a few questions.'

He gave her badge scarcely a glance, then punched the cash register to ring up a drink. 'Okay, shoot.'

'You remember seeing this woman in here?' Rizzoli laid a photo of Nina Peyton on the counter.

'Yeah, and you're not the first cop to ask about her. Some other woman detective was in here 'bout a month or so ago.'

'From the sex crimes unit?'

'I guess. Wanted to know if I saw anyone trying to pick up that woman in the picture.'

'And did you?'

He shrugged. 'In here, everyone's on the make. I don't keep track.'

'But you do remember seeing this woman? Her name is Nina Peyton.'

'I seen her in here a few times, usually with a girlfriend. I didn't know her name. Hasn't been back in a while.'

'You know why?'

'Nope.' He picked up a rag and began wiping the counter, his attention already drifting away from her.

'I'll tell you why,' said Rizzoli, her voice rising in anger. 'Because some asshole decided to have a little fun. So he came here to hunt for a victim. Looked around, saw Nina Peyton, and thought: There's some pussy. He sure didn't see a human being when he looked at her. All he saw was something he could use and throw away.'

'Look, you don't need to tell me this.'

'Yes, I do. And you need to hear it because it happened right under your nose and you chose not to see it. Some asshole slips a drug in a woman's drink. Pretty soon she's sick and staggers off to the bathroom. The asshole takes her by the arm and leads her outside. And you didn't see *any* of that?'

'No,' he shot back. 'I *didn't*.'

The room had fallen silent. She saw that people were staring at her. Without another word, she stalked off, back to the table.

After a moment, the buzz of conversation resumed.

She watched the bartender slide two whiskeys toward a man, saw the man hand one of them to a woman. She watched drink glasses lifted to lips and tongues licking off salt from Margaritas, saw heads tilted back as vodka and tequila and beer slid down throats.

And she saw men staring at women. She sipped her ginger ale, and she felt intoxicated, not with alcohol but anger. She, the lone female sitting in the corner, could see with startling clarity what this place really was. A watering hole where predator and prey came together.

Her beeper went off. It was Barry Frost paging her.

'What's all that racket?' asked Frost, barely audible over her cell phone.

'I'm sitting in a bar.' She turned and glared as a nearby table exploded with laughter. 'What did you say?'

'. . . a doctor over on Marlborough Street. I've got a copy of her medical record.'

'Whose medical record?'

'Diana Sterling's.'

At once Rizzoli was hunched forward, every ounce of attention focused on Frost's faint voice. 'Tell me again. Who's the doctor and why did Sterling see him?'

'The doctor's a she. Dr Bonnie Gillespie. A gynecologist over on Marlborough Street.'

Another noisy burst of laughter drowned out his words. Rizzoli cupped her hand over her ear so she could hear his next words. 'Why did Sterling see her?' she yelled.

But she already knew the answer; she could see it right in front of her as she stared at the bar, where two men were converging on a woman like lions stalking a zebra.

'Sexual assault,' said Frost. 'Diana Sterling was raped, too.'

'All three were sexual assault victims,' said Moore. 'But neither Elena Ortiz nor Diana Sterling reported their attacks. We found out about Sterling's rape only because we checked

179

local women's clinics and gynecologists to find out if she was ever treated for it. Sterling never even told her parents about the attack. When I called them this morning, they were shocked to find out about it.'

It was only midmorning, but the faces he saw around the conference room table looked drained. They were operating on sleep deficits, and another full day stretched ahead of them.

Lieutenant Marquette said, 'So the only person who knew about Sterling's rape was this gynecologist on Marlborough Street?'

'Dr Bonnie Gillespie. It was Diana Sterling's one and only visit. She went in because she was afraid she'd been exposed to AIDS.'

'What did Dr Gillespie know about the rape?'

Frost, who'd interviewed the physician, answered the question. He opened the folder containing Diana Sterling's medical record. 'Here's what Dr Gillespie wrote: "Thirty-year-old white female requests HIV screen. Unprotected sex five days ago, partner's HIV status unknown. When asked if her partner was in a high-risk group, patient became upset and tearful. Revealed that sex was not consensual, and she does not know assailant's name. Does not wish to report the assault. Refuses referral for rape counseling." ' Frost looked up. 'That's all the information Dr Gillespie got from her. She did a pelvic exam, tested for syphilis, gonorrhea, and HIV, and told the patient to return in two months for a follow-up HIV blood test. The patient never did. Because she was dead.'

'And Dr Gillespie never called the police? Even after the murder?'

'She didn't know her patient was dead. She never saw the news reports.'

'Was a rape kit collected? Semen?'

'No. The patient, uh . . .' Frost flushed in embarrassment. Some topics even a married man like Frost found difficult to discuss. 'She douched a few times, right after the attack.'

'Can you blame her?' said Rizzoli. 'Shit, I would've felt like douching with Lysol.'

'Three rape victims,' said Marquette. 'This is no coincidence.'

'You find the rapist,' said Zucker, 'I think you'll have your unsub. What's the status on the DNA from Nina Peyton?'

'It's on expedite,' said Rizzoli. 'Lab's had the semen sample for nearly two months, and nothing's been done with it. So I lit a fire under them. Let's just keep our fingers crossed that our perp's already in CODIS.'

CODIS, the Combined DNA Index System, was the FBI's national database of DNA profiles. The system was still in its infancy, and the genetic profiles of half a million convicted offenders had not yet been entered into the system. The chances of their getting a 'cold hit' – a match with a known offender – were slim.

Marquette looked at Dr Zucker. 'Our unsub sexually assaults the victim first. Then returns weeks later to kill her? Does that make sense?'

'It doesn't have to make sense to *us*,' said Zucker. 'Only to him. It's not uncommon for a rapist to return and attack his victim a second time. There's a sense of ownership there. A

181

relationship, however pathological, has been established.'

Rizzoli snorted. 'You call it a relationship?'

'Between abuser and victim. It sounds sick, but there it is. It's based on power. First he takes it away from her, makes her something less than a human being. She's now an object. He knows it and, more importantly, she knows it. It's the fact she's damaged, humiliated, that may excite him enough to return. First he marks her with the rape. Then he returns to claim ultimate ownership.'

Damaged women, thought Moore. That's the common link among these victims. It suddenly occurred to him that Catherine, too, was among the damaged.

'He never raped Catherine Cordell,' said Moore.

'But she *is* a rape victim.'

'Her attacker's been dead two years. How did the Surgeon identify her as a victim? How did she even show up on his radar screen? She never talks about the attack, to anyone.'

'She talked about it online, didn't she? That private chat room . . .' Zucker paused. 'Jesus. Is it possible he's *finding* his victims through the Internet?'

'We explored that theory,' said Moore. 'Nina Peyton doesn't even own a computer. And Cordell never revealed her name to anyone in that chat room. So we're right back to the question: Why did the Surgeon focus on Cordell?'

Zucker said, 'He does seem obsessed with her. He goes out of his way to taunt her. He takes risks, just to e-mail her that photograph of Nina Peyton.

And that leads to a disastrous chain of events for him. The photo brings the police right to Nina's door. He's rushed and can't complete the kill, can't achieve satisfaction. Even worse, he leaves behind a witness. The worst mistake of all.'

'That was no mistake,' said Rizzoli. 'He meant for her to live.'

Her remark elicited skeptical expressions around the table.

'How else do you explain a screwup like this?' she continued. 'That photo he e-mailed to Cordell was meant to pull us in. He sent it, and he waited for us. Waited till we called the vic's house. He knew we were on our way. And then he did a half-ass job of cutting her throat, because he *wanted* us to find her alive.'

'Oh yeah,' snorted Crowe. 'It was all part of his *plan*.'

'And his reason for this?' Zucker asked Rizzoli.

'The reason was written right on her thigh. Nina Peyton was an offering to Cordell. A gift intended to scare the shit out of her.'

There was a pause.

'If so, then it worked,' said Moore. 'Cordell is terrified.'

Zucker leaned back and considered Rizzoli's theory. 'It's a lot of risks to take, just to scare one woman. It's a sign of megalomania. It could mean he's decompensating. That's what eventually happened to Jeffrey Dahmer and Ted Bundy. They lost control of their fantasies. They became careless. That's when they made their mistakes.'

Zucker rose and went to the chart on the wall. There were three victim names there. Beneath the name Nina Peyton, he wrote in a fourth name: Catherine Cordell.

'She's not one of his victims – not yet. But in some way he's identified her as an object of interest. How did he choose her?' Zucker looked around the room. 'Have you interviewed her colleagues? Do any of them trip any alarm bells?'

Rizzoli said, 'We've eliminated Kenneth Kimball, the E.R. doc. He was on duty the night Nina Peyton was attacked. We've also interviewed most of the male surgical staff, as well as the residents.'

'What about Cordell's partner, Dr Falco?'

'Dr Falco has not been eliminated.'

Now Rizzoli had caught Zucker's attention, and he focused on her with a strange light in his eyes. The *nutso-shrink look* was what the cops in the homicide unit called it. 'Tell me more,' he said softly.

'Dr Falco looks great on paper. MIT grad in aeronautical engineering. M.D. from Harvard. Surgery residency at Peter Bent Brigham. Raised by a single mom, worked his way through college and med school. Flies his own airplane. Nice-looking guy, too. Not Mel Gibson, but he could turn a few heads.'

Darren Crowe laughed. 'Hey, Rizzoli's rating suspects by their looks. Is this how lady cops do it?'

Rizzoli shot him a hostile glance. 'What I'm *saying*', she continued, 'is this guy could have a dozen women on his arm. But I hear from the nurses that the only woman he's been interested in is Cordell. It's no secret that he keeps asking her

184

out. And she keeps turning him down. Maybe he's starting to get pissed.'

'Dr Falco bears watching,' said Zucker. 'But let's not narrow down our list too soon. Let's stick with Dr Cordell here. Are there other reasons the Surgeon might choose her as a victim?'

It was Moore who turned the question on its head. 'What if she isn't just another in a string of prey? What if she's *always* been the object of his attention? Each of these attacks has been a re-enactment of what was done to those women in Georgia. What was almost done to Cordell. We've never explained why he imitates Andrew Capra. We've never explained why he's zeroed in on Capra's only survivor.' He pointed to the list. 'These other women, Sterling, Ortiz, Peyton – what if they're merely placeholders? Surrogates for his primary victim?'

'The theory of the retaliatory target,' said Zucker. 'You can't kill the woman you really hate because she's too powerful. Too intimidating. So you kill a substitute, a woman who represents that target.'

Frost said, 'You're saying his real target's always been Cordell? But he's afraid of her?'

'It's the same reason Edmund Kemper didn't kill his mother until the very end of his murder spree,' said Zucker. '*She* was the real target all along, the woman he despised. Instead he vented his rage against other victims. With each attack he symbolically destroyed his mother again and again. He couldn't actually kill her, not at first, because she wielded too much authority over him. On some level, he was afraid of her. But with each

185

killing he gained confidence. Power. And in the end, he finally achieved his goal. He crushed his mother's skull, decapitated her, raped her. And as the final insult, he tore out her larynx and shoved it into the garbage disposal. The real target of his rage was finally dead. That's when his spree ended. That's when Edmund Kemper turned himself in.'

Barry Frost, who was usually the first cop to toss his cookies at a crime scene, looked a little queasy at the thought of Kemper's brutal finale. 'So these first three attacks,' he said, 'they could be just the warm-up for the main event?'

Zucker nodded. 'The killing of Catherine Cordell.'

It almost hurt Moore to see the smile on Catherine's face as she walked into the clinic waiting room to greet him, because he knew the questions he brought would surely destroy this welcome. Looking at her now, he did not see a victim but a warm and beautiful woman who immediately took his hand in hers and seemed reluctant to release it.

'I hope this is a convenient time to talk,' he said.

'I'll always make time for you.' Again, that bewitching smile. 'Would you like a cup of coffee?'

'No, thank you. I'm fine.'

'Let's go into my office, then.'

She settled in behind her desk and waited expectantly for whatever news he had brought. In the last few days she had learned to trust him, and her gaze was unguarded. Vulnerable. He had earned her confidence as a friend, and now he was about to shatter it.

186

'It's clear to everyone', he said, 'that the Surgeon is focused on you.'

She nodded.

'What we're wondering is *why*. Why does he reenact Andrew Capra's crimes? Why have you become the center of his attention? Do you know the answer to that?'

Bewilderment flickered in her eyes. 'I have no idea.'

'We think you do.'

'How could I possibly know the way he thinks?'

'Catherine, he could stalk any other woman in Boston. He could choose someone who's unprepared, who has no idea she's being hunted. That would be the logical thing for him to do, to go after the easy victim. You're the most difficult prey he could choose, because you're already on your guard against attack. And then he makes the hunt even more difficult by warning you. Taunting you. Why?'

The welcome was gone from her eyes. Suddenly her shoulders squared and her hands closed into fists on her desk. 'I keep telling you, I don't *know*.'

'You're the one physical connection between Andrew Capra and the Surgeon,' he said. 'The common victim. It's as if Capra is still alive, picking up where he left off. And where he left off was you. The one who got away.'

She stared down at her desk, at the files so neatly stacked in their in and out boxes. At the medical note she'd been writing in tight and precise script. Though she sat perfectly still, the knuckles of her hands stood out, stark as ivory.

'What haven't you told me about Andrew Capra?' he asked quietly.

187

'I haven't kept anything from you.'

'The night he attacked you, why did he come to your house?'

'How is this relevant?'

'You were the only victim Capra knew as a person. The other victims were strangers, women he picked up in bars. But you were different. He *chose* you.'

'He was – he may have been angry with me.'

'He came to see you about something at work. A mistake he'd made. That's what you told Detective Singer.'

She nodded. 'It was more than just one mistake. It was a series of them. Medical errors. And he'd failed to follow up on abnormal blood tests. It was a pattern of carelessness. I'd confronted him earlier in the day, in the hospital.'

'What did you tell him?'

'I told him he should seek another specialty. Because I was not going to recommend him for a second year of residency.'

'Did he threaten you? Express any anger?'

'No. That was the strange thing. He just accepted it. And he . . . smiled at me.'

'Smiled?'

She nodded. 'As though it didn't really matter to him.'

The image gave Moore a chill. She could not have known then that Capra's smile had masked an unfathomable rage.

'Later that night, in your house,' said Moore, 'when he attacked you—'

'I've already gone over what happened. It's in my statement. Everything is in my statement.'

Moore paused. Reluctantly he pressed on. 'There are things you didn't tell Singer. Things you left out.'

She looked up, her cheeks stung red with anger. 'I've left nothing out!'

He hated being forced to hound her with more questions, but he had no choice. 'I reviewed Capra's autopsy report,' he said. 'It's not consistent with the statement you gave the Savannah police.'

'I told Detective Singer exactly what happened.'

'You said you were lying with your body draped over the side of the bed. You reached under the bed for the gun. From that position you aimed at Capra and fired.'

'And that's true. I swear it.'

'According to the autopsy, the bullet tracked upward through his abdomen and passed through his thoracic spine, paralyzing him. That part is consistent with your statement.'

'Then why are you saying I lied?'

Again Moore paused, almost too sick at heart to press on. To keep hurting her. 'There's the problem of the second bullet,' he said. 'It was fired at close range, straight into his left eye. Yet you were lying on the floor.'

'He must have bent forward, and that's when I fired—'

'Must have?'

'I don't know. I don't remember.'

'You don't remember firing the second bullet?'

'No. Yes . . .'

'Which is the truth, Catherine?' He said it quietly, but he could not soften the sting of his words.

189

She shot to her feet. 'I won't be questioned this way. *I'm* the victim.'

'And I'm trying to keep you alive. I need to know the truth.'

'I've told you the truth! Now I think it's time for you to leave.' She crossed to the door, yanked it open, and gave a startled gasp.

Peter Falco stood right outside, his hand poised to knock.

'Are you okay, Catherine?' asked Peter.

'Everything is *fine*,' she snapped.

Looking at Moore, Peter's gaze sharpened. 'What is this, police harassment?'

'I'm asking Dr Cordell a few questions, that's all.'

'That's not what it sounded like in the hallway.' Peter looked at Catherine. 'Do you want me to show him out?'

'I can deal with this myself.'

'You're not obligated to answer any questions.'

'I'm well aware of that, thank you.'

'Okay. But if you need me, I'm out here.' Peter shot a last warning glance at Moore, then turned and went back to his own office. At the other end of the hallway, Helen and the billing clerk were staring at her. Flustered, she shut the door again. For a moment she stood with her back to Moore. Then her spine straightened, and she turned to him. Whether she answered him now or later, the questions would remain.

'I've kept nothing from you,' she said. 'If I can't tell you everything that happened that night, it's because I don't remember.'

'So your statement to the Savannah police was not entirely true.'

190

'I was still hospitalized when I gave that statement. Detective Singer talked me through what happened, helping me piece it together. I told him what I *thought* was correct at the time.'

'And now you're not sure.'

She shook her head. 'It's hard to know which memories are real. There's so much I can't remember, because of the drug Capra gave me. The Rohypnol. Every so often, I'll have a flashback. Something that may or may not be real.'

'And you still have these flashbacks?'

'I had one last night. It was the first one in months. I thought I was over them. I thought they'd gone away.' She walked to the window and stared out. It was a view darkened by the shadow of towering concrete. Her office faced the hospital, and one could see row upon row of patients' windows. A glimpse into the private worlds of the sick and dying.

'Two years seems like a long time,' she said. 'Time enough to forget. But really, two years is nothing. *Nothing*. After that night, I couldn't go back to my own house. I couldn't set foot in the place where it happened. My father had to pack up my things and move me into a new place. There I was, the chief resident, accustomed to the sight of blood and guts. Yet just the thought of walking up that hallway, and opening my old bedroom door – it made me break out in a cold sweat. My father tried to understand, but he's an old military man. He doesn't accept weakness. He thinks of it as just another war wound, something that heals, and then you get on with your life. He told me to grow up and get over it.' She shook her head and laughed. 'Get over it. It sounds like such an easy thing. He had no idea how hard it was for me just to step outside every morning. To walk to my car. To be so exposed. After a while, I just stopped talking to him, because I knew he was disgusted by my weakness. I haven't called him in months . . .

'It's taken me two years to finally get my fear under control. To live a reasonably normal life where I don't feel as if something's going to jump out from every bush. I had my life back.' She brushed her hand across her eyes, a swift and angry swipe at her tears. Her voice dropped to a whisper. 'And now I've lost it again . . .'

She was shaking with the effort not to cry, hugging herself, her fingers digging into her own arms as she fought for control. He rose from the chair and crossed to her. Stood behind her, wondering what would happen if he touched her. Would she pull away? Would the mere contact of a man's hand repulse her? He watched helplessly as she curled into herself, and he thought she might shatter before his eyes.

Gently he touched her shoulder. She didn't flinch, didn't pull away. He turned her toward him, his arms encircling her, and drew her against his chest. The depth of her pain shocked him. He could feel her whole body vibrating with it, the way a storm batters a swaying bridge. Though she made no sound, he felt the shaky intake of her breath, the stifled sobs. He pressed his lips to her hair. He could not help himself; her need spoke to something deep inside him. He cupped her face in his hands and kissed her forehead, her brow.

She went very still in his arms, and he thought: I've crossed the line. Quickly he released her. 'I'm sorry,' he said. 'That should not have happened.'

'No. It shouldn't have.'

'Can you forget it did?'

'Can you?' she asked softly.

'Yes.' He straightened. And said it again, more firmly, as though to convince himself. 'Yes.'

She looked down at his hand, and he knew what she was focusing on. His wedding ring. 'I hope for your wife's sake that you can,' she said. Her comment was meant to instill guilt, and it did.

He regarded his ring, a simple gold band that he had worn so long it seemed grafted to his flesh. 'Her name was Mary,' he said. He knew what Catherine had assumed: that he was betraying his wife. Now he felt almost desperate to explain, to redeem himself in her eyes.

'It happened two years ago. A hemorrhage into her brain. It didn't kill her, not right away. For six months, I kept hoping, waiting for her to wake up . . .' He shook his head. 'A chronic vegetative state was what the doctors called it. God, I hated that word, *vegetative*. As if she was a plant or some kind of tree. A mockery of the woman she used to be. By the time she died, I couldn't recognize her. I couldn't see anything left of Mary.'

Her touch took him by surprise, and he was the one who flinched at the contact. In silence they faced each other in the gray light through the window, and he thought: No kiss, no embrace, could bring two people any closer than we are right now. The most intimate emotion two people can share is neither love nor desire but pain.

The buzz of the intercom broke the spell. Catherine blinked, as though suddenly remembering where she was. She turned to her desk and pressed the intercom button.

'Yes?'

'Dr Cordell, the SICU just called. They need you upstairs STAT.'

Moore saw, from Catherine's glance, that the same thought had occurred to them both: *Something has happened to Nina Peyton.*

'Is this about Bed Twelve?' asked Catherine.

'Yes. The patient just woke up.'

Eleven

Nina Peyton's eyes were wide and frantic. Four-point restraints held her wrists and ankles to the bedrails, and the tendons of her arms stood out in thick cords as she fought to free her hands.

'She regained consciousness about five minutes ago,' said Stephanie, the SICU nurse. 'First I noticed her heart rate was up, and then I saw her eyes were open. I've been trying to calm her down, but she keeps fighting the restraints.'

Catherine looked at the cardiac monitor and saw a rapid heart rate but no arrhythmias. Nina's breathing was rapid as well, occasionally punctuated by explosive wheezes that expelled blasts of phlegm out the endotracheal tube.

'It's the ET tube,' said Catherine. 'It's making her panic.'

'Shall I give her some Valium?'

Moore said, from the doorway, 'We need her conscious. If she's sedated, we can't get any answers.'

'She can't talk to you anyway. Not with the ET tube in.' Catherine looked at Stephanie. 'How were the last blood gases? Can we extubate?'

Stephanie flipped through her papers on the clipboard. 'They're borderline. PO2's sixty-five. PCO2 thirty-two. That's on the T-tube at forty percent oxygen.'

Catherine frowned, liking none of the options. She wanted Nina awake and able to talk just as much as the police did, but she was juggling several concerns at once. The sensation of a tube lodged in the throat can induce panic in anyone, and Nina was so agitated that her restrained wrists were already chafed raw. But removing the tube carried risks as well. Fluid had accumulated in her lungs after surgery, and even while she was breathing 40 percent oxygen – twice that of room air – her blood oxygen saturation was barely adequate. That's why Catherine had left the tube in place. If they removed the tube, they would lose a margin of safety. If they left it in, the patient would continue to panic and thrash. If they sedated her, Moore's questions would go unanswered.

Catherine looked at Stephanie. 'I'm going to extubate.'

'Are you sure?'

'If there's any deterioration I'll re-intubate.' *Easier said than done* was what she saw in Stephanie's eyes. After several days with a tube in place, the laryngeal tissues sometimes swelled, making re-intubation difficult. An emergency tracheotomy would be the only option.

Catherine circled around behind her patient's head and gently cupped her face. 'Nina, I'm Dr Cordell. I'm going to take the tube out. Is that what you want?'

The patient nodded, a response that was sharp and desperate.

'I need you to be very still, okay? So we don't injure your vocal cords.' Catherine glanced up. 'Mask ready?'

Stephanie held up the plastic oxygen mask.

Catherine gave Nina's shoulder a reassuring squeeze. She peeled off the tape holding the tube in place and released air from the balloonlike inflator cuff. 'Take a deep breath and exhale,' said Catherine. She watched the chest expand, and as Nina released the breath, Catherine eased out the tube.

It emerged in a spray of mucus as Nina coughed and wheezed. Catherine stroked her hair, murmuring gently as Stephanie fastened an oxygen mask in place.

'You're doing fine,' said Catherine.

But the blips on the cardiac monitor continued to race by. Nina's frightened gaze remained focused on Catherine, as though she was her lifeline and she dared not lose sight of her. Looking into her patient's eyes, Catherine felt a disturbing flash of familiarity. *This was me two years ago. Waking up in a Savannah hospital. Surfacing from one nightmare, into another . . .*

She looked at the straps holding Nina's wrists and ankles and remembered how terrifying it was to be tied down. The way she'd been tied down by Andrew Capra.

'Take off the restraints,' she said.

'But she might pull out her lines.'

'Just take them *off.*'

Stephanie flushed at the rebuke. Without a word

she untied the straps. She did not understand; no one could understand but Catherine, who, even two years after Savannah, could not abide sleeves with tight cuffs. As the last restraint fell free, she saw Nina's lips move in a silent message.

Thank you.

Gradually the beep of the EKG slowed. Against the steady rhythm of that heartbeat, the two women gazed at each other. If Catherine had recognized a part of herself in Nina's eyes, so, too, did Nina seem to recognize herself in Catherine's. The silent sisterhood of victims.

There are more of us than anyone will ever know.

'You can come in now, Detectives,' the nurse said.

Moore and Frost stepped into the cubicle and found Catherine seated at the bedside, holding Nina's hand.

'She asked me to stay,' said Catherine.

'I can call in a female officer,' said Moore.

'No, she wants me,' said Catherine. 'I'm not leaving.'

She looked straight at Moore, her gaze unyielding, and he realized this was not the same woman he had held in his arms only a few hours ago; this was a different side of her, fierce and protective, and on this matter she would not back down.

He nodded and sat down at the bedside. Frost set up the cassette recorder and took an unobtrusive position at the foot of the bed. It was Frost's blandness, his quiet civility, that made Moore choose him to sit in on this interview. The last thing Nina Peyton needed to face was an over-aggressive cop.

Her oxygen mask had been removed and replaced with nasal prongs, and air hissed from the tube into her nostrils. Her gaze darted between the two men, eyes alert to any threats, any sudden gestures. Moore was careful to keep his voice soft as he introduced himself and Barry Frost. He guided her through the preliminaries, confirming her name and age and address. This information they already knew, but by asking her to state it on tape they established her mental status and demonstrated she was alert and competent to make a statement. She answered his questions in a hoarse, flat voice, eerily devoid of emotion. Her remoteness unnerved him; he felt as though he were listening to a dead woman.

'I didn't hear him come into my house,' she said. 'I didn't wake up until he was standing over my bed. I shouldn't have left the windows open. I shouldn't have taken the pills . . .'

'What pills?' Moore asked gently.

'I was having trouble sleeping, because of . . .' Her voice faded.

'The rape?'

She looked away, avoiding his gaze. 'I was having nightmares. At the clinic, they gave me pills. To help me sleep.'

And a nightmare, a real nightmare, walked right into her bedroom.

'Did you see his face?' he asked.

'It was dark. I could hear him breathing, but I couldn't move. I couldn't scream.'

'You were already tied down?'

199

'I don't remember him doing it. I don't remember how it happened.'

Chloroform, thought Moore, to subdue her first. Before she was fully awake.

'What happened then, Nina?'

Her breathing accelerated. On the monitor above her bed, the heart tracing blipped faster.

'He sat in a chair by my bed. I could see his shadow.'

'And what did he do?'

'He – he talked to me.'

'What did he say?'

'He said . . .' She swallowed. 'He said that I was dirty. Contaminated. He said I should be disgusted by my own filth. And that he – he was going to cut out the part that was tainted and make me pure again.' She paused. And said, in a whisper: 'That's when I knew I was going to die.'

Though Catherine's face had turned white, the victim herself looked eerily composed, as though she were talking about another woman's nightmare, not her own. She was no longer looking at Moore but staring at some point beyond him, seeing from afar a woman tied to a bed. And in a chair, hidden in the darkness, a man quietly describing the horrors he planned next. For the Surgeon, thought Moore, this is foreplay. This is what excites him. The smell of a woman's fear. He feeds on it. He sits by her bed and fills her mind with images of death. Sweat blooms on her skin, sweat that exudes the sour scent of terror. An exotic perfume he craves. He breathes it in, and he is excited.

'What happened next?' said Moore.

No answer.

'Nina?'

'He turned the lamp on my face. He put it right in my eyes, so I couldn't see him. All I could see was that bright light. And he took my picture.'

'And then?'

She looked at him. 'Then he was gone.'

'He left you alone in the house?'

'Not alone. I could hear him, walking around. And the TV – all night, I heard the TV.'

The pattern has changed, thought Moore, and he and Frost exchanged stunned looks. The Surgeon was now more confident. More daring. Instead of completing his kill within a few hours, he had delayed. All night, and the next day, he had left his prey tied to her bed, to contemplate her coming ordeal. Heedless of the risks, he had drawn out her terror. Drawn out his pleasure.

The heartbeats on the monitor had sped up again. Though her voice sounded flat and lifeless, beneath the calm facade the fear remained.

'What happened then, Nina?' he asked.

'Sometime in the afternoon, I must have fallen asleep. When I woke up, it was dark again. I was so thirsty. It was all I could think about, how much I wanted water . . .'

'Did he leave you at any time? Were you ever alone in the house?'

'I don't know. All I could hear was the TV. When he turned it off, I knew. I knew he was coming back into my room.'

'And when he did, did he turn on the light?'

'Yes.'

'Did you see his face?'

'Just his eyes. He was wearing a mask. The kind that doctors wear.'

'But you did see his eyes.'

'Yes.'

'Did you recognize him? Had you ever seen this man before in your life?'

There was a long silence. Moore felt his own heart pounding as he waited for the answer he hoped for.

Then she said, softly: 'No.'

He sank back in his chair. The tension in the room had suddenly collapsed. To this victim, the Surgeon was a stranger, a man without a name, whose reasons for choosing her remained a mystery.

Masking the disappointment in his voice, he said: 'Describe him for us, Nina.'

She took a deep breath and closed her eyes, as though to conjure up the memory. 'He had . . . he had short hair. Cut very neatly . . .'

'What color?'

'Brown. A light shade of brown.'

Consistent with the strand of hair they'd found in Elena Ortiz's wound. 'So he was Caucasian?' said Moore.

'Yes.'

'Eyes?'

'A pale color. Blue or gray. I was afraid to look straight at them.'

'And the shape of his face? Round, oval?'

'Narrow.' She paused. 'Ordinary.'

'Height and weight?'

'It's hard to—'

'Your best guess.'

She sighed. 'Average.'

Average. Ordinary. A monster who looked like any other man.

Moore turned to Frost. 'Let's show her the six-packs.'

Frost handed him the first book of mug shots, called *six-packs* because there were six photographs per page. Moore set the book on a bedside tray table and wheeled it in front of the patient.

For the next half hour they watched with sinking hopes as she flipped through the books without pausing. No one spoke; there was only the hiss of the oxygen and the sound of the pages being turned. These photos were of known sex offenders, and as Nina turned page after page it seemed to Moore that there was no end to the faces, that this parade of images represented the dark side of every man, the reptilian impulse disguised by a human mask.

He heard a tap on the cubicle window. Looking up, he saw Jane Rizzoli gesturing to him.

He stepped out to speak to her.

'Any ID yet?' she asked.

'We're not going to get one. He was wearing a surgeon's mask.'

Rizzoli frowned. 'Why a mask?'

'It could be part of his ritual. Part of what turns him on. Playing doctor is his fantasy. He told her he was going to cut out the organ that had been defiled. He knew she was a rape victim. And what did he cut out? He went right for the womb.'

Rizzoli gazed into the cubicle. She said quietly: 'I can think of another reason why he wore that mask.'

'Why?'

'He didn't want her to see his face. He didn't want her to identify him.'

'But that would mean . . .'

'It's what I've been saying all along.' Rizzoli turned and looked at Moore. 'The Surgeon fully intended for Nina Peyton to survive.'

How little we truly see into the human heart, thought Catherine as she studied the X ray of Nina Peyton's chest. Standing in semidarkness, she gazed at the film clipped to the light box, studying the shadows cast by bones and organs. The rib cage, the trampoline of diaphragm, and resting atop it the heart. Not the seat of the soul, but merely a muscular pump, unendowed with any more mystical purpose than the lungs or the kidneys. Yet even Catherine, so grounded in science, could not look at Nina Peyton's heart without being moved by its symbolism.

It was the heart of a survivor.

She heard voices in the next room. It was Peter, requesting a patient's films from the file clerk. A moment later he walked into the reading room and paused when he saw her, standing by the light box.

'You're still here?' he said.

'So are you.'

'But I'm the one on call tonight. Why don't you go home?'

Catherine turned back to Nina's chest X ray. 'I want to be sure this patient is stable first.'

He came to stand right beside her, so tall, so imposing, that she had to fight the impulse to step away. He scanned the film.

'Other than some atelectasis, I don't see much there to worry about.' He focused on the name 'Jane Doe' in the corner of the film. 'Is this the woman in Bed Twelve? The one with all the cops hanging around?'

'Yes.'

'I see you extubated her.'

'A few hours ago,' she said reluctantly. She had no wish to talk about Nina Peyton, no wish to reveal her personal involvement in the case. But Peter kept asking questions.

'Her blood gases okay?'

'They're adequate.'

'And she's otherwise stable?'

'Yes.'

'Then why don't you go home? I'll cover for you.'

'I'd like to keep an eye on this patient myself.'

He placed his hand on her shoulder. 'Since when did you stop trusting your own partner?'

At once she froze at his touch. He felt it and withdrew his hand.

After a silence, Peter moved away and began hanging his X rays on the box, shoving them briskly into place. He'd brought in an abdominal CT series, and the films took up an entire row of clips. When he had finished hanging them, he stood very still, his eyes hidden by the X ray images reflected in his glasses.

'I'm not the enemy, Catherine,' he said softly, not looking at her but focusing instead on the light box. 'I wish I could make you believe that. I keep thinking there's got to be something I did, something I said, that's changed things between us.' At

205

last he looked at her. 'We used to rely on each other. As partners, at the very least. Hell, the other day, we practically held hands in that man's chest! And now you won't even let me cover for one patient. By now, don't you know me well enough to trust me?'

'There's no other surgeon I trust more than you.'

'Then what's going on here? I get to work in the morning, and find out we've had a break-in. And you won't talk to me about it. I ask you about your patient in Bed Twelve, and you won't talk to me about her, either.'

'The police have asked me not to.'

'The police seem to be running your life these days. Why?'

'I'm not at liberty to discuss it.'

'I'm not just your partner, Catherine. I thought I was your friend.' He took a step toward her. He was a physically imposing man, and his mere approach suddenly made her feel claustrophobic. 'I can see you're scared. You lock yourself in your office. You look like you haven't slept in days. I can't stand by and watch this.'

Catherine yanked Nina Peyton's X ray off the light box and slid it into the envelope. 'It has nothing to do with you.'

'Yes, it does, if it affects you.'

Her defensiveness instantly turned to anger. 'Let's get something straight here, Peter. Yes, we work together, and yes, I respect you as a surgeon. I like you as a partner. But we don't share our lives. And we certainly don't share our secrets.'

206

'Why don't we?' he said softly. 'What are you afraid of telling me?'

She stared at him, unnerved by the gentleness of his voice. In that instant, she wanted more than anything to unburden herself, to tell him what had happened to her in Savannah in all its shameful detail. But she knew the consequences of such a confession. She understood that to be raped was to be forever tainted, forever a victim. She could not tolerate pity. Not from Peter, the one man whose respect meant everything to her.

'Catherine?' He reached out.

Through tears she looked at his outstretched hand. And like a drowning woman who chooses the black sea instead of rescue, she did not take it.

Instead she turned and walked out of the room.

Twelve

Jane Doe has moved.

I hold a tube of her blood in my hand, and am disappointed that it is cool to the touch. It has been sitting in the phlebotomist's rack too long, and the body heat this tube once contained has radiated through the glass and dissipated into the air. Cold blood is a dead thing, without power or soul, and it does not move me. It is the label I focus on, a white rectangle affixed to the glass tube, printed with the patient's name, room number, and hospital number. Though the name says 'Jane Doe,' I know who this blood really belongs to. She is no longer in the Surgical Intensive Care Unit. She has been moved to Room 538 – the surgery ward.

I put the tube back in the rack, where it sits with two dozen other tubes, capped with rubber stoppers of blue and purple and red and green, each color signifying a different procedure to be done. The purple tops are for blood counts, the blue tops for clotting tests, the red tops for chemistries and electrolytes. In some of the red-top tubes, the blood has already congealed into columns of dark gelatin. I look through the bundle of lab orders and find the slip for Jane Doe. This morning, Dr Cordell ordered two tests: a complete blood count and serum electrolytes. I dig deeper into last night's lab orders, and find the carbon copy of another requisition with Dr Cordell's name as ordering physician.

'STAT arterial blood gas, post-extubation. 2 liters oxygen by nasal prongs.'

Nina Peyton has been extubated. She is breathing on her own, taking in air without mechanical assistance, without a tube in her throat.

I sit motionless at my workstation, thinking not of Nina Peyton, but of Catherine Cordell. She thinks she has won this round. She thinks she is Nina Peyton's savior. It is time to teach her her place. It is time she learned humility.

I pick up the phone and call Hospital Dietary. A woman answers, her speech pressured, the sound of trays clanging in the background. It is near the dinner hour, and she has no time to waste in chitchat.

'This is Five West,' I lie. 'I think we may have mixed up the dietary orders on two of our patients. Can you tell me which diet you have listed for Room Five-thirty-eight?'

There is a pause as she taps on her keyboard and calls up the information.

'Clear liquids,' she answers. 'Is that correct?'

'Yes, that's correct. Thank you.' I hang up.

In the newspaper this morning, Nina Peyton was said to remain comatose and in critical condition. This is not true. She is awake.

Catherine Cordell has saved her life, as I knew

*she would. A phlebotomist crosses to my station
and sets her tray full of blood tubes on the
counter. We smile at each other, as we do every
day, two friendly coworkers who by default
assume the best about each other. She is young,
with firm high breasts that bulge like melons
against her white uniform, and she has fine,
straight teeth. She picks up a new sheaf of lab
requisitions, waves, and walks out. I wonder if her
blood tastes salty.*

*The machines hum and gurgle a continuous
lullaby.*

*I go to the computer and call up the patient list
for Five West. There are twenty rooms in that ward,
which is arranged in the shape of an H, with the
nursing station located in the crossbar of the H. I
go down the list of patients, thirty-three in all,
scanning their ages and diagnoses. I stop at the
twelfth name, in Room 521.*

*'Mr Herman Gwadowski, age 69. Attending
physician: Dr Catherine Cordell. Diagnosis: S/P
emergency laparotomy for multiple abdominal
trauma.'*

*Room 521 is located in a parallel hallway to
Nina Peyton's. From 521, Nina's room is not
visible.*

*I click on Mr Gwadowski's name and access his
lab flowsheet. He has been in the hospital two
weeks and his flowsheet goes on for screen after
screen. I can picture his arms, the veins a highway
of needle punctures and bruises. From his blood
sugar levels, I see he is diabetic. His high white
blood cell counts indicate he has an infection of
some sort. I notice, too, that there are cultures*

210

pending from a wound swab of his foot. The diabetes has affected the circulation in his limbs, and the flesh of his legs is starting to necrose. I also see a culture pending on a swab from his central venous line site.

I focus on his electrolytes. His potassium levels have been steadily climbing. 4.5 two weeks ago. 4.8 last week. 5.1 yesterday. He is old and his diabetic kidneys are struggling to excrete the everyday toxins that accumulate in the bloodstream. Toxins such as potassium.

It will not take much to tip him over the edge.

I have never met Mr Herman Gwadowski – at least, not face-to-face. I go to the rack of blood tubes which have been sitting on the counter and look at the labels. The rack is from Five East and West, and there are twenty-four tubes in the various slots. I find a red-top tube from Room 521. It is Mr Gwadowski's blood.

I pick up the tube and study it as I slowly turn it under the light. It has not clotted, and the fluid within looks dark and brackish, as though the needle that punctured Mr Gwadowski's vein has instead hit a stagnant well. I uncap the tube and sniff its contents. I smell the urea of old age, the gamey sweetness of infection. I smell a body that has already begun to decay, even as the brain continues to deny the shell is dying around it.

In this way, I make Mr Gwadowski's acquaintance. It will not be a long friendship.

Angela Robbins was a conscientious nurse, and she was irritated that Herman Gwadowski's ten o'clock dose of antibiotics had not yet arrived. She went to the Five West ward clerk and said, 'I'm still waiting for Gwadowski's IV meds. Can you call Pharmacy again?'

'Did you check the Pharmacy cart? It came up at nine.'

'There was nothing on it for Gwadowski. He needs his IV dose of Zosyn right now.'

'Oh. I just remembered.' The clerk rose and crossed to an in box on the other countertop. 'An aide from Four West brought it up a little while ago.'

'Four West?'

'The bag was sent to the wrong floor.' The clerk checked the label. 'Gwadowski, Five-twenty-one-A.'

'Right,' said Angela, taking the small IV bag. On the way back to the room, she read the label, confirming the patient's name, the ordering physician, and the dose of Zosyn that had been added to the bag of saline. It all appeared correct. Eighteen years ago, when Angela had started work as a newly minted nurse, an R.N. could simply walk into the ward's supply room, pick up a bag of IV fluid, and add to it the necessary medications. A few mistakes made by harried nurses, a few highly publicized lawsuits, had changed all that. Now even a simple IV bag of saline with added potassium had to come through the hospital pharmacy. It was another layer of administration, another cog in what was already the complicated machinery of health care, and Angela resented it. It had caused an hour's delay in this IV bag's arrival.

She switched Mr Gwadowski's IV tubing to the

new bag and hung the bag on the pole. Through it all, Mr Gwadowski lay unmoving. He'd been comatose for two weeks, and already he exuded the smell of death. Angela had been a nurse long enough to recognize that scent, like sour sweat, that was the prelude to the final passing. Whenever she detected it, she would murmur to the other nurses: 'This one's not going to make it.' That's what she thought now, as she turned up the IV flow rate and checked the patient's vital signs. *This one is not going to make it.* Still, she went about her tasks with the same care she gave to every patient.

It was time for the sponge bath. She brought a basin of warm water to the bedside, soaked a washcloth, and started by wiping Mr Gwadowski's face. He lay with mouth gaping open, the tongue dry and furrowed. If only they could let him go. If only they could release him from this hell. But the son would not even allow a change in the code status, and so the old man lived on, if you could call this living, his heart continuing to beat in its decaying shell of a body.

She peeled off the patient's hospital gown and checked the central venous line skin site. The wound looked slightly red, which worried her. They had run out of IV sites on the arms. This was their only IV access now, and Angela was conscientious about keeping the wound clean and the bandage fresh. After the bed bath, she would change the dressing.

She wiped down the torso, running her washcloth across the ridges of rib. She could tell he had never been a muscular man, and what was left

213

now of his chest was merely parchment stretched across bone.

She heard footsteps and was not happy to see Mr Gwadowski's son come into the room. With a single glance, he put her on the defensive – that's the sort of man he was, always pointing out mistakes and flaws in others. He frequently did it to his sister. Once Angela heard them arguing and had to stop herself from coming to the sister's defense. After all, it was not Angela's place to tell this son what she thought of his bullying. But she need not be overly friendly to him, either. So she merely nodded and continued with the sponge bath.

'How's he doing?' asked Ivan Gwadowski.

'There's been no change.' Her voice was cool and businesslike. She wished he would leave, would finish his little ceremony of pretending to care, and let her get on with her work. She was perceptive enough to understand that love was but a minor part of why this son was here. He had taken charge because that's what he was accustomed to doing, and he wouldn't relinquish control to anyone. Not even Death.

'Has the doctor been in to see him?'

'Dr Cordell comes in every morning.'

'What does she say about the fact he's still in a coma?'

Angela put the washcloth in the basin and straightened to look at him. 'I'm not sure what there is to say, Mr Gwadowski.'

'How long will he be like this?'

'As long as you allow him to be.'

'What does that mean?'

214

'It would be kinder, don't you think, to let him go?'

Ivan Gwadowski stared at her. 'Yes, it makes everyone's life easier, doesn't it? And it frees up another hospital bed.'

'That's not why I said it.'

'I know how hospitals get paid these days. The patient stays too long, and you eat the costs.'

'I'm only talking about what's best for your father.'

'What's best is that this hospital does its job.'

Before she could say anything she regretted, Angela turned and grabbed the washcloth from the basin. Wrung it out with shaking hands. Don't argue with him. Just do your job. *He's the kind of man who'll take it all the way to the top.*

She placed the damp cloth on the patient's abdomen. Only then did she realize that the old man was not breathing.

At once Angela felt the neck for a pulse.

'What is it?' asked the son. 'Is he okay?'

She didn't answer. Pushing right past him, she ran into the hall. 'Code Blue!' she yelled. 'Call a Code Blue, Room Five-twenty-one!'

Catherine sprinted out of Nina Peyton's room and rounded the corner into the next hallway. Personnel had already crowded into Room 521 and spilled out into the corridor, where a group of wide-eyed medical students stood craning their necks to see the action.

Catherine pushed into the room and called out, over the chaos: 'What happened?'

215

Angela, Mr Gwadowski's nurse, said: 'He just stopped breathing! There's no pulse.'

Catherine worked her way to the bedside and saw that another nurse had already clapped a mask over the patient's face and was bagging oxygen into the lungs. An intern had his hands on the chest, and with each bounce against the sternum he squeezed blood from the heart, forcing it through arteries and veins. Feeding the organs, feeding the brain.

'EKG leads are on!' someone called out.

Catherine's gaze flew to the monitor. The tracing showed ventricular fibrillation. The chambers of the heart were no longer contracting. Instead, the individual muscles were quivering, and the heart had turned into a flaccid bag.

'Paddles charged?' said Catherine.

'One hundred joules.'

'Do it!'

The nurse placed defibrillator paddles on the chest and yelled, 'Everyone back!'

The paddles discharged, sending an electrical jolt through the heart. The man's torso jerked off the mattress like a cat on a hot griddle.

'Still in V. fib!'

'One milligram epinephrine IV, then shock him again at a hundred,' said Catherine.

The bolus of epinephrine slid through the CVP line.

'Back!'

Another shock from the paddles, another jerk of the torso.

On the monitor, the EKG tracing shot straight up, then collapsed into a trembling line. The last twitches of a fading heart.

Catherine looked down at her patient and thought: How do I revive this withered pile of bones?

'You want – to keep – going?' asked the intern, panting as he pumped. A drop of sweat slid in a glistening line down his cheek.

I didn't want to code him at all, she thought, and was about to end it when Angela whispered into her ear:

'The son's here. He's watching.'

Catherine's gaze shot to Ivan Gwadowski, standing in the doorway. Now she had no choice. Anything less than a full-out effort, and the son would make sure there was hell to pay.

On the monitor, the line traced the surface of a storm-tossed sea.

'Let's do it again,' said Catherine. 'Two hundred joules this time. Get some blood sent for STAT lytes!'

She heard the code cart drawer rattle open. Blood tubes and a syringe appeared.

'I can't find a vein!'

'Use the CVP.'

'Stand back!'

Everyone stepped away as the paddles discharged.

Catherine watched the monitor, hoping that the jolt of shock-induced paralysis would jump-start the heart. Instead, the tracing collapsed to barely a ripple.

Another bolus of epinephrine slithered into the CVP line.

The intern, flushed and sweating, resumed pumping on the chest. A fresh pair of hands took

217

over the ambu-bag, squeezing air into the lungs, but it was like trying to blow life into a dried-out husk. Already Catherine could hear the change in the voices around her, the tone of urgency gone, the words flat and automatic. It was merely an exercise now, with defeat inevitable. She looked around the room, at the dozen or more people crowded around the bed, and saw that the decision was obvious to them all. They were just waiting for her word.

She gave it. 'Let's call the code,' she said. 'Eleven thirteen.'

In silence, everyone stepped back and regarded the object of their defeat, Herman Gwadowski, who lay cooling in a tangle of wires and IV tubing. A nurse turned off the EKG monitor, and the oscilloscope went blank.

'What about a pacemaker?'

Catherine, in the midst of signing the code sheet, turned and saw that the patient's son had stepped into the room. 'There's nothing left to save,' she said. 'I'm sorry. We couldn't get his heart beating again.'

'Don't they use pacemakers for that?'

'We did everything we could—'

'All you did was shock him.'

All? She looked around the room, at the evidence of their efforts, the used syringes and drug vials and crumpled packaging. The medical debris left behind after every battle. The others in the room were all watching, waiting to see how she would handle this.

She set down the clipboard she'd been writing on, angry words already forming on her lips. She never got the chance to say them. Instead she spun toward the door.

Somewhere on the ward, a woman was shrieking.

In an instant Catherine was out of the room, the nurses right behind her. Sprinting around the corner, she spotted an aide standing in the hallway, sobbing and pointing toward Nina's room. The chair outside the room was vacant.

There should be a policeman here. Where is he?

Catherine pushed open the door and froze.

Blood was the first thing she saw, bright ribbons of it streaming down the wall. Then she looked at her patient, sprawled facedown on the floor. Nina had fallen halfway between the bed and the door, as though she had managed to stagger a few steps before collapsing. Her IV was disconnected and a stream of saline dribbled from the open tube onto the floor, where it formed a clear pool next to the larger pool of red.

He was here. The Surgeon was here.

Though every instinct screamed at her to back away, to flee, she forced herself to step forward, to drop to her knees beside Nina. Blood soaked through her scrub pants, and it was still warm. She rolled the body onto its back.

One look at the white face, the staring eyes, and she knew Nina was already gone. *Only moments ago I heard your heart beating.*

Slowly emerging from her daze, Catherine looked up and saw a circle of frightened faces. 'The policeman,' she said. 'Where is the policeman?'

'We don't know—'

She rose unsteadily to her feet, and the others backed away to let her pass. Heedless of the fact she was tracking blood, she walked out of the room, her gaze darting wildly up and down the hallway.

'Oh my god,' a nurse said.

At the far end of the corridor, a dark line was creeping across the floor. Blood. It was trickling out from beneath the supply room door.

Thirteen

Rizzoli stared across the crime scene tape, into Nina Peyton's hospital room. Spurted arterial blood had dried in a celebratory pattern of tossed streamers. She continued down the corridor to the supply room, where the cop's body had been found. This doorway, too, was crisscrossed by crime scene tape. Inside was a thicket of IV poles, shelves holding bedpans and basins, and boxes of gloves, all of it zigzagged by blood. One of their own had died in this room, and for every cop in the Boston PD the hunt for the Surgeon was now deeply, intensely personal.

She turned to the patrolman standing nearby. 'Where's Detective Moore?'

'Down in Administration. They're looking at the hospital surveillance tapes.'

Rizzoli glanced up and down the hall but spotted no security cameras. They would have no video footage of this corridor.

Downstairs she slipped into the conference room where Moore and two nurses were reviewing the surveillance tapes. No one glanced her way; they were all focused on the TV monitor, where the tape was playing.

The camera was aimed at the Five West elevators. On the video, the elevator door opened. Moore froze the image.

'There,' he said. 'This is the first group to come off the elevator after the code was called. I count eleven passengers, and they all get off in a rush.'

'That's what you'd expect in a Code Blue,' said the charge nurse. 'An announcement goes over the hospital speaker system. Anyone who's available is expected to respond.'

'Take a good look at these faces,' said Moore. 'Do you recognize everyone? Is there anyone who shouldn't be there?'

'I can't see all the faces. They step off in one group.'

'How about you, Sharon?' Moore asked the second nurse.

Sharon leaned toward the monitor. 'These three here, they're nurses. And the two young men, at the side, they're medical students. I recognize that third man there—' She pointed to the top of the screen. 'An orderly. The others look familiar, but I don't know their names.'

'Okay,' said Moore, weariness in his voice. 'Let's watch the rest. Then we'll look at the stairwell camera.'

Rizzoli moved closer until she stood right behind the charge nurse.

On the screen, the images backed up, and the elevator door slid shut. Moore pressed Play and the door opened again. Eleven people stepped out, moving like a multilegged organism in their hurry to reach the code. Rizzoli saw urgency in their faces, and even without sound the sense of crisis was obvious. That knot of people vanished to the left of the screen. The elevator door closed. A moment passed, and the door re-opened, discharging another gush of personnel. Rizzoli counted thirteen passengers. So far a total of twenty-four people had arrived on the floor in under three minutes – and that was just by elevator. How many more had arrived by the stairwell? Rizzoli watched with growing amazement. The timing had been flawless. Calling a Code Blue was like setting off a stampede. With dozens of personnel from all over the hospital converging on Five West, anyone wearing a white coat could slip in unnoticed. The unsub would no doubt stand in the back of the elevator, behind everyone else. He would be careful to keep another person between him and the camera. They were up against someone who knew exactly how a hospital functioned.

She watched the second group of elevator passengers move off the screen. Two of the faces had remained hidden throughout.

Now Moore switched tapes, and the view changed. They were looking at the stairwell door. For a moment nothing happened. Then the door swung open, and a man in a white coat came barreling through.

'I know him. That's Mark Noble, one of the interns,' said Sharon.

Rizzoli took out her spiral notebook and jotted down the name.

The door flew open again, and two women emerged, both in white uniforms.

'That's Veronica Tam,' said the charge nurse,

223

pointing to the shorter of the pair. 'She works on Five West. She was on break when the code was called.'

'And the other woman?'

'I don't know. You can't see her face very well.'

Rizzoli wrote down:

10:48, stairwell camera:
Veronica Tam, nurse, Five West.
Unknown female, black hair, lab coat.

A total of seven people came through the stairwell door. The nurses recognized five of them. So far Rizzoli had counted thirty-one people who'd arrived by either elevator or stairwell. Add to that the personnel already at work on the floor, and they were dealing with at least forty people with access to Five West.

'Now watch what happens as people leave during and after the code,' said Moore. 'This time they're not rushing. Maybe you can pick up a few more faces and names.' He fast-forwarded. At the bottom of the screen, the time display advanced eight minutes. The code was still in progress, but already unneeded personnel were beginning to drift away from the ward. The camera caught only their backs as they walked to the stairwell door. First, two male medical students, followed a moment later by a third unidentified man, departing alone. Then there was a long pause, which Moore fast-forwarded through. Next a group of four men exited together into the stairwell. The time was 11:14. By then the code had officially ended, and Herman Gwadowski had been declared dead.

Moore switched tapes. Once again, they were watching the elevator.

By the time they'd run through the tapes again, Rizzoli had jotted down three pages of notes, tallying the number of arrivals during the code. Thirteen men and seventeen women had responded to the emergency. Now Rizzoli counted how many were seen leaving after the code ended.

The numbers did not add up.

At last Moore pressed Stop, and the screen went blank. They had been staring at the video for over an hour, and the two nurses looked shell-shocked.

Cutting through the silence, Rizzoli's voice seemed to startle them both. 'Do you have any male employees working on Five West during your shift?' she asked.

The charge nurse focused on Rizzoli. She seemed surprised that another cop had somehow slipped into the room without her realizing it. 'There's a male nurse who comes on at three. But I have no men during day shift.'

'And no men were working on Five West at the time the code was called?'

'There might have been surgical residents on the floor. But no male nurses.'

'Which residents? Do you remember?'

'They're always in and out, making rounds. I don't keep track of them. We have our own work to do.' The nurse looked at Moore. 'We really need to get back to the floor.'

Moore nodded. 'You can go. Thank you.'

Rizzoli waited until the two nurses had left the room. Then she said to Moore, 'The Surgeon was already on the ward. Before the code was even called. Wasn't he?'

Moore rose to his feet and went to the VCR. She could see anger in his body language, the way he jerked the tape out of the machine, the way he shoved in the second tape.

'Thirteen men arrived on Five West. And fourteen men left. There's an extra man. He had to be there the whole time.'

Moore pressed Play. The stairwell tape began rolling again.

'Damn it, Moore. Crowe was in charge of arranging protection. And now we've lost our only witness.'

Still he said nothing but stared at the screen, watching the by-now familiar figures appear and disappear through the stairwell door.

'This unsub walks through walls,' she said. 'He hides in thin air. They had nine nurses working on that floor, and none of them realized he was there. He was with them *the whole goddamn time*.'

'That's one possibility.'

'So how did he get to that cop? Why would any cop let himself be talked into leaving the patient's door? Stepping into a supply room?'

'It would have to be someone he was familiar with. Or someone who posed no threat.'

And in the excitement of a code, with everyone scrambling to save a life, it would be natural for a hospital employee to turn to the one guy who's just standing there in the hallway – the cop. Natural to ask that cop to help you with something in the supply room.

Moore pressed Pause. 'There,' he said softly. 'I think that's our man.'

Rizzoli stared at the screen. It was the lone man who'd walked out the stairwell door early in the code. They could see only his back. He wore a white coat and an O.R. cap. A narrow swath of trimmed brown hair was visible beneath the cap. He had a slender build, his shoulders not at all impressive, his whole posture stooped forward like a walking question mark.

'This is the only place we see him,' said Moore. 'I couldn't spot him in the elevator footage. And I don't see him coming up through this stairwell door. But he leaves this way. See how he pushes the door open with his hip, never touching it with his hands? I'm betting he left no prints anywhere. He's too careful. And see how he hunches over, as though he knows he's on camera. He knows we're looking for him.'

'We got any ID?'

'None of the nurses can name him.'

'Shit, he was on their floor.'

'So were a lot of other people. Everyone was focused on saving Herman Gwadowski. Everyone except *him*.'

Rizzoli approached the video screen, her gaze frozen on that lone figure framed in the white hallway. Though she could not see his face, she felt as chilled as though she were looking into the eyes of evil. *Are you the Surgeon?*

'No one remembers seeing him,' said Moore. 'No one remembers riding up with him in the elevator. Yet there he is. A ghost, who appears and vanishes at will.'

'He left eight minutes after the code started,' said Rizzoli, looking at the time on the screen. 'There were two medical students who walked out right before him.'

'Yes, I spoke to them. They had to get to a lecture at eleven. That's why they left the code early. They didn't notice our man follow them into the stairwell.'

'So we have no witnesses at all.'

'Just this camera.'

She was still focused on the time. Eight minutes into the code. Eight minutes was a long time. She tried to choreograph it in her head. Walk up to the cop: ten seconds. Talk him into following you a few feet up the hallway, into the supply room: thirty seconds. Cut his throat: ten seconds. Walk out, shut the door, enter Nina Peyton's room: fifteen seconds. Dispatch the second victim, walk out: thirty seconds. That added up to two minutes, tops. That still left six minutes. What did he use that extra time for? To clean up? There was a lot of blood; he may well have been splattered with it.

He'd had plenty of time to work with. The nurse's aide did not discover Nina's body until ten minutes after the man on that video screen walked out the stairwell door. By then, he could have been a mile away, in his car.

Such perfect timing. This unsub moves with the accuracy of a Swiss watch.

Abruptly she sat up straight, the realization zinging through her like a bolt of electricity. 'He knew. Jesus, Moore, he *knew* there'd be a Code Blue.' She looked at him and saw, by his calm reaction, that he had already reached that conclusion. 'Did Mr Gwadowski have any visitors?'

'The son. But the nurse was in the room the whole time. And she was there when the patient coded.'

'What happened just prior to the code?'

'She changed the IV bag. We've sent the bag for analysis.'

Rizzoli looked back at the video screen, where the image of the man in a white coat remained frozen in mid-stride. 'This makes no sense. Why would he take such a risk?'

'This was a mop-up job, to get rid of a loose end – the witness.'

'But what did Nina Peyton actually witness? She saw a masked face. He knew she couldn't identify him. He knew she posed almost no danger. Yet he went to a lot of trouble to kill her. He exposed himself to capture. What does he gain by it?'

'Satisfaction. He finally finished his kill.'

'But he could have finished it at her house. Moore, he *let* Nina Peyton live that night. Which means he planned to end it this way.'

'In the hospital?'

'Yes.'

'To what purpose?'

'I don't know. But I find it interesting that of all the patients on that ward, it was Herman Gwadowski he chose as his diversion. A patient of Catherine Cordell's.'

Moore's beeper went off. As he took the call Rizzoli turned her attention back to the monitor. She pressed Play and watched the man in the white coat approach the door. He tilted his hip to hit the door's opening bar and stepped into the stairwell. Not once did he allow any part of his face to be visible on camera. She hit Rewind, viewed the sequence again. This time, as his hip rotated slightly, she saw it: the bulge under his white coat. It was on his right side, at the level of his waist. What was he concealing there? A change of clothes? His murder kit?

She heard Moore say into the phone: 'Don't touch it! Leave it right where it is. I'm on my way.'

As he disconnected, Rizzoli asked: 'Who's that?'

'It's Catherine,' said Moore. 'Our boy's just sent her another message.'

'It came up in interdepartmental mail,' said Catherine. 'As soon as I saw the envelope, I knew it was from him.'

Rizzoli watched as Moore pulled on a pair of gloves – a useless precaution, she thought, since the Surgeon had never left his prints on any evidence. It was a large brown envelope with a string-and-button closure. On the top blank line was printed in blue ink: 'To Catherine Cordell. Birthday greetings from A.C.'

Andrew Capra, thought Rizzoli.

'You didn't open it?' asked Moore.

'No. I put it right down, on my desk. And I called you.'

'Good girl.'

Rizzoli thought his response was condescending, but Catherine clearly didn't take it that way, and she flashed him a tense smile. Something passed between Moore and Catherine. A look, a warm current, that Rizzoli registered with a twinge of painful jealousy. *It's gone further than I realized between these two.*

'It feels empty,' he said. With gloved hands, he unwound the string clasp. Rizzoli slid a sheet of plain white paper on the countertop to catch the contents. He lifted the flap and turned the envelope upside down.

Silky red-brown strands slid out and lay in a gleaming clump on the sheet of paper.

A chill shot up Rizzoli's spine. 'It looks like human hair.'

'Oh god. Oh *god* . . .'

Rizzoli turned and saw Catherine backing away in horror. Rizzoli stared at Catherine's hair, then looked back at the strands that had fallen from the envelope. *It's hers. The hair is Cordell's.*

'Catherine.' Moore spoke softly, soothingly. 'It may not be yours at all.'

She looked at him in panic. 'What if it is? How did he—'

'Do you keep a hairbrush in your O.R. locker? Your office?'

'Moore,' said Rizzoli. 'Check out these strands. They weren't pulled off a hairbrush. The root ends have been cut.' She turned to Catherine. 'Who last cut your hair, Dr Cordell?'

Slowly Catherine approached the countertop and regarded the clipped strands as though staring at a poisonous viper. 'I know when he did it,' she said softly. 'I remember.'

'When?'

'It was that night . . .' She looked at Rizzoli with a stunned expression. 'In Savannah.'

* * *

231

Rizzoli hung up the phone and looked at Moore. 'Detective Singer confirms it. A clump of her hair was cut.'

'Why didn't that appear in Singer's report?'

'Cordell didn't notice it until the second day of her hospitalization, when she looked in a mirror. Since Capra was dead, and no hair was found at the crime scene, Singer assumed the hair was cut by hospital personnel. Maybe during emergency treatment. Cordell's face was pretty bruised up, remember? The E.R. may have snipped away some hair to clean her scalp.'

'Did Singer ever confirm it was someone in the hospital who cut it?'

Rizzoli tossed down her pencil and sighed. 'No. He never followed up.'

'He just left it at that? Never mentioned it in his report because it didn't make sense.'

'Well, it *doesn't* make sense! Why weren't the clippings found at the scene, along with Capra's body?'

'Catherine doesn't remember a large part of that night. The Rohypnol wiped out a significant chunk of her memory. Capra may have left the house. Returned later.'

'Okay. Here's the biggest question of all. Capra's dead. How did this souvenir end up in the Surgeon's hands?'

For this, Moore had no answer. Two killers, one alive, one dead. What bound these two monsters to each other? The link between them was more than merely psychic energy; it had now taken on a physical dimension. Something they could actually see and touch.

232

He looked down at the two evidence bags. One was labeled: *Unknown hair clippings*. The second bag contained a sample of Catherine's hair for comparison. He himself had snipped the coppery strands and had placed them into the Ziploc bag. Such hair would indeed make a tempting souvenir. Hair was so very personal. A woman wears it, sleeps with it. It carries fragrance and color and texture. A woman's very essence. No wonder Catherine had been horrified to learn that a man she did not know possessed such an intimate part of her. To know that he had stroked it, sniffed it, acquainting himself like a lover with her scent.

By now, the Surgeon knows her scent well.

It was nearly midnight, but her lights were on. Through the closed curtains, he saw her silhouette glide past, and he knew she was awake.

Moore walked over to the parked cruiser and bent to talk to the two patrolmen inside. 'Anything to report?'

'She hasn't stepped outta the building since she got home. Doing a lot of pacing. Looks like she's in for a restless night.'

'I'm going in to talk to her,' said Moore, and turned to cross the street.

'Staying all night?'

Moore halted. Turned stiffly to look at the cop. 'Excuse me?'

'Are you staying all night? 'Cause if you are, we'll pass it along to the next team. Just to let 'em know it's one of ours upstairs with her.'

Moore swallowed back his anger. The patrolman's question had been a reasonable one,

233

so why had he been so quick to take offense?

Because I know how it must look, to be walking in her door at midnight. I know what must be going through their heads. It's the same thing that's going through my head.

The instant he stepped into her apartment, he saw the question in her eyes, and he answered with a grim nod. 'I'm afraid the lab confirmed it. It was your hair he sent.'

She accepted the news in stunned silence.

In the kitchen, a kettle whistled. She turned and walked out of the room.

As he locked the door, his gaze lingered on the shiny new dead bolt. How insubstantial even tempered steel seemed, against an opponent who could walk through walls. He followed her into the kitchen and watched her turn off the heat to the squealing kettle. She fumbled with a box of tea bags, gave a startled gasp as they spilled out and scattered across the countertop. Such a minor mishap, yet it seemed to be the crushing blow. All at once she sagged against the counter, hands clenched, white knuckles against white tiles. She was fighting not to cry, not to fall apart before his eyes, and she was losing the battle. He saw her draw in a deep breath. Saw her shoulders knot up, her whole body straining to stifle the sob.

He could stand to watch this no longer. He went to her, pulled her against him. Held her as she shook in his embrace. All day he had thought about holding her, had longed for it. He had not wanted it to be like this, with her driven by fear into his arms. He wanted to be more than a safe haven, a reliable man to turn to.

234

But that was exactly what she needed now. So he wrapped himself around her, shielding her from the terrors of the night.

'Why is this happening again?' she whispered.

'I don't know, Catherine.'

'It's Capra—'

'No. He's dead.' He cupped her wet face, made her look at him. 'Andrew Capra is dead.'

Staring back at him, she went very still in his arms. 'Then why has the Surgeon chosen *me*?'

'If anyone knows the answer, it's you.'

'I *don't* know.'

'Maybe not on a conscious level. But you yourself told me you don't remember everything that happened in Savannah. You don't remember firing the second shot. You don't remember who cut your hair, or when. What *else* don't you remember?'

She shook her head. Then blinked, startled, at the sound of his beeper.

Why can't they leave me alone? He crossed to the phone on the kitchen wall to answer the page.

Rizzoli's voice greeted him with what sounded like an accusation. 'You're at her place.'

'Good guess.'

'No, caller ID. It's midnight. Have you thought about what you're doing?'

He said, irritably, 'Why did you page me?'

'Is she listening?'

He watched Catherine walk out of the kitchen. Without her, the room suddenly seemed empty. Bled of any interest. 'No,' he said.

'I've been thinking about the hair clipping. You know, there's one more explanation for how she got it.'

'And that would be?'

'She sent it to herself.'

'I can't believe I'm hearing this.'

'And I can't believe it never even crossed your mind.'

'What would be the motive?'

'The same motive that makes men walk in off the street and confess to murders they never committed. Look at all the attention she's getting! Your attention. It's midnight, and you're right there, fussing over her. I'm not saying the Surgeon *hasn't* been stalking her. But this hair thing makes me step back and say *whoa*. It's time to look at what else might be going on. How did the Surgeon get that hair? Did Capra *give* it to him two years ago? How could he do that when he's lying dead on her bedroom floor? You saw the inconsistencies between her statement and Capra's autopsy report. We both know she didn't tell the whole truth.'

'That statement was coaxed out of her by Detective Singer.'

'You think he fed her the story?'

'Think of the pressure Singer was under. Four murders. Everyone screaming for an arrest. And he had a nice, neat solution: the perp is dead, shot by his intended victim. Catherine closed the case for him, even if he had to put the words in her mouth.' Moore paused. 'We need to know what really happened that night in Savannah.'

'She's the only one who was there. And she claims she doesn't remember it all.'

Moore looked up as Catherine came back into the room. 'Not yet.'

236

Fourteen

'You're certain Dr Cordell's willing to do this?' asked Alex Polochek.

'She's here and waiting for you,' said Moore.

'You didn't talk her into this? Because hypnosis won't work if the subject is resistant. She has to be fully cooperative, or it'll be a waste of time.'

A waste of time was what Rizzoli had already called this session, and her opinion was shared by more than a few of the other detectives in the unit. They considered hypnosis a lounge act, the purview of Vegas entertainers and parlor magicians. At one time, Moore had agreed with them.

The Meghan Florence case had changed his mind.

On October 31, 1998, ten-year-old Meghan had been walking home from school when a car pulled up beside her. She was never again seen alive.

The only witness to the abduction was a twelve-year-old boy standing nearby. Although the car was in plain view and he could recount its shape and color, he could not remember the license plate. Weeks later, with no new developments in the case, the girl's parents had insisted on hiring a hypnotherapist to interview the boy. With every avenue of investigation exhausted, the police reluctantly agreed.

Moore was present during the session. He watched Alex Polochek gently ease the boy into a hypnotic state and listened in amazement as the boy quietly recited the license number.

Meghan Florence's body was recovered two days later, buried in the abductor's backyard.

Moore hoped that the magic Polochek had worked on that boy's memory could now be repeated on Catherine Cordell's.

The two men now stood outside the interview room, looking through the one-way mirror at Catherine and Rizzoli, seated on the other side of the window. Catherine appeared uneasy. She shifted in her chair and glanced at the window, as though aware she was being watched. A cup of tea sat untouched on the small table beside her.

'This is going to be a painful memory to retrieve,' said Moore. 'She may *want* to cooperate, but it won't be pleasant for her. At the time of the attack, she was still under the influence of Rohypnol.'

'A drugged memory from two years ago? Plus you said it's not pure.'

'A detective in Savannah may have planted a few suggestions through questioning.'

'You know I can't work miracles. And nothing we get from this session is going to be admissible as evidence. This will invalidate any future testimony she gives in court.'

'I know.'

'And you still want to proceed?'

'Yes.'

Moore opened the door and the two men stepped into the interview room. 'Catherine,' said Moore, 'this is the man I told you about, Alex Polochek. He's a forensic hypnotist for the Boston PD.'

As she and Polochek shook hands, she gave a nervous laugh.

'I'm sorry,' she said. 'I guess I wasn't sure what to expect.'

'You thought I'd have a black cape and a magician's wand,' said Polochek.

'It's a ridiculous image, but yes.'

'And instead you get a chubby little bald guy.'

Again she laughed, her posture relaxing a bit.

'You've never been hypnotized?' he asked.

'No. Frankly, I don't think I can be.'

'Why do you think that?'

'Because I don't really believe in it.'

'Yet you've agreed to let me try.'

'Detective Moore thought I should.'

Polochek sat down in a chair facing her. 'Dr Cordell, you don't have to believe in hypnosis for this session to be useful. But you have to *want* it to work. You have to trust me. And you have to be willing to relax and let go. To let me guide you into an altered state. It's a lot like the phase you go through just before you fall asleep at night. You won't *be* asleep. I promise, you'll be aware of what's happening around you. But you'll be so relaxed you'll be able to reach into parts of your memory you don't normally have access to. It's like unlocking a filing cabinet that's there, in your

239

brain, and finally being able to open the drawers and take out the files.'

'That's the part I don't believe. That hypnosis can make me remember.'

'Not make you remember. Allow you to.'

'All right, *allow* me to remember. It strikes me as unlikely that this can help me pull out a memory I can't reach on my own.'

Polochek nodded. 'Yes, you're right to be skeptical. It doesn't seem likely, does it? But here's an example of how memories can be blocked. It's called the Law of Reversed Effect. The harder you try to remember something, the less likely it is you'll be able to recall it. I'm sure you've experienced it yourself. We all have. For instance, you see a famous actress on the TV screen, and you *know* her name. But you just can't retrieve it. It drives you crazy. You spend an hour wracking your brain for her name. You wonder if you've got early Alzheimer's. Tell me it's happened to you.'

'All the time.' Catherine was smiling now. It was clear she liked Polochek and was comfortable with him. A good beginning.

'Eventually, you do remember the actress's name, don't you?' he said.

'Yes.'

'And when is that likely to happen?'

'When I stop trying so hard. When I relax and think about something else. Or when I'm lying in bed about to fall asleep.'

'Exactly. It's when you relax, when your mind stops desperately clawing at that filing cabinet drawer. That's when, magically, the drawer opens and the file pops out. Does this make the

240

concept of hypnosis seem more plausible?'

She nodded.

'Well, that's what we're going to do. Help you relax. Allow you to reach into that filing cabinet.'

'I'm not sure I can relax enough.'

'Is it the room? The chair?'

'The chair is fine. It's . . .' She looked uneasily at the video camera. 'The audience.'

'Detectives Moore and Rizzoli will leave the room. And as for the camera, it's just an object. A piece of machinery. Think of it that way.'

'I suppose . . .'

'You have other concerns?'

There was a pause. She said, softly: 'I'm afraid.'

'Of me?'

'No. Of the memory. Reliving it.'

'I would never make you do that. Detective Moore told me it was a traumatic experience, and we're not going to make you relive it. We'll approach it a different way. So fear won't block out the memories.'

'And how do I know they'll be real memories? Not something I made up?'

Polochek paused. 'It's a concern, that your memories may no longer be pure. A lot of time has passed. We'll just have to work with what's there. I should tell you now that I myself know very little about your case. I try not to know too much, to avoid the danger of influencing your recall. All I've been told is that the event was two years ago, that it involved an attack against you, and that the drug Rohypnol was in your system. Other than that, I'm in the dark. So whatever memories come

241

out are yours. I'm only here to help you open that filing cabinet.'

She sighed. 'I guess I'm ready.'

Polochek looked at the two detectives.

Moore nodded; then he and Rizzoli stepped out of the room. From the other side of the window, they watched as Polochek took out a pen and a pad of paper and placed them on the table beside him. He asked a few more questions. What she did for relaxation. Whether there was a special place, a special memory, that she found particularly peaceful.

'In the summertime, when I was growing up,' she said, 'I used to visit my grandparents in New Hampshire. They had a cabin on a lake.'

'Describe it for me. In detail.'

'It was very quiet. Small. With a big porch facing the water. There were wild raspberry bushes next to the house. I used to pick the berries. And on the path leading down to the dock, my grandmother planted daylilies.'

'So you remember berries. Flowers.'

'Yes. And the water. I love the water. I used to sunbathe on the dock.'

'That's good to know.' He scribbled notes on the pad, put down the pen again. 'All right. Now let's start by taking three deep breaths. Let each one out slowly. That's it. Now close your eyes and just concentrate on my voice.'

Moore watched as Catherine's eyelids slowly closed. 'Start recording,' he said to Rizzoli.

She pressed the video Record button, and the tape began to spin.

In the next room, Polochek guided Catherine

toward complete relaxation, instructing her to focus first on her toes, the tension flowing away. Now her feet were going limp as the sense of relaxation slowly spread up her calves.

'You really believe this shit?' said Rizzoli.

'I've seen it work.'

'Well, maybe it does. Because it's putting me to sleep.'

He looked at Rizzoli, who stood with arms crossed, her lower lip stuck out in stubborn skepticism. 'Just watch,' he said.

'When does she begin to levitate?'

Polochek had guided the focus of relaxation to higher and higher muscles of Catherine's body, moving up her thighs, her back, her shoulders. Her arms now hung limp at her sides. Her face was smooth, unworried. The rhythm of her breathing had slowed, deepened.

'Now we are going to visualize a place you love,' said Polochek. 'Your grandparents' cottage, on the lake. I want you to see yourself standing on that big porch. Looking out toward the water. It's a warm day, and the air is calm and still. The only sound is the chirping of birds, nothing else. It is quiet here, and peaceful. The sunlight sparkles on the water . . .'

A look of such serenity came across her face that Moore could scarcely believe it was the same woman. He saw warmth there and all the rosy hopes of a young girl. I am looking at the child she once was, he thought. Before the loss of innocence, before all the disappointments of adulthood. Before Andrew Capra had left his mark.

'The water is so inviting, so beautiful,' said Polochek. 'You walk down the porch steps and start along the path, toward the lake.'

Catherine sat motionless, her face completely relaxed, her hands limp in her lap.

'The ground is soft beneath your feet. The sunlight shines down, warm on your back. And birds chirp in the trees. You are at complete ease. With every step you take, you are growing more and more peaceful. You feel a deepening calm come over you. There are flowers on either side of the path, daylilies. They have a sweet scent, and as you brush past them, you breathe in the fragrance. It is a very special, magical fragrance that pulls you toward sleep. As you walk, you feel your legs growing heavy. The scent of the flowers is like a drug, making you more relaxed. And the sun's warmth is melting away all the remaining tension from your muscles.

'Now you are nearing the water's edge. And you see a small boat at the end of the dock. You walk onto that dock. The water is calm, like a mirror. Like glass. The little boat in the water is so still, it just floats there, as stable as can be. It's a magic boat. It can take you places all by itself. Wherever you want to go. All you have to do is get in. So now you lift your right foot to step into the boat.'

Moore looked at Catherine's feet and saw that her right foot had actually lifted and was suspended a few inches off the floor.

'That's right. You step in with your right foot. The boat is stable. It holds you securely, safely. You are utterly confident and comfortable. Now you put in your left foot.'

244

Catherine's left foot rose from the floor, slowly lowered again.

'Jesus, I don't believe this,' said Rizzoli.

'You're looking at it.'

'Yeah, but how do I know she's really hypnotized? That she's not faking it?'

'You don't.'

Polochek was leaning closer to Catherine, but not touching her, using only his voice to guide her through the trance. 'You untie the boat's line from the dock. And now the boat is free and moving on the water. You are in control. All you have to do is think of a place, and the boat will take you there by magic.' Polochek glanced at the one-way mirror and gave a nod.

'He's going to take her back now,' said Moore.

'All right, Catherine.' Polochek jotted on his pad of paper, noting the time that the induction had been completed. 'You are going to take the boat to another place. Another time. You are still in control. You see a mist rising on the water, a warm and gentle mist that feels good on your face. The boat glides into it. You reach down and touch the water, and it's like silk. So warm, so still. Now the mist begins to lift and just ahead, you see a building on the shore. A building with a single door.'

Moore found himself leaning close to the window. His hands had tensed, and his pulse quickened.

'The boat brings you to shore and you step out. You walk up the path to the house and open the door. Inside is a single room. It has a nice thick carpet. And a chair. You sit down in the chair, and it's the most comfortable chair you've ever been in. You are completely at ease. And in control.'

Catherine sighed deeply, as though she had just settled onto thick cushions.

'Now, you look at the wall in front of you and you see a movie screen. It's a magic movie screen, because it can play scenes from any time in your life. It can go back as far as you want it to. You are in control. You can make it go forward or backward. You can stop it at a particular instant in time. It's all up to you. Let's try it now. Let's go back to a happy time. A time when you were at your grandparents' cottage on the lake. You are picking raspberries. Do you see it, on the screen?'

Catherine's answer was a long time in coming. When at last she spoke, her words were so soft Moore could barely hear them.

'Yes. I see it.'

'What are you doing? On the screen?' asked Polochek.

'I'm holding a paper sack. Picking berries and putting them in the sack.'

'And do you eat them as you pick?'

A smile on her face, soft and dreamy. 'Oh, yes. They're sweet. And warm from the sun.'

Moore frowned. This was unexpected. She was experiencing taste and touch, which meant she was reliving the moment. She was not just watching it on a movie screen; she was *in* the scene. He saw Polochek glance at the window with a look of concern. He had chosen the movie screen imagery as a device to detach her from the trauma of her experience. But she was not detached. Now Polochek hesitated, considering what to do next.

'Catherine,' he said, 'I want you to concentrate on the cushion you are sitting on. You are in the chair, in the room, watching the movie screen. Notice how soft the cushion is. How the chair hugs your back. Do you feel it?'

A pause. 'Yes.'

'Okay. Okay, now you're going to stay in that chair. You are not going to leave it. And we're going to use the magic screen to watch a different scene in your life. You will still be in the chair. You will still be feeling that soft cushion against your back. And what you're going to see is just a movie on the screen. All right?'

'All right.'

'Now.' Polochek took a deep breath. 'We're going to go back to the night of June fifteenth, in Savannah. The night Andrew Capra knocked on your front door. Tell me what is happening on the screen.'

Moore watched, scarcely daring to breathe.

'He is standing on my front porch,' said Catherine. 'He says he needs to speak to me.'

'About what?'

'About the mistakes he made. In the hospital.'

What she said next was no different from the statement she had given to Detective Singer in Savannah. Reluctantly she invited Capra into her home. It was a hot night, and he said he was thirsty, so she offered him a beer. She opened a beer for herself as well. He was agitated, worried about his future. Yes, he had made mistakes. But didn't every doctor? It was a waste of his talent, to cut him from the program. He knew a medical student at Emory, a brilliant young man who'd

247

made just one mistake, and it had ended that student's career. It wasn't right that Catherine should have the power to make or break a career. People should get second chances.

Though she tried to reason with him, she heard his mounting anger, saw how his hands shook. At last she left to use the bathroom, to give him time to calm down.

'And when you returned from the bathroom?' asked Polochek. 'What happens in the movie? What do you see?'

'Andrew is quieter. Not so angry. He says he understands my position. He smiles at me when I finish my beer.'

'Smiles?'

'Strange. A very strange smile. Like the one he gave me in the hospital . . .'

Moore could hear her breathing begin to quicken. Even as a detached observer, watching the scene in an imaginary movie, she was not immune to the approaching horror.

'What happens next?'

'I'm falling asleep.'

'Do you see this on the movie screen?'

'Yes.'

'And then?'

'I don't see anything. The screen is black.'

The Rohypnol. She has no memory of this part.

'All right,' said Polochek. 'Let's fast-forward through the black part. Move ahead, to the next part of the movie. To the next image you see on the screen.'

Catherine's breathing grew agitated.

'What do you see?'

248

'I—I'm lying in my bed. In my room. I can't move my arms or my legs.'

'Why not?'

'I'm tied to the bed. My clothes are gone, and he's lying on top of me. He's inside me. Moving inside me . . .'

'Andrew Capra?'

'Yes. Yes . . .' Her breathing was erratic now, the sound of fear catching in her throat.

Moore's fists clenched and his own breathing accelerated. He fought the urge to pound on the window and put an immediate halt to the proceedings. He could barely stand to listen to this. They must not force her to relive the rape.

But Polochek was already aware of the danger, and he quickly guided her away from the painful memory of that ordeal.

'You are still in your chair,' said Polochek. 'Safe in that room with the movie screen. It's only a movie, Catherine. Happening to someone else. You are safe. Secure. Confident.'

Her breathing calmed again, slowing into a steady rhythm. So did Moore's.

'All right. Let's watch the movie. Pay attention to what *you* are doing. Not Andrew. Tell me what happens next.'

'The screen has gone black again. I don't see anything.'

She has not yet shaken off the Rohypnol.

'Fast-forward, past this black part. To the next thing you see. What is it?'

'Light. I see light . . .'

Polochek paused. 'I want you to zoom out,

Catherine. I want you to pull back, to see more of the room. What is on the screen?'

'Things. Lying on the nightstand.'

'What things?'

'Instruments. A scalpel. I see a scalpel.'

'Where is Andrew?'

'I don't know.'

'He's not there in the room?'

'He's gone. I can hear water running.'

'What happens next?'

She was breathing fast, her voice agitated. 'I pull on the ropes. Try to get myself free. I can't move my feet. But my right hand – the rope is loose around my wrist. I pull. I keep pulling and pulling. My wrist is bleeding.'

'Andrew is still out of the room?'

'Yes. I hear him laughing. I hear his voice. But it's somewhere else in the house.'

'What is happening to the rope?'

'It's coming off. The blood makes it slippery, and my hand slides out . . .'

'What do you do then?'

'I reach for the scalpel. I cut the rope on my other wrist. Everything takes so long. I'm sick to my stomach. My hands don't work right. They're so slow, and the room keeps going dark and light and dark. I can still hear his voice, talking. I reach down and cut my left ankle free. Now I hear his footsteps. I try to climb off the bed, but my right ankle is still tied. I roll over the side and fall on the floor. On my face.'

'And then?'

'Andrew is there, in the doorway. He looks surprised. I reach under the bed. And I feel the gun.'

'There's a gun under your bed?'

'Yes. My father's gun. But my hand is so clumsy, I can barely hold it. And things are starting to go black again.'

'Where is Andrew?'

'He is walking toward me . . .'

'And what happens, Catherine?'

'I'm holding the gun. And there's a sound. A loud sound.'

'The gun has fired?'

'Yes.'

'Did you fire the gun?'

'Yes.'

'What does Andrew do?'

'He falls. His hands are on his stomach. There's blood leaking through his fingers.'

'And what happens next?'

A long pause.

'Catherine? What do you see on the movie screen?'

'Black. The screen has gone black.'

'And when does the next image appear on that screen?'

'People. So many people in the room.'

'Which people?'

'Policemen . . .'

Moore almost groaned in disappointment. This was the vital gap in her memory. The Rohypnol, combined with the aftereffects of that blow on her head, had dragged her back into unconsciousness. Catherine did not remember firing the second shot. They still did not know how Andrew Capra had ended up with a bullet in his brain.

Polochek was looking at the window, a question

251

in his eyes. Were they satisfied?

To Moore's surprise, Rizzoli suddenly opened the door and gestured to Polochek to come into the next room. He did, leaving Catherine alone, and shut the door.

'Make her go back, to before she shot him. When she's still lying on the bed,' said Rizzoli. 'I want you to focus on what she's hearing in the other room. The water running. Capra's laughter. I want to know every sound she hears.'

'Any particular reason?'

'Just do it.'

Polochek nodded and went back to the interview room. Catherine had not moved; she sat absolutely still, as though Polochek's absence had left her in suspended animation.

'Catherine,' he said gently, 'I want you to rewind the movie. We're going to go back, before the gunshot. Before you've gotten your hands free and rolled onto the floor. We're at a point in the movie where you're still lying on the bed and Andrew is not in the room. You said you heard water running.'

'Yes.'

'Tell me everything you hear.'

'Water. I hear it in the pipes. The hiss. And I hear it gurgling down the drain.'

'He's running water into a sink?'

'Yes.'

'And you said you heard laughter.'

'Andrew is laughing.'

'Is he talking?'

A pause. 'Yes.'

'What does he say?'

252

'I don't know. He's too far away.'

'Are you sure it's Andrew? Could it be the TV?'

'No, it's him. It's Andrew.'

'Okay. Slow down the movie. Go second by second. Tell me what you hear.'

'Water, still running. Andrew says, "Easy." The word "easy." '

'That's all?'

'He says, "See one, do one, teach one." '

' "See one, do one, teach one"? That's what he says?'

'Yes.'

'And the next words you hear?'

'" It's my turn, Capra." '

Polochek paused. 'Can you repeat that?'

' "It's my turn, Capra." '

'*Andrew* says that?'

'No. Not Andrew.'

Moore froze, staring at the motionless woman in the chair.

Polochek glanced sharply at the window, amazement in his face. He turned back to Catherine.

'Who says those words?' asked Polochek. 'Who says, "It's my turn, Capra"?'

'I don't know. I don't know his voice.'

Moore and Rizzoli stared at each other.

There was someone else in the house.

Fifteen

He's with her now.

Rizzoli's knife moved clumsily on the cutting board, and pieces of chopped onion skittered off the counter onto the floor. In the next room, her dad and two brothers had the TV blaring. The TV was always blaring in this house, which meant that everyone was always yelling above it. If you didn't yell in Frank Rizzoli's house, you didn't get heard, and just a normal family conversation sounded like an argument. She swept the chopped onion into a bowl and started on the garlic, her eyes burning, her mind still wrapped around the troubling image of Moore and Catherine Cordell.

After the session with Dr Polochek, Moore had been the one to take Cordell home. Rizzoli had watched them walk together to the elevator, had seen his arm go around Cordell's shoulder, a gesture that struck her as more than just protective. She could see the way he looked at Cordell, the expression that came over his face, the spark in his eyes. He was no longer a cop guarding a citizen; he was a man falling in love.

Rizzoli pulled the garlic cloves apart, smashed

them one by one with the flat of her blade, and peeled off the skin. Her knife slammed hard against the cutting board, and her mother, standing at the stove, glanced at her but said nothing.

He's with her now. In her home. Maybe in her bed.

She released some of her pent-up frustration by whacking the cloves, *bang-bang-bang*. She didn't know why the thought of Moore and Cordell disturbed her so much. Maybe it was because there were so few saints in the world, so few people who played strictly by the rules, and she'd thought Moore was one of them. He had given her hope that not all of humanity was flawed, and now he'd disappointed her.

Maybe it was because she saw this as a threat to the investigation. A man with intensely personal stakes cannot think or act logically.

Or maybe it's because you're jealous of her. Jealous of a woman who can turn a man's head with just a glance. Men were such suckers for women in distress.

In the next room, her father and brothers gave a noisy cheer at the TV. She longed to be back in her own quiet apartment and began formulating excuses to leave early. At the very least she'd have to sit through dinner. As her mom kept reminding her, Frank Jr didn't get home very often, and how could Janie not want to spend time with her brother? She'd have to endure an evening of Frankie's boot camp stories. How pitiful the new recruits were this year, how the youth of America was going soft and he had to kick a lot more butt just to get those girly-men through the obstacle course. Mom and Dad hung on his every word. What ticked her off was that the family asked so little about *her* work. So far in his career, Frankie the macho Marine had only played at war. She saw battle every day, against real people, real killers.

Frankie swaggered into the kitchen and got a beer from the refrigerator. 'So when's dinner?' he asked, popping off the tab. Acting as though she were just the maid.

'Another hour,' said their mom.

'Jesus, Ma. It's already seven-thirty. I'm starved.'

'Don't curse, Frankie.'

'You know,' said Rizzoli, 'we'd be eating a lot sooner if we had a little help from the guys.'

'I can wait,' said Frankie, and turned back to the TV room. In the doorway he stopped. 'Oh, I almost forgot. You got a message.'

'What?'

'Your cell phone rang. Some guy named Frosty.'

'You mean Barry Frost?'

'Yeah, that's his name. He wants you to call him back.'

'When was this?'

'You were outside moving the cars.'

'Goddamnit, Frankie! That was an hour ago!'

'Janie,' said their mother.

Rizzoli untied her apron and threw it on the counter. 'This is my job, Ma! Why the hell doesn't anyone respect that?' She grabbed the kitchen phone and punched in Barry Frost's cell phone number.

He answered on the first ring.

'It's me,' she said. 'I just got the message to call back.'

256

'You're gonna miss the takedown.'

'What?'

'We got a cold hit on that DNA from Nina Peyton.'

'You mean the semen? The DNA's in CODIS?'

'It matches a perp named Karl Pacheco. Arrested 1997, charged with sexual assault, but acquitted. He claimed it was consensual. The jury believed him.'

'He's Nina Peyton's rapist?'

'And we got the DNA to prove it.'

She gave a triumphant punch in the air. 'What's the address?'

'Four-five-seven-eight Columbus Ave. The team's just about all here.'

'I'm on my way.'

She was already running out the door when her mother called: 'Janie! What about dinner?'

'Gotta go, Ma.'

'But it's Frankie's last night!'

'We're making an arrest.'

'Can't they do it without you?'

Rizzoli stopped, her hand on the doorknob, her temper hissing dangerously toward detonation. And she saw, with startling clarity, that no matter what she achieved or how distinguished her career might be, this one moment would always represent her reality: Janie, the trivial sister. The *girl*.

Without a word, she walked out and slammed the door.

Columbus Avenue was on the northern edge of Roxbury, smack in the center of the Surgeon's killing grounds. To the south was Jamaica Plain,

257

the home of Nina Peyton. To the southeast was Elena Ortiz's residence. To the northeast was the Back Bay, and the homes of Diana Sterling and Catherine Cordell. Glancing at the tree-lined streets, Rizzoli saw brick row houses, a neighborhood populated by students and staff from nearby Northeastern University. Lots of coeds.

Lots of good hunting.

The traffic light ahead turned yellow. Adrenaline spurting, she floored the accelerator and barreled through the intersection. The honor of making this arrest should be hers. For weeks, Rizzoli had lived, breathed, even dreamed of the Surgeon. He had infiltrated every moment of her life, both awake and asleep. No one had worked harder to catch him, and now she was in a race to claim her prize.

A block from Karl Pacheco's address, she screeched to a halt behind a cruiser. Four other vehicles were parked helter-skelter along the street.

Too late, she thought, running toward the building. They've already gone in.

Inside she heard thudding footsteps and men's shouts echoing in the stairwell. She followed the sound to the second floor and stepped into Karl Pacheco's apartment.

There she confronted a scene of chaos. Splintered wood from the door littered the threshold. Chairs had been overturned, a lamp smashed, as though wild bulls had raged through the room, trailing destruction. The air itself was poisoned with testosterone, cops on a rampage, hunting for the perp who a few days before had slaughtered one of their own.

On the floor, a man lay facedown. Black – not the Surgeon. Crowe had his heel brutally pressed to the back of the black man's neck.

'I asked you a question, asshole,' yelled Crowe. 'Where's Pacheco?'

The man whimpered and made the mistake of trying to lift his head. Crowe brought his heel down, hard, slamming the prisoner's chin against the floor. The man made a choking sound and began to thrash.

'Let him up!' yelled Rizzoli.

'He won't hold still!'

'Get off him and maybe he'll talk to you!' Rizzoli shoved Crowe aside. The prisoner rolled onto his back, gasping like a landed fish.

Crowe yelled, 'Where's Pacheco?'

'Don't – don't know—'

'You're in his apartment!'

'Left. He left—'

'When?'

The man began to cough, a deep, violent hacking that sounded like his lungs were ripping apart. The other cops had gathered around, staring with undisguised hatred at the prisoner on the floor. The friend of a cop-killer.

Disgusted, Rizzoli headed up the hall to the bedroom. The closet door hung open and clothes on the hangers had been thrown to the floor. The search of the flat had been thorough and brutish, every door flung open, every possible hiding place exposed. She pulled on gloves and began going through dresser drawers, poking through pockets, searching for a datebook, an address book, anything that could tell her where Pacheco might have fled.

She looked up as Moore came into the room. 'You in charge of this mess?' she asked.

He shook his head. 'Marquette gave the go-ahead. We had information that Pacheco was in the building.'

'Then where is he?' She slammed the drawer shut and crossed to the bedroom window. It was closed but unlatched. The fire escape was right outside. She opened the window and stuck her head out. A squad car was parked in the alley below, radio chattering, and she saw a patrolman shining his flashlight into a Dumpster.

She was about to pull her head back in when she felt something tap her on the back of the scalp, and she heard the faint clatter of gravel bouncing off the fire escape. Startled, she looked up. The night sky was awash with city lights, and the stars were barely visible. She stared for a moment, scanning the outline of the roof against that anemic black sky, but nothing moved.

She climbed out the window onto the fire escape and started up the ladder to the third story. On the next landing she stopped to check the window of the flat above Pacheco's; the screen had been nailed in place, and the window was dark.

Again she looked up, toward the roof. Though she saw nothing, heard nothing from above, the hairs on the back of her neck were standing up.

'Rizzoli?' Moore called out the window. She didn't answer but pointed to the roof, a silent signal of her intentions.

She wiped her damp palms on her slacks and quietly started up the ladder leading to the roof. At the last rung she paused, took a deep breath, and slowly, slowly raised her head to peer over the edge.

Beneath the moonless sky, the rooftop was a forest of shadows. She saw the silhouette of a table and chairs, a tangle of arching branches. A rooftop garden. She scrambled over the edge, dropped lightly onto the asphalt shingles, and drew her weapon. Two steps, and her shoe hit an obstacle, sent it clattering. She inhaled the pungent scent of geraniums. Realized she was surrounded by plants in clay pots. An obstacle course of them at her feet.

Off to her left, something moved.

She strained to make out a human form in that jumble of shadows. Saw him then, crouching like a black homunculus.

She raised her weapon and commanded: 'Freeze!'

She did not see what he already held in his hand. What he was preparing to hurl at her.

A split second before the garden trowel hit her face, she felt the air rush toward her, like an evil wind whistling out of the darkness. The blow slammed into her left cheek with such force she saw lights explode.

She landed on her knees, a tidal wave of pain roaring up her synapses, pain so terrible it sucked her breath away.

'*Rizzoli?*' It was Moore. She hadn't even heard him drop onto the rooftop.

'I'm okay. I'm okay . . .' She squinted toward where the figure had been crouching. It was gone. 'He's here,' she whispered. 'I want that son of a bitch.'

261

Moore eased into the darkness. She clutched her head, waiting for the dizziness to pass, cursing her own carelessness. Fighting to keep her head clear, she staggered to her feet. Anger was a potent fuel; it steadied her legs, strengthened her grip on the weapon.

Moore was a few yards to her right; she could just make out his silhouette, moving past the table and chairs.

She moved left, circling the roof in the opposite direction. Every throb in her cheek, every poker stab of pain, was a reminder that she'd screwed up. *Not this time*. Her gaze swept the feathery shadows of potted trees and shrubs.

A sudden clatter made her whirl to her right. She heard running footsteps, saw a shadow dart across the roof, straight toward her.

Moore yelled, 'Freeze! Police!'

The man kept coming.

Rizzoli dropped to a crouch, weapon poised. The throbbing in her face crescendoed into bursts of agony. All the humiliation she'd endured, the daily snubs, the insults, the never-ending torment dished out by the Darren Crowes of the world, seemed to shrink into a single pinpoint of rage.

This time, bastard, you're mine. Even as the man suddenly halted before her, even as his arms lifted toward the sky, the decision was irreversible.

She squeezed the trigger.

The man twitched. Staggered backward.

She fired a second time, a third, and each kick of the weapon was a satisfying snap against her palm.

'*Rizzoli! Cease fire!*'

Moore's shout finally penetrated the roaring in her ears. She froze, her weapon still aimed, her arms taut and aching.

The perp was down, and he was not moving. She straightened and slowly walked toward the crumpled form. With each step came the mounting horror of what she'd just done.

Moore was already kneeling at the man's side, checking for a pulse. He looked up at her, and although she could not read his expression on that dark roof, she knew there was accusation in his gaze.

'He's dead, Rizzoli.'

'He was holding something – in his hand—'

'There was nothing.'

'I saw it. I know I did!'

'His hands were up in the air.'

'Goddamnit, Moore. It was a good shooting! You've got to back me up on this!'

Other voices suddenly broke in as cops scrambled onto the roof to join them. Moore and Rizzoli said nothing more to each other.

Crowe shone his flashlight on the man. Rizzoli caught a nightmarish glimpse of open eyes, a shirt black with blood.

'Hey, it's Pacheco!' said Crowe. 'Who brought him down?'

Rizzoli said, tonelessly, 'I did.'

Someone gave her a slap on the back. 'Girl cop does okay!'

'Shut up,' said Rizzoli. 'Just *shut up*!' She stalked away, clambered down the fire escape, and retreated numbly to her car. There she sat, huddled behind the steering wheel, her pain giving way to nausea. Mentally she kept playing and replaying the scene on the rooftop. What Pacheco had done, what she had done. She saw him running again, just a shadow, flitting toward her. She saw him stop. Yes, stop. She saw him look at her.

A weapon. Jesus, please, let there be a weapon.

But she had seen no weapon. In that split second before she'd fired, the image had been seared into her brain. A man, frozen. A man with hands raised in submission.

Someone knocked on the window. Barry Frost. She rolled down the glass.

'Marquette's looking for you,' he said.

'Okay.'

'Something wrong? Rizzoli, you feeling okay?'

'I feel like a truck ran over my face.'

Frost leaned in and stared at her swollen cheek. 'Wow. That asshole really had it coming.'

That was what Rizzoli wanted to believe, too: that Pacheco deserved to die. Yes, he did, and she was tormenting herself for no reason. Wasn't the evidence clear on her face? He had attacked her. He was a monster, and by shooting him she had dispensed swift, cheap justice. Elena Ortiz and Nina Peyton and Diana Sterling would surely applaud. No one mourns the scum of the world.

She stepped out of the car, feeling better because of Frost's sympathy. Stronger. She walked toward the building and saw Marquette standing near the front steps. He was talking to Moore.

Both men turned to face her as she approached. She noticed Moore was not meeting her gaze but was focused elsewhere, avoiding her eyes. He looked sick.

Marquette said, 'I need your weapon, Rizzoli.'

'I fired in self-defense. The perp attacked me.'

'I understand that. But you know the drill.'

She looked at Moore. *I liked you. I trusted you.* She unbuckled her holster and thrust it at Marquette. 'Who's the fucking enemy here?' she said. 'Sometimes I wonder.' And she turned and walked back to the car.

Moore stared into Karl Pacheco's closet and thought: This is all wrong. On the floor were half a dozen pairs of shoes, size 11, extra wide. On the shelf were dusty sweaters, a shoebox of old batteries and loose change, and a stack of *Penthouse* magazines.

He heard a drawer slide open and turned to look at Frost, whose gloved hands were rifling through Pacheco's socks drawer.

'Anything?' asked Moore.

'No scalpels, no chloroform. Not even a roll of duct tape.'

'Ding ding ding!' announced Crowe from the bathroom, and he sauntered out waving a Ziploc bag of plastic vials containing a brown liquid. 'From sunny Mexico, land of pharmaceutical plenty.'

'Roofies?' asked Frost.

Moore glanced at the label, printed in Spanish. 'Gamma hydroxybutyrate. Same effect.'

Crowe shook the bag. 'At least a hundred date rapes in here. Pacheco must've had a very busy dick.' He laughed.

The sound grated on Moore. He thought of that busy dick and the damage it had done, not just the physical damage, but the spiritual destruction. The souls it had cleaved in two. He remembered what Catherine had told him: that every rape victim's life was divided into *before* and *after*. A sexual assault turns a woman's world into a bleak and unfamiliar landscape in which every smile, every bright moment, is tainted with despair. Weeks ago he might scarcely have registered Crowe's laughter. Tonight, he heard it only too well, and he recognized its ugliness.

He went into the living room, where the black man was being questioned by Detective Sleeper.

'I'm telling you, we were just hanging out,' the man said.

'You just hang out with six hundred bucks in your pocket?'

'I like to carry cash, man.'

'What'd you come to buy?'

'Nothin'.'

'How do you know Pacheco?'

'I just do.'

'Oh, a real *close* friend. What was he selling?'

GHB, thought Moore. The date rape drug. That's what he'd come to buy. Another busy dick.

He walked out into the night and felt immediately disoriented by the pulsing lights of the cruisers. Rizzoli's car was gone. He stared at the empty space and the burden of what he'd done, what he'd felt compelled to do, suddenly weighed so heavily on his shoulders that he could not move. Never in his career had he faced such a terrible choice, and even though he knew in his

266

heart he'd made the right decision, he was tormented by it. He tried to reconcile his respect for Rizzoli with what he had seen her do on the rooftop. It wasn't too late to retract what he'd said to Marquette. It *had* been dark and confusing on the roof; maybe Rizzoli really thought Pacheco had been holding a weapon. Maybe she had seen some gesture, some movement, that Moore had missed. But try as he might, he could not retrieve any memory that justified her actions. He could not interpret what he'd witnessed as anything but a cold-blooded execution.

When he saw her again, she was hunched at her desk, holding a bag of ice to her cheek. It was after midnight, and he was in no mood for conversation. But she looked up as he walked past and her gaze froze him to the spot.

'What did you tell Marquette?' she asked.

'What he wanted to know. How Pacheco ended up dead. I didn't lie to him.'

'You son of a bitch.'

'You think I wanted to tell him the truth?'

'You had a choice.'

'So did you, up on that roof. You made the wrong one.'

'And you never make the wrong choice, do you? You *never* make a mistake.'

'If I do, I own up to it.'

'Oh, yeah. Fucking Saint Thomas.'

He moved to her desk and gazed straight down at her. 'You're one of the best cops I've ever worked with. But tonight, you shot a man in cold blood, and I saw it.'

'You didn't have to see it.'

267

'But I did.'

'What did we really see up there, Moore? A lot of shadows, a lot of movement. The separation between a right choice and a wrong choice is *this* thin.' She held up two fingers, nearly touching. 'And we allow for that. We allow each other the benefit of the doubt.'

'I tried to.'

'You didn't try hard enough.'

'I won't lie for another cop. Even if she's my friend.'

'Let's remember who the fucking bad guys are here. Not *us*.'

'If we start lying, how do we draw the line between *them* and *us*? Where does it end?'

She took the bag of ice off her face and pointed to her cheek. One eye was swollen shut and the entire left side of her face was blown up like a mottled balloon. The brutal appearance of her injury shocked him. 'This is what Pacheco did to me. Not just a friendly little slap, is it? You talk about *them* and *us*. Which side was *he* on? I did the world a favor by blowing him away. No one's going to miss the Surgeon.'

'Karl Pacheco was not the Surgeon. You blew away the wrong man.'

She stared at him, her bruised face a lurid Picasso that was half-grotesque, half-normal. 'We had a DNA match! He was the one—'

'The one who raped Nina Peyton, yes. Nothing about him matches the Surgeon.' He dropped a Hair and Fiber report on her desk.

'What's this?'

'The microscopic on Pacheco's head hair.

Different color, different curl, different cuticle density from the strand in Elena Ortiz's wound margin. No evidence of bamboo hair.'

She sat motionless, staring at the lab report. 'I don't understand.'

'Pacheco raped Nina Peyton. That's all we can say about him with any certainty.'

'Both Sterling and Ortiz were raped—'

'We can't prove Pacheco did it. Now that he's dead, we'll never know.'

She looked up at him, and the uninjured side of her face was twisted with anger. 'It *had* to be him. Pick three random women in this city, and what are the chances all of them have been raped? That's what the Surgeon's managed to do. He's batted three out of three. If he's not the one raping them, how does he know which ones to choose, which ones to slaughter? If it's not Pacheco, then it's a buddy, a partner. Some fucking vulture feeding off the carrion Pacheco leaves behind.' She thrust the lab report back at him. 'Maybe I didn't shoot the Surgeon. But the man I *did* shoot was scum. Everyone seems to forget that fact. *Pacheco was scum*. Do I get a medal?' She rose to her feet and shoved her chair, hard, against the desk. 'Administrative duty. Marquette's turned me into a fucking desk jockey. Thanks a lot.'

In silence he watched her walk away and could think of nothing to say, nothing he could do to repair the rift between them.

He went to his own workstation and sank into the chair. I'm a dinosaur, he thought, lumbering through a world where truth-tellers are despised. He could not think about Rizzoli now. The case against Pacheco had disintegrated, and they were back at square one, hunting for a nameless killer.

Three raped women. It kept coming back to that. How was the Surgeon finding them? Only Nina Peyton had reported her rape to the police. Elena Ortiz and Diana Sterling had not. Theirs was a private trauma, known only to the rapists, their victims, and the medical professionals who had treated them. But the three women had sought medical attention in different places: Sterling in the office of a Back Bay gynecologist. Ortiz in the Pilgrim Hospital E.R. Nina Peyton in the Forest Hills Women's Clinic. There was no overlap of personnel, no doctor or nurse or receptionist who had come into contact with more than one of these women.

Somehow the Surgeon knew those women were damaged, and he was attracted by their pain. Sexual killers choose their prey from among the most vulnerable members of society. They seek women they can control, women they can degrade, women who do not threaten them. And who is more fragile than a woman who has been violated?

As Moore walked out, he paused to look at the wall where the photos of Sterling, Ortiz, and Peyton were tacked. Three women, three rapes.

And a fourth. Catherine was raped in Savannah.

He blinked as the image of her face suddenly flashed into mind, an image that he could not help adding to that victims' gallery on the wall.

Somehow, it all goes back to what happened that night in Savannah. It all goes back to Andrew Capra.

270

Sixteen

In the heart of Mexico City, human blood once ran in rivers. Beneath the foundations of the modern metropolis lie the ruins of Templo Mayor, the great Aztec site which dominated ancient Tenochtitlán. Here, tens of thousands of unfortunate victims were sacrificed to the gods.

The day I walked those temple grounds, I felt some measure of amusement that nearby loomed a cathedral, where Catholics light candles and whisper prayers to a merciful God in heaven. They kneel near the very place where the stones were once slippery with blood. I visited on a Sunday, not knowing that on Sundays admission is free to the public, and the Museum of Templo Mayor was as warm with children, their voices echoing brightly in the halls. I do not care for children, or for the disorder they stir; if ever I return, I will remember to avoid museums on Sundays.

But it was my last day in the city, so I put up with the irritating shards of noise. I wanted to see the excavation, and I wanted to tour Hall Two. The Hall of Ritual and Sacrifice.

The Aztecs believed that death is necessary for

271

life. To maintain the sacred energy of the world, to ward off catastrophe and ensure that the sun continues to rise, the gods must be fed human hearts. I stood in the Hall of Ritual and saw, in the glass case, the sacrificial knife which had carved flesh. It had a name: Tecpatl Ixcuahua. The Knife with the Broad Forehead. The blade was made of flint, and the handle was in the shape of a kneeling man.

How, I wondered, does one go about cutting out a human heart when equipped with only a flint knife?

That question consumed me as I walked later that afternoon in the Alameda Central, ignoring the filthy urchins who trailed behind me, begging for coins. After a while they realized I could not be seduced by brown eyes or toothy smiles, and they left me alone. At last I was allowed some measure of peace – if such a thing is possible in the cacophony of Mexico City. I found a cafe, and sat at an outdoor table sipping strong coffee, the only patron who chose to be outside in the heat. I crave the heat; it soothes my cracking skin. I seek it the way a reptile seeks a warm rock. And so, on that sweltering day, I drank coffee and considered the human chest, puzzling over how best to approach the beating treasure within.

The Aztec sacrificial ritual has been described as swift, with a minimum of torture, and this presents a dilemma. I know it is hard work to crack through the sternum and separate the breastbone, which protects the heart like a shield. Cardiac surgeons make a vertical incision down the center of the chest, and split the sternum in two with a saw. They have assistants who help *them separate the bony halves, and they use a variety of sophisticated instruments to widen the field, every tool fashioned of gleaming stainless steel.*

An Aztec priest, with only a flint knife, would have problems using such an approach. He would need to pound on the breastbone with a chisel to split it down the center, and there would be a great deal of struggling. A great deal of screaming.

No, the heart must be taken through a different approach.

A horizontal cut running between two ribs, along the side? This, too, has its problems. The human skeleton is a sturdy structure, and to spread two ribs apart, wide enough to insert a hand, requires strength and specialized tools. Would an approach from below make more sense? One swift slice down the belly would open the abdomen, and all the priest would have to do is slice through the diaphragm and reach up to grasp the heart. Ah, but this is a messy option, with intestines spilling out upon the altar. Nowhere in the Aztec carvings are sacrificial victims depicted with loops of bowel protruding.

Books are wonderful things; they can tell you anything, everything, even how to cut out a heart using a flint knife, with a minimum of fuss. I found my answer in a textbook with the title Human Sacrifice and Warfare, written by an academic (my, universities are interesting places these days!), a man named Sherwood Clarke, whom I would very much like to meet someday.

I think we could teach each other many things.

The Aztecs, Mr Clarke says, used a transverse

273

thoracotomy to cut out the heart. The wound slices across the front of the chest, starting between the second and third rib, on one side of the sternum, cutting across the breastbone to the opposite side. The bone is broken transversely, probably with a sharp blow and a chisel. The result is a gaping hole. The lungs, exposed to outside air, instantly collapse. The victim quickly loses consciousness. And while the heart continues to beat, the priest reaches into the chest and severs the arteries and veins. He grasps the organ, still pulsating, from its bloody cradle and lifts it to the sky.

And so it was described in Bernardino de Sahagan's Codex Florentio, *The General History of New Spain:*

An offering priest carried the eagle cane,
Set it standing on the captive's breast, there
    where the heart had been, stained it with
    blood, indeed submerged it in the blood.
Then he also raised the blood in dedication to
    the sun.
It was said: 'Thus he giveth the sun to drink.'
And the captor thereupon took the blood of his
    captive
In a green bowl with a feathered rim.
The sacrificing priests poured it in for him there.
In it went the hollow cane, also feathered,
And then the captor departed to nourish the
    demons.

Nourishment for the demons.
How powerful is the meaning of blood.

I think this as I watch a thread of it being sucked into a needle-thin pipette. All around me are racks of test tubes, and the air hums with the sound of machines. The ancients considered blood a sacred substance, sustainer of life, food for monsters, and I share their fascination with it, even though I understand it is merely a biological fluid, a suspension of cells in plasma. The stuff with which I work every day.

The average seventy-kilogram human body possesses only five liters of blood. Of that, 45 percent is cells and the rest is plasma, a chemical soup made up of 95 percent water, the rest proteins and electrolytes and nutrients. Some would say that reducing it to its biological building blocks peels away its divine nature, but I do not agree. It is by looking at the building blocks themselves that you recognize its miraculous properties.

The machine beeps, a signal that the analysis is complete, and a report rolls out of the printer. I tear off the sheet and study the results.

With just a glance, I know many things about Mrs Susan Carmichael, whom I have never met. Her hematocrit is low – only 28, when it should be 40. She is anemic, lacking a normal supply of red blood cells, which are the carriers of oxygen. It is the protein hemoglobin, packed within these disk-shaped cells, that makes our blood red, that pinkens the nailbeds and brings a pretty flush to a young girl's cheeks. Mrs Carmichael's nailbeds are sallow, and if one peeled back her eyelid, the conjunctiva would appear only the palest shell-pink. Because she is anemic, her heart must work all the faster to pump diluted blood through her arteries, and so she pauses at every flight of stairs to catch her breath, to calm her racing pulse. I picture her stooping forward, her hand to her throat, her chest heaving like a bellows. Anyone passing her on the stairs can see she is not well.

I can see it just by looking at this sheet of paper.

There is more. On the roof of her mouth are flecks of red – petechiae, where blood has broken through capillaries and lodged in the mucous membrane. Perhaps she's unaware of these pin-point bleeds. Perhaps she has noticed them elsewhere on her body, beneath her fingernails, or on her shins. Perhaps she finds bruises she cannot account for, startling islands of blue on her arms or her thighs, and she thinks hard about when she might have injured herself. Was it a bump against the car door? The child clinging to her leg with sturdy fists? She seeks external reasons, when the real cause lurks in her bloodstream.

Her platelet count is twenty thousand; it should be ten times higher. Without platelets, the tiny cells that help form clots, the slightest bump may leave a bruise.

There is yet more to be learned from this flimsy sheet of paper.

I look at her white blood cell differential, and I see the explanation for her woes. The machine has detected the presence of myeloblasts, primitive white blood cell precursors that do not belong in the bloodstream. Susan Carmichael has acute myeloblastic leukemia.

I picture her life as it will play out in the months to come. I see her lying prone on a treatment table,

276

her eyes closed in pain as the bone marrow needle penetrates her hip.

I see her hair falling out in clumps, until she surrenders to the inevitable, and the electric shaver.

I see mornings with her crouched over the toilet bowl, and long days of staring at the ceiling, her universe shrunken to the four walls of her bedroom.

Blood is the giver of life, the magic fluid that sustains us. But Susan Carmichael's blood has turned against her; it flows in her veins like poison.

All these intimate details I know about her, without ever having met her.

I transmit the STAT results by fax to her physician, place the lab report in the out basket for later delivery, and reach for the next specimen. Another patient, another tube of blood.

The connection between blood and life has been known since the dawn of man. The ancients did not know that blood is made in the marrow, or that most of it is merely water, but they did appreciate its power in ritual and sacrifice. The Aztecs used bone perforators and agave needles to pierce their own skin and draw blood. They poked holes through their lips or tongue or the flesh of their chest, and the blood that resulted was their personal offering to the gods. Today such self-mutilation would be called sick and grotesque, the hallmark of insanity.

I wonder what the Aztecs would think of us.

Here I sit, in my sterile surroundings, garbed in white, my hands gloved to protect them from an accidental splash. How far we have strayed from our essential natures. Just the sight of blood can make some men faint, and people scurry to hide such horrors from the public eye, hosing down sidewalks where blood has spilled, or covering children's eyes when violence erupts on the television. Humans have lost touch with who, and what, they really are.

Some of us, however, have not.

We walk among the rest, normal in every respect; perhaps we are more normal than anyone else because we have not allowed ourselves to be wrapped and mummified in civilization's sterile bandages. We see blood, and we do not turn away. We recognize its lustrous beauty; we feel its primitive pull.

Everyone who drives past an accident and cannot help but look for the blood understands this. Beneath the revulsion, the urge to turn away, throbs a greater force. Attraction.

We all want to look. But not all of us will admit it.

It is lonely, walking among the anesthetized. In the afternoon, I wander the city and breathe in air so thick I can almost see it. It warms my lungs like heated syrup. I search the faces of people on the street, and I wonder which among them is my dearest blood brother, as once you were. Is there anyone else who has not lost touch with the ancient force that flows through us all? I wonder if we would recognize each other if we met, and I fear we would not, because we have hidden ourselves so deeply beneath the cloak that passes for normality.

So I walk alone. And I think of you, the only one who ever understood.

Seventeen

As a physician, Catherine had looked at death so many times that its visage was familiar to her. She had stared into a patient's face and watched life drain from the eyes, turning them blank and glassy. She had seen skin fade to gray, the soul in retreat, seeping away like blood. The practice of medicine is as much about death as it is about life, and Catherine had long ago made Death's acquaintance over the cooling remains of a patient. She was not afraid of corpses.

Yet as Moore turned onto Albany Street and she saw the neat brick building of the Medical Examiner's office, her hands broke out in a sweat.

He parked in the lot behind the building, next to a white van with the words 'Commonwealth of Massachusetts, Office of the Medical Examiner' printed on the side. She did not want to leave the car, and only when he came around to open her door did she finally step out.

'Are you ready for this?' he asked.

'I'm not looking forward to it,' she admitted. 'But let's get it over with.'

Though she had viewed dozens of autopsies, she

was not fully prepared for the smell of blood and ruptured intestines that hit her as they walked into the lab. For the first time in her medical career, she thought she would be sick at the sight of a body.

An older gentleman, eyes protected by a plastic face shield, turned to look at them. She recognized the M.E., Dr Ashford Tierney, whom she had met at a forensic pathology conference six months before. A trauma surgeon's failures were often the very subjects who ended up on Dr Tierney's autopsy table, and she had last spoken to him only a month ago, regarding the disturbing circumstances surrounding a child's death from a ruptured spleen.

Dr Tierney's gentle smile contrasted jarringly with the blood-streaked rubber gloves he was wearing. 'Dr Cordell, it's good to see you again.' He paused, as the irony of that statement struck him. 'Though it could be under more pleasant circumstances.'

'You've already started cutting,' Moore noted in dismay.

'Lieutenant Marquette wants immediate answers,' said Tierney. 'Every police shooting, the press is at his throat.'

'But I called ahead to arrange this viewing.'

'Dr Cordell's seen autopsies before. This is nothing new for her. Just let me finish this excision, and she can take a look at the face.'

Tierney turned his attention to the abdomen. With the scalpel, he finished slicing free the small bowel, pulled out loops of intestine, and dropped them into a steel basin. Then he stepped away from the table and nodded to Moore. 'Go ahead.'

Moore touched Catherine's arm. Reluctantly she approached the corpse. At first she focused on the gaping incision. An open abdomen was familiar territory, the organs impersonal landmarks, lumps of tissue that could belong to any stranger. Organs held no emotional significance, carried no personal stamp of identity. She could study them with the cool eye of a professional, and so she did, noting that the stomach and pancreas and liver were still in situ, waiting to be removed in a single bloc. The Y-incision, extending from the neck to the pubis, revealed both the chest and the abdominal cavity. The heart and lungs had already been excised, leaving the thorax an empty bowl. Visible in the chest wall were two bullet wounds, one entry just above the left nipple, the other a few ribs beneath it. Both bullets would have entered the thorax, piercing either heart or lung. In the left upper abdomen was yet a third entrance wound, tracking straight toward where the spleen would have been. Another catastrophic injury. Whoever had fired on Karl Pacheco had meant to kill him.

'Catherine?' said Moore, and she realized she had been silent too long.

She took a deep breath, inhaling the odor of blood and chilled flesh. By now she was well acquainted with Karl Pacheco's internal pathology; it was time to confront his face.

She saw black hair. A narrow face, the nose as sharp as a blade. Flaccid jaw muscles, the mouth gaping. Straight teeth. She focused, at last, on the eyes. Moore had told her almost nothing about this man, just his name and the fact he had been

281

shot by police while resisting arrest. *Are you the Surgeon?*

The eyes, corneas clouded by death, stirred no memory. She studied his face, trying to sense some trace of evil still lingering in Karl Pacheco's corpse, but she felt nothing. This mortal shell was empty, and no trace of its former inhabitant remained.

She said, 'I don't know this man,' and she walked out of the room.

She was already waiting outside by his car when Moore emerged from the building. Her lungs had been fouled by the stench of that autopsy room, and she was taking breaths of scorchingly hot air, as though to wash out the contamination. Though she was now sweating, the chill of that air-conditioned building had settled in her bones, deep as the marrow.

'Who was Karl Pacheco?' she asked.

He looked off in the direction of Pilgrim Hospital, listening to the crescendoing wail of an ambulance. 'A sexual predator,' he said. 'A man who hunted women.'

'Was he the Surgeon?'

Moore sighed. 'It appears not.'

'But you thought he might be.'

'DNA links him to Nina Peyton. Two months ago, he sexually assaulted her. But we have no evidence that connects him to Elena Ortiz or Diana Sterling. Nothing that places him in their lives.'

'Or in my life.'

'You're sure you've never seen him?'

'I'm only sure that I don't remember him.'

The sun had baked the car to oven heat, and

they stood with the doors open, waiting for the interior to cool. Gazing across the car roof at Moore, she saw how tired he was. Already his shirt was blotted with sweat. A fine way to spend his Saturday afternoon, driving a witness to the morgue. In many respects, cops and doctors led similar lives. They worked long hours, at jobs for which there was no five o'clock whistle. They saw humanity in its darkest, most painful hours. They witnessed nightmares and learned to live with the images.

And what images did he carry? she wondered as he drove her home. How many victims' faces, how many murder scenes, were stored like filed photographs in his head? She was only one element of this case, and she wondered about all the other women, living and dead, who had vied for his attention.

He pulled up in front of her building and turned off the engine. She looked up at her apartment window and was reluctant to step out of the car. To leave his company. They had spent so much time together over the last few days that she had come to rely on his strength and his kindness. Had they met under happier circumstances, his good looks alone would have caught her eye. Now what mattered most to her wasn't his attractiveness, nor even his intelligence, but what lay in his heart. This was a man she could trust.

She considered her next words and what those words could lead to. And decided that she didn't give a damn about the consequences.

She asked, softly: 'Will you come in for a drink?'

He didn't answer right away, and she felt her face flush as his silence took on unbearable significance. He was struggling to make a decision; he, too, understood what was happening between them, and was uncertain what to do about it.

When at last he looked at her and said, 'Yes, I'd like to come in,' they both knew that more than a drink was on their minds.

They walked to the lobby door and his arm came around her. It was little more than a protective gesture, his hand resting casually on her shoulder, but the warmth of his touch, and her response to it, made her fumble with the security keypad. Anticipation made her slow and clumsy. Upstairs, she unlocked her apartment door with shaking hands, and they stepped through, into the delicious coolness of her flat. He paused only long enough to close the door and turn the dead bolts.

And then he took her in his arms.

It had been so long since she'd let herself be held. Once, the thought of a man's hands on her body had filled her with panic. But in Moore's embrace, panic was the last thing on her mind. She responded to his kisses with a need that surprised them both. She'd been deprived of love so long that she'd lost all sense of hunger. Only now, as every part of her came alive, did she remember what desire felt like, and her lips sought his with the eagerness of a starved woman. She was the one who tugged him up the hall toward the bedroom, kissing all the way. She was the one who unbuttoned his shirt and unfastened his belt buckle. He knew, somehow he knew, that he could not be the aggressor for it would frighten her. That for this, their first time, she must lead the way. But he could not hide his arousal, and she felt it as she opened the zipper, as his trousers slipped off.

He reached for the buttons on her blouse and stopped, his gaze searching hers. The look she gave him, the sound of her quickening breath, left no doubt that this was what she wanted. The blouse slowly parted, and slid off her shoulders. The bra whispered to the floor. He did it with the utmost gentleness, not a stripping away of her defenses, but a welcome release. A liberation. She closed her eyes and sighed with pleasure as he bent to kiss her breast. Not an assault, but an act of reverence.

And so, for the first time in two years, did Catherine allow a man to make love to her. No thoughts of Andrew Capra intruded as she and Moore lay together on the bed. No flashes of panic, no frightening memories, returned as they shed the last of their clothes, as the weight of him pressed her into the mattress. What another man had done to her was an act so brutal it held no connection to this moment, to this body she inhabited. Violence is not sex, and sex is not love. Love was what she felt as Moore entered her, his hands cupping her face, his gaze on hers. She had forgotten what pleasure a man could give, and she lost herself in the moment, experiencing joy as though for the very first time.

It was dark when she awakened in his arms. She felt him stir and heard him ask: 'What time is it?'

'Eight-fifteen.'

'Wow.' He gave a dazed laugh and rolled onto

285

his back. 'I can't believe we slept all afternoon. I guess it caught up with me.'

'You haven't been getting much sleep, either.'

'Who needs sleep?'

'Spoken like a doctor.'

'Something we have in common,' he said, and his hand slowly traced her body. 'We've both been deprived too long . . .'

They lay still for a moment. Then he asked softly: 'How was it?'

'Are you asking me how good a lover are you?'

'No. I meant, how was it for *you*. Having me touch you.'

She smiled. 'It was good.'

'I didn't do anything wrong? I didn't scare you?'

'You make me feel safe. That's what I need, most of all. To feel safe. I think you're the only man who ever understood that. The only man I've been able to trust.'

'Some men are worth trusting.'

'Yes, but which ones? I never know.'

'You won't know until push comes to shove. He'll be the one still standing beside you.'

'Then I guess I never found him. I've heard other women say that as soon as you tell a man what happened to you, as soon as you use the word *rape*, the men back away. As though we're damaged goods. Men don't want to hear about it. They prefer silence to confession. But the silence spreads. It takes over, until you can't talk about anything at all. All of life becomes a taboo subject.'

'No one can live that way.'

'It's the only way other people can stand to be

286

around us. If we keep our silence. But even when I don't talk about it, it's *there*.'

He kissed her, and that simple act was more intimate than any act of love could be, because it came on the heels of confession.

'Will you stay with me tonight?' she whispered.

His breath was warm in her hair. 'If you'll let me take you to dinner.'

'Oh. I completely forgot about eating.'

'There's the difference between men and women. A man never forgets to eat.'

Smiling, she sat up. 'You make us drinks, then. I'll feed you.'

He mixed two martinis, and they sipped as she tossed a salad, slid steaks under the broiler. Masculine food, she thought with amusement. Red meat for the new man in her life. The act of cooking had never seemed as pleasurable as it was tonight, Moore smiling as he handed her the salt and pepper shakers, her head buzzing from the gin. Nor could she remember the last time food had tasted so good. It was as if she'd just emerged from a sealed bottle and was experiencing the full vibrancy of tastes and smells for the very first time.

They ate at the kitchen table and sipped wine. Her kitchen, with its white tiles and white cabinets, suddenly seemed bright with color. The ruby wine, the crisp green lettuce, the blue-checked cloth napkins. And Moore sitting across from her. She had once thought him colorless, like all the other featureless men who walk past you on a city street, outlines sketched on a flat canvas. Only now did she really see him, the warm ruddiness of his skin, the web of laugh lines around his eyes. All the charming imperfections of a face well lived in.

We have all night, she thought, and the prospect of what lay ahead brought a smile to her lips. She rose, and held her hand out to him.

Dr Zucker stopped the videotape of Dr Polochek's session and turned to Moore and Marquette. 'It could be a false memory. Cordell has conjured up a second voice that didn't exist. You see, that's the problem with hypnosis. Memory is a fluid thing. It can be altered, rewritten to match expectations. She went into that session *believing* Capra had a partner. And presto, the memory's there! A second voice. A second man in the house.' Zucker shook his head. 'It's not reliable.'

'It's not just her memory that supports a second perp,' said Moore. 'Our unsub sent hair clippings that could only have been collected in Savannah.'

'She *says* the hair was taken in Savannah,' Marquette pointed out.

'You don't believe her, either?'

'The lieutenant raises a valid point,' said Zucker. 'We're dealing with an emotionally fragile woman here. Even two years after the attack, she may not be entirely stable.'

'She's a trauma surgeon.'

'Yes, and she functions fine in the workplace. But she *is* damaged. You know that. The attack has left its mark.'

Moore fell silent, thinking about the first day he'd met Catherine. How her movements were precise, controlled. A different person from the carefree girl who had appeared during the hypnosis session, the young Catherine basking in the sunlight of her grandparents' dock. And last night, that joyous young Catherine had re-emerged in his arms. She had been there all along, trapped inside that brittle shell, waiting to be released.

'So what do we make of this hypnosis session?' asked Marquette.

Zucker said, 'I'm not saying she doesn't believe it. Doesn't remember it vividly. It's like telling a child there was an elephant in the backyard. After a while, the child believes it so strongly she can describe the elephant's trunk, the pieces of straw on the back. The broken tusk. The memory becomes reality. Even when it never happened.'

'We can't completely discount the memory,' said Moore. 'You may not believe Cordell is reliable, but she *is* the focus of our unsub's interest. What Capra started – the stalking, the killing – it hasn't stopped. It's followed her here.'

'A copycat?' said Marquette.

'Or a partner,' said Moore. 'There are precedents.'

Zucker nodded. 'Partnerships of killers aren't all that uncommon. We think of serial killers as being lone wolves, but up to a quarter of serial killings are done by partners. Henry Lee Lucas had one. Kenneth Bianchi had one. It makes everything easier for them. Abduction, control. It's cooperative hunting, to ensure success.'

'Wolves hunt together,' said Moore. 'Maybe Capra did, too.'

Marquette picked up the VCR remote, pressed

Rewind and then Play. On the TV screen, Catherine sat with eyes closed, arms limp.

Who says those words, Catherine? Who says, 'It's my turn, Capra'?

I don't know. I don't know his voice.

Marquette pressed Pause and Catherine's face froze on the screen. He looked at Moore. 'It's been over two years since she was attacked in Savannah. If he was Capra's partner, why has he waited this long to come after her? Why is it happening now?'

Moore nodded. 'I wondered the same thing. I think I know the answer.' He opened the folder he'd brought into the meeting and took out a tear sheet from the *Boston Globe*. 'This appeared seventeen days before Elena Ortiz's murder. It's an article about women surgeons in Boston. A third of it is devoted to Cordell. Her success. Her achievements. Plus there's a color photo of her.' He handed the sheet to Zucker.

'Now this is interesting,' said Zucker. 'What do you see when you look at this photo, Detective Moore?'

'An attractive woman.'

'Besides that? What does her posture, her expression, say to you?'

'Confidence.' Moore paused. 'Distance.'

'That's what I see, too. A woman at the top of her game. A woman who's untouchable. Arms crossed, her chin high. Out of reach to most mortals.'

'What's your point?' asked Marquette.

'Think about what turns on our unsub. Damaged women, contaminated by rape. Women who've symbolically been destroyed. And here is Catherine Cordell, the woman who killed his partner, Andrew Capra. She doesn't look damaged. She doesn't look like a victim. No, in this photo, she looks like a conqueror. What do you think he felt when he saw this?' Zucker looked at Moore.

'Anger.'

'Not just anger, Detective. Sheer, uncontrollable rage. After she left Savannah, he follows her to Boston, but he can't get at her because she's protected herself. So he bides his time, killing other targets. He probably imagines Cordell as a traumatized woman. A subhuman creature, just waiting around to be harvested as a victim. Then one day he opens the newspaper, and comes face-to-face, not with a victim, but with this conquering *bitch*.' Zucker handed the article back to Moore. 'Our boy is trying to bring her back down. He's using terror to do it.'

'What would be his end goal?' said Marquette.

'To reduce her to a level he can once again deal with. He only assaults women who act like victims. Women who are so damaged and humiliated, he doesn't feel threatened by them. And if indeed Andrew Capra was his partner, then our unsub has another motivation as well. Revenge, for what she destroyed.'

Marquette said, 'So where do we go with this hidden partner theory?'

'If Capra had a partner,' said Moore, 'then this takes us right back to Savannah. We're coming up empty-handed here. We've conducted nearly a thousand interviews so far, and have turned up no viable suspects. I think it's time to take a look at everyone associated with Andrew Capra. See if one of those names has turned up here in Boston. Frost is already on the phone to Detective Singer, the Savannah lead. He can fly down and review the evidence.'

'Why Frost?'

'Why not?'

Marquette looked at Zucker. 'We on a wild-goose chase?'

'Sometimes, you *do* catch a wild goose.'

Marquette nodded. 'Okay. Let's do Savannah.'

Moore rose to leave but stopped when Marquette said: 'Can you stay a minute? I need to talk to you.' They waited until Zucker had left the office; then Marquette closed the door and said, 'I don't want Detective Frost to go.'

'May I ask why?'

'Because I want you to go to Savannah.'

'Frost is ready to go. He's already prepared for it.'

'This isn't about Frost. It's about you. You need some separation from this case.'

Moore fell silent, knowing where this was leading.

'You've been spending a lot of time with Catherine Cordell,' said Marquette.

'She's key to this investigation.'

'Too many evenings in her company. You were with her at midnight on Tuesday.'

Rizzoli. Rizzoli knew that.

'And Saturday, you stayed all night with her. What, exactly, is going on?'

Moore said nothing. What could he say? *Yes,*

I've crossed the line. But I couldn't help myself.

Marquette sank into his chair with a look of profound disappointment. 'I can't believe I'm talking to *you* about this. You, of all people.' He sighed. 'It's time for you to pull back. We'll have someone else deal with her.'

'But she trusts me.'

'Is that all it is between you, *trust*? What I've heard goes way beyond that. I don't need to tell you how inappropriate this is. Look, we've both seen this happen before to other cops. It never works out. It won't work out this time, either. Right now, she needs you, and you happen to be handy. You two get hot and heavy for a few weeks, a month. Then you both wake up one morning and bam, it's over. Either she's hurt or you're hurt. And everyone's sorry it ever happened.' Marquette paused, waiting for a response. Moore had none.

'Aside from the personal issues,' continued Marquette, 'this complicates the investigation. And it's fucking embarrassing to the whole unit.' He gave a brusque wave toward the door. 'Go to Savannah. And stay the hell away from Cordell.'

'I need to explain to her—'

'Don't even call her. We'll see she gets the message. I'll assign Crowe in your place.'

'*Not* Crowe,' Moore said sharply.

'Who, then?'

'Frost.' Moore sighed. 'Let Frost be the one.'

'Okay, Frost. Now go catch a plane. Getting out of town is just what you need to cool things down. You're probably pissed at me now. But you know I'm only asking you to do the right thing.'

Moore did know, and it was painful to have a mirror held up to his own behavior. What he saw in that mirror was Saint Thomas the Fallen, brought down by his own desires. And the truth enraged him, because he could not rail against it. He could not deny it. He managed to hold his silence until he walked out of Marquette's office, but when he saw Rizzoli sitting at her desk he could no longer contain his fury.

'Congratulations,' he said. 'You got your payback. Feels good to draw blood, does it?'

'Have I?'

'You told Marquette.'

'Yeah, well, if I did, I wouldn't be the first cop to rat on a partner.'

It was a stinging comeback, and it had its intended effect. In cold silence he turned and walked away.

Stepping out of the building, he paused in the breezeway, desolate at the thought of not seeing Catherine tonight. Yet Marquette was right; this was how it had to be. How it *should* have been from the start, a careful separation between them, the forces of attraction ignored. But she had been vulnerable, and he, foolishly enough, had been drawn to that. After years of walking the straight and narrow, he now found himself in unfamiliar territory, a disturbing place ruled not by logic but by passion. He was not comfortable in this new world. And he did not know how to find his way out of it.

Catherine sat in her car, collecting the courage to walk into One Schroeder Plaza. All afternoon, through a succession of clinic appointments, she'd mouthed the usual pleasantries as she'd examined patients, consulted colleagues, and tackled the minor annoyances that always arose in the course of her workday. But her smiles had been hollow, and beneath her cordial mask had lurked a rip current of despair. Moore was not returning her calls, and she did not know why. Only one night together, and already something had gone wrong between them.

At last she stepped out of the car and walked into Boston Police Headquarters.

Though she had been here once before, for the session with Dr Polochek, the building still seemed like a forbidding fortress where she did not belong. That impression was reinforced by the uniformed officer who eyed her from behind the reception desk.

'Can I help you?' he asked. Neither friendly nor unfriendly.

'I'm looking for Detective Thomas Moore in Homicide.'

'Let me call upstairs. Your name, please?'

'Catherine Cordell.'

As he made the call, she waited in the lobby, feeling overwhelmed by the polished granite, by all the men, both in uniform and in plainclothes, walking past, throwing curious glances her way. This was Moore's universe, and she was a stranger here, trespassing in a place where hard men stared and guns gleamed in holsters. Suddenly she realized this was a mistake, that she should never have come, and she started toward the exit. Just as she reached the door, a voice called out:

'Dr Cordell?'

She turned and recognized the blond man with the mild and pleasant face who had just stepped off the elevator. It was Detective Frost.

'Why don't we go upstairs?' he said.

'I came to see Moore.'

'Yes, I know. I came down to get you.' He motioned toward the elevator. 'Shall we?'

On the second floor, he led her up the hallway, into Homicide. She had not been in this area before, and she was surprised by how much it looked like any business office, with its computer terminals and desks grouped into workpods. He led her to a chair and sat her down. His eyes were kind. He could see she was uncomfortable in this alien place, and he tried to put her at ease.

'A cup of coffee?' he asked.

'No, thank you.'

'Is there anything I can get you? A soda? A glass of water?'

'I'm fine.'

He sat down as well. 'So. What do you need to talk about, Dr Cordell?'

'I was hoping to see Detective Moore. I spent the whole morning in surgery, and I thought that he might have tried to reach me . . .'

'Actually . . .' Frost paused, discomfort plainly in his eyes. 'I left a message with your office staff around noontime. From now on, you should call me with any concerns. Not Detective Moore.'

'Yes, I got that message. I just want to know . . .' She swallowed back tears. 'I want to know why things have changed.'

'It's to, uh, streamline the investigation.'

'What does that mean?'

'We need Moore to focus on other aspects of the case.'

'Who decided that?'

Frost was looking more and more unhappy. 'I don't really know, Dr Cordell.'

'Was it Moore?'

Another pause. 'No.'

'So it's not that he doesn't want to see me.'

'I'm sure that's not the case.'

She did not know if he was telling her the truth or simply trying to soothe her. She noticed that two detectives in another workpod were staring in her direction, and she flushed with sudden anger. Did everyone but her know the truth? Was that pity she saw in their eyes? All morning she had savored the memories of last night. She had waited for Moore to call, had longed to hear his voice and know that he was thinking of her. But he had not called.

And at noon, she'd been handed Frost's telephoned message that in the future she should direct all concerns to him.

It was all she could do now to hold her head up and keep the tears under control as she asked: 'Is there some reason I can't talk to him?'

'I'm afraid he's not in town right now. He left this afternoon.'

'I see.' She understood, without being told, that this was as much as he would reveal. She didn't ask where Moore had gone, nor did she ask how to reach him. Already she had embarrassed herself by coming here, and now pride took over. For the last two years, the sheer force of pride had been her main source of strength. It had kept her marching forward, day after day, refusing to wear the cloak of victimhood. Others looking at her saw only cool competence and emotional distance, because it was all she allowed them to see.

Only Moore saw me as I really am. Damaged and vulnerable. And this is the result. This is why I can't ever be weak again.

When she rose to leave, her spine was straight, her gaze steady. As she walked out of the work-pod, she passed Moore's desk. She knew it was his because of the nameplate. She paused just long enough to focus on the photograph displayed there, of a smiling woman, with the sun in her hair.

She walked out, leaving behind Moore's world, and returned in sorrow to her own.

Eighteen

Moore had thought the heat in Boston was unbearable; he was unprepared to deal with Savannah. Walking out of the airport late that afternoon was like instant submersion in a hot bath, and he felt as though he were wading through liquid, his limbs sluggish as he proceeded toward the rental car parking lot, where watery air rippled above the macadam. By the time he checked into his hotel room, his shirt was drenched in sweat. He stripped off his clothes, lay down on the bed for just a few minutes' rest, and ended up sleeping through the afternoon.

When he awakened, it was dark, and he was shivering in the over-cooled room. He sat up on the side of the bed, his head pounding.

He pulled a fresh shirt from his suitcase, got dressed, and left the hotel.

Even at night, the air was like steam, but he drove with his window open, inhaling the damp smells of the South. Though he'd never been to Savannah before, he'd heard of its charm, its fine old homes and wrought-iron benches and *Midnight in the Garden of Good and Evil*. But tonight he was not on a quest for tourist sites. He was driving to a particular address in the northeast corner of town. It was a pleasant neighborhood of small but tidy homes with front porches and fenced gardens and trees with spreading branches. He found his way to Ronda Street and pulled to a stop in front of the house.

Inside the lights were on, and he could see the blue glow of a TV.

He wondered who lived there now and whether the current occupants knew the history of their house. When they turned off the lights at night and climbed into bed, did they ever think about what had happened in that very room? Lying in the darkness, did they listen for the echoes of terror still reverberating within those walls?

A silhouette moved past the window – a woman's, slender and long-haired. Very much like Catherine's.

He saw it now, in his mind's eye. The young man on the porch, knocking on the front door. The door opening, spilling golden light into the darkness. Catherine standing there, haloed by that light, inviting in the young colleague she knew from the hospital, never suspecting the horrors he had in mind for her.

And the second voice, the second man – where does he come in?

Moore sat for a long time, studying the house, noting the windows and the shrubbery. He stepped out of his car and walked along the sidewalk, to see around the side of the house. The shrubbery was mature and dense, and he could not see past it, into the backyard.

Across the street, a porch light came on.

He turned and saw a stout woman standing at her window, staring at him. She was holding a telephone to her ear.

He got back in his car and drove away. There was one more address he wished to see. It was near the State College, several miles south. He wondered how often Catherine had driven this very road, whether that little pizza shop on the left or that dry-cleaning shop on the right was a place she had frequented. Everywhere he looked, he seemed to see her face, and this disturbed him. It meant he'd allowed his emotions to become entwined in this investigation, and it would serve no one well.

He arrived at the street he'd been looking for. After a few blocks, he stopped at what should have been the address. What he found was merely an empty lot, thick with weeds. He had expected to find a building here, owned by Mrs Stella Poole, a widow, age fifty-eight. Three years ago, Mrs Poole had rented out her upstairs apartment to a surgical intern named Andrew Capra, a quiet young man who always paid his rent on time.

He stepped out of his car and stood on the sidewalk where Andrew Capra had surely walked. He gazed up and down the street that had been Capra's neighborhood. It was only a few blocks from the State College, and he assumed that many of the houses on this street were rented to students – short-term tenants who might not know the story of their infamous neighbor.

A wind stirred the soupy air, and he did not like the smell that arose. It was the damp odor of decay. He looked up at a tree in Andrew Capra's old front yard and saw a clump of Spanish moss drooping from a branch. He shuddered and thought: *Strange fruit*, remembering a grotesque Halloween from his childhood, when a neighbor, thinking it a fine display to scare trick-or-treaters, had tied a rope around a scarecrow's neck and hung it from a tree. Moore's father had been livid when he saw it. Immediately he'd stormed next door and, ignoring the protests of the neighbor, cut down the scarecrow.

Moore felt the same impulse now, to climb into the tree and yank down that dangling moss.

Instead he returned to his car and drove back to the hotel.

Detective Mark Singer set a carton on the table and clapped dust from his hands. 'This is the last one. Took us the weekend to track 'em down, but they're all here.'

Moore eyed the dozen evidence boxes lined up on the table and said, 'I should bring a sleeping bag and just move in.'

Singer laughed. 'Might as well, if you expect to get through every piece of paper in those there boxes. Nothin' leaves the building, okay? Photocopier's down the hall; just log in your name and agency. Bathroom's thataway. Most times, there'll be doughnuts and coffee in the squad room. If you take any doughnuts, the boys'd surely 'preciate it if you'd slip a few bucks in the jar.' Though all this was said with a smile, Moore heard the underlying message in that soft southern drawl: *We have our ground rules, and even you big boys from Boston have to follow them.*

Catherine had not liked this cop, and Moore understood why. Singer was younger than he'd expected, not yet forty, a muscular overachiever who would not take kindly to criticism. There can be only one alpha dog in a pack, and for the moment Moore would let Singer be that dog.

'These here four boxes, they hold the investigation control files,' said Singer. 'Might want to start with 'em. Cross-index files're in that box, action files are in this one here.' He walked along the table, slapping boxes as he spoke. 'And this has the Atlanta files on Dora Ciccone. It's just photocopies.'

'Atlanta PD has those originals?'

Singer nodded. 'First victim, only one he killed there.'

'Since they're photocopies, may I take that box out? Review the documents in my hotel?'

'Long as you bring 'em back.' Singer sighed, looking around at the boxes. 'Y'know, I'm not sure what you think you're lookin' for. Never get a more open-and-shut case. Every one of them, we got Capra's DNA. We got fiber matches. We got the timeline. Capra's living in Atlanta, Dora Ciccone gets killed in Atlanta. He moves to Savannah, our ladies here start turning up dead. He was always in the right place, at the right time.'

'I don't question for a minute that Capra was your man.'

'So why you diggin' through this now? Some of this stuff is three, four years old.'

Moore heard defensiveness in Singer's voice and knew diplomacy was key here. Any hint that

Singer had made mistakes during the Capra investigation, that he'd missed the vital detail that Capra had a partner, and there'd be no hope of cooperation from the Savannah PD.

Moore chose an answer that would in no way cast blame. 'We have a copycat theory,' he said. 'Our unsub in Boston appears to be an admirer of Capra's. He's reproducing his crimes in painstaking detail.'

'How would he know the details?'

'They may have corresponded while Capra was still alive.'

Singer seemed to relax. Even laughed. 'A sick fucker's fan club, huh? Nice.'

'Since our unsub is intimately familiar with Capra's work, I need to be, as well.'

Singer waved at the table. 'Y'all go for it, then.'

After Singer had left the room, Moore surveyed the labels on the evidence boxes. He opened the one marked: IC #1. The Savannah Investigation Control Files. Inside were three accordion file folders, each pocket filled to capacity. And this was just one of four IC boxes. The first accordion folder contained the occurrence reports for the three Savannah attacks, witness statements, and executed warrants. The second accordion folder held suspects files, criminal record checks, and lab reports. There was enough, just in this first box, to keep him reading all day.

And there were eleven more boxes to go.

He started by reviewing Singer's final summary. Once again he was struck by how airtight the evidence was against Andrew Capra. There were a total of five attacks on record, four of them fatal. The first victim was Dora Ciccone, killed in Atlanta. One year later, the murders began in Savannah. Three women in one year: Lisa Fox, Ruth Voorhees, and Jennifer Torregrossa.

The killings ended when Capra was shot to death in Catherine Cordell's bedroom.

In every case, sperm was found in the victim's vaginal vault and the DNA matched Capra's. Hair strands left at the Fox and Torregrossa crime scenes matched Capra's. The first victim, Ciccone, was killed in Atlanta the same year Capra was finishing his final year of medical school in Atlanta's Emory University.

The murders followed Capra to Savannah.

Every thread of evidence wove neatly into a tight pattern, and the fabric appeared indestructible. But Moore realized he was reading only a case summary, which pulled together the elements in favor of Singer's conclusions. Contradictory details might be left out. It was these very details, the small but significant inconsistencies, that he hoped to ferret out of these evidence boxes. Somewhere in here, he thought, the Surgeon has left his footprints.

He opened the first accordion folder and began to read.

When he finally rose from his chair three hours later and stretched the kinks from his back, it was already noon and he had barely begun to scale the mountain of paper. He had not caught even a whiff of the Surgeon's scent. He walked around the table, eyeing the labels on the boxes that had not yet been opened, and spotted one that said:

305

'#12 Fox/Torregrossa/Voorhees/Cordell. Press clippings/Videos/Misc.'

He opened the box and found half a dozen videotapes on top of a thick stack of folders. He took out the video labeled: *Capra Residence*. It was dated June 16. The day after the attack on Catherine.

He found Singer at his desk, eating a sandwich. A deli special, piled high with roast beef. The desk itself told him much about Singer. It was organized to the nth degree, the stacks of papers lined up with corners squared. A cop who was great with details but probably a pain in the ass to work with.

'Is there a VCR I could use?' said Moore.

'We keep it locked up.'

Moore waited, his next request so obvious he didn't bother to voice it. With a dramatic sigh, Singer reached into his desk for the keys and stood up. 'I guess you want it right now, don't you?'

From the storage room, Singer took out the cart with the VCR and TV and rolled it into the room where Moore had been working. He plugged in the cords, pressed the power buttons, and grunted in satisfaction when everything came on.

'Thanks,' said Moore. 'I'll probably need it for a few days.'

'You come up with any big-time revelations yet?' There was no mistaking the note of sarcasm in his voice.

'I'm just getting started.'

'I see you got the Capra video.' Singer shook his head. 'Man, was there weird shit in that house.'

'I drove past the address last night. There's only an empty lot.'

'Building burned down 'bout a year ago. After Capra, the landlady couldn't rent out the upstairs apartment. So she started chargin' for tours, and believe it or not, she got herself a lot of takers. Y'know, the sick as shit Anne Rice crowd, come to worship at the monster's den. Hell, landlady herself was somethin' weird.'

'I'll need to speak to her.'

'Not unless you can talk to the dead.'

'The fire?'

'Crispy critter.' Singer laughed. 'Smokin' is bad for your health. She sure proved it.'

Moore waited until Singer walked out. Then he inserted the 'Capra Residence' tape into the VCR slot.

The first images were exterior, daylight, a view of the front of the house where Capra had lived. Moore recognized the tree in the front yard with the Spanish moss. The house itself was charmless, a two-story box in need of paint. The voice-over of the cameraman gave the date, time, and location. He identified himself as Savannah detective Spiro Pataki. Judging by the quality of daylight, Moore guessed the video had been shot in the early morning. The camera panned the street, and he saw a jogger run past, face turned toward the lens in curiosity. Traffic was heavy (the morning commute hour?) and a few neighbors stood on the sidewalk, staring at the cameraman.

Now the view swung back to the house and approached the front door with handheld jerkiness. Once inside, Detective Pataki briefly panned the first floor, where the landlady, Mrs Poole, lived. Moore glimpsed faded carpets, dark furniture, an ashtray overflowing with cigarettes. The fatal habit of a future crispy critter. The camera moved up some narrow stairs, and through a door with a heavy dead bolt installed, into the upstairs apartment of Andrew Capra.

Moore felt claustrophobic just looking at it. The second floor had been cut into small rooms, and whoever had done this 'renovation' must have gotten a special deal on wood paneling. Every wall was covered in dark veneer. The camera moved up a hallway so narrow it seemed to be burrowing through a tunnel. 'Bedroom on the right,' said Pataki on camera, swinging the lens through the doorway to catch a view of a twin bed, neatly made up, a nightstand, a dresser. All the furniture that would fit in that dim little cave.

'Moving toward the rear living area,' said Pataki as the camera jerked once again into the tunnel. It emerged in a larger room where other people stood around, looking grim. Moore spotted Singer by a closet door. Here's where the action was.

The camera focused on Singer. 'This door was padlocked,' Singer said, pointing to the broken lock. 'We had to pry off the hinges. Inside we found this.' He opened the closet door and yanked on the light chain.

The camera went briefly out of focus, then abruptly sharpened again, the image filling the screen with startling clarity. It was a black-and-white photograph of a woman's face, eyes wide and lifeless, the neck slashed so deeply the tracheal cartilage was laid open.

'I believe this is Dora Ciccone,' said Singer. 'Okay, focus on this one now.'

The camera moved to the right. Another photograph, another woman.

'These appear to be postmortem photos, taken of four different victims. I believe we are looking at the death images of Dora Ciccone, Lisa Fox, Ruth Voorhees, and Jennifer Torregrossa.'

It was Andrew Capra's private photo gallery. A retreat in which to relive the pleasure of his slaughters. What Moore found more disturbing than the images themselves was the remaining blank space on the walls, and the little package of thumbtacks sitting on a shelf. Plenty of room for more.

The camera shifted dizzyingly out of the closet and was once again in the larger room. Slowly Pataki swung around, capturing on camera a couch, a TV, a desk, a phone. Bookshelves filled with medical textbooks. The camera continued its pan until it came to the kitchen area. It focused on the refrigerator.

Moore leaned closer, his throat suddenly dry. He already knew what that refrigerator contained, yet he found his pulse quickening, his stomach turning in dread, as he saw Singer walk to the refrigerator. Singer paused and looked at the camera.

'This is what we found inside,' he said, and opened the door.

Nineteen

He took a walk around the block, and this time he scarcely noticed the heat, he was so chilled by the images on that videotape. He felt relieved just to be out of the conference room, which was now intimately associated with horror. Savannah itself, with its syrupy air and its soft green light, made him uneasy. The city of Boston had sharp edges and jarring voices, every building, every scowling face, in harsh focus. In Boston, you knew you were alive, if only because you were so irritated. Here, nothing seemed in focus. He saw Savannah as though through gauze, a city of genteel smiles and sleepy voices, and he wondered what darkness lay hidden from view.

When he returned to the squad room, he found Singer typing at a laptop. 'Hold on,' said Singer, and he hit Spellcheck. God forbid there be any misspellings in his reports. Satisfied, he looked at Moore. 'Yeah?'

'Did you ever find Capra's address book?'

'What address book?'

'Most people keep a personal address book near their telephone. I didn't see one in the video of his

310

apartment, and I didn't find one on your property list.'

'You're talking over two years ago. If it wasn't on our list, then he didn't have one.'

'Or it was removed from his apartment before you got there.'

'What're you fishing for? I thought you came to study Capra's technique, not solve the case again.'

'I'm interested in Capra's friends. Everyone who knew him well.'

'Hell, no one did. We interviewed the doctors and nurses he worked with. His landlady, the neighbors. I drove out to Atlanta to talk to his aunt. His only living relative.'

'Yes, I read the interviews.'

'Then you know he had 'em all fooled. I kept hearing the same comments: "Compassionate doctor! Such a *polite* young man!"' Singer snorted.

'They had no idea who Capra really was.'

Singer swiveled back to his laptop. 'Hell, no one ever knows who the monsters are.'

Time to view the last videotape. Moore had put this one off till the very end, because he had not been ready to deal with the images. He had managed to watch the others with detachment, taking notes as he studied the bedrooms of Lisa Fox and Jennifer Torregrossa and Ruth Voorhees. He had viewed, again and again, the pattern of blood splatters, the knots in the nylon cord around the victims' wrists, the glaze of death in their eyes. He could look at the tapes with a minimum of emotion because he did not know these women and he heard no echo of their voices in his memory. He was focused not on the victims but on the malevolent presence that had passed through their rooms. He ejected the tape of the Voorhees crime scene and set it on the table. Reluctantly he picked up the remaining tape. On the label was the date, the case number, and the words: 'Catherine Cordell Residence.'

He thought about putting it off, waiting until tomorrow morning, when he'd be fresh. It was now nine o'clock, and he had been in this room all day. He held the tape, weighing what to do.

It was a moment before he realized Singer was standing in the doorway, watching him.

'Man. You're still here,' said Singer.

'I've got a lot to go over.'

'You watched all the tapes?'

'All except this one.'

Singer glanced at the label. 'Cordell.'

'Yeah.'

'Go ahead; play it. Maybe I can fill in a few details.'

Moore inserted it into the VCR slot and pressed Play. They were looking at the front of Catherine's house. Night-time. The porch was lit up and the lights all on inside. On audio, he heard the videographer give the date and time – 2:00 A.M. – and his name. Again, it was Spiro Pataki, who seemed to be everyone's favorite cameraman. Moore heard a lot of background noise – voices, the fading wail of a siren. Pataki did his routine pan of the surroundings, and Moore saw a grim gathering of neighbors staring over crime scene tape, their faces illuminated by the lights of several police cruisers parked on the street. This surprised him, knowing the hour of night. It must have been a considerable disturbance to awaken so many neighbors.

Pataki turned back to the house and approached the front door.

'Gunshots,' said Singer. 'That's the initial report we got. The woman across the street heard the first shot, then a long pause, and then a second shot. She called nine-one-one. First officer on the scene was there in seven minutes. Ambulance was called two minutes later.'

Moore remembered the woman across the street, staring at him through her window.

'I read the neighbor's statement,' said Moore. 'She said she didn't see anyone come out the front door of the house.'

'That's right. Just heard the two shots. She got out of bed after the first one, looked out the window. Then, maybe five minutes later, she heard the second gunshot.'

Five minutes, thought Moore. What accounted for the gap?

On the screen, the camera entered the front door and was now just inside the house. Moore saw a closet, the door opened to reveal a few coats on hangers, an umbrella, a vacuum cleaner. The view shifted now, sweeping around to show the living room. On the coffee table next to the couch sat two drinking glasses, one of them still containing what looked like beer.

'Cordell invited him inside,' said Singer. 'They had a few drinks. She went to the bathroom, came back, finished her beer. Within an hour the Rohypnol took effect.'

The couch was peach-colored, with a subtle floral design woven into the fabric. Moore did not see Catherine as a floral-fabric kind of woman, but there it was. Flowers on the curtains, on the cushions in the end chair. Color. In Savannah, she had lived with lots of color. He imagined her sitting on that couch with Andrew Capra, listening sympathetically to his concerns about work, as the Rohypnol slowly passed from her stomach into her bloodstream. As the drug's molecules swirled their way toward her brain. As Capra's voice began to fade away.

They were moving into the kitchen now, the camera making a sweep of the house, recording every room as they'd found it at two o'clock on that Saturday morning. In the kitchen sink sat a single water glass.

Suddenly Moore leaned forward. 'That glass – you have DNA analysis on the saliva?'

'Why would we?'

'You don't know who drank from it?'

'There were only two people in the house when the first officer responded. Capra and Cordell.'

'Two glasses were on the coffee table. Who drank from this third glass?'

'Hell, it could've been in that kitchen sink all day. It was not relevant to the situation we found.'

The cameraman finished his sweep of the kitchen and now turned up the hallway.

Moore grabbed the remote control and pressed Rewind. He backed up the tape to the beginning of the kitchen segment.

'What?' said Singer.

Moore didn't answer. He leaned closer, watching the images play once again on the screen. The refrigerator, dotted with bright magnets in the shapes of fruits. The flour and sugar canisters on the kitchen counter. The sink, with the single water glass. Then the camera swept past the kitchen door, toward the hallway.

Moore hit Rewind again.

'What are you looking at?' Singer asked.

The tape was back at the water glass. The camera started its pan toward the hallway. Moore hit Pause. 'This,' he said. 'The kitchen door. Where does it lead?'

'Uh – the backyard. Opens to a lawn.'

'And what's beyond that backyard?'

'Adjoining yard. Another row of houses.'

'Did you talk to the owner of that adjoining yard? Did he or she hear the gunshots?'

'What difference does it make?'

Moore rose and went to the monitor. 'The kitchen door,' he said, tapping on the screen. 'There's a chain. It isn't fastened.'

Singer paused. 'But the door's locked. See the position of the knob button?'

'Right. It's the kind of button you can push on your way out, locking the door behind you.'

'And your point is?'

'Why would she push that button but not fasten the chain? People who lock up for the night do it all at once. They press in the button, slide in the chain. She left out that second step.'

'Maybe she just forgot.'

'There'd been three women murdered in

315

Savannah. She was worried enough to keep a gun under her bed. I don't think she'd forget.' He looked at Singer. 'Maybe someone walked *out* that kitchen door.'

'There were only two people in that house. Cordell and Capra.'

Moore considered what he should say next. Whether he had more to gain or lose if he was perfectly forthright.

By now Singer knew where this conversation was headed. 'You're sayin' Capra had a partner.'

'Yes.'

'That's a mighty big conclusion to draw from one unlocked chain.'

Moore took a breath. 'There's more. The night Catherine Cordell was attacked, she heard another voice in her house. A man, speaking to Capra.'

'She never told me that.'

'It came out during a forensic hypnosis session.'

Singer burst out laughing. 'Did you get a psychic to back that up? 'Cause then I'd really be convinced.'

'It explains why the Surgeon knows so much about Capra's technique. The two men were partners. And the Surgeon is carrying on the legacy, to the point of stalking their only surviving victim.'

'The world's full of women. Why focus on her?'

'Unfinished business.'

'Yeah, well, I got a better theory.' Singer rose from his chair. 'Cordell forgot to lock the chain on her kitchen door. Your boy in Boston is copying what he read in the newspapers. And your forensic hypnotist pulled up a false memory.' Shaking his head, he started toward the door. Tossed back a sarcastic parting shot: 'Let me know when you catch the *real* killer.'

Moore allowed the exchange to bother him only briefly. He knew Singer was defending his own work on the case, and he could not blame him for being skeptical. He was beginning to wonder about his own instincts. He had come all the way to Savannah to either prove or disprove the partner theory, and thus far he had nothing to back it up.

He focused his attention on the TV screen and pressed Play.

The camera left the kitchen, advanced up the hallway. A pause to look into the bathroom – pink towels, a shower curtain with multicolored fish. Moore's hands were sweating. He dreaded watching what came next, but he could not tear his gaze from the screen. The camera turned from the bathroom and continued up the hallway, past a framed watercolor of pink peonies hanging on the wall. On the wood floor, bloody shoeprints had been smeared and tracked over by the first officers on the scene and later by frantic paramedics. What was left was a confusing abstract in red. A doorway loomed ahead, the view jiggling in an unsteady hand.

Now the camera moved into the bedroom.

Moore felt his stomach turn, not because what he was staring at was any more shocking than other crime scenes he had witnessed. No, this horror was deeply visceral because he knew, and cared deeply about, the woman who had suffered here. He had studied the still photos of this room, but they did not convey the same lurid quality as this video. Even though Catherine was not in the frame – by this time she had already been taken to the hospital – the evidence of her ordeal shouted at him from the TV screen. He saw the nylon cord, which had bound her wrists and ankles, still attached to the four bedposts. He saw surgical instruments – a scalpel and retractors – left on the nightstand. He saw all this and the impact was so powerful that he actually swayed back in his chair, as though shoved by a fist.

When the camera lens shifted, at last, to Andrew Capra's body lying on the floor, he felt barely a twitch of emotion; he was already numbed by what he'd seen seconds earlier. Capra's abdominal wound had bled profusely, and a large pool had collected beneath his torso. The second bullet, into his eye, had inflicted the fatal wound. He remembered the five-minute gap between the two gunshots. The image he saw reinforced that timeline. Judging by the amount of pooling, Capra had lain alive and bleeding for at least a few minutes.

The videotape came to an end.

He stared at the blank screen, then stirred from his paralysis and turned off the VCR. He felt too drained to rise from the chair. When at last he did, it was only to escape this place. He picked up the box containing the photocopied documents from the Atlanta investigation. Since these papers were not originals but copies of documents on file in Atlanta, he could review them elsewhere.

Back in his hotel, he showered, ate a room-service hamburger and fries. Gave himself an hour with the TV to decompress. But the whole time he sat flipping between channels, what his hand really itched to do was call Catherine. Watching the last crime scene video had brought home exactly what sort of monster now stalked her, and he could not rest easy.

Twice he picked up the phone and put it down again. He picked it up yet again, and this time his fingers moved of their own accord, punching in a number he knew so well. Four rings, and he got Catherine's answering machine.

He hung up without leaving a message.

He stared at the phone, ashamed by how easily his resolve had crumbled. He had promised himself to hold fast, had agreed to Marquette's demand that he maintain his distance from Catherine for the duration of the investigation. *When all this is over, somehow I will make things right between us.*

He looked at the stack of Atlanta documents on the desk. It was midnight and he had not even started. With a sigh, he opened the first file from the Atlanta box.

The case of Dora Ciccone, Andrew Capra's first victim, did not make for appetizing reading. He already knew the general details; they'd been summarized in Singer's final report. But Moore had not read the raw reports from Atlanta, and now he was going back in time, examining the earliest work of Andrew Capra. This was where it all started. In Atlanta.

He read the initial crime report, then progressed through files of interviews. He read statements from Ciccone's neighbors, from the bartender in the local watering hole where she was last seen alive, and from the girlfriend who discovered the body. There was also a file with a list of suspects and their photographs; Capra was not among them.

Dora Ciccone was a twenty-two-year-old grad student at Emory. On the night of her death, she was last seen around midnight, sipping a Margarita at La Cantina. Forty hours later, her body was discovered in her home, nude and tied to the bed with nylon cord. Her uterus had been removed and her neck slashed.

He found the police timeline. It was only a rough sketch in barely legible writing, as though the Atlanta detective had put it together merely to satisfy some internal checklist. He could almost smell failure in these pages, could read it in the depressive droop of the detective's handwriting. He himself had experienced that heavy feeling that builds in your chest as you pass the twenty-four-hour mark, then a week, then a month, and you still have no tangible leads. This was what the Atlanta detective had – nothing. Dora Ciccone's killer remained an unknown subject.

He opened the autopsy report.

The butchery of Dora Ciccone had been neither as swift nor as skillful as Capra's later killings. Incisional jags indicated Capra lacked the confidence to make a single clean cut across the lower abdomen. Instead he had hesitated, his blade backtracking, macerating the skin. Once through the skin layer, the procedure degenerated to amateurish hacking, the blade deeply nicking both bladder and bowel as he excavated his prize.

On this, his first victim, no suture was used to tie off any arteries. The bleeding was profuse, and Capra would have been working blind, his anatomical landmarks submerged in an ever-deepening pool of crimson.

Only the coup de grace was performed with any skill. It had been done in one clean slash, left to right, as though, with his hunger now sated and the frenzy fading, he was finally in control and could finish the job with cold efficiency.

Moore set aside the autopsy report and confronted the remains of his dinner, sitting on a tray beside him. Suddenly queasy, he carried the tray to the door and set it outside in the hall. Then he returned to the desk and opened the next folder, which contained the crime lab reports.

The first sheet was a microscopic: *Spermatozoa identified in swab from victim's vaginal vault.*

He knew that DNA analysis of this sperm later confirmed it was Capra's. Prior to killing Dora Ciccone, he had raped her.

Moore turned to the next page and found a bundle of reports from Hair and Fiber. The victim's pubic area had been combed and the hairs examined. Among the samples was a reddish-brown pubic hair that matched Capra's. He flipped through the next few pages of Hair and Fiber reports, which examined various stray hairs found at the crime scene. Most of the samples were from the victim herself, either pubic or head hairs. There was also a short blond strand retrieved from the blanket, later identified as non-human, based on the complex structural pattern of the medulla. A handwritten addendum said:

'Vic's mother owns Golden Retriever. Similar hairs found on backseat of vic's car.'

He turned to the last page from Hair and Fiber, and stopped. It was an analysis of yet another hair, this one human but never identified. It had been found on the pillow. In any home, a variety of stray hairs can be found. Humans shed dozens of hairs a day, and depending on how fastidious a housekeeper you are and how often you vacuum, blankets and carpets and couches accumulate a microscopic record of every visitor who has ever spent significant time in your home. This single hair, found on the pillow, could have come from a lover, a house-guest, a relative. It was not Andrew Capra's.

Single human head hair, light brown, A0 (curved), shaft length: 5 centimeters. Telogen phase. Trichorrhexis invaginata noted. Unidentified origin.

Trichorrhexis invaginata. Bamboo hair.
The Surgeon was there.
He sat back, stunned. Earlier that day he had read the Savannah lab reports for Fox, Voorhees, Torregrossa, and Cordell. In none of those crime scenes had a hair with *Trichorrhexis invaginata* been found.

But Capra's partner had been there all along. He had remained invisible, leaving no semen, no DNA, behind. The only evidence of his presence was this single strand of hair, and Catherine's buried memory of his voice.

Their partnership began with the very first killing. In Atlanta.

322

Twenty

Peter Falco was up to his elbows in blood. He glanced up from the table as Catherine pushed into the trauma room. Whatever tensions had grown between them, whatever uneasiness she felt in Peter's presence, were instantly shoved aside. They had assumed the roles of two professionals working together in the heat of battle.

'Another one coming in!' said Peter. 'That makes four. They're still cutting him out of the car.'

Blood spurted from the incision. He grabbed a clamp from the tray and thrust it into the open abdomen.

'I'll assist,' said Catherine, and broke the tape seal on a sterile gown.

'No, I can handle this. Kimball needs you in Room Two.'

As if to emphasize his statement, an ambulance wail pierced the hubbub of the room.

'That one's yours,' said Falco. 'Have fun.'

Catherine ran out to the ambulance loading dock. Already, Dr Kimball and two nurses were waiting outside as the beeping vehicle backed up.

Even before Kimball yanked the ambulance door open, they could hear the patient screaming.

He was a young man, tattoos mapping his arms and shoulders. He thrashed and cursed as the crew rolled out his stretcher. Catherine took one glance at the blood-soaked sheet covering his lower extremities and knew why he was shrieking.

'We gave him a ton of morphine at the scene,' said the paramedic as they wheeled him into Trauma Two. 'Didn't seem to touch him!'

'How much?' said Catherine.

'Forty, forty-five milligrams IV. We stopped when his BP started dropping.'

'Transfer on my count!' said a nurse. 'One, two, three!'

'Jesus fucking *CHRIST! IT HURTS!*'

'I know, sweetie; I know.'

'You don't know a FUCKING THING!'

'You'll feel better in a minute. What's your name, son?'

'Rick . . . Oh Jesus, my leg—'

'Rick what?'

'Roland!'

'Do you have any allergies, Rick?'

'What's wrong with you *FUCKING PEOPLE?*'

'We have vitals?' cut in Catherine as she pulled on gloves.

'BP one-oh-two over sixty. Pulse a hundred thirty.'

'Ten milligrams morphine, IV push,' said Kimball.

'*SHIT! GIMME A HUNDRED!*'

As the rest of the staff scurried around drawing bloods and hanging IV bags, Catherine peeled back the blood-soaked sheet and caught her breath when she saw the emergency tourniquet tied around what was barely recognizable as a limb. 'Give him thirty,' she said. The lower right leg was attached by only a few shreds of skin. The nearly severed limb was a pulpy red mass, the foot twisted nearly backward.

She touched the toes and they were stone cold; of course there would be no pulse.

'They said the artery was pumping out,' said the paramedic. 'First cop on the scene put on the tourniquet.'

'That cop saved his life.'

'Morphine's in!'

Catherine directed the light onto the wound. 'Looks like the popliteal nerve and artery are both severed. He's lost vascular supply to this leg.' She looked at Kimball, and they both understood what had to be done.

'Let's get him to O.R.,' said Catherine. 'He's stable enough to be moved. That'll free up this trauma room.'

'Just in time,' said Kimball as they heard another ambulance siren wailing closer. He turned to leave.

'Hey. *Hey!*' The patient grabbed Kimball's arm. 'Aren't you the doctor? It fucking *hurts!* Tell these bitches to *do something!*'

Kimball shot Catherine a wry look. And he said, 'Be nice to 'em, bud. These bitches are running the show.'

Amputation was not a choice Catherine ever made lightly. If a limb could be saved, she would do everything in her power to reattach it. But when she stood in the O.R. a half hour later, scalpel in hand, and looked down at what remained of her patient's right leg, the choice was obvious. The calf was macerated and both the tibia and fibula crushed to splinters. Judging by the uninjured left leg, his right limb had once been well formed and muscular, a leg deeply bronzed by the sun. The bare foot – strangely intact despite the shocking angle at which it pointed – had the tan lines of sandal straps, and there was sand under the toenails. She did not like this patient and had not appreciated his cursing or the insults he'd hurled in his pain at her and the other women on the hospital staff, but as her scalpel sliced through his flesh, shaping a posterior skin flap, as she sawed off the sharp edges of the fractured tibia and fibula, she worked with a sense of sadness.

The O.R. nurse removed the severed leg from the table and wrapped a drape over it. A foot that had once savored the warmth of beach sand would soon be reduced to ash, cremated with all the other sacrificed organs and limbs that found their way to the hospital's pathology department.

The operation left Catherine depressed and drained. When at last she stripped off her gloves and gown and walked out of the O.R., she was not in any mood to see Jane Rizzoli waiting for her.

She went to the sink to wash the smell of talc and latex from her hands. 'It's midnight, Detective. Don't you ever sleep?'

'Probably about as much as you do. I have some questions for you.'

'I thought you were no longer on the case.'

'I'll never be off this case. No matter what any-one says.'

Catherine dried her hands and turned to look at Rizzoli. 'You don't like me much, do you?'

'Whether or not I like you isn't important.'

'Was it something I said to you? Something I did?'

'Look, are you finished up here for the night?'

'It's because of Moore, isn't it? That's why you resent me.'

Rizzoli's jaw squared. 'Detective Moore's personal life is his business.'

'But you don't approve.'

'He never asked my opinion.'

'Your opinion's clear enough.'

Rizzoli eyed her with undisguised distaste. 'I used to admire Moore. I thought he was one of a kind. A cop who never crossed the line. It turns out he's no better than anyone else. What I can't believe is that the reason he messed up was a woman.'

Catherine pulled off her O.R. cap and dropped it in the rubbish bin. 'He knows it was a mistake,' she said, and she pushed out of the O.R. wing, into the hallway.

Rizzoli followed her. 'Since when?'

'Since he left town without a word. I guess I was just a temporary lapse in judgement for him.'

'Is that what he was for you? A lapse in *your* judgement?'

Catherine stood in the hallway, blinking away tears. *I don't know. I don't know what to think*.

'You seem to be at the center of everything, Dr Cordell. You're right up there onstage, the focus of

327

everyone's attention. Moore's. The Surgeon's.'

Catherine turned in anger to Rizzoli. 'You think I want any of this? I never asked to be a victim!'

'But it keeps happening to you, doesn't it? There's some kind of weird bond between you and the Surgeon. I didn't see it at first. I thought he killed those other victims to play out his sick fantasies. Now I think it was all about you. He's like a cat, killing birds and bringing them home to his mistress, to prove his worth as a hunter. Those victims were offerings meant to impress you. The more scared you get, the more successful he feels. That's why he waited to kill Nina Peyton until she was in this hospital, under your care. He wanted you to witness his skill firsthand. You're his obsession. I want to know why.'

'He's the only one who can answer that.'

'You have no idea?'

'How could I? I don't even know who he is.'

'He was in your house with Andrew Capra. If what you said under hypnosis is true.'

'Andrew was the only one I saw that night. Andrew's the only one . . .' She stopped. 'Maybe *I'm* not his real obsession, Detective. Have you thought about that? Maybe *Andrew* is.'

Rizzoli frowned, struck by that statement. Catherine suddenly realized that she had hit on the truth. The center of the Surgeon's universe was not her but Andrew Capra. The man he emulated, perhaps even worshiped. The partner Catherine had wrenched from him.

She glanced up as her name was called over the hospital address system.

'Dr Cordell, STAT, E.R. Dr Cordell, STAT, E.R.'

God, will they never leave me alone?

She punched the Down button for the elevator.

'Dr Cordell?'

'I don't have time for any of your questions. I have patients to see.'

'When will you have the time?'

The door slid open and Catherine stepped in, the weary soldier called back to the front lines. 'My night's just begun.'

By their blood will I know them.

I survey the racks of test tubes the way one lusts over chocolates in a box, wondering which will be tastiest. Our blood is as unique as we are, and my naked eye discerns varying shades of red, from bright cardinal to black cherry. I am familiar with what gives us this broad palette of colors; I know the red is from hemoglobin, in varying states of oxygenation. It is chemistry, nothing more, but ah, such chemistry has the power to shock, to horrify. We are all moved by the sight of blood.

Even though I see it every day, it never fails to thrill me.

I look over the racks with a hungry gaze. The tubes have come from all over the greater Boston area, funneled in from doctors' offices and clinics and the hospital next door. We are the largest diagnostic lab in the city. Anywhere in Boston, should you open your arm to the phlebotomist's needle, the chances are your blood will find its way here. To me.

I log in the first rack of specimens. On each tube is a label with the patient's name, the doctor's name, and the date. Next to the rack is the bundle of accompanying requisition forms. It is the forms I reach for, and I flip through them, scanning the names.

Halfway through the stack, I stop. I am looking at a requisition for Karen Sobel, age twenty-five, who lives at 7536 Clark Road in Brookline. She is Caucasian and unmarried. All this I know because it appears on the form, along with her Social Security number and employer's name and insurance carrier.

The doctor has requested two blood tests: an HIV screen, and a VDRL, for syphilis.

On the line for diagnosis, the doctor has written: 'Sexual assault.'

In the rack, I find the tube containing Karen Sobel's blood. It is a deep and somber red, the blood of a wounded beast. I hold it in my hand, and as it warms to my touch, I see her, feel her, this woman named Karen. Broken and stumbling. Waiting to be claimed.

Then I hear a voice that startles me, and I look up.

Catherine Cordell has just walked into my lab.

She is standing so close, I can almost reach out and touch her. I am stunned to see her here, especially at this remote hour between darkness and dawn. Seldom do any physicians venture into our basement world, and to see her now is an unexpected thrill, as arresting as the vision of Persephone descending into Hades.

I wonder what has brought her. Then I see her hand several tubes of straw-colored fluid to the technician at the next bench, and hear the words 'pleural effusion,' and I understand why she has

330

deigned to visit us. Like many physicians, she does not trust the hospital couriers with certain precious body fluids, and she has personally carried the tubes down the tunnel that connects Pilgrim Hospital with the Interpath Labs building.

I watch her walk away. She passes right by my bench. Her shoulders sag, and she sways, her legs wobbly, as though she is struggling through deep mud. Fatigue and the fluorescent lights make her skin look like little more than a milky wash over the fine bones of her face. She vanishes out the door, never knowing that I've been watching her.

I look down at Karen Sobel's tube, which I am still holding, and suddenly the blood seems dull and lifeless. A prey not even worth the hunt. Not when compared to what has just walked past me.

I can still smell Catherine's scent.

I log onto the computer, and under 'doctor's name' I type: 'C. Cordell.' On the screen appear all the lab tests she has ordered in the last twenty-four hours. I see that she has been in the hospital since 10:00 P.M. It is now 5:30 A.M., and a Friday. She faces a whole clinic day ahead of her.

My workday is now coming to an end.

When I step out of the building, it is 7:00 A.M., and the morning sunlight slices straight into my eyes. Already the day is warm. I walk to the medical center parking garage, take the elevator to the fifth level, and head along the row of cars to stall # 541, where her car is parked. It is a lemon-yellow Mercedes, this year's model. She keeps it sparkling clean.

I take the key ring from my pocket, the ring I

have been guarding for two weeks now, and slip one of the keys into her trunk lock.

The trunk pops open.

I glance inside and spot the trunk release lever, an excellent safety feature to prevent children from being accidentally locked inside.

Another car growls up the garage ramp. I quickly close the Mercedes trunk and walk away.

For ten brutal years, the Trojan War waged on. The virgin blood of Iphigenia that was spilled upon the altar at Aulis had sped the thousand Greek ships on a fair wind toward Troy, but a swift victory did not await the Greeks, for on Olympus the gods were divided. On Troy's side stood Aphrodite and Ares, Apollo and Artemis. On the Greek side stood Hera and Athena and Poseidon. Victory fluttered from one side to the other and back again, as fickle as the breezes. Heroes slew and were slain, and the poet Virgil says the earth streamed with blood.

In the end, it was not force but cunning that brought Troy to her knees. On the dawn of Troy's last day, her soldiers awakened to the sight of a great wooden horse, abandoned at her scaean gates.

When I think of the Trojan Horse, I am puzzled by the foolishness of Troy's soldiers. As they wheeled the behemoth into the city, how could they not know the enemy was burrowed within? Why did they bring it within the city walls? Why did they spend that night in revels, clouding their minds in drunken celebration of victory? I like to think I would have known better.

Perhaps it was their impregnable walls that lulled them into complacency. Once the gates are closed, and the barricades are tight, how can the enemy attack? He is shut out, beyond those walls.

No one stops to consider the possibility that the enemy is inside the gates. That he is right there, beside you.

I am thinking of the wooden horse as I stir cream and sugar into my coffee.

I pick up the telephone.

'Surgery office; this is Helen,' the receptionist answers.

'Could I see Dr Cordell this afternoon?' I ask.

'Is it an emergency?'

'Not really. I've got this soft lump on my back. It doesn't hurt, but I want her to look at it.'

'I could fit you into her schedule in about two weeks.'

'Can't I see her this afternoon? After her last appointment?'

'I'm sorry, Mr – what is your name, please?'

'Mr Troy.'

'Mr Troy. But Dr Cordell's booked until five o'clock, and she's going right home after that. Two weeks is the best I can do.'

'Never mind then. I'll try another doctor.'

I hang up. I know now that sometime after five o'clock, she will walk out of her office. She is tired; surely she will drive straight home.

It is now 9:00 A.M. This will be a day of waiting, of anticipation. For ten bloody years, the Greeks laid siege to Troy. For ten years, they persevered, flinging themselves against the enemy's walls, as their fortunes rose and fell with the favor of the gods.

I have waited only two years to claim my prize. It has been long enough.

Twenty-one

The secretary in the Emory University Medical School Office of Student Affairs was a Doris Day lookalike, a sunny blonde who'd matured into a gracious southern matron. Winnie Bliss kept a coffeepot brewing by the students' mail slots and a crystal bowl of butterscotch candies on her desk, and Moore could imagine how a stressed-out medical student might find this room a welcome retreat. Winnie had worked in this office for twenty years, and since she had no children of her own, she'd focused her maternal impulses on the students who visited this office every day to pick up their mail. She fed them cookies, passed along tips about apartment vacancies, counseled them through bad love affairs and failing test scores. And every year, at graduation, she shed tears because 110 of her children were leaving her. All this she told Moore in a soft Georgia accent as she plied him with cookies and poured him coffee, and he believed her. Winnie Bliss was all magnolia and no steel.

'I couldn't believe it when the Savannah police called me two years ago,' she said, settling gracefully into her chair. 'I told them it had to be a mistake. I saw Andrew come into this office every day for his mail, and he was just about the nicest boy you could hope to meet. Polite, never a bad word from that boy's lips. I make a point of looking people in the eye, Detective Moore, just to let them know I'm really *seeing* them. And I saw a good boy in Andrew's eyes.'

A testament, thought Moore, to how easily we are deceived by evil.

'During the four years Capra was a student here, do you remember any close friendships he had?' Moore asked.

'You mean, like a sweetheart?'

'I'm more interested in his male friends. I spoke to his ex-landlady here in Atlanta. She said there was a young man who occasionally visited Capra. She thought he was another medical student.'

Winnie rose to her feet and crossed to the filing cabinet, where she retrieved a computer printout. 'This is the class roster for Andrew's year. There were one hundred ten students in his freshman class. About half of them were men.'

'Did he have any close friends among them?'

She scanned the three pages of names and shook her head. 'I'm sorry. I just don't recall anyone on this list being particularly close to him.'

'Are you saying he didn't have any friends?'

'I'm saying I don't *know* of any friends.'

'May I see the list?'

She handed it to him. He went down the page but saw no name except Capra's that struck him as familiar. 'Do you know where all these students are living now?'

'Yes. I update their mailing addresses for the alumni newsletter.'

'Are any of them in the Boston area?'

'Let me check.' She swiveled to face her computer, and her polished pink nails clicked on the keys. Winnie Bliss's innocence made her seem like a woman from an older, more gracious era, and it struck him as odd to watch her navigating computer files with such skill. 'There's one in Newton, Massachusetts. Is that close to Boston?'

'Yes.' Moore leaned forward, his pulse suddenly quickening. 'What's his name?'

'It's a she. Latisha Green. Very nice girl. She used to bring me these big bags of pecans. Course, it was really naughty of her, since she knew I was watching my figure, but I think she liked to feed people. It was just her way.'

'Was she married? Did she have a boyfriend?'

'Oh, she has a *wonderful* husband! Biggest man I ever did see! Six foot five, with this beautiful black skin.'

'Black,' he repeated.

'Yes. Pretty as patent leather.'

Moore sighed and looked back at the list. 'And there's no one else from Capra's class living near Boston, as far as you know?'

'Not according to my list.' She turned to him. 'Oh. You look disappointed.' She said it with a note of distress, as though she felt personally responsible for failing him.

'I'm batting a lot of zeros today,' he admitted.

'Have a candy.'

'Thank you, but no.'

'Watching your weight, too?'

'I don't have a sweet tooth.'

'Then you are clearly *not* a southerner, Detective.'

He couldn't help laughing. Winnie Bliss, with her wide eyes and soft voice, had charmed him, as she surely charmed every student, male and female, who walked into her office. His gaze lifted to the wall behind her, hung with a series of group photographs. 'Are those the medical school classes?'

She turned to look at the wall. 'I have my husband take one every graduation. It's not an easy thing, to get those students together. It's like herding cats, my husband likes to say. But I want that picture, and I *make 'em* do it. Aren't they just the nicest group of young people?'

'Which is Andrew Capra's graduating class?'

'I'll show you the yearbook. It has the names, too.' She rose and went to a bookcase covered with glass doors. With reverence she removed a slim volume from the shelf and lightly ran her hand across the cover, as though to brush away dust. 'This is the year Andrew graduated. It has pictures of all his classmates, and tells you where they were accepted for internship.' She paused, then held out the book to him. 'It's my only copy. So please, if you could just look at it here, and not take it out?'

'I'll sit right over there in that corner, out of your way. You can keep an eye on me. How about that?'

'Oh, I'm not sayin' I don't trust you!'

'Well, you shouldn't,' he said, and winked. She blushed like a schoolgirl.

He took the book over to the corner of the room, where the coffeepot and a plate of cookies were set in the small sitting area. He sank into a worn easy chair and opened the Emory Medical School student yearbook. The noon hour came, and a parade of fresh-faced students in white coats began dropping in to check their mail. Since when had kids become doctors? He could not imagine submitting his middle-aged body to the care of these youngsters. He saw their curious glances, heard Winnie Bliss whisper: 'He's a *homicide* detective, from Boston.' Yes, that decrepit old man sitting in the corner.

Moore hunched deeper into the chair and focused on the photos. Next to each was the student's name, hometown, and the internship he or she had been accepted to. When he came to Capra's photo, he paused. Capra looked straight at the camera, a smiling young man with an earnest gaze, hiding nothing. This was what Moore found most chilling – that predators walked unrecognized among prey.

Next to Capra's photo was the name of his residency program. *Surgery, Riverland Medical Center, Savannah, Georgia.*

He wondered who else from Capra's class had gone to a residency in Savannah, who else had lived in that town while Capra was butchering women. He flipped through the pages, scanning the listings, and found that three other medical students had been accepted into programs in the Savannah area. Two of them were women; the third was an Asian male.

Yet another blind alley.

He leaned back, discouraged. The book fell open in his lap, and he saw the medical school dean's photograph smiling up at him. Beneath it was his printed graduation message: 'To heal The World.'

Today, 108 fine young people take the solemn oath that completes a long and difficult journey. This oath, as physician and healer, is not taken lightly, for it is meant to last a lifetime . . .

Moore sat up straight and re-read the dean's statement.

Today, 108 fine young people . . .

He rose and went to Winnie's desk. 'Mrs Bliss?'

'Yes, Detective?'

'You said that Andrew had one hundred ten students in his freshman class.'

'We admit one hundred ten every year.'

'Here, in the dean's speech, he says one hundred eight graduated. What happened to the other two?'

Winnie shook her head sadly. 'I still haven't gotten over it, what happened to that poor girl.'

'Which girl?'

'Laura Hutchinson. She was working in a clinic down in Haiti. One of our elective courses. The roads there, well, I hear they're just awful. The truck went into a ditch and turned right over on her.'

'So it was an accident.'

'She was riding in the back of the truck. They couldn't evacuate her for ten hours.'

340

'What about the other student? There's one more who didn't graduate with the class.'

Winnie's gaze fell to her desk, and he could see she was not anxious to talk about this particular topic.

'Mrs Bliss?'

'It happens, every so often,' she said. 'A student drops out. We try to help them stay in the program, but you know, some of them *do* have problems with the material.'

'So this student – what was the name?'

'Warren Hoyt.'

'He dropped out?'

'Yes, you could say that.'

'Was it an academic problem?'

'Well . . .' She looked around, as though seeking help and not finding any. 'Perhaps you should talk to one of our professors, Dr Kahn. He'll be able to answer your questions.'

'You don't know the answer?'

'It's something of a . . . private matter. Dr Kahn should be the one to tell you.'

Moore glanced at his watch. He had thought to catch a plane back to Savannah tonight, but it didn't look like he would make it. 'Where do I find Dr Kahn?'

'The anatomy lab.'

He could smell the formalin from the hallway. Moore paused outside the door labeled *ANATOMY*, bracing himself for what came next. Though he thought he was prepared, when he stepped through the door he was momentarily stunned by the view. Twenty-eight tables, laid out in four rows, stretched the length of the room. On the tables were corpses in advanced stages of dissection. Unlike the corpses Moore was accustomed to viewing in the Medical Examiner's lab, these bodies looked artificial, the skin tough as vinyl, the exposed vessels embalmed bright blue or red. Today the students were focusing on the heads, teasing apart the muscles of the face. There were four students assigned to each corpse, and the room was abuzz with voices reading aloud to one another from textbooks, trading questions, offering advice. If not for the ghastly subjects on the table, these students might be factory workers, laboring over mechanical parts.

A young woman glanced up curiously at Moore, the business-suited stranger who had wandered into their room. 'Are you looking for someone?' she asked, her scalpel poised to slice into a corpse's cheek.

'Dr Kahn.'

'He's at the other end of the room. See that big guy with the white beard?'

'I see him, thank you.' He continued down the row of tables, his gaze inexorably drawn to each cadaver as he passed. The woman with wasted limbs like shriveled sticks on the steel table. The black man, skin splayed open to reveal the thick muscles of his thigh. At the end of the row, a group of students listened attentively to a Santa Claus lookalike who was pointing out the delicate fibers of the facial nerve.

'Dr Kahn?' said Moore.

Kahn glanced up, and all semblance to Santa Claus vanished. This man had dark, intense eyes, without a trace of humor. 'Yes?'

'I'm Detective Moore. Mrs Bliss in Student Affairs sent me.'

Kahn straightened, and suddenly Moore was looking up at a mountain of a man. The scalpel looked incongruously delicate in his huge hand. He set the instrument down, stripped off his gloves. As he turned to wash his hands in a sink, Moore saw that Kahn's white hair was tied back in a ponytail.

'So what's this all about?' asked Kahn, reaching for a paper towel.

'I have a few questions about a freshman medical student you taught here seven years ago. Warren Hoyt.'

Kahn's back was turned, but Moore could see the massive arm freeze over the sink, dripping water. Then Kahn yanked the paper towel from the dispenser and silently dried his hands.

'Do you remember him?' asked Moore.

'Yes.'

'Remember him well?'

'He was a memorable student.'

'Care to tell me more?'

'Not really.' Kahn tossed the crumpled paper towel in the trash can.

'This is a criminal investigation, Dr Kahn.'

By now, several students were staring at them. The word *criminal* had drawn their attention.

'Let's go into my office.'

Moore followed him into an adjoining room. Through a glass partition, they had a view of the lab and all twenty-eight tables. A village of corpses.

Kahn closed the door and turned to him. 'Why

are you asking about Warren? What's he done?'

'Nothing to our knowledge. I just need to know about his relationship with Andrew Capra.'

'Andrew Capra?' Kahn snorted. 'Our most famous graduate. Now there's something a medical school loves to be known for. Teaching psychos how to slice and dice.'

'Did you think Capra was crazy?'

'I'm not sure there is a psychiatric diagnosis for men like Capra.'

'What was your impression of him, then?'

'I saw nothing out of the ordinary. Andrew struck me as perfectly normal.'

A description that seemed more chilling every time Moore heard it.

'What about Warren Hoyt?'

'Why do you ask about Warren?'

'I need to know if he and Capra were friends.'

Kahn thought it over. 'I don't know. I can't tell you what happens outside this lab. All I see is what goes on in that room. Students struggling to cram an enormous amount of information into their overworked brains. Not all of them are able to deal with the stress.'

'Is that what hapened to Warren? Is that why he withdrew from medical school?'

Kahn turned toward the glass partition and gazed into the anatomy lab. 'Do you ever wonder where cadavers come from?'

'Excuse me?'

'How medical schools get them? How they end up on those tables out there, to be cut open?'

'I assume people will their own bodies to the school.'

'Exactly. Every one of those cadavers was a human being who made a profoundly generous decision. They willed their bodies to us. Rather than spend eternity in some rosewood coffin, they chose to do something useful with their remains. They are teaching our next generation of healers. It can't be done without real cadavers. Students need to see, in three dimensions, all the variations of the human body. They need to explore, with a scalpel, the branches of the carotid artery, the muscles of the face. Yes, you can learn some of it on a computer, but it's not the same thing as actually cutting open the skin. Teasing out a delicate nerve. For that, you need a human being. You need people with the generosity and the grace to surrender the most personal part of themselves – their own bodies. I consider every one of those cadavers out there to have been an extraordinary person. I treat them as such, and I expect my students to honor them as well. There's no joking or horsing around in that room. They are to treat the bodies, and all body parts, with respect. When the dissections are completed, the remains are cremated and disposed of with dignity.' He turned to look at Moore. 'That's the way it is in my lab.'

'How does this relate to Warren Hoyt?'

'It has everything to do with him.'

'The reason he withdrew?'

'Yes.' He turned back to the window.

Moore waited, his gaze on the professor's broad back, allowing him the time to form the right words.

'Dissection', said Kahn, 'is a lengthy process.

Some students can't complete the assignments during scheduled class hours. Some of them need extra time to review complicated anatomy. So I allow them access to the lab at all hours. They each have a key to this building, and they can come in and work in the middle of the night, if they need to. Some of them do.'

'Did Warren?'

A pause. 'Yes.'

A horrifying suspicion was beginning to prickle Moore's neck.

Kahn went to the filing cabinet, opened the drawer, and began searching through the crammed contents. 'It was a Sunday. I'd spent the weekend out of town, and had to come in that night to prepare a specimen for Monday's class. You know these kids, many of them are clumsy dissectors, and they make mincemeat of their specimens. So I try to have one good dissection on display, to show them the anatomy they may have damaged on their own cadavers. We were working on the reproductive system, and they'd already begun dissecting those organs. I remember it was late when I drove onto campus, sometime after midnight. I saw lights in the lab windows, and thought it was just some compulsive student, here to get a leg up on his classmates. I let myself in the building. Came up the hall. Opened the door.'

'Warren Hoyt was here,' ventured Moore.

'Yes.' Kahn found what he was looking for in the filing cabinet drawer. He took out the folder and turned to Moore. 'When I saw what he was doing, I – well, I lost control. I grabbed him by the shirt and shoved him up against the sink. I was not

346

gentle, I admit it, but I was so angry I couldn't help myself. I still get angry, just thinking about it.' He released a deep breath, but even now, nearly seven years later, he could not calm himself. 'After – after I finished yelling at him, I dragged him here, into my office. I had him sit down and sign a statement that he would withdraw from this school effective eight a.m. the next morning. I would not require him to give a reason for it, but he had to withdraw, or I would release my written report of what I saw in this lab. He agreed, of course. He didn't have a choice. Nor did he even seem very disturbed by the whole thing. That's what struck me as the strangest thing about him – nothing disturbed him. He could take it all calmly and rationally. But that was Warren. Very rational. Never upset by anything. He was almost . . .' Kahn paused. 'Mechanical.'

'What was it you saw? What was he doing in the lab?'

Kahn handed Moore the folder. 'It's all written there. I've kept it on file all these years, just in case there's ever any legal action on Warren's part. You know, students can sue you for just about anything these days. If he ever tried to be readmitted to this school, I wanted to have a response prepared.'

Moore took the folder. It was labeled simply: *Hoyt, Warren.* Inside were three typewritten pages.

'Warren was assigned to a female cadaver,' said Kahn. 'He and his lab partners had started the pelvic dissection, exposing the bladder and uterus. The organs were not to be removed, just laid bare.

That Sunday night, Warren came in to complete the work. But what should have been a careful dissection turned into mutilation. As if he got his hand on the scalpel and lost control. He didn't just expose the organs. He carved them out of the body. First he severed the bladder and left it lying between the cadaver's legs. Then he hacked out the uterus. He did this without any gloves on, as though he wanted to *feel* the organs against his own skin. And that's how I found him. In one hand, he was holding the dripping organ. And in his other hand . . .' Kahn's voice trailed off in disgust.

What Kahn could not bring himself to say was printed on the page that Moore now read. Moore finished the sentence for him. 'He was masturbating.'

Kahn went to the desk and sank into his chair. 'That's why I couldn't let him graduate. God, what kind of doctor would he make? If he did that to a corpse, what would he do to a live patient?'

I know what he does. I've seen his work with my own eyes.

Moore turned to the third page in Hoyt's file and read Dr Kahn's final paragraph.

Mr Hoyt agrees that he will voluntarily withdraw from school, effective 8:00 A.M. tomorrow. In return, I will maintain confidentiality regarding this incident. Due to cadaver damage, his lab partners at table 19 will be reassigned to other teams for this stage of dissection.

Lab partners.

Moore looked at Kahn. 'How many lab partners did Warren have?'

'There are four students to a table.'

'Who were the other three students?'

Kahn frowned. 'I don't recall. It was seven years ago.'

'You don't keep records of those assignments?'

'No.' He paused. 'But I do remember one of his partners. A young woman.' He swiveled around to face his computer and called up his medical student enrollment files. The class list from Warren Hoyt's freshman year appeared onscreen. It took Kahn a moment to scan down the names; then he said:

'Here she is. Emily Johnstone. I remember her.'

'Why?'

'Well, first because she was a real cutie. A Meg Ryan lookalike. Second because after Warren withdrew, she wanted to know why. I didn't want to tell her the reason. So she came out and asked if it had something to do with women. It seems Warren had been following Emily around campus, and she was getting the willies. Needless to say, she was relieved when he left school.'

'Do you think she'd remember her other two lab partners?'

'There's a chance.' Kahn picked up the phone and called Student Affairs. 'Hey, Winnie? Do you have a current contact number for Emily Johnstone?' He reached for a pen and jotted the number, then hung up. 'She's in private practice in Houston,' he said, dialing again. 'It's eleven o'clock her time, so she should be in . . . Hello, Emily? . . . This is a voice from your past. Dr

349

Kahn at Emory . . . Right, anatomy lab. Ancient history, huh?'

Moore leaned forward, his pulse quickening.

When Kahn at last hung up and looked at him, Moore saw the answer in his eyes.

'She does remember the other two anatomy partners,' said Kahn. 'One was a woman named Barb Lippman. And the other . . .'

'Capra?'

Kahn nodded. 'The fourth partner was Andrew Capra.'

Twenty-Two

Catherine paused in the doorway to Peter's office. He sat at his desk, unaware she was watching him, his pen scratching in a chart. She had never taken the time to truly observe him before, and what she saw now brought a faint smile to her lips. He worked with fierce concentration, the very picture of the dedicated physician, except for one whimsical touch: the paper airplane lying on the floor. Peter and his silly flying machines.

She knocked on the door frame. He glanced up over his glasses, startled to see her there.

'Can I talk to you?' she asked.

'Of course. Come in.'

She sat down in the chair facing his desk. He said nothing, just waited patiently for her to speak. She had the impression that no matter how long she took, he would still be there, waiting for her.

'Things have been ... tense between us,' she said.

He nodded.

'I know it bothers you as much as it does me. And it bothers me a lot. Because I've always liked

351

you, Peter. It may not seem so, but I do.' She drew in a breath, struggling to come up with the right words. 'The problems between us, they have nothing to do with you. It's all because of me. There are so many things going on in my life right now. It's hard for me to explain.'

'You don't have to.'

'It's just that I see us falling apart. Not just our partnership, but our friendship. It's funny how I never realized it was there between us. I didn't realize how much it meant to me until I felt it slipping away.' She rose to her feet. 'Anyway, I'm sorry. That's what I came to say.' She started toward the door.

'Catherine,' he said softly, 'I know about Savannah.'

She turned and stared at him. His gaze was absolutely steady.

'Detective Crowe told me,' he said.

'When?'

'A few days ago, when I talked to him about the break-in here. He assumed I already knew.'

'You didn't say anything.'

'It wasn't my place to bring it up. I wanted you to feel ready to tell me. I knew you needed time, and I was willing to wait, as long as it took for you to trust me.'

She released a sharp breath. 'Well, then. Now you know the worst about me.'

'No, Catherine.' He stood up to face her. 'I know the *best* about you! I know how strong you are, how brave you are. All this time I had no idea what you were dealing with. You could have told me. You could have trusted me.'

'I thought it would change everything between us.'

'How could it?'

'I don't want you to feel sorry for me. I don't ever want to be pitied.'

'Pitied for what? For fighting back? For coming out alive against impossible odds? Why the hell would I pity you?'

She blinked away tears. 'Other men would.'

'Then they don't really know you. Not the way I do.' He stepped around his desk, so that it was no longer separating them. 'Do you remember the day we met?'

'When I came for the interview.'

'What do you remember about it?'

She gave a bewildered shake of her head. 'We talked about the practice. About how I'd fit in here.'

'So you recall it as just a business meeting.'

'That's what it was.'

'Funny. I think of it quite differently. I hardly remember any of the questions I asked you, or what you asked me. What I remember is looking up from my desk and seeing you walk into my office. And I was stunned. I couldn't think of anything to say that wouldn't sound trite or stupid or just plain ordinary. I didn't want to be ordinary, not for you. I thought: Here's a woman who has it all. She's smart; she's beautiful. And she's standing right in front of me.'

'Oh god, you were so wrong. I didn't have it all.' She blinked away tears. 'I never have. I'm just barely holding it together . . .'

Without a word he took her in his arms. It all

353

happened so naturally, so easily, without the awkwardness of a first embrace. He was simply holding her, and making no demands. One friend comforting another.

'Tell me what I can do to help,' he said. 'Anything.'

She sighed. 'I'm so tired, Peter. Could you just walk me to my car?'

'That's all?'

'That's what I really need right now. Someone I can trust to walk with me.'

He stood back and smiled at her. 'Then I'm definitely your man.'

The fifth floor of the hospital parking garage was deserted, and the concrete echoed back their footsteps like the sound of trailing ghosts. Had she been alone, she would have been glancing over her shoulder the whole way. But Peter was beside her, and she felt no fear. He walked her to her Mercedes. Stood by while she slid behind the wheel. Then he shut her door and pointed to the lock.

Nodding, she pressed the lock button and heard the comforting click as all the doors were secured.

'I'll call you later,' he said.

As she drove away, she saw him in her rearview mirror, his hand raised in a wave. Then he slid from view as she turned down the ramp.

She found herself smiling as she drove home to the Back Bay.

Some men are worth trusting, Moore had told her.

Yes, but which ones? I never know.

You won't know until push comes to shove. He'll be the one still standing beside you.

354

Whether as a friend or a lover, Peter would be one of those men.

Slowing down at Commonwealth Avenue, she turned into the driveway for her building and pressed the garage remote. The security gate rumbled open and she drove through. In her rearview mirror she saw the gate close behind her. Only then did she swing into her stall. Caution was second nature to her, and these were rituals she never failed to perform. She checked the elevator before stepping in. Scanned the hallway before stepping out again. Secured all her locks as soon as she'd stepped into her apartment. Fortress secure. Only then could she allow the last of her tension to drain away.

Standing at her window she sipped iced tea and savored the coolness of her apartment as she looked down at people walking on the street, sweat glistening on their foreheads. She'd had three hours of sleep in the last thirty-six hours. I have earned this moment of comfort, she thought as she pressed the icy glass to her cheek. I've earned an early night to bed and a weekend of doing nothing at all. She wouldn't think of Moore. She wouldn't let herself feel the pain. Not yet.

She drained her glass and had just set it on the kitchen counter when her beeper went off. A page from the hospital was the last thing she wanted to deal with. When she called the Pilgrim Hospital operator, she could not keep the irritation out of her voice.

'This is Dr Cordell. I know you just paged me, but I'm not on call tonight. In fact, I'm going to turn off my beeper right now.'

'I'm sorry to disturb you, Dr Cordell, but there was a call from the son of a Herman Gwadowski. He insists on meeting with you this afternoon.'

'Impossible. I'm already home.'

'Yes, I told him you were off for the weekend. But he said this is the last day he'll be in town. He wants to see you before he visits his attorney.'

An attorney?

Catherine sagged against the kitchen counter. God, she had no strength to deal with this. Not now. Not when she was so tired she could barely think straight.

'Dr Cordell?'

'Did Mr Gwadowski say when he wants to meet?'

'He said he'll wait in the hospital cafeteria until six.'

'Thank you.' Catherine hung up and stared numbly at the gleaming kitchen tiles. How meticulous she was about keeping those tiles clean! But no matter how hard she scrubbed or how thoroughly she organized every aspect of her life, she could not anticipate the Ivan Gwadowskis of the world.

She picked up her purse and car keys and once again left the sanctuary of her apartment.

In the elevator she glanced at her watch and was alarmed to see it was already 5:45. She would not make it to the hospital in time, and Mr Gwadowski would assume she'd stood him up.

The instant she slid into the Mercedes, she picked up the car phone and called the Pilgrim operator.

'This is Dr Cordell again. I need to reach Mr

Gwadowski to let him know I'll be late. Do you know which extension he was calling from?'

'Let me check the phone log . . . Here it is. It wasn't a hospital extension.'

'A cell phone, then?'

There was a pause. 'Well, this is strange.'

'What is?'

'He was calling from the number you're using now.'

Catherine went still, fear blasting like a cold wind up her spine. *My car. The call was made from my car.*

'Dr Cordell?'

She saw him then, rising like a cobra in the rearview mirror. She took a breath to scream, and her throat burned with the fumes of chloroform.

The receiver dropped from her hand.

Jerry Sleeper was waiting for him at the curb outside airport baggage claim. Moore threw his carry-on into the backseat, stepped into the car, and yanked the door shut with a slam.

'Have you found her?' was the first question Moore asked.

'Not yet,' said Sleeper as he pulled away from the curb. 'Her Mercedes has vanished, and there's no evidence of any disturbance in her apartment. Whatever happened, it was fast, and it was in or near her vehicle. Peter Falco was the last one to see her, around five-fifteen in the hospital garage. About a half hour later, the Pilgrim operator paged Cordell and spoke to her on the phone. Cordell called back again from her car. That conversation was abruptly cut off. The operator

357

claims it was the son of Herman Gwadowski who called in the original page.'

'Confirmation?'

'Ivan Gwadowski was on a plane to California at twelve noon. He didn't make that call.'

They did not need to say who *had* called in the page. They both knew. Moore stared in agitation at the row of taillights, strung as densely as bright red beads in the night.

He's had her since 6:00 P.M. What has he done to her in those four hours?

'I want to see where Warren Hoyt lives,' said Moore.

'We're headed there now. We know he got off his shift at Interpath Labs around seven A.M. this morning. At ten A.M., he called his supervisor to say he had a family emergency and wouldn't be back at work for at least a week. No one's seen him since. Not at his apartment, not at the lab.'

'And the family emergency?'

'He has no family. His only aunt died in February.'

The row of taillights blurred into a streak of red. Moore blinked and turned his gaze so that Sleeper would not see his tears.

Warren Hoyt lived in the North End, a quaint maze of narrow streets and redbrick buildings that made up the oldest neighborhood in Boston. It was considered a safe part of town, thanks to the watchful eyes of the local Italian population, who owned many of the businesses. Here, on a street where tourists and residents alike walked with little fear of crime, a monster had lived.

Hoyt's apartment was on the third floor of a

brick walk-up. Hours before, the team had combed the place for evidence, and when Moore stepped inside and saw the sparse furnishings, the nearly bare shelves, he felt he was standing in a room that had already been swept clean of its soul. That he'd find nothing left of whoever – whatever – Warren Hoyt might be.

Dr Zucker emerged from the bedroom and said to Moore, 'There's something wrong here.'

'Is Hoyt our unsub or not?'

'I don't know.'

'What *do* we have?' Moore looked at Crowe, who had met them at the door.

'We've got a bingo on shoe size. Eight and a half, matches the footprints from the Ortiz crime scene. We've got several hair strands from the pillow – short, light brown. Also looks like a match. Plus we found a long black hair on the bathroom floor. Shoulder-length.'

Moore frowned. 'There was a woman here?'

'Maybe a friend.'

'Or another victim,' said Zucker. 'Someone we don't know about yet.'

'I spoke to the landlady, who lives downstairs,' said Crowe. 'She last saw Hoyt this morning, coming home from work. She has no idea where he is now. Bet you can guess what she has to say about him. *Good tenant. Quiet man, never any trouble.*'

Moore looked at Zucker. 'What did you mean when you said there's something wrong here?'

'There's no murder kit. No tools. His car's parked right outside, and there's no kit in there, either.' Zucker gestured to the nearly empty living room. 'This apartment looks barely lived in. There are only a few items in the refrigerator. The bath-room has soap, a toothbrush, and a razor. It's like a hotel room. A place to sleep, nothing more. It's not where he keeps his fantasies alive.'

'This *is* where he lives,' said Crowe. 'His mail comes here. His clothes are here.'

'But this place is missing the most important thing of all,' Zucker said. 'His trophies. There are no trophies here.'

A feeling of dread had seeped into Moore's bones. Zucker was right. The Surgeon had carved an anatomical trophy out of each of his victims; he would keep them around to remind him of his kills. To tide him over between hunts.

'We're not looking at the whole picture,' said Zucker. He turned to Moore. 'I need to see where Warren Hoyt worked. I need to see the lab.'

Barry Frost sat down at the computer keyboard and typed in the patient's name: *Nina Peyton*. A new screen appeared, filled with data.

'This terminal is his fishing hole,' said Frost. 'This is where he finds his victims.'

Moore stared at the monitor, startled by what he saw. Elsewhere in the lab, machines whirred and phones rang and medical technicians processed their clattering racks of blood tubes. Here, in this antiseptic world of stainless steel and white coats, a world devoted to the healing sciences, the Surgeon had quietly hunted for prey. At this computer terminal, he could call up the names of every woman whose blood or body fluids had been processed at Interpath Labs.

'This is the primary diagnostic lab in the city,'

said Frost. 'Get your blood drawn at any doctor's office or any outpatient clinic in Boston, and the chances are, that blood will come right here to be analyzed.'

Right here, to Warren Hoyt.

'He had her home address,' said Moore, scanning the information on Nina Peyton. 'Her employer's name. Her age and marital status—'

'And her diagnosis,' said Zucker.' He pointed to two words on the screen: *sexual assault*. 'This is exactly what the Surgeon hunts for. It's what turns him on. Emotionally damaged women. Women marked by sexual violence.'

Moore heard the lilt of excitement in Zucker's voice. It was the game that fascinated Zucker, the contest of wits. At last he could see his opponent's moves, could appreciate the genius behind them.

'Here he was,' said Zucker. 'Handling their blood. Knowing their most shameful secrets.' He straightened and gazed around the lab, as though seeing it for the first time. 'Did you ever stop to think what a medical lab knows about you?' he said. 'All the personal information you give them when you open your arm and let them stick a needle in your vein? Your blood reveals your most intimate secrets. Are you dying of leukemia or AIDS? Did you smoke a cigarette or drink a glass of wine in the last few hours? Are you taking Prozac because you're depressed, or Viagra because you can't get it up? He was holding the very *essence* of those women. He could study their blood, touch it, smell it. And they never knew. They never knew that part of their own body was being fondled by a stranger.'

361

'The victims never knew him,' said Moore. 'Never met him.'

'But the Surgeon knew *them*. And on the most intimate of terms.' Zucker's eyes were feverishly bright. 'The Surgeon doesn't hunt like any serial killer I've ever come across. He is unique. He stays hidden from view, because he chooses his prey sight unseen.' He stared in wonder at a rack of tubes on the countertop. 'This lab is his hunting ground. This is how he finds them. By their blood. By their pain.'

When Moore stepped out of the medical center, the night air felt cooler, crisper, than it had in weeks. Across the city of Boston, fewer windows would be left open, fewer women lying vulnerable to attack.

But tonight, the Surgeon will not be hunting. Tonight, he'll be enjoying his latest catch.

Moore came to a sudden halt beside his car and stood there, paralyzed by despair. Even now, Warren Hoyt might be reaching for his scalpel. Even now . . .

Footsteps approached. He summoned the strength to raise his head, to look at the man standing a few feet away in the shadows.

'He has her, doesn't he?' said Peter Falco.

Moore nodded.

'God. Oh, god.' Falco looked up in anguish at the night sky. 'I walked her to her car. She was right *there* with me, and I let her go home. I let her drive away . . .'

'We're doing everything we can to find her.' It was a stock phrase. Even as he said it, Moore

362

heard the hollowness of his own words. It's what you said when matters are grim, when you know that even your best efforts will likely come to nothing.

'What *are* you doing?'

'We know who he is.'

'But you don't know where he's taken her.'

'It will take time to track him down.'

'Tell me what I can do. Anything at all.'

Moore fought to keep his voice calm, to hide his own fears, his own dread. 'I know how hard it is to stand on the sidelines and let others do the work. But this is what we're trained to do.'

'Oh yes, *you're* the professionals! So what the hell went wrong?'

Moore had no answer.

In agitation, Falco crossed toward Moore and came to stand beneath the parking lot lamp. The light fell on his face, haggard with worry. 'I don't know what happened between you two,' he said. 'But I do know she trusted you. I hope to god that means something to you. I hope she's more than just another case. Just another name on the list.'

'She is,' said Moore.

The men stared at each other, acknowledging in silence what they both knew. What they both felt.

'I care more than you'll ever know,' said Moore.

And Falco said softly, 'So do I.'

Twenty-three

'He's going to keep her alive for a while,' said Dr Zucker. 'The way he kept Nina Peyton alive for a whole day. He is now in complete control of the situation. He can take all the time he wants.'

A shudder went through Rizzoli as she considered what that meant, *All the time he wants.* She considered how many tender nerve endings the human body possessed and wondered how much pain must be endured before Death took pity. She looked across the conference room and saw Moore drop his head into his hands. He looked sick, exhausted. It was after midnight, and the faces she saw around the conference table looked sallow and discouraged. Rizzoli stood outside that circle, her back sagging against the wall. The invisble woman, whom no one acknowledged, allowed to listen in but not participate. Restricted to administrative duty, deprived of her service weapon, she was now little more than an observer in a case that she knew better than anyone at this table.

Moore's gaze lifted in her direction, but he

looked straight through her, not at her. As though he didn't *want* to look at her.

Dr Zucker summarized what they'd learned about Warren Hoyt. The Surgeon.

'He's been working toward this one goal for a long time,' said Zucker. 'Now that he's attained it, he's going to prolong the pleasure as long as possible.'

'Then Cordell's always been his goal?' said Frost. 'The other victims – they were just for practice?'

'No, they gave him pleasure as well. They tided him over, helped him release sexual tension while he worked toward this prize. In any hunt, the predator's excitement is most intense when he's stalking the most difficult of prey. And Cordell was probably the one woman he could not easily reach. She was always on alert, always careful about security. She barricaded herself behind locks and alarm systems. She avoided close relationships. She seldom went out at night, except to work at the hospital. She was the most challenging prey he could pursue, and the one he wanted most. He made his hunt even more difficult by letting her *know* she was prey. He used terror as part of the game. He wanted her to feel him closing in. The other women were just the buildup. Cordell was the main event.'

'*Is*,' said Moore, his voice tight with rage. 'She's not dead yet.'

The room suddenly hushed, all eyes averted from Moore.

Zucker nodded, icy calm unbroken. 'Thank you for correcting me.'

Marquette said, 'You've read his background files?'

'Yes,' said Zucker. 'Warren was an only child. Apparently an adored child, born in Houston. Father was a rocket scientist – I kid you not. His mother came from an old oil family. Both of them are dead now. So Warren was blessed with smart genes and family money. There's no record of criminal behavior as a child. No arrests, no traffic tickets, nothing that raised a red flag. Except for that one incident in medical school, in the anatomy lab, I find no warning signs. No clues that tell me he was destined to be a predator. By all accounts, he was a perfectly normal boy. Polite and reliable.'

'Average,' said Moore softly. 'Ordinary.'

Zucker nodded. 'This is a boy who never stood out, never alarmed anyone. This is the most frightening killer of all, because there's no pathology, no psychiatric diagnosis. He's like Ted Bundy. Intelligent, organized, and, on the surface, quite functional. But he has one personality quirk: he enjoys torturing women. This is someone you might work with every day. And you'd never suspect that when he's looking at you, smiling at you, he's thinking about some new and creative way to rip out your guts.'

Shuddering at Zucker's hiss of a voice, Rizzoli looked around the room. *What he's saying is true. I see Barry Frost every day. He seems like a nice guy. Happily married. Never in a foul mood. But I have no idea what he's really thinking.*

Frost caught her gaze, and he reddened.

Zucker continued. 'After the incident in medical

school, Hoyt was forced to withdraw. He entered a med tech training program, and followed Andrew Capra to Savannah. It appears their partnership lasted several years. Airline and credit card records indicate they often traveled together. To Greece and Italy. To Mexico, where they both volunteered at a rural clinic. It was an alliance of two hunters. Blood brothers who shared the same violent fantasies.'

'The catgut suture,' said Rizzoli.

Zucker gave her a puzzled look. 'What?'

'In third world countries, they still use catgut in surgery. That's how he got his supply.'

Marquette nodded. 'She could be right.'

I am right, thought Rizzoli, prickling with resentment.

'When Cordell killed Andrew Capra,' said Zucker, 'she destroyed the perfect killing team. She took away the one person Hoyt felt closest to. And that's why she became his ultimate goal. His ultimate victim.'

'If Hoyt was in the house that night Capra died, why didn't he kill her then?' asked Marquette.

'I don't know. There's a lot about that night in Savannah that only Warren Hoyt knows. What we do know is that he moved to Boston two years ago, shortly after Catherine Cordell came here. Within a year, Diana Sterling was dead.'

At last Moore spoke, his voice haunted. 'How do we find him?'

'You can keep his apartment under surveillance, but I don't think he'll be returning there soon. It's not his lair. That's not where he indulges his fantasies.' Zucker sat back, eyes unfocused.

Channeling what he knew about Warren Hoyt into words and images. 'His real lair will be a place he keeps separate from his day-to-day life. A place he retreats to in anonymity, possibly quite distant from his apartment. It may not be rented under his real name.'

'You rent a place, you have to pay for it,' said Frost. 'We follow the money.'

Zucker nodded. 'You'll know it's his lair when you find it, because his trophies will be there. The souvenirs he took from his kills. It's possible he's even prepared this lair as a place to eventually bring his victims. The ultimate torture chamber. It's a place where privacy is assured, where he won't be interrupted. A stand-alone building. Or an apartment that's well insulated for sound.'

So no one can hear Cordell screaming, thought Rizzoli.

'In this place, he can become the creature he truly is. He can feel relaxed and uninhibited. He's never left semen at any of the crime scenes, which tells me he's able to delay sexual gratification until he's in a safe place. This lair is that place. He probably visits it from time to time, to re-experience the thrill of the slaughter. To sustain himself between kills.' Zucker looked around the room. 'That's where he's taken Catherine Cordell.'

The Greeks call it dere, *which refers to the front of the neck, or the throat, and it is the most beautiful, the most vulnerable, part of a woman's anatomy. In the throat pulses life and breath, and beneath the milky white skin of Iphigenia, blue veins would have throbbed at the point of her father's knife. As Iphigenia lay stretched upon the altar, did Agamemnon pause to admire the delicate lines of his daughter's neck? Or did he study the landmarks, to choose the most efficient point at which his blade should pierce her skin? Though anguished by this sacrifice, at the instant his knife sank in, did he not feel just the slightest frisson in his loins, a jolt of sexual pleasure as he thrust his blade into her flesh?*

Even the ancient Greeks, with their hideous tales of parents devouring offspring and sons coupling with mothers, do not mention such details of depravity. They did not need to; it is one of those secret truths we all understand without benefit of words. Of those warriors who stood with stony expressions and hearts hardened against a maiden's screams, of those who watched as Iphigenia was stripped naked, and her swan neck was bared to the knife, how many of those soldiers felt the unexpected heat of pleasure flood their groins? Felt their cocks harden?

How many would ever again look at a woman's throat, and not feel the urge to cut it?

Her throat is as pale as Iphigenia's must have been. She has protected herself from the sun, as every redhead should, and there are only a few freckles marring the alabaster translucence of her skin. These two years, she has kept her neck flawless for me. I appreciate that.

I have waited patiently for her to regain consciousness. I know she is now awake and aware of me, because her pulse has quickened. I touch her throat, at the hollow just above the breastbone, and she takes in a sharp breath. She does not release it as I stroke up the side of her neck, tracing the course of her carotid artery. Her pulse throbs, heaving the skin with rhythmic quakes. I feel the gloss of her sweat beneath my finger. It has bloomed like mist on her skin, and her face glows with its sheen. As I stroke up to the angle of her jaw, she finally releases her breath; it comes out in a whimper, muffled by the tape over her mouth. This is not like my Catherine to whimper. The others were stupid gazelles, but Catherine is a tigress, the only one who ever struck back and drew blood.

She opens her eyes and looks at me, and I see that she understands. I have finally won. She, the worthiest of them all, is conquered.

I lay out my instruments. They make a pleasant clang as I set them on the metal tray by the bed. I feel her watching me, and know her gaze is drawn to the sharp reflection off stainless steel. She knows what each one is for, as she has certainly used such instruments many times. The retractor is to spread apart the edges of an incision. The hemostat is to clamp tissues and blood vessels. And the scalpel – well, we both know what a scalpel is used for.

I set the tray near her head, so she can see, and contemplate, what comes next. I don't have to say a word; the glitter of the instruments says everything.

I touch her naked belly and her abdominal muscles snap tight. It is a virgin belly, without any scars marring its flat surface. The blade will part her skin like butter.

I pick up the scalpel, and press its tip to her abdomen. She gasps in a breath and her eyes go wide.

Once, I saw a photograph of a zebra just as a lion's fangs have sunk into its throat, and the zebra's eyes are rolled back in mortal terror. It is an image I will never forget. That is the look I see now, in Catherine's eyes.

Oh god, oh god, oh god.

Catherine's breaths roared in and out of her lungs as she felt the scalpel tip prick her skin. Drenched in sweat, she closed her eyes, dreading the pain that was about to come. A sob caught in her throat, a cry to the heavens for mercy, even for a quick death, but not this. Not the slicing of flesh.

Then the scalpel lifted away.

She opened her eyes and looked into his face. So ordinary, so forgettable. A man she might have seen a dozen times and never registered. Yet he knew *her*. He had hovered on the edges of her world, had placed her at the bright center of his universe, while he circled around her, unseen in the darkness.

And I never knew he was there.

He set the scalpel down on the tray. And smiling, he said, 'Not yet.'

Only when he'd walked out of the room did she know the torment was postponed, and she gave a sharp gasp of relief.

So this was his game. Prolong the terror, prolong the pleasure. For now he would keep her alive, giving her time to contemplate what came next.

Every minute alive is another minute to escape.

The effect of the chloroform had dissipated, and she was fully alert, her mind racing on the potent fuel of panic. She was lying spreadeagled on a steel-framed bed. Her clothes had been stripped off; her wrists and ankles were bound to the bed-frame with duct tape. Though she yanked and strained against the bindings until her muscles quivered from exhaustion, she could not free herself. Four years ago, in Savannah, Capra had used nylon cord to bind her wrists, and she had managed to slip one hand free; the Surgeon would not repeat that mistake.

Drenched with sweat, too tired to keep struggling, she focused on her surroundings.

A single bare lightbulb hung above the bed. The scent of earth and dank stone told her she was in a cellar. Turning her head, she could make out, just beyond the circle of light, the cobbled surface of the stone foundation.

Footsteps creaked overhead, and she heard chair legs scrape. A wooden floor. An old house. Upstairs, a TV went on. She could not remember how she had arrived in this room or how long the drive had taken. They might be miles away from Boston, in a place where no one would think to look.

The gleam of the tray drew her gaze. She stared at the array of instruments, neatly laid out for the procedure to come. Countless times she herself had wielded such instruments, had thought of them as tools of healing. With scalpels and clamps she had excised cancers and bullets, had staunched the hemorrhage from ruptured arteries and drained chest cavities drowning in blood. Now she stared at the tools she had used to save lives and saw the instruments of her own death. He had put them close to the bed, so she could study them and contemplate the razor edge of the scalpel, the steel teeth of the hemostats.

Don't panic. Think. Think.

She closed her eyes. Fear was like a living thing, wrapping its tentacles around her throat.

You beat them before. You can do it again.

She felt a drop of perspiration slide down her breast, into the sweat-soaked mattress. There was a way out. There had to be a way out, a way to fight back. The alternative was too terrible to contemplate.

Opening her eyes, she stared at the lightbulb overhead and focused her scalpel-sharp mind on what to do next. She remembered what Moore had told her: that the Surgeon fed on terror. He attacked women who were damaged, who were victims. Women to whom he felt superior.

He will not kill me until he has conquered me.

She drew in a deep breath, understanding now what game had to be played. *Fight the fear. Welcome the rage. Show him that no matter what he does to you, you cannot be defeated.*

Even in death.

Twenty-four

Rizzoli jerked awake, and pain stabbed her neck like a knife. Lord, not another pulled muscle, she thought as she slowly raised her head and blinked at the sun-light in the office window. The other workstations in her pod were deserted; she was the only one sitting at a desk. Sometime around six, she'd put her head down in exhaustion, promising herself just a short nap. It was now nine-thirty. The stack of computer printouts she'd used as a pillow was damp with drool.

She glanced at Frost's workstation and saw his jacket hanging over the back of the chair. A dough-nut bag sat on Crowe's desk. So the rest of the team had come in while she was sleeping and had surely seen her slack-jawed and leaking spittle. What an entertaining sight that must have been.

She stood and stretched, trying to work the crick out of her neck, but knew it was futile. She'd just have to go through the day with her head askew.

'Hey, Rizzoli. Get your beauty sleep?'

Turning, she saw a detective from one of the other teams grinning at her across the partition.

'Don't I look it?' she growled. 'Where is everyone?'

'Your team's been in conference since eight.'

'What?'

'I think the meeting just broke up.'

'No one bothered to tell *me*.' She headed up the hall, the last cobwebs of sleep blasted away by anger. Oh, she knew what was going on. This was how they drove you out, not with a frontal assault but with the drip, drip of humiliation. Leave you out of the meetings, out of the loop. Reduce you to cluelessness.

She walked into the conference room. The only one there was Barry Frost, gathering his papers from the table. He looked up, and a faint flush spread across his face when he saw her.

'Thanks for letting me know about the meeting,' she said.

'You looked so wiped out. I figured I could catch you up on all this later.'

'When, next week?'

Frost looked down, avoiding her gaze. They'd worked together as partners long enough for her to recognize the guilt in his face.

'So I'm out in the cold,' she said. 'Was that Marquette's decision?'

Frost gave an unhappy nod. 'I argued against it. I told him we needed you. But he said, with the shooting and all . . .'

'He said what?'

Reluctantly Frost finished: 'That you were no longer an asset to the unit.'

No longer an asset. Translation: her career was finished.

Frost left the room. Suddenly dizzy from lack of sleep and food, she dropped into a chair and just sat there, staring at the empty table. For an instant she had a flashback to being nine years old, the despised sister, wanting desperately to be accepted as one of the boys. But the boys had rejected her, as they always did. She knew Pacheco's death was not the real reason she'd been shut out. Bad shootings had not ruined the careers of other cops. But when you were a woman and better than anyone else and you had the nerve to let them know it, a single mistake like Pacheco was all it took.

When she returned to her desk, she found the workpod deserted. Frost's jacket was now gone; so was Crowe's doughnut bag. She, too, might as well split. In fact, she ought to just clean out her desk right now, since there was no future for her here.

She opened her drawer to take out her purse and paused. An autopsy photo of Elena Ortiz stared up at her from a jumble of papers. *I'm his victim, too,* she thought. Whatever resentments she might hold against her colleagues, she did not lose sight of the fact the Surgeon was responsible for her downfall. The Surgeon was the one who had humiliated her.

She slammed the drawer shut. *Not yet. I'm not ready for surrender.* She glanced at Frost's desk and saw the stack of papers that he'd gathered from the conference table. She looked around to make sure no one was watching her. The only other detectives were at another pod at the far end of the room.

She grabbed Frost's papers, took them to her desk, and sat down to read.

They were Warren Hoyt's financial records. This was what the case had come down to: a paper chase. Follow the money, find Hoyt. She saw credit card charges, bank checks, deposits and withdrawals. A lot of big numbers. Hoyt's parents had left him a wealthy young man, and he'd indulged in travel every winter to the Caribbean and Mexico. She found no evidence of another residence, no rent checks, no fixed monthly payments.

Of course not. He was not stupid. If he maintained a lair, he'd pay for it in cash.

Cash. You can't always predict when you'll run out of cash. ATM withdrawals were often unplanned or spontaneous transactions.

She flipped through the bank records, searching for every ATM use, and jotted them down on a separate piece of paper. Most were cash withdrawals from locations near Hoyt's residence or the medical center, areas within his normal field of activity. It was the unusual she was searching for, the transactions that didn't fit his pattern.

She found two of them. One at a bank in Nashua, New Hampshire, on June 26. The other was at an ATM in Hobb's FoodMart in Lithia, Massachusetts, on May 13.

She leaned back, wondering if Moore was already chasing down these two transactions. With so many other details to follow up on and all the interviews with Hoyt's colleagues at the lab, a pair of ATM withdrawals might be way down on the team's priority list.

She heard footsteps and glanced up with a start, panicked that she'd been caught reading Frost's papers, but it was only a clerk from the lab who walked into the pod. The clerk gave Rizzoli a smile, dropped a folder on Moore's desk, and walked out again.

After a moment, Rizzoli rose from her chair and went to Moore's desk to peek inside the folder. The first page was a report from Hair and Fiber, an analysis of the light brown strands found on Warren Hoyt's pillow.

Trichorrhexis invaginata, compatible with hair strand found in wound margin of victim Elena Ortiz. Bingo. Confirmation that Hoyt was their man.

She flipped to a second page. This, too, was a report from Hair and Fiber, on a strand found on Hoyt's bathroom floor. This one did not make sense. This did not fit in.

She closed the folder and walked to the lab.

Erin Volchko was sitting in front of the gamma-tech prism, shuffling through a series of photomicrographs. As Rizzoli came into the lab, Erin held up a photo and challenged: 'Quick! What is it?'

Rizzoli frowned at the black-and-white image of a scaly band. 'It's ugly.'

'Yeah, but what is it?'

'Probably something gross. Like a cockroach leg.'

'It's a hair from a deer. Cool, isn't it? It doesn't look a thing like human hair.'

'Speaking of human hair.' Rizzoli handed her the report that she'd just read. 'Can you tell me more about this?'

'From Warren Hoyt's apartment?'

'Yeah.'

'The short brown hairs on Hoyt's pillow show *Trichorrhexis invaginata*. He does appear to be your unsub.'

'No, the other hair. The black strand from his bathroom floor.'

'Let me show you the photo.' Erin reached for a bundle of photomicrographs. She shuffled through them like cards and pulled one from the deck. 'This is the hair from the bathroom. You see the numerical scores there?'

Rizzoli looked at the sheet, at Erin's neat handwriting. *A00-B00-C05-D33*. 'Yeah. Whatever it means.'

'The first two scores, A00 and B00, tell you the strand is straight and black. Under the compound microscope, you can see additional details.' She handed Rizzoli the photo. 'Look at the shaft. It's on the thick side. Notice the cross-sectional shape is nearly round.'

'Meaning?'

'It's one feature that helps us distinguish between races. A hair shaft from an African subject, for instance, is nearly flat, like a ribbon. Now look at the pigmentation, and you'll notice it's very dense. See the thick cuticle? These all point to the same conclusion.' Erin looked at her. 'This hair is characteristic of East Asian heritage.'

'What do you mean by East Asian?'

'Chinese or Japanese. The Indian subcontinent. Possibly Native American.'

'Can that be confirmed? Is there enough hair root for DNA tests?'

'Unfortunately, no. It appears to have been clipped, not shed naturally. There's no follicular tissue on this strand. But I'm confident this hair comes from someone of non-European, non-African descent.'

An Asian woman, thought Rizzoli as she walked back to the homicide unit. How does this come into the case? In the glass-walled corridor leading to the north wing she paused, her tired eyes squinting against the sunlight as she looked out over the neighborhood of Roxbury. Was there a victim whose body they had yet to find? Had Hoyt clipped her hair as a souvenir, the way he'd clipped Catherine Cordell's?

She turned and was startled to see Moore walk right past her, on his way to the south wing. He might never have acknowledged her presence had she not called out to him.

He stopped and reluctantly turned to face her.

'That long black strand on Hoyt's bathroom floor,' she said. 'The lab says it's East Asian. There could be a victim we've missed.'

'We discussed that possibility.'

'When?'

'This morning, at the meeting.'

'Goddamnit, Moore! Don't leave me out of the loop!'

His cold silence served to amplify the shrillness of her outburst.

'I want him, too,' she said. Slowly, inexorably, she approached him until she was right in his face. 'I want him as much as you do. Let me back in.'

'It's not my decision. It's Marquette's.' He turned to leave.

'Moore?'

Reluctantly he stopped.

'I can't stand this,' she said. 'This feud between us.'

'This isn't the time to talk about it.'

'Look, I'm *sorry*. I was pissed off at you about Pacheco. I know it's a lousy excuse for what I did. For telling Marquette about you and Cordell.'

He turned to her. 'Why did you do it?'

'I just told you why. I was pissed off.'

'No, there's more to it than Pacheco. It's about Catherine, isn't it? You've disliked her from the very first day. You couldn't stand the fact—'

'That you were falling in love with her?'

A long silence passed.

When Rizzoli spoke, she could not keep the sarcasm from her voice. 'You know, Moore, for all your high-minded talk about respecting women's *minds*, admiring women's *abilities*, you still fall for the same thing every other man does. Tits and ass.'

He went white with anger. 'So you hate her for the way she looks. And you're pissed at me for falling for it. But you know what, Rizzoli? What man's going to fall for you, when you don't even like yourself?'

She stared in bitterness as he walked away. Only weeks ago, she'd thought Moore was the last person on earth who would say something so cruel. His words stung worse than if they'd come from anyone else.

That he might have spoken the truth was something she refused to consider.

Downstairs, passing through the lobby, she paused at the memorial to Boston PD's fallen cops. The names of the dead were engraved on the wall in chronological order, starting with Ezekiel Hodson in 1854. A vase of flowers sat on the granite floor in tribute. Get yourself killed in the line of duty, and you're a hero. How simple, how permanent. She didn't know anything about these men whose names were now immortalized. For all she knew, some of them might have been dirty cops, but death had made their names and reputations untouchable. Standing there, before that wall, she almost envied them.

She walked out to her car. Rooting around in her glove compartment, she found a New England map. She spread it on the seat and eyed her two choices: Nashua, New Hampshire, or Lithia, in western Massachusetts. Warren Hoyt had used ATM's at both locations. It was down to pure guesswork. A toss of a coin.

She started the car. It was ten-thirty; she didn't reach the town of Lithia until noon.

Water. It was all Catherine could think about, the cool, clean taste of it streaming into her mouth. She thought of all the fountains from which she had drunk, the stainless-steel oases in the hospital corridors spouting icy water that splashed her lips, her chin. She thought of crushed ice and the way post-op patients would crane their necks and open their parched mouths like baby birds to receive a few precious chips of it.

And she thought of Nina Peyton, bound in a bedroom, knowing she was doomed to die, yet able to think only of her terrible thirst.

This is how he tortures us. How he beats us down. He wants us to beg for water, beg for our lives. He wants complete control. He wants us to acknowledge his power.

All night she had been left to stare at that lone lightbulb. Several times she had dozed off, only to startle awake, her stomach churning in panic. But panic cannot be sustained, and as the hours passed and no amount of struggling could loosen her bonds, her body seemed to shut down into a state of suspended animation. She hovered there, in the nightmarish twilight between denial and reality, her mind focused with exquisite concentration on her craving for water.

Footsteps creaked. A door squealed open.

She snapped fully awake. Her heart was suddenly pounding like an animal trying to beat its way out of her chest. She sucked in dank air, cool cellar air that smelled of earth and moist stone. Her breaths came in quickening gasps as the footsteps moved down the stairs and then *he* was there, standing above her. The light from the lone bulb cast shadows on his face, turning it into a smiling skull with hollows for eyes.

'You want a drink, don't you?' he said. Such a quiet voice. Such a sane voice.

She could not speak because of the tape over her mouth, but he could see the answer in her feverish eyes.

'Look what I have, Catherine.' He held up a tumbler and she heard the delicious clink of ice cubes and saw bright beads of water sweating on the cold surface of the glass. 'Wouldn't you like a sip?'

She nodded, her gaze not on him but on the tumbler. Thirst was driving her mad, but she was already thinking ahead, beyond that first glorious sip of water. Plotting her moves, weighing her chances.

He swirled the water, and the ice rang like chimes against the glass. 'Only if you behave.'

I will, her eyes promised him. The tape stung as it was peeled off. She lay completely passive, let him slip a straw into her mouth. She took a greedy sip, but it was barely a trickle against the raging fire of her thirst. She drank again and immediately began to cough, precious water dribbling from her mouth.

'Can't – can't drink lying down,' she gasped. 'Please, let me sit up. Please.'

He set down the glass and studied her, his eyes bottomless pools of black. He saw a woman on the verge of fainting. A woman who had to be revived if he wanted the full pleasure of her terror.

He began to cut the tape that bound her right wrist to the bedframe.

Her heart was thumping hard, and she thought that surely he would see it surging against her breastbone. The right bond came free, and her hand lay limp. She did not move, did not tense a single muscle.

There was an endless silence. *Come on. Cut my left hand free. Cut it!*

Too late she realized she'd been holding her breath and he had noticed it. In despair she heard the screech of fresh duct tape peeling off the roll.

It's now or never.

She grabbed blindly at the instrument tray, and

the glass of water went flying, ice cubes clattering to the floor. Her fingers closed around steel. The scalpel!

Just as he lunged at her, she swung the scalpel and felt the blade strike flesh.

He flinched away, howling, clutching his hand.

She twisted sideways, slashed the scalpel across the tape that bound her left wrist. Another hand free!

She shot upright in bed, and her vision suddenly dimmed. A day without water had left her weak, and she fought to focus, to direct the blade at the tape binding her right ankle. She slashed blindly and pain nipped her skin. One hard kick and her ankle was free.

She reached out toward the last binding.

The heavy retractor slammed into her temple, a blow so brutal she saw bright flashes of light.

The second blow caught her on the cheek, and she heard bone crack.

She never remembered dropping the scalpel.

When she surfaced back to consciousness, her face was throbbing and she could not see out her right eye. She tried to move her limbs and found her wrists and ankles were once again bound to the bedframe. But he had not yet taped her mouth; he had not yet silenced her.

He was standing above her. She saw the stains on his shirt. *His* blood, she realized with a feral sense of satisfaction. His prey had lashed back and had drawn blood. *I am not so easily conquered. He feeds on fear; I will show him none of it.*

He picked up a scalpel from the tray and came toward her. Though her heart was slamming

385

against her chest, she lay perfectly still, her gaze on his. Taunting him, daring him. She now knew her death was inevitable, and with that acceptance came liberation. The courage of the condemned. For two years she'd cowered like a wounded animal in hiding. For two years, she had let Andrew Capra's ghost rule her life. No longer.

Go ahead, cut me. But you will not win. You will not see me die defeated.

He touched the blade to her abdomen. Involuntarily her muscles snapped taut. He was waiting to see fear on her face.

She showed him only defiance. 'You can't do it without Andrew, can you?' she said. 'You can't even get it up on your own. Andrew had to do the fucking. All you could do was watch him.'

He pressed the blade, pricking her skin. Even through her pain, even as the first drops of blood trickled out, she kept her gaze locked on his, showing no fear, denying him all satisfaction.

'You can't even fuck a woman, can you? No, your hero Andrew had to do it. And he was a loser, too.'

The scalpel hesitated. Lifted. She saw it hovering there, in the dim light.

Andrew. The key is Andrew, the man he worships. His god.

'Loser. Andrew was a loser,' she said. 'You know why he came to see me that night, don't you? He came to beg.'

'No.' The word was barely a whisper.

'He asked me not to fire him. He pleaded with me.' She laughed, a harsh and startling sound in that dim place of death. 'It was pitiful. That was

Andrew, your hero. Begging *me* to help him.'

The hand on the scalpel tightened. The blade pressed down on her belly again, and fresh blood oozed out and trickled down her flank. Savagely she suppressed the instinct to flinch, to cry out. Instead she kept talking, her voice as strong and confident as though *she* were the one holding the scalpel.

'He told me about you. You didn't know that, did you? He said you couldn't even *talk* to a woman, you were such a coward. *He* had to find them for you.'

'Liar.'

'You were nothing to him. Just a parasite. A worm.'

'Liar.'

The blade sank into her skin, and though she fought against it, a gasp escaped her throat. *You will not win, you bastard. Because I'm no longer afraid of you. I'm not afraid of anything.*

She stared, her eyes burning with the defiance of the damned, as he made the next slice.

Twenty-five

Rizzoli stood eyeing the row of cake mixes and wondered how many of the boxes were infested with mealybugs. Hobbs' FoodMart was that kind of grocery store – dark and musty, a real Mom and Pop establishment, if you pictured Mom and Pop as a pair of mean geezers who'd sell spoiled milk to school kids. 'Pop' was Dean Hobbs, an old Yankee with suspicious eyes who paused to study a customer's quarters before accepting them as payment. Grudgingly he handed back two pennies' worth of change, then slammed the register shut.

'Don't keep track of who uses that ATM thingamajig,' he said to Rizzoli. 'Bank put it in, as a convenience to my customers. I got nothing to do with it.'

'The cash was withdrawn back in May. Two hundred dollars. I have a photo of the man who—'

'Like I told that state cop, that was May. This is August. You think I remember a customer from that far back?'

'The state police were here?'

'This morning, asking the same questions. Don't you cops talk to each other?'

So the ATM transaction had already been followed up on, not by Boston PD but by the staties. Shit, she was wasting her time here.

Mr Hobbs's gaze suddenly shot to a teenage boy studying the candy selection. 'Hey, you gonna pay for that Snickers bar?'

'Uh . . . yeah.'

'Then take it outta your pocket, why don't ya?'

The boy put the candy bar back on the shelf and slunk out of the store.

Dean Hobbs grunted. 'That one's always been trouble.'

'You know that kid?' asked Rizzoli.

'Know his folks.'

'How about the rest of your customers? You know most of them?'

'You had a look around town?'

'A quick one.'

'Yeah, well, a *quick one's* all it takes to see Lithia. Twelve hundred people. Nothing much to see.'

Rizzoli took out Warren Hoyt's photo. It was the best they could come up with, a two-year-old image from his driver's license. He was looking straight at the camera, a thin-faced man with trim hair and a strangely generic smile. Though Dean Hobbs had already seen it, she held it out to him anyway. 'His name is Warren Hoyt.'

'Yeah, I seen it. The state police showed me.'

'Do you recognize him?'

'Didn't recognize him this morning. Don't recognize him now.'

'Are you sure?'

'Don't I sound sure?'

Yes, he did. He sounded like a man who never changed his mind about anything.

Bells chimed as the door opened, and two teenage girls walked in, summer blondes with long legs bare and tanned in their short shorts. Dean Hobbs was momentarily distracted as they strolled by, giggling, and wandered toward the gloomy back end of the store.

'They sure have grown,' he murmured in wonder.

'Mr Hobbs.'

'Huh?'

'If you see the man in that photo, I want you to call me immediately.' She handed him her card. 'I can be reached twenty-four hours a day. Pager or cell phone.'

'Yeah, yeah.'

The girls, now carrying a bag of potato chips and a six-pack of Diet Pepsi, came back to the register. They stood in all their braless teenage magnificence, nipples poking against sleeveless tee shirts. Dean Hobbs was getting an eyeful, and Rizzoli wondered if he'd already forgotten she was there.

The story of my life. Pretty girl walks in; I turn invisible.

She left the grocery store and went back to her car. Just that short time in the sun had baked the interior, so she opened the door and waited for the car to air out. On Lithia's main street, nothing moved. She saw a gas station, a hardware store, and a cafe, but no people. The heat had driven

390

everyone indoors, and she could hear the rattle of air conditioners up and down the street. Even in small-town America, no one sat outside fanning themselves anymore. The miracle of air conditioning had made the front porch irrelevant.

She heard the grocery store door tinkle shut and saw the two girls stroll lazily out into the sun, the only creatures moving. As they walked up the street, Rizzoli saw curtains flick aside in a window. People noticed things in small towns. They certainly noticed pretty young women.

Would they notice if one had gone missing?

She shut the car door and went back into the grocery store.

Mr Hobbs was in the vegetable aisle, cunningly burying the fresh lettuce heads at the back of the cooler bin, moving the wilted heads to the front.

'Mr Hobbs?'

He turned. 'You back again?'

'Another question.'

'Don't mean I have an answer.'

'Do any Asian women live in this town?'

This was a question he had not anticipated, and he just looked at her in bafflement. 'What?'

'A Chinese or Japanese woman. Or maybe a Native American.'

'We got a coupla black families,' he offered, as though they might do instead.

'There's a woman who may be missing. Long black hair, very straight, past her shoulders.'

'And you say she's Oriental?'

'Or possibly Native American.'

He laughed. 'Hell, I don't think she's any of those.'

Rizzoli's attention perked up. He had turned back to the vegetable bin and began layering old zucchinis on top of the fresh shipment.

'Who's *she*, Mr Hobbs?'

'Not Oriental, that's for sure. Not Indian, either.'

'You know her?'

'Seen her in here, once or twice. She's renting the old Sturdee Farm for the summer. Tall girl. Not all that pretty.'

Yes, he would notice that last fact.

'When was the last time you saw her?'

He turned and yelled: 'Hey, Margaret!'

The door to a back room swung open and Mrs Hobbs came out. 'What?'

'Didn't you drop off a delivery at the Sturdee place last week?'

'Yeah.'

'That gal out there look okay to you?'

'She paid me.'

Rizzoli asked, 'Have you seen her since, Mrs Hobbs?'

'Haven't had a reason to.'

'Where is this Sturdee Farm?'

'Out on West Fork. Last place on the road.'

Rizzoli looked down as her beeper went off. 'Can I use your telephone?' she asked. 'My cell phone just died.'

'It's not a long-distance call, is it?'

'Boston.'

He grunted and turned back to his zucchini display. 'Pay phone's outside.'

Cursing under her breath, Rizzoli stalked out again into the heat, found the pay phone, and thrust coins into the slot.

'Detective Frost.'

'You just paged me.'

'Rizzoli? What're you doing out in Western Mass?'

To her dismay, she realized he knew her location, thanks to caller ID. 'I took a little drive.'

'You're still working the case, aren't you?'

'I'm just asking a few questions. Not a big deal.'

'Shit, if—' Frost abruptly lowered his voice. 'If Marquette finds out—'

'You're not gonna tell him, are you?'

'No way. But get back in here. He's looking for you and he's pissed.'

'I've got one more place to check out here.'

'Listen to me, Rizzoli. *Let it go*, or you'll blow whatever chance you've still got in the unit.'

'Don't you see? I've already blown it! I'm already fucked!' Blinking away tears, she turned and stared bitterly up the empty street, where dust blew like hot ash. 'He's all I've got now. The Surgeon. There's nothing left for me except to nail him.'

'The staties have already been out there. They came up empty-handed.'

'I know.'

'So what are *you* doing there?'

'Asking the questions they *didn't* ask.' She hung up. Then she got in her car and drove off to find the black-haired woman.

Twenty-Six

The Sturdee Farm was the only house at the end of a long dirt road. It was an old Cape with chipping white paint and a porch that sagged in the middle beneath a burden of stacked firewood.

Rizzoli sat in her car for a moment, too tired to step out. And too demoralized by what her once-promising career had come down to: sitting alone on this dirt road, contemplating the uselessness of walking up those steps and knocking on that door. Talking to some bewildered woman who just happened to have black hair. She thought of Ed Geiger, another Boston cop who'd also parked his car on a dirt road one day, and had decided, at the age of forty-nine, that it really was the end of the road for him. Rizzoli had been the first detective to arrive on the scene. While all the other cops had stood around that car with its blood-splattered windshield, shaking their heads and murmuring sadly about poor Ed, Rizzoli had felt little sympathy for a cop pathetic enough to blow his own brains out.

It's so easy, she thought, suddenly aware of the weapon on her hip. Not her service weapon, which she'd turned over to Marquette, but her own, from home. A gun could be your best friend or your worst enemy. Sometimes both at once.

But she was no Ed Geiger; she was no loser who'd eat her gun. She turned off the engine and reluctantly stepped out of the car to do her job.

Rizzoli had lived all her life in the city, and the silence of this place was eerie to her. She climbed the porch steps, and every creak of the wood seemed magnified. Flies buzzed around her head. She knocked on the door, waited. Gave the knob an experimental twist and found it locked. She knocked again, then called out, her voice ringing with startling loudness: 'Hello?'

By now the mosquitoes had found her. She slapped at her face and saw a dark smear of blood on her palm. To hell with country life; at least in the city the bloodsuckers walked on two legs and you could see them coming.

She gave the door a few more loud knocks, slapped at a few more mosquitoes, then gave up. No one seemed to be home.

She circled around to the back of the house, scanning for signs of forced entry, but all the windows were shut; all the screens were in place. The windows were too high for an intruder to climb through without a ladder, as the house was built upon a raised stone foundation.

She turned from the house and surveyed the backyard. There was an old barn and a farm pond, green with scum. A lone mallard drifted dejectedly in the water – probably the reject of his flock. There was no sign of any attempt at a garden – just knee-high weeds and grass and more mosquitoes. A lot of them.

Tire ruts led to the barn. A swath of grass had been flattened by the recent passage of a car.

One last place to check.

She tramped along the track of squashed grass to the barn and hesitated. She had no search warrant, but who was going to know? She'd just take a peek to confirm there was no car inside.

She grasped the handles and swung open the heavy doors.

Sunlight streamed in, slicing a wedge through the barn's gloom, and motes of dust swirled in the abrupt disturbance of air. She stood frozen, staring at the car parked inside.

It was a yellow Mercedes.

Icy sweat trickled down her face. So quiet; except for a fly buzzing in the shadows, it was too damn quiet.

She didn't remember unsnapping her holster and reaching for her weapon. But suddenly there it was in her hand, as she moved toward the car. She looked in the driver's window, one quick glance to confirm it was unoccupied. Then a second, longer look, scanning the interior. Her gaze fell on a dark clump lying on the front passenger seat. A wig.

Where does the hair for most black wigs come from? The Orient.

The black-haired woman.

She remembered the hospital surveillance video on the day Nina Peyton was killed. In none of the tapes had they spotted Warren Hoyt arriving on Five West.

Because he walked onto the surgical ward as a woman, and walked out as a man.

A scream.

She spun around to face the house, her heart pounding. *Cordell?*

She was out of the barn like a shot, sprinting through the knee-high grass, straight toward the back door of the house.

Locked.

Lungs heaving like bellows, she backed up, eyeing the door, the frame. Kicking open doors had more to do with adrenaline than muscle power. As a rookie cop and the only female on her team, Rizzoli had been the one ordered to kick down a suspect's door. It was a test, and the other cops expected, perhaps even hoped, that she would fail. While they stood waiting for her to humiliate herself, Rizzoli had focused all her resentment, all her rage, on that door. With only two kicks, she'd splintered it open, and charged through like the Tasmanian Devil.

That same adrenaline was roaring through her now as she pointed her weapon at the frame and squeezed off three shots. She slammed her heel against the door. Wood splintered. She kicked it again. This time it flew open and she was through, wheeling in a crouch, gaze and weapon simultaneously sweeping the room. A kitchen. Shades down, but enough light to see there was no one there. Dirty dishes in the sink. The refrigerator humming, burbling.

Is he here? Is he in the next room, waiting for me?

Christ, she should have worn a vest. But she had not expected this.

Sweat slid between her breasts, soaking into her sports bra. She spotted a phone on the wall. Edged toward it and lifted the receiver off the hook. No dial tone. No chance to call for backup.

She left it hanging and sidled to the doorway. Glanced into the next room and saw a living room, a shabby couch, a few chairs.

Where was Hoyt? Where?

She moved into the living room. Halfway across, she gave a squeak of fright as her beeper vibrated. Shit. She turned it off and continued across the living room.

In the foyer she halted, staring.

The front door hung wide open.

He's out of the house.

She stepped onto the porch. As mosquitoes whined around her head, she scanned the front yard, looking beyond the dirt driveway, where her car was parked, to the tall grass and the nearby fringe of woods with its ragged edge of advancing saplings. Too many places out there to hide. While she'd been battering like a stupid bull at the back door, he'd slipped out the front door and fled into the woods.

Cordell is in the house. Find her.

She stepped back into the house and hurried up the stairs. It was hot in the upper rooms, and airless, and she was sweating rivers as she quickly searched the three bedrooms, the bath-room, the closets. No Cordell.

God, she was going to suffocate in here.

She went back down the stairs, and the silence of the house made the hairs on the back of her neck stand on end. All at once, she knew that

Cordell was dead. That what she'd heard from the barn must have been a mortal cry, the last sound uttered from a dying throat.

She returned to the kitchen. Through the window over the sink, she had an unobstructed view of the barn.

He saw me walk through the grass, cross to that barn. He saw me open those doors. He knew I'd find the Mercedes. He knew his time was up.

So he finished it. And he ran.

The refrigerator clunked a few times and fell silent. She heard her own heartbeat, pattering like a snare drum.

Turning, she saw the door to the cellar. The only place she hadn't searched.

She opened the door and saw darkness gaping below. Oh hell, she hated this, walking from the light, descending down those steps to what she knew would be a scene of horror. She didn't want to do it, but she knew Cordell had to be down there.

Rizzoli reached into her pocket for the mini-Maglite. Guided by its narrow beam, she took a step down, then another. The air felt cooler, moister.

She smelled blood.

Something brushed across her face and she jerked back, startled. Let out a sharp breath of relief when she realized it was only a pull chain for a light, swinging above the stairs. She reached up and gave the chain a tug. Nothing happened.

The penlight would have to do.

She aimed the beam at the steps again, lighting her way as she descended, holding her weapon close to her body. After the stifling heat upstairs, the air down here felt almost frigid, chilling the sweat on her skin.

She reached the bottom of the stairs, her shoes landing on packed earth. Even cooler down here, the smell of blood stronger. The air thick and damp. Silent, so silent; still as death. The loudest sound was her own breath, rushing in and out of her lungs.

She swung the beam in an arc, almost screamed when her reflection flashed right back at her. She stood with weapon aimed, her heart hammering, as she saw what it was that reflected the light.

Glass jars. Large apothecary jars, lined up on a shelf. She did not need to look at the objects floating inside to know what those jars contained.

His souvenirs.

There were six jars, each one labeled with a name. More victims than they ever knew.

The last one was empty, but the name was already written on the label, the container ready and waiting for its prize. The best prize of all.

Catherine Cordell.

Rizzoli swung around, her Maglite zigzagging around the cellar, flitting past massive posts and foundation stones, and coming to an abrupt halt on the far corner. Something black was splashed on the wall.

Blood.

She shifted the beam, and it fell directly on Cordell's body, wrists and ankles bound with duct tape to the bed. Blood glistened, fresh and wet, on her flank. On one white thigh was a single crimson handprint where the Surgeon had pressed his glove onto her flesh, as though to leave his mark. The tray of surgical instruments was still there by the bed, a torturer's assortment of tools.

Oh god. I was so close to saving you . . .

Sick with rage, she moved the beam of her light up the length of Cordell's blood-splashed torso until it stopped at the neck. There was no gaping wound, no coup de grace.

The light suddenly wavered. No, not the light; Cordell's chest had moved!

She's still breathing.

Rizzoli ripped the duct tape off Cordell's mouth and felt warm breath against her hand. Saw Cordell's eyelids flutter.

Yes!

Felt a burst of triumph yet at the same time a niggling sense that something was terribly wrong. No time to think about it. She had to get Cordell out of here.

Holding the Maglite between her teeth, she swiftly cut both Cordell's wrists free and felt for a pulse. She found one – weak, but definitely present.

Still, she could not shake the sense that something was wrong. Even as she started to cut the tape binding Cordell's right ankle, even as she reached toward the left ankle, the alarms were going off in her head. And then she knew why.

That scream. She'd heard Cordell's scream all the way from the barn.

But she'd found Cordell's mouth covered with tape.

He took it off. He wanted her to scream. He wanted me to hear it.

A trap.

Instantly her hand went for her gun, which she'd laid on the bed. She never reached it.

The two-by-four slammed into her temple, a blow so hard it sent her sprawling facedown on the packed earthen floor. She struggled to rise to her hands and knees.

The two-by-four came whistling at her again, whacked into her side. She heard ribs crack, and the breath whooshed out of her. She rolled onto her back, the pain so terrible she could not draw air into her lungs.

A light came on, a single bulb swaying far overhead.

He stood above her, his face a black oval beneath the cone of light. The Surgeon, eyeing his new prize.

She rolled onto her uninjured side and tried to push herself off the ground.

He kicked her arm out from under her and she collapsed onto her back again, the impact jarring her broken ribs. She gave a cry of agony and could not move. Even as he stepped closer. Even as she saw the two-by-four looming over her head.

His boot came down on her wrist, crushing it against the ground.

She screamed.

He reached toward the instrument tray and picked up one of the scalpels.

No. God, no.

He dropped to a crouch, his boot still holding down her wrist, and raised the scalpel. Brought it down in a merciless arc toward her open hand.

A shriek this time, as steel penetrated her flesh

and pierced straight through to the earthen floor, skewering her hand to the ground.

He picked up another scalpel from the tray. Grabbed her right hand and pulled, extending her right arm. He stamped his boot down, pinning her wrist. Again he raised the scalpel. Again, he brought it down, stabbing through flesh and earth.

This time, her scream was weaker. Defeated.

He rose and stood gazing at her for a moment, the way a collector admires the bright new butterfly he has just pinned to the board.

He went to the instrument tray and picked up a third scalpel. With both her arms stretched out, her hands staked to the ground, Rizzoli could only watch and wait for the final act. He walked around behind her and crouched down. Grasped the hair at the crown of her head and yanked it backward, hard, extending her neck. She was staring straight up at him, and still his face was little more than a dark oval. A black hole, devouring all light. She could feel her carotids bounding at her throat, pulsing with each beat of her heart. Blood was life itself, flowing through her arteries and veins. She wondered how long she would stay conscious after the blade did its work. Whether death would be a gradual fadeout to black. She saw its inevitability. All her life she had been a fighter, all her life she had raged against defeat, but in this she was conquered. Her throat lay bare, her neck arched backward. She saw the gleam of the blade and closed her eyes as he touched it to her skin.

Lord, let it be quick.

She heard him take a preparatory breath, felt his grip suddenly tighten on her hair.

The blast of the gun shocked her.

Her eyelids flew open. He was still crouched above her, but he was no longer gripping her hair. The scalpel fell from his hand. Something warm dribbled onto her face. Blood.

Not hers, but his.

He toppled backward and vanished from her line of vision.

Already resigned to her own death, now Rizzoli lay stunned by the prospect that she would live. She struggled to take in a host of details at once. She saw the lightbulb swaying like a bright moon on a string. On the wall, shadows moved. Turning her head, she saw Catherine Cordell's arm drop weakly back to the bed.

Saw the gun slide from Cordell's hand and thud to the floor.

In the distance, a siren wailed.

Twenty-Seven

Rizzoli was sitting up in her hospital bed, glowering at the TV. Bandages encased her hands so thoroughly they looked like boxing gloves. A large bald spot had been shaved on the side of her head, where the doctors had stitched up a scalp laceration. She fussed with the TV remote, and at first she did not notice Moore standing in the doorway. Then he knocked. When she turned and looked at him he saw, just for an instant, a glimmer of vulnerability. Then her usual defenses sprang back into place and she was the old Rizzoli, her gaze wary as he walked into the room and took the chair by her bed.

On the TV whined the annoying background theme of a soap opera.

'Can you turn off that crap?' she blurted in frustration and gestured to the remote control with one bandaged paw. 'I can't press the buttons. They expect me to use my goddamn nose or something.'

He took the remote and pressed the Off button.

'*Thank* you,' she huffed. And winced from the pain of three broken ribs.

With the TV off, a long silence stretched between them. Through the open doorway, they heard a doctor's name paged and the rattle of the meal cart wheeling down the hall.

'They taking good care of you out here?' he asked.

'It's okay, for a hick hospital. Probably better than being in the city.'

While both Catherine and Hoyt had been air-lifted to Pilgrim Medical Center in Boston due to their more serious injuries, Rizzoli had been brought by ambulance to this small regional hospital. Despite its distance from the city, just about every detective in the Boston Homicide Unit had already made the pilgrimage here to visit Rizzoli.

And they'd all brought flowers. Moore's bouquet of roses was almost lost among the many arrangements displayed on the tray tables and the nightstand, even on the floor.

'Wow,' he said. 'You've picked up a lot of admirers.'

'Yeah. Can you believe it? Even Crowe sent flowers. Those lilies over there. I think he's trying to tell me something. Doesn't it look like a funeral arrangement? See those nice orchids here? Frost brought those in. Hell, I should've sent *him* flowers for saving my ass.'

It was Frost who'd called the state police for assistance. When Rizzoli failed to answer his pages, he'd contacted Dean Hobbs at the FoodMart to track down her whereabouts and learned she'd driven out to the Sturdee Farm to talk to a black-haired woman.

Rizzoli continued her inventory of the flower arrangements. 'That huge vase with those tropical things came from Elena Ortiz's family. The carnations are from Marquette, the cheapskate. And Sleeper's wife brought in that hibiscus plant.'

Moore shook his head in amazement. 'You remember all that?'

'Yeah, well, nobody ever sends me flowers. So I'm committing this moment to memory.'

Again he caught a glimpse of vulnerability shining through her brave mask. And he saw something else that he had never noticed before, a luminosity in her dark eyes. She was bruised, bandaged, and sporting an ugly bald patch on her head. But once you overlooked the flaws of her face, the square jaw, the boxy forehead, you saw that Jane Rizzoli had beautiful eyes.

'I just spoke to Frost. He's over at Pilgrim,' said Moore. 'He says Warren Hoyt is going to recover.'

She said nothing.

'They removed the breathing tube from Hoyt's throat this morning. He's still got another tube in his chest, because of a collapsed lung. But he's breathing on his own.'

'Is he awake?'

'Yes.'

'Talking?'

'Not to us. To his attorney.'

'God, if I'd had the chance to finish off that son of a bitch—'

'You wouldn't have done it.'

'You don't think so?'

'I think you're too good a cop to make that mistake again.'

She looked him straight in the eye. 'You'll never know.'

And neither will you. We never know until the beast of opportunity is staring us in the face.

'I just thought you should know that,' he said, and rose to leave.

'Hey, Moore.'

'Yes?'

'You didn't say anything about Cordell.'

He had, in fact, purposely avoided bringing up the subject of Catherine. She was the main source of conflict between Rizzoli and him, the unhealed wound that had crippled their partnership.

'I hear she's doing okay,' said Rizzoli.

'She came through surgery fine.'

'Did he – did Hoyt—'

'No. He never completed the excision. You arrived before he could do it.'

She leaned back, looking relieved.

'I'm going to Pilgrim to see her now,' he said.

'And what happens next?'

'Next, we get you back to work so you can start answering your own damn phone.'

'No, I mean, what happens between you and Cordell?'

He paused, and his gaze shifted to the window, where sunlight spilled over the vase of lilies, turning the petals aglow. 'I don't know.'

'Marquette still giving you grief about it?'

'He warned me not to get involved. And he's right. I shouldn't have. But I couldn't help myself. It makes me wonder if . . .'

'You're not Saint Thomas after all?'

He gave a sad laugh and nodded.

'There's nothing as boring as perfection, Moore.'

He sighed. 'There are choices to make. Hard ones.'

'The important choices are always tough.'

He mulled it over for a moment. 'Maybe it's not my choice at all,' he said, 'but hers.'

As he walked to the door, Rizzoli called out: 'When you see Cordell, tell her something for me, willya?'

'What shall I say?'

'Next time, aim higher.'

I don't know what happens next.

He drove east toward Boston with his window open, and the air blowing in felt cooler than it had in weeks. A Canadian front had rolled in during the night, and on this crisp morning the city smelled clean, almost pure. He thought of Mary, his own sweet Mary, and of all the ties that would forever bind him to her. Twenty years of marriage, with all its countless memories. The whispers late at night, the private jokes, the history. Yes, the history. A marriage is made up of such little things as burned suppers and midnight swims, yet it's those little things that bind two lives into one. They had been young together, and together they had grown into middle age. No woman but Mary could own his past.

It was his future that lay unclaimed.

I don't know what will happen next. But I do know what would make me happy. And I think I could make her happy as well. At this time in our lives, could we ask for any greater blessing?

409

With each mile he drove, he shed another layer of uncertainty. When at last he stepped out of his car at Pilgrim Hospital, he could walk with the sure step of a man who knows he has made the right decision.

He rode the elevator to the fifth floor, checked in at the nursing station, and walked down the long hall to Room 523. He knocked softly and stepped inside.

Peter Falco was sitting at Catherine's bedside.

This room, like Rizzoli's, smelled of flowers. The morning light flooded Catherine's window, bathing the bed and its occupant in a golden glow. She was asleep. An IV bottle hung over her bed, and the saline glistened like liquid diamonds as it dripped into the line.

Moore stood across from Falco, and for a long time the two men did not speak.

Falco leaned over to kiss Catherine's forehead. Then he stood up, and his gaze met Moore's. 'Take care of her.'

'I will.'

'And I'll hold you to it,' Falco said, and walked out of the room.

Moore took his place in the chair at Catherine's side and reached for her hand. Reverently he pressed it to his lips. Said again, softly: 'I will.'

Thomas Moore was a man who kept his promises; he would keep this one as well.

Epilogue

It is cold in my cell. Outside, the harsh winds of February are blowing and I am told it has once again begun to snow. I sit on my cot, a blanket draped over my shoulders, and remember how the delicious heat had enveloped us like a cloak on the day we walked the streets of Livadia. To the north of that Greek town, there are two springs which were known in ancient times as Lethe and Mnemosyne. Forgetfulness and Memory. We drank from both springs, you and I, and then we fell asleep in the dappled shade of an olive grove.

I think of this now, because I do not like this cold. It makes my skin dry and cracked, and I cannot slather on enough cream to counter winter's effects. It is only the lovely memory of heat, of you and me walking in Livadia, the sunbaked stones warming our sandals, that comforts me now.

The days go slowly here. I am alone in my cell, shielded from the other inmates by my notoriety. Only the psychiatrists talk to me, but they are losing interest, because I can offer them no thrilling glimpse of pathology. As a child I tortured no animals, set no fires, and I never wet my bed. I attended church. I was polite to my elders.

I wore sunscreen.

I am as sane as they are, and they know this.

It is only my fantasies that set me apart, my fantasies that have led me to this cold cell, in this cold city, where the wind blows white with snow.

As I hug the blanket to my shoulders, it's hard to believe there are places in the world where golden bodies lie glistening with sweat on warm sand, and beach umbrellas flutter in the breeze. But that is just the sort of place where she has gone.

I reach under the mattress and take out the scrap which I have torn from today's cast-off newspaper, which the guard so kindly slipped me for a price.

It is a wedding announcement. At 3:00 P.M. on February 15, Dr Catherine Cordell was married to Thomas Moore.

The bride was given away by her father, Col. Robert Cordell. She wore an ivory beaded gown with an Empire waist. The groom wore black.

A reception followed at the Copley Plaza Hotel in the Back Bay. After a lengthy honeymoon in the Caribbean, the couple will reside in Boston.

I fold up the scrap of newspaper and slip it under my mattress, where it will be safe.

A lengthy honeymoon in the Caribbean.

She is there now.

I see her, lying with eyes closed on the beach, bits of sand sparkling on her skin. Her hair is like red silk splayed across the towel. She drowses in the heat, her arms boneless and relaxed.

And then, in the next instant, she jerks awake. Her eyes snap wide open, and her heart is *pounding. Fear bathes her in cold sweat.*

She is thinking of me. Just as I am thinking of her.

We are forever linked, as intimately as two lovers. She feels the tendrils of my fantasies, winding around her. She can never break the bindings.

In my cell, the lights go out; the long night begins, with its echoes of men asleep in cages. Their snores and coughs and breathing. Their mumblings as they dream. But as the night falls quiet, it is not Catherine Cordell I think of, but you. You, who are the source of my deepest pain.

For this, I would drink deeply from the spring of Lethe, the spring of forgetfulness, just to wipe clean the memory of our last night in Savannah. The last night I saw you alive.

The images float before me now, forcing themselves before my retinas, as I stare into the darkness of my cell.

I am looking down at your shoulders, and admiring how your skin gleams so much darker against hers, how the muscles of your back contract as you thrust into her again and again. I watch you take her that night, the way you took the others before her. And when you are done, and have spilled your seed inside her, you look at me and smile.

And you say: 'There, now. She's ready for you.'

But the drug has not yet worn off, and when I press the blade to her belly, she barely flinches.

No pain, no pleasure.

'We have all night,' you say. 'Just wait.'

My throat is dry, so we go into the kitchen, where I fill a glass of water. The night has just begun, and my hands shake with excitement. The thought of what comes next has engorged me, and as I sip the water, I remind myself to prolong the pleasure. We have all night, and we want to make it last.

See one, do one, teach one, you tell me. Tonight, you've promised, the scalpel is mine.

But I am thirsty, and so I lag behind in the kitchen, while you return to see if she is awake yet. I am still standing by the sink when the gun goes off.

Here time freezes. I remember the silence that followed. The ticking of the kitchen clock. The sound of my own heart pounding in my ears. I am listening, straining to hear your footsteps. To hear you tell me it is time to leave, and quickly. I am afraid to move.

At last I force myself to walk down the hall, into her bedroom. I stop in the doorway.

It takes a moment for me to comprehend the horror.

She lies with her body draped over the side of the bed, struggling to pull herself back onto the mattress. A gun has fallen from her hand. I cross to the bed, grasp a surgical retractor from the nightstand, and slam it against her temple. She falls still.

I turn and focus on you.

Your eyes are open, and you lie on your back, staring up at me. A pool of blood spreads around you. Your lips move, but I can't hear any words. You do not move your legs, and I realize the bullet has damaged your spinal cord. Again you try to speak, and this time I understand what you are telling me:

Do it. Finish it.

You are not talking about her, but about your-self. I shake my head, appalled by what you ask me to do. I cannot. Please don't expect me to do this! I stand trapped between your desperate request and my panic to flee.

Do it now, *your eyes plead with me.* Before they come.

I look at your legs, splayed out and useless. I consider the horrors that lie ahead for you, should you live. I could spare you all of this.

Please.

I look at the woman. She doesn't move, doesn't register my presence. I would like to wrench her hair back, to bare her neck and sink the blade deep in her throat, for what she has done to you. But they must find her alive. Only if she is alive will I be able to walk away, unpursued.

My hands are sweating inside the latex gloves, and when I pick up the gun it feels clumsy, foreign in my grasp.

I stand at the edge of the pool of blood, looking down at you. I think of that magical evening, when we wandered the Temple of Artemis. It was misty, and in the gathering dusk I caught fleeting glimpses of you, walking among the trees. Suddenly you stopped, and smiled at me through the twilight. And our gazes seemed to meet across the great divide that stretches between the world of the living and the world of the dead.

I am looking across that divide now, and I feel your gaze on mine.

This is all for you, Andrew, I think. I do this for you.

415

I see gratitude in your eyes. It is there even as I raise the gun in my shaking hands. Even as I pull the trigger.

Your blood flicks against my face, warm as tears.

I turn to the woman who still sprawls senseless over the side of the bed. I place the gun by her hand. I grasp her hair, and with the scalpel, I slice off a lock near the nape of her neck, where its absence will not be noticed. With this lock, I will remember her. By its scent will I remember her fear, as heady as the smell of blood. It will tide me over until I meet her again.

I walk out the back door, into the night.

I no longer possess that precious lock of hair. But I do not need it now, because I know her scent as well as I know my own. I know the taste of her blood. I know the silken glaze of sweat on her skin. All this do I carry in my dreams, where pleasure shrieks like a woman and walks with bloody footprints. Not all souvenirs can be held in one's hand, or fondled with a touch. Some we can only store in that deepest part of our brains, our reptilian core, from which we have all sprung.

That part inside us all which so many of us would deny. I have never denied it. I acknowledge my essential nature; I embrace it. I am as God created me, as God created us all.

As the lamb is blessed, so is the lion. So is the hunter.

THE END